A SILENT RECKONING

Sinner's Empire Book 2

NIKITA SLATER

To my best friend and beta reader, Jennifer. Your infectious excitement for my books gives me life.

Dear readers,

Thank you for purchasing A Silent Reckoning. This is the second book in the Sinner's Empire trilogy, following Sin of Silence. If you haven't read Sin of Silence, you will want to go back and start with the first book before continuing with A Silent Reckoning. Each book must be read in order for the full reading experience.

A Silent Reckoning takes place one year after the events of Sin of Silence. This book will continue the pattern of the first book, with all sign language conversation taking place in italics. This book is a work of fiction and while some aspects will seem realistic, this book was written from the author's imagination. I am not an expert in sign language, medicine, mercenary work, mafia, geography, or any other subject written into the book. I do research the subjects and themes within my books and try to write as realistically as possible, but this book should not be taken as an accurate representation on any of the above subjects. Having said that, it is important to me, as an author, to shed light on experiences that are not necessarily mainstream in romance writing. I hope that you enjoy my diverse characters and the situations I thrust them into.

Please note, some of the scenes in this book contains elements of PTSD and panic attacks, which can be distressing for some readers. Please read with caution. I hope you enjoy A Silent Reckoning, the second book in my Sinner's Empire Series.

Thank you,
Nikita Slater

KOBA FAMILY TREE

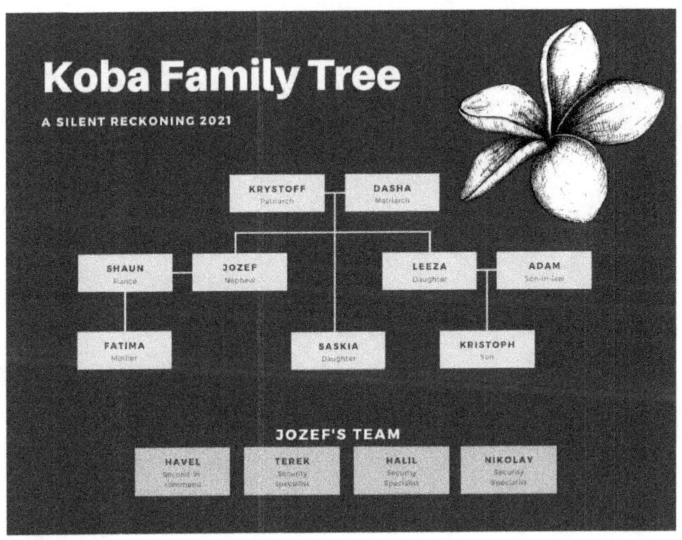

The People's Republic of Luhansk - The first time Jozef saw Shaun

Jozef watched his target leave the bookstore and walk north on Pavlivska Street. He followed the man as he headed toward the Optovyy Rynok market. It was mid-afternoon on a Wednesday. The streets weren't deserted but they weren't filled with people either. Jozef and his team could easily grab Gustav now, as he cut through a side street on his way to pick up groceries, but that wasn't the plan.

Jozef refused to do a job without the proper surveillance and equipment. It was something he and his team had become well known for throughout the mafia underworld. They were unparalleled when it came to completing operations to their client's satisfaction. Though this particular mission was personal, Jozef wouldn't fuck it up by snatching his target too early. He was in Luhansk for surveillance only.

As he walked, he started to give Gustav more space, not wanting to spook the man. In the five days since Jozef's uncle, Krystoff Koba, had been kidnapped, Jozef had come up with only one lead. Gustav. The man responsible for mailing a finger to Dasha Koba, Jozef's aunt. The desire to cut the man's throat, to avenge this insult to Jozef's family was strong. His time would come. The courier was living on borrowed time.

"Excuse me."

Jozef's gaze snapped from Gustav's back to a woman who'd stepped out of a small store and into Jozef's path. He was about to grunt a response and move on, when his gaze landed on her face. He froze, stunned by the exotic beauty of the stranger as she passed him without lifting her eyes. She was looking down at the phone in her hand.

Jozef turned to watch her walk away, his gaze taking in the gentle swell of her hips, the confidence in her walk and her unusual complexion. There were so few black women in that part of Ukraine that he had to blink a few times to be sure he was seeing her right. She stopped on the sidewalk next to a child and crouched down, smiling and holding out her hand. The boy hesitated and then took her proffered hand, giving it a shake.

She said something to him, but he shook his head and pointed at his ears. She shifted so Jozef could see her face again. He was so drawn to her that he found himself taking a few steps toward the pair before forcing himself to stop. He watched her smile fade into a frown of concern as she carefully set her bag on the pavement and sat next to the boy on the curb.

Jozef didn't want to look away, he wanted to see every expression her mobile face made, every tiny movement of her graceful hands, but he wasn't here for her. He was here for Gustav. Jozef glanced over his shoulder and saw Gustav heading toward a corner. Jozef would have to jog to catch up.

Yet, he couldn't seem to tear himself away from the woman. Finally, he let Gustav go, shaking his head in frustration. What was wrong with him? He was a duty first kind of guy. Women were interesting for sex only, but not beyond. Not a single one had yet tempted him toward marriage.

His gaze strayed back to the woman and what he saw next stunned him. He couldn't blink, couldn't breathe, could only watch as she used sign language to speak to the child. It became quickly obvious the child didn't understand but she patiently showed the boy several signs that he was able to pick up easily, grinning his happiness as he showed her.

Jozef knew exactly what they were saying.

Hello.

Boy.

Food.

Hospital.

Doctor.

Then she signed her name. S-H-A-U-N.

Jozef stared as her beautiful fingers moved to create each shape, showing the child until he understood. Her patience and kindness astounded him. As far as Jozef could tell, she hadn't known the child before sitting down with him, yet she was taking time out of her day to teach him an important skill. A skill Jozef knew too.

Jozef rarely met people outside of his family who understood or used sign language. It was so rare, in fact, that he'd given up finding anyone who could and started teaching the people around him, particularly his security team, how to sign.

This woman was different. She was unique and beautiful.

A powerful bolt of lust shot through his body. He hungered for her. A total stranger he hadn't met.

She showed the child the sign for goodbye and then she stood, stretching her back. She picked up her groceries, ruffled the boy's hair and set off down the street.

Jozef had to make a decision. Follow the mysterious woman or go find Gustav in the market and record the man's routine. They would pick him up soon, take him to their borrowed house outside of the city and force the where-abouts of Jozef's uncle from him.

He watched her walk until she disappeared. She was not his mission and never would be. She would be better off if she never met Jozef. He was the harbinger of death. Jozef rarely spent time with anyone outside of his inner circle unless they were a target. Those that he did spend time with didn't survive long.

If he became involved with the woman, her mortality would become a question and he couldn't bring himself to imagine anything happening to her. She was special.

He turned away and headed toward the market. He would hold her image close to his heart until she faded. Her ghost would be his comfort during the lonely nights when he paced his rooms, his mind occupied with death, strategy and war.

She would be his angel of mercy.

The woman he would never know.

One year later.

"Koba, you have a visitor."

Jozef's muscles strained with effort as he dragged his body up to the ceiling, tilting his head to the side as he lifted himself and held the pose for 40 seconds while the guard stood behind him, waiting quietly. Jozef let go, dropping to the floor of his cell. He'd intended to do four sets of ten pull-ups and was only halfway through.

Who is it? he signed, reaching for the towel on his bed and mopping the sweat off his face and chest.

Two of the guards at Prison Karvina had learned sign language after Jozef had been transferred from Prague after his sentencing.

Within a month of imprisonment, it became clear to the authorities that Jozef had too much support in the Pankrác Remand Prison outside of Prague. During his first week he'd stabbed his cellmate. It'd been a calculated move. Inmates and guards alike who hadn't known of him and his reputation would have preyed on what they saw as a weakness; his inability to speak or scream for help. After the stabbing, he'd been moved to solitary until his trial, which suited him. It was a good way to avoid Krystoff and his lawyers while giving Jozef the uninterrupted time he needed to strategize his next moves.

The prison officials hoped that by moving him closer to the Polish border he'd have fewer allies and serve his time quietly. They hadn't counted on Jozef's global mindset. He had men in prisons throughout Czechia and surrounding countries. If they transferred him to Siberia, he'd still have all the support he needed on the inside.

Jozef effectively ran Prison Kavina. He'd always had a policy of treating his men well and caring for their families if they got picked up and jailed. His family-inclusive mentality had won him the undying loyalty of some of the most hardened men in Eastern Europe. All it took was checking in on their mamas while they were inside.

He brought the guards alongside by padding their salaries and paying off the local authorities and politicians to look the other way as he rose through the ranks in prison. It hadn't all been tea-time chats. A few of the more tenacious bosses hadn't wanted to give up their positions to the enforcer of the Koba clan, but Jozef had convinced them otherwise. The prison guards simply looked the other way as Jozef cut a bloody path through the system, working his way up until he had enough power to ensure his every need was met both inside and out.

"Krystoff Koba is here to see you."

Jozef dropped the towel and pulled on a T-shirt. He'd been waiting for this moment. His uncle had visited Pankrác before Jozef had gone into solitary, but the conversation hadn't gone well and Jozef had declined any more visits. Krystoff refused to believe anyone in the family was responsible for Shaun's poisoning.

Jozef's single-minded purpose while in prison, besides climbing his way to the top, was finding the person who'd nearly killed his fiancé, put Jozef in prison, and tore him from the woman he loved.

He'd spent every night for a year fantasizing about what he would do to the traitor when he got hold of them. Peel the skin from thier body one strip at a time, drain every drop of blood, dismember them while they were still alive. He didn't care who it was, when he found the traitor, he was going to take his revenge in the worst possible way. Each family member took turns in his fantasies, swapping out depending on who he settled on as the would-be murderer. Sometimes Krystoff, sometimes Dasha, sometimes Leeza.

The guard led him to a dank room one floor above Jozef's cell. A metal table took up most of the small room, along with two metal chairs. The fluorescent lights cast a harsh glow. A barred window allowed a weak amount of sunlight to filter through a dirty windowpane.

"Let me know if you need anything," the guard said, motioning Jozef inside.

Jozef dipped his head in a nod and stepped into the visitor's room. The door slammed shut behind him, the click of the lock echoing in the small space.

Krystoff looked the same as he remembered, except for a few more lines around his eyes. His beard obscured the lower half of his face, but his dark blue eyes, the same shade as Jozef's, spoke eloquently. Jozef saw compassion and concern there, but he wasn't convinced it was real.

What do you want? Jozef asked, dragging the metal chair away from the table, scraping it across the concrete floor and dropping into it.

It's time to come home, son.

Jozef narrowed his eyes. If his uncle was using Jozef's method of communication, then he wanted something. They hadn't parted on good terms and when Krystoff was annoyed, he wouldn't sign. It put distance between him and his nephew. Jozef hated when people did that to him. Whether subconscious or not, it never sat well when he was unceremoniously cut off from his chosen language.

What's that supposed to mean? Jozef asked. *Last I checked I have two life sentences to serve.*

I pulled some strings with the higher-ups. Krystoff leaned on the table, his face settling into earnest lines. *The justice office agreed to look over your case two months ago and they found some inconsistencies.*

What inconsistencies? Jozef demanded. *I killed the two men I was accused of taking out, I earned prison.*

"Fuck Jozef, what's wrong with you?" Krystoff exploded, smacking his palm down on the table and switching to verbal in his agitation. "You can't say shit like that. Our official position is not guilty."

Krystoff ran a hand through his steel grey hair and took a breath, calming himself. "The justice department wasn't able to find more than circumstantial evidence linking you to the death of Danilo Melnychuk. The witnesses at the hospital were proven to be unreliable and the evidence found in the basement outside of Luhansk, while linking you to the scene, wasn't enough to prove you killed Gustav. Without a body, they have nothing."

Yet, here I am, incarcerated. If the evidence doesn't hold up, why was I convicted?

Jozef had been stupid to leave evidence at the house. He'd been preoccupied by Shaun and hadn't disposed of the bucket. He'd taken his gloves off for a few minutes while filling it with water, leaving his fingerprints on the side.

They both knew the witnesses at the hospital were infallible. A nurse and a patient had described Jozef right down to his combat boots, leather jacket and the tattoos on his neck. If they'd been proven unreliable, it was likely due to coercion or a fabricated drug problem. Jozef knew the drill because he'd used the method himself. Discredit a witness by planting evidence to make it look like they were a drug abuser.

"The justice department has decided otherwise; you get out on Saturday. The Prime Minister doesn't want to make a fuss, so you'll be released quietly. No media, no questions. I'll have a car sent for you." He leaned over to emphasize his point. "You get out in two days and you'll come back home where you belong."

Jozef felt numb. Not at the news that he was getting out. He'd been expecting that, but not from his uncle. Havel was close to reaching an agreement with the justice department as well. It would have been a matter of weeks before he was freed.

He'd been numb for a year, since losing Shaun. Since taking the fall for Krystoff's rescue and joining the ranks of the men who filled Czechia's crowded prisons. Somehow, he knew he wouldn't feel a damn thing again until he could touch her. Look at her face, feel the heat of her sunshine as she smiled at him.

"You don't seem pleased by my news." Krystoff's tone indicated disgruntlement. He expected gratitude from his nephew.

His uncle could go to hell. There had to be trust before there could be gratitude. Jozef was short on both.

He leveled a narrow-eyed glare at his uncle and clenched his fists beneath the table. Perhaps his uncle hadn't directly tried to kill Shaun, but he was responsible for keeping his house in order and he'd failed. Someone had tried to kill Jozef's woman under Krystoff's roof, while she was under his protection.

I won't be coming home, Jozef signed. *When I'm released, I'll be moving to the club*.

Jozef referred to the building he owned in Prague where the club was located. An old five-story brick and concrete structure in the heart of the downtown sector. Prior to his imprisonment he'd used the non-club floors for meetings and storage. After his imprisonment, knowing he couldn't go back to the Koba estate, he'd ordered Havel to overhaul the top floors as both work and living space. As far as he knew, he had an apartment ready and waiting for him in Prague.

Jozef pushed away from the table and stood. *Let Havel know how much you spent greasing the authorities. The money will be transferred back to you tomorrow. Don't bother sending a car. I'll find my own way.*

Jozef turned to leave.

"Jozef Koba!" Krystoff snapped, also rising from the table, his chair clattering as he shoved it back. "This is ridiculous. You're imagining this vendetta. Not a single member of our family would have betrayed you. Please come home, your aunt has been distraught."

Jozef turned back to face his uncle. *Find the person who poisoned my woman and we'll talk. Until then, I'm removing myself from your organization. You can keep your business in the city, I will take the international contracts.*

"Generous of you," Krystoff couldn't keep the sarcasm from his voice.

I don't wish to go to war.

"Then don't," Krystoff growled. "Don't splinter everything we've worked for."

Jozef wanted to point out that most of what the Kobas had came from the work of Jozef and his team. Instead, he said, *I will have to maintain a few legitimate businesses in Prague for appearances. Other than those, you can keep Prague.*

"You can't walk away from us, Jozef," Krystoff growled, frustrated with Jozef's refusal to compromise. "We're family. You don't leave family for a piece of ass."

Jozef tensed, the breath freezing in his lungs. He forced every muscle in his body to lock so he wouldn't end his uncle's life in a fit of rage. He was closer to the edge than he'd ever been. Jozef was the picture of control in every situation, but when it came to Shaun, he was on the razor's edge of slaughtering every single person in between him and her.

He turned to face his uncle.

You don't speak of her again, understand? His blazing eyes must've alerted Krystoff that the feral dog was about to go offleash. *A threat to her is a threat to me.*

Krystoff nodded and reassured Jozef, "I care about the girl too, son. She helped my grandson when he was injured and was kind to every member of our family while residing with us. This isn't about her, it's about your position in my organization. You can't give it up."

Jozef didn't bother speaking. His silent *why* echoed through the room louder than a clap of thunder.

"You'll lose everything." Krystoff spoke quickly, desperately. "Not just the family, but the money, the prestige, the power."

Jozef laughed, the sound cool and unpleasant. His face quickly straightened. *The difference between us, is that I never cared about the prestige and power. I only cared about my family. I would have given my life for any member of the Koba family, but you tried to take someone I love more than any amount of money.*

"So that's it," Krystoff demanded. "You go your own way now, to hell with the people who took you in and raised you?"

Jozef stalked back to the table, pointing at his uncle, then at his throat, touching his finger to the scar marring his flesh. *Whoever did this was trying to steal my voice without killing me. Who would want to do such a thing, Uncle? Who would want to kill the parents and leave the child, voiceless but alive? I can think of only one person.*

Krystoff drew his eyebrows downward in a thunderous frown. "Now you go too far. I grieved for my brother, for both of your parents. I took you into my home and raised you as my own."

Despite Krystoff's protests, Jozef noticed his uncle didn't deny the charge.

Then tell me what happened the night my parents died. You've only ever told me an enemy killed them and somehow you managed to rescue me before I could be killed too, but not before I was disfigured. What happened?

"I've told you what happened. An enemy of your father's killed your parents and tried to kill you too." Krystoff shook his head. "I don't know why you're rehashing history. This has nothing to do with us. We took you in, we raised you into the man you've become, a strong and powerful enforcer. Don't throw it all away, son."

Jozef thought over what he was doing, what he was giving up. As the Koba's enforcer he had unlimited resources and power. What his uncle didn't know was that, while still loyal to the Kobas, Jozef had been quietly building his own empire. He'd never been quite sure why but had chalked up his desire to become financially and emotionally independent after the loss of his parents. Now he wondered if it had more to do with a subconscious mistrust of the family who had taken him in.

I'm sorry, uncle. I'm not ungrateful for the sacrifices you've made for me over the years. My love for you, my aunt, and my cousins remains intact. If you wish to invite me to your home strictly as family, then I will come. But we are no longer business associates.

Krystoff's shoulders slumped and he nodded. "So be it. I'll cut you loose, as you wish. But if you ever need an ally, you must come to us. We will always have your back, son."

Perhaps he was being too harsh. These were the people who'd raised him. They nurtured and loved him, learned sign language for him and backed his ambitions. Perhaps he should reconsider his position.

Shaun's face filled his imagination. He could remember every detail, from the flawless ebony skin to the arched eyebrows, expressive golden eyes and quick-to-smile lips. Even in the worst of circumstances, she'd been able to find happiness. They'd been happy together... sometimes.

Jozef hadn't known happiness until Shaun. He would do anything to hold on to that feeling. Including cutting his family off.

Without looking at his uncle, Jozef banged on the door and left.

CHAPTER TWO

"Move the light about an inch to my left and tilt 45 degrees." Shaun lifted her shoulder to catch a bead of sweat pooling against her neck, then rolled her shoulders to ease the strain.

Shaun and her team had been in surgery for three hours working to remove a glioblastoma from a 62-year-old female patient. There was an estimated three more hours left in the surgery. They would take a ten-minute break to drink something and walk off the muscular tension before returning to surgery. The surgery itself wasn't complex for someone of Shaun's experience, but she had to be incredibly careful not to do any damage while removing the mass from her patient's brain.

Doctor Olivia King, one of the resident surgeons moved the light as requested, then glanced up at the clock on the wall. "Fifteen minutes until break."

Shaun blinked several times and took a few deep breaths before easing the scalpel back into her patient's brain. "Make it twenty and we should be able to remove the larger section before break."

They worked for exactly twenty more minutes until Shaun felt her patient was stable enough to be left. Stepping back, she spoke to her team. "Ten minutes then scrub back in." She glanced at her anesthesiologist, one of the best in the country. "You good without a break?"

He nodded. "We'll be fine, she's doing great. Go work the kinks out and we'll get this finished."

Shaun smiled gratefully behind her surgical goggles and backed out of the operating room. She removed her gloves, goggles and mask and tossed them in the hazardous materials disposal bin. She would have to start over fresh, but it was worth getting a few minutes of fresh air after a long surgery.

Shaun headed for the nearest exit, flexing her fingers to ease the stiffness. It didn't matter how many surgeries she did, nervous tension always wracked her body. She managed to push the emotion aside until her job was completed, but the stiffness always got to her after.

She pushed her way through the exit and stepped out into the cool Montréal afternoon. Her mother greeted her on the other side with a wry look and a smile. She extended the lunch bag she was holding, and Shaun took it with a grateful smile. Since Shaun's return to the city, Fatima had made it her mission to stalk her daughter. She wanted to be as close to Shaun as she could, calling often throughout the day and spending most nights in the guest room of Shaun's townhouse.

Shaun had to admit that her mother's vigilance was a balm to her soul. She'd been so screwed up after returning home from Prague that she hadn't been able to leave the house for weeks. It had been Fatima's patient, unquestioning, undemanding care that had pulled Shaun through her fear and depression. Gradually the nightmares subsided, and, after a few months, life returned to normal. Or as close as it was going to get.

They'd had one discussion about Jozef, which had gone so badly they hadn't spoken about him since.

Fatima didn't understand why Shaun refused to testify against him. She thought Shaun was being selfish by not wanting to help put a killer in prison.

Shaun had argued that she wasn't needed to help put Jozef in prison, that there was plenty of evidence. She'd lied and told her mother she couldn't stomach going back to Prague for the court appearance.

The truth was that Shaun couldn't handle the thought of being a party to imprisoning Jozef. He'd been her lover…. they had been in love with each other. Maybe she was selfish, maybe she was a monster, but she couldn't be the final nail in his coffin. She couldn't think of him as a murderer, even though she'd seen it with her own eyes. The real Jozef was a blend of intense lover and hardened killer who felt remorse for the lives he took.

"I was starting to get worried," Fatima admitted as she sank onto the concrete step next to Shaun, who was pulling a sandwich out of the lunch bag.

"It's a complicated surgery. I couldn't leave until I was sure the patient was stable." Shaun took a big bite out of the pastrami sandwich and chewed hungrily. She'd lost her appetite for months after returning home and had lost enough weight to worry her mother and colleagues. Lately, she'd been eating and sleeping better, though she still had bad days.

Fatima sighed and nodded. "I know, and you were only a few minutes late. I just worry about you."

Of course Shaun knew her mother worried, which was why she hadn't gotten impatient with Fatima's overbearing mothering.

"Thanks, mom." She grinned at her mother and finished her sandwich as fast as she could, her mind on her incomplete operation. Surgeries, especially the complex ones, consumed her completely. Obsessed her mind. She loved pulling her patients from the brink of death and giving them a new lease on life.

Wiping her hands together to get rid of the crumbs, Shaun stood up, handing the bag back to her mother.

Fatima shook her head. "There are some carrots and a pudding cup in there. Keep it and eat after the operation. I'm sure you'll want to stay until the patient wakes up, and who knows how long that might take. Bring the bag home with you."

Shaun thanked her mother, gave her a quick hug and flashed her hospital identification card over the metal reader. The door lock clicked open and Shaun went back into the hospital. As she strode down the corridor, her mind back in the OR, she nearly ran headfirst into a man walking toward her. Barely glancing up, Shaun murmured an apology and stepped around the man.

Then his scent hit her; leather mixed with Jozef's brand of aftershave. She looked over her shoulder and saw a tall man, around Jozef's height, with dark hair, a leather jacket, jeans and boots, striding away from her. She froze, her heart taking flight and her body going into a cold sweat. Dread and anticipation slammed into her, stealing her breath.

He made it to the end of the hall before she was able to find her voice. "Jozef!" she called out.

Without pausing, the stranger walked through the door she'd come in and out into the cool afternoon. She stared, battling the urge to run after him. To look into his face and assure herself that it wasn't Jozef in the hospital, in Montréal, Canada. How could it be? He was in prison, somewhere in the Czech Republic.

Slowly, she turned away and walked down the hall towards the OR, her thoughts on the mystery man. She *knew* it wasn't

Jozef. Her mind had been playing tricks on her since she felt safe enough to resume her old life. Whenever she left the house, she felt as though someone was following her, watching her. When she looked up, she saw Jozef. Everywhere she went she saw him. Standing in line at the grocery store, sitting in the waiting room at her dentist's office, even once at a playground while she was playing with her cousin's children. Every time she stepped foot in the hospital, she saw him. Whenever she picked up an implement in the operating room, she would turn her head to the side, expecting to see the barrel of a gun.

Of course, it was never Jozef. Her counsellor assured her that the hallucinations were normal. They were a manifestation of her fears. Her fear of being kidnapped again, held at gunpoint, forced to take part in a sham engagement. The counsellor was partly right. Shaun feared all those things, but what she feared most was never seeing Jozef again. Her heart had broken when she'd opened her eyes to strangers in the hospital in Prague.

The first word out of her mouth had been his name. That was when she'd discovered the men surrounding her were police.

"You're safe now, ma'am," one had kindly reassured her, touching her arm. She'd jerked it away, still confused and upset. "Jozef Koba has been arrested. You won't have to see him again."

Over the following week, Shaun had been reunited with her mother and forced to answer question after question. She'd been too upset by the poisoning and Jozef's arrest to pay much attention to what was going on around her. Thankfully, the hospital staff had become protective of Shaun once they realized she was the missing doctor from Luhansk. They kept the investigators at bay and allowed only the guests Shaun wanted to see into her hospital room.

Knowing she wouldn't be able to leave the country unless she made some kind of statement about her ordeal, Shaun had sat down with the two lead investigators and given them a statement. She'd told them everything that she could remember surrounding her kidnapping from the hospital and the murder of Danilo Melnychuk. Though guilt ate at her, she couldn't do Danilo the injustice of lying. Her heart might belong to a killer, but she could still tell right from wrong.

Though the police officers were happy with her statement regarding the actual kidnapping, they were less happy when it came to her lack of details about the Koba family. This was the only time Shaun had lied. She told them the truth about her engagement to Jozef but refused to tell them that her cooperation was forced. She also refused to give any details about the family. Though the entire Koba clan had certainly been complicit in her kidnapping, they were not involved in Danilo's murder, which meant she could protect them by muddying the truth of her time with them.

She told the men pressuring her into giving up more details, that she'd been locked in a room for almost her entire stay with Jozef. She hadn't known where she was, and she never saw single member of his family. Only Jozef. None of it was true.

Shaun played the Stockholm card. She didn't go overboard by professing her love, but she allowed the police to think a bond had formed between Shaun and Jozef due to the shared experience and his care of her. They tried to keep her for questioning, even going so far as to ask for her passport, for safekeeping they said. Shaun knew better. She knew it was time to leave the country.

Her saviour had come in the form of an unlikely source.

Havel had met her outside of the hotel where Fatima was staying. He'd opened the door to one of the family's black SUVs and stood silently until she got in. Shaun had halfway expected to find Jozef, but the vehicle was empty except for the driver. Havel got in beside her.

Shaun stiffened and reached for the other door. Havel terrified her more than any other member of the Koba organization. He was big, gruff and liked his weapons way too much. He'd argued with Jozef when Jozef had hesitated in killing her. He'd called her a 'job' and Shaun hadn't been able to bring herself to forgive him, though he was completely loyal to Jozef, and wouldn't harm her unless ordered to by Jozef. This fact didn't make Shaun feel any less uneasy in his presence.

Havel put his hand on her arm to stop her from climbing out of the car. He wasn't exactly restraining her, but silently asking her to stay. Shaun took a deep breath and turned to Havel, asking him the one thing she'd been dying to ask since waking up in the hospital and finding out she'd been poisoned.

"How is Jozef?"

She'd found out he'd been in prison for a week, having been arrested at the hospital.

"He'll be fine," Havel assured her, then his gaze sharpened, and he added, "You know he did it for you?"

Shaun nodded. "I figured it out. Taking me to the hospital was a risk. He had to have known I'd be recognized and he'd be linked to the kidnapping."

Havel's shoulders seemed to relax. "Smart girl."

"Doctor," Shaun automatically corrected. "Do you think he'll actually be convicted?"

Havel dipped his big bald head in a nod. "Yes. Interpol has become involved and they've been salivating over him for years. He travels, works on a global level, which makes him more exposed to authorities."

Shaun's stomach took a dive at hearing that Jozef would likely do hard time. She quickly ran her fingers under her eyes, drying them before the tears could fall. Now was the time for strength, not falling apart. She would do that when she got home.

"Is there anything I can do?" she asked.

Havel's eyes softened as he looked at her. Perhaps he was seeing the desperate love for Jozef that was twisting Shaun up inside. Though she didn't like Havel, she trusted him. They were bound by their love for the same man.

"You can leave." Havel pulled an envelope from his jacket pocket and handed it to Shaun. "Two tickets to Montréal; one for you and one for your mother. The plane takes off in five hours."

Shaun grasped the envelope, staring blankly at it while blinking back a fresh wave of tears. What had she thought was going to happen? That the authorities would forget the crimes Jozef committed and release him so he could marry her? It was ridiculous. Even if he somehow got out, Shaun had a life to get back to. She hadn't worked every moment of every day for the past sixteen years just to walk away now. She was a surgeon, and her career was her life.

"You don't have to worry, we'll take the flight." She gave Havel a half-smile and reached for the door. "Thank you..." she wasn't sure why she was thanking him. It took her a moment to settle on the reason. She was thanking him for being the family Jozef needed, for taking care of the man she loved when she couldn't.

"He'll be fine," Havel said as she got out of the car. She turned to look at him. He lowered his sunglasses, showing her the earnestness in his eyes. "Jozef has many friends inside the system, both behind bars and on the other side. He is elite in the underworld. He won't be harmed."

Shaun nodded and closed the door. As she stepped back to the curb, the SUV pulled away. When she turned to go into the hotel, she caught sight of a man watching her. He had undercover policeman written all over him. He was tall, broad-shouldered, perfectly manicured hair, jeans, leather jacket, sunglasses. Not handsome, but not ugly. Non-descript. Yet something about him made him stand out more than Shaun thought he'd want to if he was surveilling her.

She wondered if he recognized Jozef's second-in-command, then decided she didn't care. She was leaving all this behind. And though she might leave half her heart in Prague, she would be going home to the things she loved.

As Shaun began scrubbing her hands and arms in the big metal sink next to her OR, she forced the memories back into the tidy little box in her mind where she kept all of her memories of Prague. They were a year old, starting to get fuzzy. They didn't matter. The only memory that mattered was Jozef's face, and she saved it for when she went to bed every night. She fell asleep with his image keeping her safe.

One of the RNs helped Shaun with her gloves, gown, mask and goggles. Pushing all thoughts of her time in the Ukraine and Czech Republic out of her head, she walked into the operating room with confidence, determined to give her patient a few more years of life.

CHAPTER THREE

Jozef accepted the bag that was handed to him from across the desk. He glanced inside. It contained clothes, a phone, his watch and wallet. He pulled Shaun's gold chain from the bag, holding the heart in the palm of his hand before closing his fist and turning away. He changed in the dingy prison guest washroom, then emerged to join the officer who would walk him off the premises.

He signed the release log and stepped through the doors into the open air. His first breath after spending a year in prison was sweet. Freedom. It didn't matter that the prisoners got to spend an hour in the yard, working out and socializing. Prison air was more restrictive than the air breathed by a free man.

Jozef didn't know if he could call himself truly free. He was being released because palms had been greased, certain politicians had been threatened and, ultimately, they hadn't wanted Jozef on the inside. He wreaked havoc, killing the top Vory and liquidating their assets all while locked behind bars.

He'd worked his way to the top, determined to be the one

man every single person in the Eastern European underworld feared. His name would be whispered like the bogeyman. With each death, Jozef sent his team of men out to ensure a smooth transition to his organization. Any resistance was dealt with swiftly and brutally. No one knew what he planned, and everyone was afraid. Jozef was shaking up the entire continent and, though he was behind bars, he'd become untouchable.

It had taken Jozef a few months to sort out his reasons for systematically taking out one Vory after another and forcing their followers to bow to him. At first, he believed he was building an army so when he discovered who had betrayed him, he would be able to execute them with ease. But after many hours of internal introspection, time that was easy to come by during his incarceration, Jozef realized he was doing it for her.

For Shaun.

Before Shaun, he hadn't cared if he lived or died. That day in the hospital when he'd given himself up to the police, he would have happily finished the whole thing in a shootout that ended in his death, except he had to stay alive. What if she needed him? What if the person who poisoned her tried again? He had to live long enough to give the order that she be watched at all times. Then he had to live long enough to ensure his orders were carried out.

Eventually, he realized he had to live long enough to see her face again. Happy and healthy. Only the reports coming into him indicated she wasn't happy or healthy. After returning to Montréal, she became a near recluse, refusing to leave her home. She'd admitted to her counsellor, whose records Jozef was easily able to access through a hacker on his payroll, that she was floating through life, unable to concentrate. Nightmares haunted her nights and anxiety had turned her days unbearable.

When she finally returned to her work at the hospital, she allowed it to consume her. The only two places she went were the hospital and her home. Occasionally she would go to her mother's house, but more often Fatima would come to her. The few times Shaun left her house to go to the store or an appointment, she rushed back home as if a demon was chasing her.

Jozef wondered if he was her bogeyman.

The prison guard left Jozef after escorting him through the final gate. As expected, Havel was parked on the road next to the prison. He stood leaning against his SUV, a cigarette clenched between his teeth. Though half his face was obscured by aviator sunglasses, Jozef could tell Havel was happy to see him.

Havel rounded the vehicle and grabbed Jozef by the shoulders, pulling him in for bear hug.

Jozef was surprised, having never gotten a hug from Havel before. It took a moment, but eventually he relaxed and hesitantly wrapped his arms around the bigger man, squeezing.

You look good, old man, Jozef signed, stepping back.

"You don't seem too bad off for a stint in this place. You're coming out a much richer man than you went in." Havel waved his hand at the prison, a huge concrete and metal monstrosity. Then he turned his gaze back to Jozef. "I see you got some new ink."

Jozef touched the side of his neck and nodded. A Kizlyar blade had been seamlessly inked in among his other tattoos. It was the knife favoured by Russian Spetsnaz for its light-weight durability. Jozef had inherited one from his father, who had once worked for the Russian special forces.

Jozef had used the blade, which had been illicitly mailed to him by Havel while guards looked the other way, to dispatch each of the three Vory he'd taken out in prison. Each man was represented by a drop of blood tattooed beneath the tip of the blade.

Jozef reached for the passenger door and slid inside the car, sighing as his ass hit the plush leather seat. It would be a while before he took his life of privilege for granted again. He might be one of the toughest motherfuckers in that part of the world, but his ass liked a good cushiony seat.

Havel didn't have to ask where Jozef wanted to be taken. They were going to Ostrava airport, the nearest international airport to the prison.

Jozef had been planning his and Shaun's reunion since the moment he went in. There was a private jet waiting for them at the airport. They would leave once Jozef was on board. In less than twelve hours he would be landing in the city where his woman resided.

He'd thought about leaving her alone, letting her heal so she could get on with her life, but he couldn't do it. His obsession was too compelling. It was unhealthy, it made no sense, but he knew that living without her would be like living without his own heart. He had transferred his loyalty from the family who had raised him but had also treated him like the family guard dog. He was raised to become their first line of defense against the dark and deadly underworld.

No more. Now he lived for Shaun.

Perhaps if there had been some proof that she was happy in Montréal without him, he would consider tearing out his own heart and living without her. The daily reports on her movements were consistent. She rarely smiled and walked with her head down and shoulders slumped. She was pale and jumpy, and she only left her house for work. She talked to her counsellor about feelings of hopelessness and depression.

Jozef would take her back. He would take care of her and help her find joy again. He would make sure the sacrifice of her career and family were well compensated. She would want for nothing for the rest of her life, he would make sure of it.

As though reading his thoughts, Havel verbalized the thing that Jozef couldn't. "She's going to hate you for this, man."

CHAPTER FOUR

S haun was exhausted in every conceivable way: mentally, physically, even her aura was dragging behind her on the floor. It had been a long surgery, but so far, her patient was recovering well. Tomorrow, Shaun would check in on her and determine if the tumour and subsequent surgery had caused any permanent damage. Though the surgery itself was fairly routine for Shaun, the placement of the tumour was not. It had been difficult to reach and had grown into normal brain tissue, making the resection more difficult.

"Have a good night, Doctor." One of the RN's who had assisted in surgery picked up her lunch kit and coat and headed for the exit.

"Same to you," Shaun said warmly. "Good job in there today, Sam."

Shaun gathered her belongings, wrapping a thick jacket around her thin frame. She'd lost weight after returning from Europe even though her mother made all kinds of tempting dishes to perk up Shaun's appetite. Despite her lack of appetite, Shaun loved going home to a warm home-cooked meal. It made her think she should eventually find a house husband who was content to stay home to cook and clean.

A picture of Jozef in an apron teased her imagination and she laughed out loud, her first spontaneous laugh in almost a year. She stopped, pressing her fingers to her lips as the smile faded. The image of the hardened gangster wearing an apron *was* funny, but the fact that he was the first person who jumped into her brain when she thought about marriage was upsetting. She needed to let him go.

Not him... his ghost. It had been haunting her for long enough. She needed to learn to live again, without the spectre of Jozef following her everywhere she went.

Shaun was so engrossed in her own thoughts that she didn't see a man step in front of her until she walked straight into him. He gripped her arms, steadying her. The scent of leather filled her head, and she tipped her head back, expectation filling her heart.

The disappointment of seeing her colleague, Dr. Simon Lee, was so intense it stole her breath and sparked tears in her eyes. He continued to hold her, his expression turning from annoyance at having someone nearly knock him over to admiration as his eyes ran up and down Shaun's body.

The man was incorrigible, the playboy of the neurology department. Tall, smoothly handsome and talented. He'd slept with every female nurse who would let him, most of the female doctors and even a few patients. He considered himself an ethical man, so he poached other doctors' patients to fill his dating pool, never his own.

He'd asked Shaun out no less than a dozen times and if his expression was anything to go by, she was about to be asked out again. She sighed internally, preparing a polite but decisive refusal. If she was anything less than absolutely sure, he would push until she became annoyed. She didn't want to risk her professional relationship with the man, especially because they occasionally worked the OR together.

"Simon." She smiled at him.

"Hey, how's it going, Doc?" He dropped his hands from her arms.

Shaun took a step back to put some space between them. "I'm good. You?"

She hoped he didn't want to talk long, she wanted nothing more than to see what her mom was cooking for dinner, crack a bottle of Merlot and cuddle with her cat, Fitzy, on her comfortable couch. It was the same thing she did almost every night, but she appreciated the mundane predictable pattern her life had taken.

"I'm good, really good." His gaze crawled over her, prompting her to cross her arms over her chest.

Once, a long time ago, she'd agreed to a date. He'd spent the night talking about himself and doing with his hands what his eyes were doing now. She'd made an excuse and walked out of the restaurant. If she hadn't had to continue working with the man, she would have told him exactly what she thought of his handsiness and followed it up with an ice-cold glass of water in his lap for emphasis.

"Hey, you think maybe you'd want to..." His voice drifted off as his gaze fixed on something over Shaun's shoulder.

Shaun glanced behind her and her vision filled with a leather jacket stretched over a broad chest, tattoos peeking out from the neckline of his T-shirt. Her heart started pumping blood through her body faster and faster until she felt faint. She hardly dared to breathe as she slowly turned on the spot and tipped her head back, her gaze travelling the tattooed throat to the perfectly chiseled features and the scar across his lips. Her heart stopped entirely.

Jozef.

Standing right there, in her hospital.

It couldn't be true. She saw him every single day, but he was never real. She would blink and he would go away, disappearing like the figment of her imagination he was. Tears filled her eyes as she waited for him to fade away, leaving her with the hollow loneliness that always followed.

Only he didn't disappear. He continued to block her path, his scent invading her nose, his beautiful dark blue eyes on her face.

His expression gave nothing away. He looked bigger, more muscular than he had a year ago. His face was harder, more lined.

He was real. Oh god, he was actually there.

Shaun couldn't breathe.

"I don't know who you are, but you can't be in here," Simon interjected, moving to stand beside Shaun, his shoulder brushing hers. "This area is for staff only."

Jozef's eyes followed the movement and settled on the man standing next to Shaun. Touching her. Shaun tried to ease away from the doctor, but he just shuffled along with her, clearly trying to project a united front.

"You'll have to leave, or we'll call security," Simon continued, oblivious of the very real threat to his life.

Shaun wanted to say something, to step between the two men. She could lie and tell Simon Jozef was her boyfriend, that she'd told him to come to the hospital, anything to ease the tension, but the words wouldn't come. They were frozen in her throat, along with her breath. She was struggling for air, her world spinning, her entire being focused on the man who had taken her every waking thought, and some of her sleeping ones, for the past year.

Simon frowned and eased himself further into Shaun's comfort zone, his arm going around her lower back. "You have ten seconds to leave this floor or we'll call security."

Jozef's eyes followed every move Simon made, landing on

the hand wrapped around her hip. Shaun knew what was coming. She didn't know how Simon couldn't sense the deadly rage rapidly overtaking the hulking man standing in front of them.

Jozef moved so fast it was like watching lightning strike. He shoved Simon against the wall, pulling his gun from the holster under his jacket and pressing the muzzle to Simon's head. The movement sent Shaun tumbling back and she had to catch herself before she fell to the floor.

"No!" Shaun gasped, righting herself and grabbing Jozef's arm, trying to pull him away from the other doctor. Dark spots were floating through her vision and she knew she had to try to breathe through her constricted airway or risk passing out. A very dangerous thing to do around a man like Jozef.

Jozef turned his head to stare down at Shaun. His gaze softened and he allowed her to see some of the emotion raging inside. He couldn't tell her, but she knew, from that look, that he still loved her, and he'd come to Montréal to collect her. Then his pointed gaze fell to her hip where Simon had touched her. Jozef didn't give a shit about security arresting him, he cared about another man touching Shaun.

Shaun's heart sang while her brain screamed in panic. Not again, she couldn't do this again. She couldn't be the victim of another kidnapping. She couldn't watch as another colleague died violently.

"Please don't hurt him, he didn't do anything," Shaun managed to gasp, sucking air into starved lungs, begging for Simon's life, knowing how easily Jozef could and would pull the trigger if she didn't stop him. The life of a man he never met would mean nothing to him. But as much as Simon was a terrible date, he didn't deserve to die and the hospital needed him. "Please, Jozef, for me."

Jozef's eyes narrowed and she realized she'd said the

wrong thing. His finger tightened on the trigger. Shaun slid her hand up his arm, shivering at the sensation of his supple leather jacket, the muscle of his bicep hard beneath the material.

"I don't care about him," she reassured Jozef, ignoring the throat clearing from the man pinned to the wall. "But I don't want you to kill him either. Please, put the gun away."

She knew she'd gotten through to him when he dipped his head slightly, his shoulders relaxing. Shaun relaxed too and was unprepared for the strike when it came.

Jozef swung his gun hand back and hit Simon in the temple with a sickening crunch. Shaun gasped as Jozef wrapped an arm around her waist and swung her away from her falling colleague.

Shaun immediately reached for the fallen man, her fingers seeking the bloody wound, but Jozef dragged her back and walked swiftly down the corridor, his gun still in his hand. Shaun was forced to straighten and follow him or risk falling on her face. She twisted in his grasp trying to see if Simon was moving, but his body lay limp on the cold hospital tiles.

Jozef shoved the door to the stairwell open and pushed Shaun inside. She yanked on her arm and when he refused to release her, she gripped the door handle before he could haul her down the stairs.

"No!" she yelled. "We're not doing this again."

Jozef let her arm go and swung around to face her. She flinched and cowered against the door as his gun hand came up. He might care about her still, but that didn't make him predictable. Jozef was called *vztekl'y pes*, feral dog, for a reason. He was vicious and unpredictable, ready to strike at any moment.

Jozef followed her gaze to the gun and quickly shoved it into the holster under his jacket before holding his hands up to show they were empty. He hadn't forgotten his promise. He wouldn't turn the gun on her.

Shaun collapsed, her legs folding underneath her. She reached for the wall as she fell but missed. Jozef's warm grasp wrapped around her instead as he controlled her fall, crouching next to her. She was panicking; she couldn't breathe. The harder she tried to pull air in, the worse it felt.

Tears gathered in her eyes as she struggled to pull in the oxygen she desperately needed.

Shaun pressed her forehead to her knees, squeezing her body into as tight a space as she could. It had taken months of counselling, once a week, but she'd finally managed to put the panic attacks behind her.

They'd started shortly after arriving in Canada. The first one had been triggered by her first visit to a place outside of her home. She'd decided to go for a walk and had slipped into a Starbucks for a coffee. The crowd, the sounds, everything amplified in her head until she was positive she would die if she didn't leave. She'd run home, gasping for breath, tears streaming down her face. She'd managed to calm herself eventually, but the incident had prompted her to seek a therapist. She couldn't risk having an attack while her hands were in a patient's brain.

Luckily, the attacks rarely came when she was in the hospital. They mostly happened when she felt vulnerable, or if something reminded her of the violence she'd experienced. Once, when her mother dropped a book and it hit the floor with a bang, Shaun had such a bad panic attack Fatima had called the Healthline for advice.

Now, here she was, sitting on the cold concrete floor in the stairwell of the hospital, the author of her waking nightmare crouched in front of her. Every feeling of terror surfaced, mixing with the longing she felt each and every night as she went to bed and dreamed of him. His hard sexy body, his beautiful eyes, his elegant and brutal hands as he touched her.

Jozef took her head in his hands and forced her to look up at him. She had to blink several times before his face stopped swimming in her vision. Slowly he dropped his hands, making sure she followed them with her eyes.

You need to breathe.

She wanted to laugh bitterly, but no sound came out. No shit she needed to breathe. What did he think she was trying to do? Die of spontaneous asphyxiation so he couldn't terrorize her anymore?

"How....?" It was all she could manage, but he seemed to understand.

I was released from prison yesterday. I came straight here.

His admission ignited a spark of heat in her chest, like a glowing fireball that had resided inside her since they were last together but had gone dormant during their time apart. Now it was coming to life. For him.

He'd come for her. Once, he'd told her he would come for her if she ever tried to leave him. Now he was here, in her city. He was risking his life and his freedom.

It's time to go, S-H-A-U-N. He signed each letter of her name, not something he often did. Jozef was spare with his words, probably years of trying to make the most of people's attention when he had it. By spelling her name, he was making this personal. He was here for her and he wasn't going to let her go.

CHAPTER FIVE

Breathe, breathe, breathe.

Shaun's eyes followed Jozef's hands as he told her to keep breathing. Shaun wanted to warn him that he needed to get out of there before hospital security arrived, then she remembered he would be far deadlier than any security who showed up. She should urge him to leave before he hurt someone else.

Instead, he sat with her in the stairwell as though he had all the time in the world.

Jozef touched her face, cupping her head and holding her. He breathed with her, one long breath in and a longer breath out. She fell into the deep pools of his velvet blue eyes, unable to concentrate on anything but his touch, his face and the energy he was pushing into her.

After another minute, the constriction in her chest eased and she was able to draw in a deep breath without feeling choked. She blinked the tears back and gave Jozef a tight smile. He seemed to realize she was better. He slid an arm around her back and eased her to her feet. She let out a strangled yelp when he lifted her off the ground, holding her in his arms.

"Jozef..." Her voice trailed off hoarsely as he began descending the stairs at a dizzying pace. He didn't look down at her but kept running.

"Jozef." She forced some strength into her voice and this time when he glanced down at her she was able to say what she needed to say. "I know what you're doing and I won't go along with it. Put me down and leave. Please."

Her heart tore as she spoke. She didn't want him to leave without her, but she couldn't go with him. If he forced her to leave then she would resent him for taking away her free will. She would never be able to forgive him for once more taking her away from her mother and her career. There were extenuating circumstances the first time he kidnapped her; he'd done it for his uncle. This was different. He was taking Shaun because he wanted her.

When he ignored her and continued running, Shaun began to struggle, pushing against his chest and trying to get him to let her down. Again, he didn't pay any attention to her struggles, but held her tighter. She wanted to scream for help, but if she did, it would attract unwanted attention and someone might get hurt.

If Shaun wanted to avoid another kidnapping, she was going to have to do something and do it quick. She twisted violently in his arms and flailed her arms, striking him in the head. He tried to hang on to her, but he couldn't keep his grip when she started thrashing in earnest.

It became clear that he was trying to avoid hurting her, which Shaun appreciated. She didn't want to hurt him either, but she was going to have to do something extreme to get out of the situation. If she had to use his desire not to hurt her against him then she would.

As she started to tumble to the ground, Shaun punched

him in the leg, directly over his femoral artery. It wouldn't cripple him, but it would cause a fair amount of discomfort and the leg would go dead for a few precious seconds. Jozef was forced to release her as his leg collapsed. Shaun blindly reached out, trying to catch herself, but hit the concrete steps hard and rolled down to the next landing.

Pain radiated through her body, but she didn't have time to take stock of her bruises. She didn't think anything was broken. She shoved herself to her feet and, without a backward glance at Jozef, who was recovering from her strike, she launched herself down the stairs, running as fast as she could.

She'd learned in that clearing in the woods outside of Luhansk that Jozef could run fast. Faster than she could. She pushed herself harder than she'd ever done before, hoping the head start she had and the fear pushing adrenalin through her body would give her enough of a boost to escape him. She had no idea what she would do after that. Turn him in to the authorities? Go into hiding until he lost interest? She would have to figure it out later. At the moment, she needed to concentrate on escape.

She didn't dare turn to see if Jozef was behind her, and she couldn't hear anything over the thundering of her own heart. She knew Jozef though; he would be close behind. She'd cleared the last two flights of stairs to the main floor and was heading for the door leading to the parking garage when the dark shape of a man stepped through. She opened her mouth to scream at him to get out of the way, flashbacks of Jozef shooting at people in the Luhansk hospital filling her mind. The guy looked up and she realized she was running toward Havel.

Shaun stopped abruptly, thinking to turn around and head back to the first-floor door. She was too late though. Before she could whirl around and run in the other direction, arms closed around her and she was lifted off her feet.

"No – " Her scream was abruptly cut off as Jozef's hand landed over her mouth.

The smell of leather and aftershave filled her head. His arms, hard but yielding, were familiar. She struggled, kicking out at him, her running shoes making contact with his shins as he hauled her off the floor and carried her toward Havel.

"Told you she wasn't going to be happy." Havel gave Shaun a grim smile as Jozef carried her past him. "Good to see you again, Doc."

Jozef grunted as the heel of Shaun's foot got him in the knee. His arms tightened in warning, but she only fought harder. A dark SUV loomed in front of them, the rear passenger door open. Hands reached for her as Jozef lifted her into the vehicle.

Shaun braced her feet on either side of the door, pushing back hard enough to make Jozef stumble. He didn't drop her though and Havel reached out to grab her legs so she couldn't brace and thrust back again.

The hands reached for her again once she was in the vehicle, pulling her further into the interior so Jozef could climb in behind her. The moment Havel slid into the driver's seat and the doors slammed shut they were moving. Shaun threw an elbow into the man holding her and he let her go with a grunt.

Jozef reached for her and she went into his arms with a sob. She'd fought as hard as she could, now she needed the comfort only he could provide. It was screwed up, needing comfort from the very person who was terrorizing her, but Shaun was beyond questioning how she felt. Her therapist had spent a year trying to help her screw her head back on straight and now here she was, right back in the same situation that had landed her in therapy.

Shaun cried into Jozef's neck while he held her, running his hand over her short curls and down her back. She cried for her lost independence, for the fear her mother and colleagues would experience, and she cried for her lost year. She'd missed Jozef with every fiber of her being. She'd worried over the prison conditions where he was being kept; worried that he would be hurt or killed.

As the tears subsided, she was finally able to look around and assess her situation. She was in the back seat of an SUV with tinted windows, sitting on Jozef's lap. Neither of them was buckled in. One of Jozef's men, Halil, nodded at her from the other seat. He'd been the one to pull her into the vehicle.

The drive to the airport was uneventful compared to their violent meeting in the hospital. Shaun kept twisting in her seat and staring out the back window of the SUV, searching for the police who should be following them, but there was no one.

Jozef must've grabbed her fast enough that the hospital was still scrambling. Or Simon hadn't woken up yet to tell everyone she'd been taken.

Oh god. She was being kidnapped again. It felt surreal, but here she was in the back of a vehicle with Jozef and two members of his security team. They were concentrated but relaxed. The lack of tension in the vehicle felt wrong considering they were kidnapping her.

She turned on Jozef's lap to face him and spoke in a low voice, meant for only him to hear, but of course everyone could hear her. "Don't do this, Jozef. Just pull over and let me out."

His eyes lifted to hers and, ignoring her words, he cupped her cheek in the palm of his hand and ran his thumb over her skin. He used the back of his fingers to brush the last traces of her tears away.

She sighed and tilted her head into his hand. The feel of him combined with his scent was too much for her to ignore.

She closed her eyes for a few seconds and enjoyed the touch of the man she thought she would never see again.

She breathed in deeply and allowed the first moment of peace she'd felt in more than a year wash over her. When she opened her eyes again, he was staring back at her, his gaze mirroring hers.

Shaun had never believed in fate or soul mates before. Yet, she couldn't explain the feeling she had when she was with Jozef, other than to say her soul called out to his.

One year ago, during an impossible situation, they'd found each other. But they'd been on borrowed time. Now it seemed Jozef was determined to steal more time for them.

Shaun shook her head and whispered. "We can't."

Jozef's gaze changed, becoming closed off. He pushed her back into the seat next to him and ignored her pleas as they closed in on the airport. When the tower came into focus, Shaun's panic ratcheted up again. They were really doing this. They were planning on taking a Canadian citizen off Canadian soil.

Shaun stared in desperation as they drove past the airport around to the private section. Her heart pounded frantically as they approached the security gate.

What should she do? She had to try to get someone's attention, but she didn't want to be the reason Jozef was arrested again. She wasn't sure how he got out of prison after being handed two life sentences, but she suspected if he were arrested in Canada, he would have a much more difficult time securing his release.

She was happy to see him, her heart sang with joy at knowing he was alive and well, but her responsibility lay elsewhere. She had an obligation to herself, her mother and her profession to fight tooth and nail against whatever Jozef was planning. She'd committed her life to fighting the evils in the world. Yet wouldn't she become the evil she despised if she quietly went with Jozef simply because her heart wanted him?

She had to do something.

As they approached the security gates, a guard stepped out of the booth. The SUV slowed and Shaun frantically tried to plan what she would say, how she would get the guard's attention.

Jozef must've anticipated her intention because he grabbed her by the head and kissed her, a lightning fast, intense kiss that took her by surprise. As soon as his lips touched hers, sparks shot through her. Precious seconds passed.

Dimly she heard Havel speaking to the guard, laughing and exchanging a joke. Shaun pushed against Jozef's chest, trying to break contact so she could shout at the guard.

Jozef twisted on the seat, using his broad leather-clad shoulders to block her view of the guard. He gripped her head, cupping her ears and holding her still.

They stared at each other though Jozef continued to kiss her. His eyes spoke as eloquently as his lips. He wanted her and nothing was going to stop him from taking her. Passion clashed with anger as the sparks flew between them.

Havel's conversation with the guard ended and they were driving again. Once they'd cleared the barrier and Havel rolled up his window, Jozef released her.

Without considering the consequences, Shaun slapped Jozef, her palm striking his cheek in a sharp crack. Her hand stung, which meant his face must've felt worse. She cringed as Jozef swung his gaze back to hers. She could see the beginnings of anger stirring in the lake-blue depths.

Shaun was shocked. She'd never been a violent person, had never in her life hit another human being. She'd pushed Jozef, refused to do his bidding and kicked and fought when he grabbed her, but she'd never deliberately hit anyone. She hated the feeling and regretted it immediately. Yes, she was in an extreme circumstance, but it was no excuse to lash out. Especially in a way that wouldn't improve her situation.

I'm sorry, she mouthed.

Jozef's expression softened and he reached out, wrapping a big hand around her neck and dragging her into his chest, holding her as they drove across the tarmac toward the plane that would take her back to Eastern Europe and the new life she suspected Jozef was going to force her into.

CHAPTER SIX

Shaun thought she might have another opportunity to call for help during the confusion of getting out of the vehicle and onto the airplane. She should have realized, with a man like Jozef and his well-trained team, there would be no confusion.

As soon as the car came to a halt, Jozef's side facing the plane, his door opened and Shaun was pulled from the vehicle. She took in a lungful of air, ready to scream, but Jozef held her tight against his chest, dropping a hand over her mouth. He hoisted her off the ground and climbed the steps up to the plane, Havel covering their backs, his hand on the butt of his gun.

Once they were on the airplane, Jozef dropped into a seat, Shaun's squirming body on top of his. He didn't remove his hand from her mouth until the door was closed and sealed.

Jozef's men took their seats and Jozef set Shaun on the seat next to his. He reached across her to buckle the belt.

Shaun's heart felt like it was bursting from her chest, her breaths were rushing in and out of her lungs and she felt on the verge of another anxiety attack.

The airplane vibrated as the engines were started.

Shaun looked around her in panic. None of Jozef's men would look at her, their eyes on the floor, their faces grim. There was one flight attendant, who was speaking rapid Czech into a phone. The door to the cockpit was firmly shut, closing them off from the pilots.

Shaun was trapped.

She tipped forward, pressing her forehead to her knees and trying to force herself to breathe properly. She clutched her head as the plane taxied down the runway.

She straightened and looked at Jozef.

"If you do this, I will hate you." She enunciated each word, hoping this was the one thing she could say to him to get through.

It wasn't.

His gaze turned pitying and he shook his head. *You won't. You aren't capable of hate.*

She laughed bitterly. "Of course I'm capable of hate. Any human being can be pushed to hate." When he didn't respond, she added, "You're forcing me into an impossible situation. If you do this, I won't be able to forgive you."

It's done. You have no choice but to accept the situation, and hopefully, one day, forgive me.

He looked sad to be causing her pain but determined. He wasn't going to change course. The plane lifted off the runway, startling Shaun. She turned in her seat to watch the Montréal airport falling away beneath them. The more distance they travelled, the higher they climbed, the more agitated Shaun felt. Like something was trying to claw its way up her throat.

"No," she moaned, shaking her head and trying to stop the rush of nausea that threatened. She turned accusing eyes to Jozef. "If you love me, you won't do this."

He looked like she'd slapped him again, only worse. Guilt

flashed across his face, followed by genuine remorse. But none of it replaced the determined set to his jaw and shoulders. No matter how she felt, he was still going to do this.

"My mother," she sobbed, the tears overflowing onto her cheeks.

Thinking about her mother was a whole other layer of pain that threatened to cripple Shaun. She moaned and wrapped her arms around herself, rocking in her seat. Her mother was going to be devastated. Shaun's first kidnapping and subsequent recovery had been as hard on Fatima as it had been on her daughter. She'd been there every step of the way with Shaun when she was forced to relearn how to live, how to survive without Jozef, how to resolve her feelings surrounding the kidnapping.

Fatima had held Shaun while she cried, had listened to the words spilling from her daughter's mouth. Had patiently lent an ear to all of Shaun's misery. And now she would find out her daughter had been taken again.

As if reading her distress, Jozef reached for her.

Shaun pushed his hands away, not wanting him to touch her. He hadn't earned the right to touch her, to comfort her.

She had to get up. She couldn't stay in her seat. She couldn't breathe, couldn't settle down. Her world was falling away beneath her feet and the hardened soldiers who were the cause of her distress could do nothing except stare at the floor and try to swallow their shame. Well, she wasn't going to let them. They would damn well know exactly what they were complicit in.

Her fingers scrambled over her seatbelt until she was finally able to get it unbuckled. She leapt to her feet and flung herself away from Jozef, toward the front of the plane. He launched himself out of his seat, reaching for her, probably afraid she was going to do something stupid like open the door.

Instead of fighting him, she stood stiffly in his embrace, forcing him to make the next move. Gradually his muscles relaxed and he eased his grip, allowing her to step away from him. He placed himself between her and the cabin door. She didn't care. She might be angry, devastated, completely crushed, but she wasn't suicidal.

"Don't you have mothers?" she demanded accusingly, staring around at Jozef's team. "Do you have any idea what this will do to my mother? This will kill her."

At first no one said anything. She could feel the heat of Jozef's body at her back.

"It won't kill her," Havel finally answered, his eyes lifting to hers. "I've spent the past year observing both of you. She's a strong woman. Persistent. She won't give up on you."

"Is that what you think?" she snarled, impatiently swiping at the tears on her cheeks. "And she can't have a heart attack while she's holding out hope? She won't collapse under the stress? Maybe bankrupt herself while she searches for me? You haven't just ruined my life; you've taken hers as well."

Havel dropped his gaze, nodding his head slowly. "I'm sorry, Doc."

Shaun wanted to yell at him, but he wasn't the right target. Havel was following orders. She was fairly certain that if it was up to him, she would've stayed in Canada and their paths would've never again crossed.

She whirled to give Jozef the most accusing glare she could manage. "I want to call my mother. Right. Fucking. Now."

Jozef's eyes were hard chips of ice. He wasn't going to let her call. When he lifted his hands to sign his refusal to her, she stepped away from him, shaking her head. She wouldn't listen. She didn't have to. She didn't care if she was being an asshole by ignoring his signs; didn't care if she cut him off. He was the bigger asshole for kidnapping her. Again.

"You either let me call my mother or I will spend every waking minute of my life trying to find a way to leave."

Anger flared in his eyes at her ultimatum. His muscles tightened, as though he was about to grab her. Shaun held her ground, glaring at him. This time she didn't interrupt when he signed his response.

You will not threaten me in front of my men.

"Why?" she demanded, crossing her arms over her chest. "Are you going to kill me? Hold a gun to my head?"

He didn't answer. He couldn't, because she was right; he wasn't going to do any of the things she mentioned. He'd promised he wouldn't, and he didn't break his promises. At least, not to her.

She poked her finger into his chest. "Unless you can come up with a consequence you can live with, you had better be prepared for life with a woman who hates you. I will make damn sure you never rest."

If you think death is the only consequence I can give you, then you would do well to remember who you are speaking to.

Pure righteous indignation flared to life inside her.

"Is this what you want, Jozef?" she demanded. "War between us? Is this what you imagined when you were locked up? Did you fantasize about our reunion? Because whenever I imagined seeing you again, this isn't what I pictured."

He glared back at her.

No, I did not imagine our reunion would be like this, he admitted.

"Me neither." Her voice was impassioned as she placed her hand over her chest. "I thought you cared about me enough not to put me through something like this again."

He flushed and glanced away, telling her she'd scored a hit. Her anger fled, leaving behind despair. She hadn't wanted to hurt him. Not really. This wasn't the meeting either of them wanted, but this was what they had. Seeing him again, seeing his face and feeling his arms wrapped around her, she knew she didn't love him any less than she had a year ago.

"Please let me call my mother," she whispered, her eyes shimmering pools of sadness.

Jozef stared at her for a minute without saying anything.

It was Havel who finally broke the silence.

"Give her a phone call," he said quietly, looking up from his seat where he was bent forward with his hands slung between his knees. "We all have family. None of us would want them to suffer. It won't hurt to let her explain."

Jozef's hard gaze turned to his second-in-command. He didn't look pleased. *Explain what?* Jozef signed, anger making his movements quick and jerky. *That her daughter has been kidnapped for a second time? That she won't be coming home? It's better to leave her guessing.*

"No, it's not." Shaun jumped in, seizing on the tiny bit of hope Havel was giving her. "I promise, I'll be careful. I won't tell her anything. I just need her to hear my voice and know I'm okay. Once she hears about what happened at the hospital, she'll freak out. I can calm her down."

Jozef swung his hard stare back to Shaun. Finally, after long seconds ticked by, he nodded his head. *You can call, but make it brief, and don't give her any information.*

"I won't, I promise."

He pulled his phone from his back pocket and handed it to her. She took it gratefully. It was warm from his body heat. She sat back down and stared at it trying to gather her thoughts. What would she say? It didn't really matter. She couldn't tell her mother anything, other than that she was okay.

Before she could lose her nerve, she tapped the phone. It was locked. She looked up at him expectantly.

He signed, *0614.*

Her birthday.

She ducked her head and entered the number, unlocking the phone. With shaking hands, she typed in Fatima's cell phone number.

Jozef took the phone and hit the speakerphone button before handing it back. It rang twice before Fatima picked up.

"Hello?" Her voice sounded out of breath, as though she'd been running.

"Mom, it's me."

There was a pause, and then Fatima burst into speech. "My god, Shaun, they're saying you were taken from the hospital, like in Ukraine. Are you alright? What happened?"

"I'm okay, mom," Shaun was quick to reassure her. She glanced up at Jozef who was watching her steadily, his expression inscrutable. "I w-wasn't taken." She choked on the lie. "I left the hospital on my own."

Jozef's brows drew down in a thunderous look and he shook his head, telling her not to lie. She suspected Jozef didn't want her taking the fall too, if there were any charges laid after the incident with Simon.

Fatima unknowingly answered the question for them. "Do you realize you're wanted for questioning over the assault of a doctor at the hospital?"

A flutter of guilt went through Shaun. "Is Simon okay?"

"Of course," Fatima said impatiently. "He was barely tapped on the head. I think he wants to press charges for his ego more than his head, but he said you were upset, that the man who accosted him was there for you."

"I don't know what you're talking about," Shaun lied again. She hated lying to anyone but lying to Fatima felt like she was trying to swallow a bagful of acrid rocks.

"Don't play with me, Shaun Soraya Patterson." Fatima pulled out her mom voice and included Shaun's middle name, which made Shaun smile in spite of her situation. "I know something's going on and you're going to tell me exactly what it is. I won't have my daughter disappearing again without a word."

"I'm not disappearing without a word," Shaun tried to assure her mother. "I'm calling so you know I'm okay. I have to go away for a while, but I don't want you to worry."

"Where?" Fatima demanded.

Shaun sighed and rubbed the bridge of her nose. She should've anticipated Fatima's reaction. Her mother was a fierce defender of the people she loved. She wasn't about to allow Shaun to disappear again without making damn sure she knew what was going on.

"I can't tell you where I'm going," Shaun said quietly. "Please don't ask me again or I will hang up."

When she glanced up at Jozef, he nodded his approval.

Then Fatima threw a wrench into the conversation. "It's him, isn't it?" she asked. "The guy who kidnapped you before. Does Jozef Koba have you?"

Shaun looked up at Jozef, but he didn't give her any indication of what she should say. He simply looked at her grimly.

As if she was able to divine the entire situation from the few facts she knew, Fatima guessed what was happening.

"He wasn't able to let you go, was he?" she demanded, anger making her voice louder. "He's obsessed with you. He came back for you and now he's taking you away forever, isn't he? Answer me, Shaun. Tell me I'm wrong."

Tears filled Shaun's eyes and she bowed her head, stifling a sob. "No, mom." Her voice cracked as she spoke. "You've got it wrong."

"I don't," Fatima said sharply. "Somehow he got out of prison and came after you. I know it. God, Shaun, how is this possible?"

Shaun couldn't speak anymore, and Jozef, sensing her

distress, took the phone from her limp fingers. Before he could hang up, Fatima addressed him directly.

"Did he let you use a phone? Put him on," she snapped, her rage igniting with every word. "Jozef Koba, if you're listening, you bring my daughter back. She doesn't deserve this. You're destroying her life by doing this to her. Do you hear me?" Fatima's voice cracked as the words rushed out in short desperate sentences. "Just bring her back to me."

Jozef hung up the phone and tucked it into his pocket. He reached for Shaun, but she shoved his hands away, the tears now streaming unchecked down her face.

"Don't touch me." She pulled her legs up onto the seat and curled in on herself, letting the sobs flow free. "Don't ever touch me again."

CHAPTER SEVEN

Shaun spent the rest of the flight in silent misery, guilt eating her up every time she thought of her mother. Maybe she shouldn't have called. But then, the call hadn't been for Shaun, it had been for her mother. Fatima knew her daughter was alive, which was the only thing that mattered. If Shaun had to feel shame and guilt so her mother could rest easy, then so be it.

She couldn't explain why she was in love with a man who was more monster than human, and the tailspin of emotion was eating her up. The darkness that had shaped most of Jozef's life had also shaped their relationship. For him, kidnapping, beating people, killing them, it was all part of his job. For her, it was unthinkable.

How on earth did he think they could be compatible together? She would be utterly miserable if she were forced to accept the type of life he lived. She would become a shadow of herself. All her convictions, values, her life's work, would mean nothing. She would be trading it all in for the wealth Jozef could provide. Which, in her opinion, wasn't good enough.

She could console herself with the fact that she had no choice. She hadn't chosen to leave the Montréal hospital in the back of a tinted SUV, nor had she agreed to get on an airplane and leave immediately for Prague. Or at least that's where she assumed they were going.

How long could she use kidnapping as an excuse? When she stopped trying to run away? When she admitted that she loved her captor and couldn't bring herself to turn him in or testify against him? Her guilt lay in Danilo's coffin.

The moment that she relaxed in Jozef's presence and accepted the things he wanted for her, she would become an accessory to his criminal life. And she simply couldn't agree to that kind of life. She was raised better than that.

"Where are we going?" Her voice was hoarse.

They'd been in the air for two hours, but she'd only recently stopped crying. Her head was swimming and she felt like she had a bad cold. She held a wad of crushed tissues in her hand. Jozef had quietly handed them to her while she cried.

Home.

She blinked the tears away so she could see his signs.

"Where is home?" she asked quietly. "The mansion?"

He shook his head. *I no longer live with my aunt and uncle. I have a place in the city. An apartment building.*

The rest of their flight passed mostly in silence, but somewhere along the way the quiet went from tension-filled to relaxed. Shaun fell asleep at some point and when she woke up, her seat was reclined so that she was laying down and a blanket was tucked around her. She yawned and sat up, blinking as she looked for Jozef. He was behind her, giving his men instructions on what to do once they landed.

It was then, as she tried to catch what he was telling them, that she realized he hadn't been home at all. He had left prison and got on an airplane. To go see her. He hadn't waited even a single day. He must be exhausted and eager to see his new home.

Warmth crept into her as once again he proved the depth of his feelings. It didn't help Shaun though. His love for her was creating a world of difficulties for them and the people around them. They would be so much better off if he let her go and they lived their separate lives. It was a devastating thought and her sadness lingered throughout the journey from the airport to her new home.

Shaun thought Jozef meant a single apartment when he told her he had a place in the city, but it turned out he owned the entire building.

Jozef's home was in the building where the Koba-owned nightclub, Zmatek, was located. The old stone and brick building was sprawling, taking up nearly half the block. It was five floors high with windows on all sides.

Jozef explained that the nightclub took up the first two floors, while the third floor housed the offices for his new organization, the fourth floor was living space for his men and the top floor was Jozef's condo and a private gym for him and his men. He told her there was a rooftop terrace, but it was unused.

As they travelled to the top floor, Shaun shivered, prompting Jozef to put his arm around her. She thought about pulling away, setting the precedent that he wasn't allowed to touch her.

Maybe later.

For now, she needed him too much to push him away. The déjà vu of being back in Prague made her feel vulnerable.

It was 3:00 AM and between her long day and the time difference, Shaun was swaying on her feet.

Jozef entered a code into the panel next to his apartment, then unlocked the door and pushed it open, waving her inside.

Shaun glanced over her shoulder as two of Jozef's men took up positions in the hallway. She didn't recognize either of them. When she'd lived in the mansion, she'd gotten to know some of the security, but not all. One thing she had come to understand was that Jozef's elite team didn't do the menial security jobs. They certainly didn't stand sentry next to apartment doors.

Jozef closed the door, shutting out her view of the guards.

She turned, curious about his apartment. Her mouth opened in surprise as she took in the beautifully decorated modern room. Two entire walls were dedicated to windows, showcasing most of downtown Prague, the Vltava river below and the districts surrounding it.

Shaun couldn't help herself. She was drawn to the stunning view, momentarily forgetting where she was and why she was there.

Jozef followed her as she stood in front of the windows, gazing at the brightly lit buildings, the bridges, the dark winding river and the moving cars.

"It's really beautiful," she murmured, looking at him in the glass.

He didn't touch her or try to say anything. Instead, he stood silently, watching her watch the rest of the city. It felt like she and Jozef were the only people on earth, the silence wrapping them in a frozen cocoon while the world went busily by on the other side of the glass.

She turned to face him, her gaze travelling over the apartment. It was huge, with an industrial feel. Pipes lined the ceiling overhead, but they weren't ugly. In fact, they'd been integrated into the artfully decorated space. Modern paintings decorated the walls, giving splashes of colour to the otherwise austere room. The stainless-steel appliances were shined to perfection and the furniture was plush and inviting. A large glass-top table stood between the kitchen and one wall of windows. The living room, on the other side of the room, was filled with plush leather furniture, a glass coffee table, a large fluffy white rug and a floor-to-ceiling fireplace.

Shaun would bet her life savings that this place hadn't been decorated by Dasha, Jozef's aunt. The woman's style tended toward obvious wealth and heavy opulence, while Jozef's condo had a light, airy feel to it. The paintings were probably very expensive, but they'd been chosen as a complement to the room, not to show off Jozef's wealth.

Shaun turned a serious look on her captor. "Last time I was in Prague, someone tried to kill me."

His face darkened. *I know.*

"What if they still want me dead? What if they try again?"

They'll have to go through me.

She nodded, feeling the truth of his words to her bones. Though she trusted him to protect her, the thought of her would-be killer, who had targeted her a year ago, still on the loose was a disturbing one.

The police had only wanted to talk to her about her experience in Ukraine, her kidnapping from the hospital and her time with Jozef. They asked her a couple of questions about the poisoning and then dropped the line of questioning. They quickly veered away from inquiries about the Koba family and estate and set their sights on the Koba enforcer.

Once she realized the police weren't going to prosecute the family, Shaun had been both pleased and offended. It was obvious that the Koba money kept law enforcement on the side of the crime family. Unable to shake the image of Saskia, the youngest Koba, from her head, Shaun hadn't wanted to press charges anyway.

Then there had been the question of testifying against Jozef. A question that hadn't ever really been a question. She couldn't do it. She'd been a mess after her ordeal and weak from the poisoning. With every passing second, her confused and bruised heart had called out for him. She'd kept it to herself, but the emotional pain had been as real as the physical pain she'd went through. The authorities clearly had a plan when it came to Jozef, one that hadn't required her presence. They weren't upset about her departure from the Czech Republic.

"I'm tired." She didn't realize she'd said the words out loud until Jozef touched her arm, wrapping his long fingers around her elbow. He pointed toward a door that she assumed led to the bedroom.

"It is your room or mine?" she asked, smothering a yawn.

Jozef gave her an impatient look and dropped his hand so he could make his position, and hers, abundantly clear.

You sleep in my bed. You will always sleep with me unless I'm away.

Shaun really wasn't in the mood for an argument. She was tired, she was hungry, her clothes were rumpled and smelled like body odor and antiseptic. Her hair had become an unholy mess during the hospital struggle and her restless napping on the airplane. But, if she didn't stand up for herself now, she would lose out in the future. She couldn't allow Jozef to assume he could kidnap her, AGAIN, and that she would fall in line with his plans.

"No." Her voice was clear and final.

Jozef raised an eyebrow.

She shook her head. "I'm not sleeping with you."

Why? He demanded. *We've already been together. There's no reason for you to sleep anywhere else.*

His response was so typically Jozef that she almost laughed out loud. Was he serious? Just because they'd already slept together, didn't mean she planned on doing it now. He needed a lesson in women's rights. Then again, kidnapping was definitely a no-no when it came to feminism, or really any other kind of movement, so she was pretty sure he wasn't going to listen.

"I'll take the couch," she said insistently, walking around Jozef and heading toward the couch. "I'll need a T-shirt. I've been in these scrubs for nearly 24 hours."

He grunted, but instead of responding, strode to where she was standing next to the couch. He bent over, gripped her around the knees, and stood, tossing her over his shoulder. Her stomach hit his shoulder blade, driving the air from her lungs and turning her shriek into a squeak.

He walked with her into the bedroom, flicking the light on as he walked past the switch.

Shaun was about to start wailing and beating him with her fists when he dragged her off his shoulder and threw her on the bed like she was a handful of feathers. It was a testament to his strength that he could toss her around so easily.

She pushed herself up with her hands and glared at Jozef's back while he rummaged through the drawer of a big beautiful old wooden wardrobe. He flung a T-shirt over his shoulder.

Shaun caught it and held it against her chest. She thought about arguing, about getting off the bed and leaving the room, despite Jozef's declaration that she would sleep with him. She also knew he wasn't going to hurt her. If she kicked up a fuss, he might eventually give in.

She didn't argue though. The soft cushioning of the bed beneath her butt and the smooth, silky softness of his comforter made her want to lay down and rub her cheek against the fabric until she fell into a deep sleep.

"This isn't over." She glared at Jozef, pulling herself toward the side of the bed and standing. She glanced around and headed toward a door that she hoped led to a washroom.

She half expected Jozef to stop her, to insist she change in front of him, but he let her go, his sharp eyes following her as she opened the door and slipped into the dark washroom. She closed the door behind herself and breathed a sigh of relief, reaching for the light.

She blinked and looked around, both shocked by the opulence of the room and unsurprised. The amount of money in the Koba family, and she suspected with Jozef himself, took everything to the next level.

The washroom was spacious and filled with modern glass amenities. Unlike the mansion, where everything had been classy and smooth, this room was all angles and modern styling. Even the huge bathtub was made out of thick frosted glass with a slight blue sheen to it. A glass-walled shower stood next to it with multiple shower heads. The vanity sink, which sat on the white marble vanity was made out of the same kind of frosted glass. The oddly angled mirror was backlit by blue light, which gave the whole room a soft glow.

Instead of flowers, there was a tall vase filled with blue and clear crystals sitting on the floor next to the vanity. The towels were big, fluffy and white. She rubbed one against her cheek, the longing for a shower pulling at her. She resisted the urge, her exhaustion beating out her desire to feel clean.

Shaun quickly pulled off her scrubs and changed into Jozef's oversized white T-shirt. It contrasted vividly with her skin and she blushed when she looked down and realized her dark nipples were easily visible through the fabric.

She crossed her arms over her chest and re-entered the bedroom. She stopped, standing in the doorway and squinting into the gloom.

Jozef had turned out the light. She was about to call out to him, tell him to turn the light back on, when a hand reached for her in the darkness.

Jozef stepped out of the shadows and stood in front of her, his beautiful face thrown into sharp relief from the dim streetlights filtering in through the windows. His cheekbones stood out in jagged edges and his nose was a long, thin blade. He'd never been more handsome or more terrifying to her. It was like looking at a stranger.

Then his scent reached her, leather and man wrapped around her, holding her with its familiarity. She was so enthralled by him that she didn't try to pull away when he slipped his hand into hers and tugged her forward. He pulled her around the end of the bed, easily picking out a path in the darkness.

He led her to the windows and stood behind her, one arm wrapping around her waist, while the other reached past her to brace against the window, his arm brushing the side of her head.

She breathed in and out, nice and slow, drawing his scent deep into her lungs. Together they watched the world below.

CHAPTER EIGHT

Shaun was so deeply asleep, that when she finally woke up it took her several minutes to figure out where she was, let alone what the sound was that had woken her up. She squinted at the unholy bright sunlight streaming in through the windows.

She was starting to see a distinct drawback to the floor-to-ceiling type of windows. While they provided spectacular views at night, they were eye-searing devils during the harsh light of day.

Bang, bang, bang.

Shaun jumped and looked around, still disoriented, tangled in a pile of blankets and wondering where Jozef was. The sound came again, and she realized that someone was knocking on the apartment door.

Kicking the blankets away, Shaun climbed off the bed and stood, swaying on the spot. She'd slept so hard she hadn't woken up once, apparently not even when Jozef left. She was a little annoyed at his disappearance. He went straight from prison to an airport, flew to Canada to collect Shaun and flew all the way back home with her. One would think he would be interested in spending a little time with his reclaimed fiancé.

Then again, she was grumpy from spending the night sleeping like the dead and waking up to the brightest sunlight she'd ever experienced and banging on the door. Actually, now that she listed the issues, she was starting to realize that she felt hungover without the benefit of alcohol.

"I'm coming, I'm coming," she mumbled.

A quick search produced a soft white bathrobe hanging from the back of the washroom door. She pulled it on and tied the belt around her waist. It swam on her, but it covered all the necessary bits. She headed for the apartment door.

She was about to jerk it open and blast whoever was standing on the other side, but hesitated. Jozef had enemies. She knew firsthand that there were people out there targeting both him and her. She'd been safe in Canada but suspected that she would no longer be protected by distance now that she was back in Prague.

Then again, what kind of murderer knocked on a door to announce their presence? Shaun didn't really know. Jozef was the only murderer she could say for sure she'd met, and he almost never knocked.

Finally, she decided to open the door. It appeared to be the only way to stop the person on the other side from banging on it until it splintered. When Jozef got back, she would ask him why a career criminal hadn't invested in a peephole.

Then she realized there was a panel next to the door with a screen on it. She tapped it and the screen immediately lit up with an image of the hallway. Of course. There were cameras.

She was able to see Saskia Koba clear as day, chatting animatedly with a man who looked familiar. Shaun opened the door, startling the two on the other side.

Saskia didn't give her a chance to say anything but shoved

the door all the way open and pushed her way inside, flinging her arms around a startled Shaun and hugging her tightly.

Shaun was so stunned it took her a moment to return the hug, gently squeezing the younger woman until she finally pulled back.

"I missed you," Saskia announced, turning away from Shaun and tossing a purse stuffed to the seams on the kitchen island. She pulled a heavy backpack off her shoulders and let it thunk to the floor. It sounded like it had a bowling ball inside. "Have you seen your hair? It's pretty special this morning."

"I missed you too." Shaun tried to smooth her hair down, but she could tell from touching it that she was experiencing a bad case of bed head.

Then she realized, as she looked Saskia over, that she really had missed the other woman. Saskia had been irrepressible, challenging and often annoying when Shaun had lived in the mansion, but she had also been Shaun's only real friend and ally. Saskia told Shaun the truth, did her best to protect her and helped Shaun connect with her mother, something Shaun would be forever grateful for.

"How did you know I was back?" Shaun asked, peeking into the hallway. She was surprised to find a man she recognized standing stoic and staring forward. "Karl, how are you?"

He turned his head to look at her and though he didn't smile she recognized the good-natured twinkle in his eye. "I'm doing well, thank you, Dr. Patterson."

"Shaun, please."

He nodded and returned his gaze to the opposite wall. Shaun closed the door to the apartment, frowning in thought. Karl seemed different. Why wasn't he on the Koba estate?

As if reading her mind, Saskia answered, "He got fired after you were poisoned." When Shaun continued to look blank, Saskia rolled her eyes and shook her head. "He was family security... he allowed someone in the family to get poisoned. He's lucky dad didn't have him killed."

Saskia's words were a stark reminder of how out of her depth Shaun felt around the Kobas. "But that makes no sense, he couldn't have known someone would try to poison me."

Saskia gave Shaun a sharp look as she opened the refrigerator and started digging. "It's his job to protect the family. Not knowing about an attack isn't an excuse. If he allows harm to fall to any member of the family, it's his fault."

Shaun's lips twitched with amusement as Saskia took a container out of the fridge, opened it, sniffed, nodded and allowed the fridge to close. "Then why is he here?" Shaun asked, watching as Saskia went unerringly to a drawer and pulled a fork out.

Saskia shrugged, peeling the lid off her container and digging in. Shaun suspected it was cold spaghetti. She didn't know why there were leftovers in the fridge, since Jozef hadn't occupied the apartment prior to now. Perhaps he had a cook or a housekeeper who stocked up for him.

"I don't know for sure since no one in this family tells me anything, but I think it's because Jozef thinks someone in the family tried to poison you. He thinks that's why Karl wasn't able to prevent what happened. Jozef hired him from prison and asked him to work with the mercs and then take over family security once you arrived. Plus, Karl actually likes following family around, carrying bags, organizing security detail. That kind of stuff." Saskia stared hard at Shaun. "I never asked... are you okay? Did the poisoning, you know, have any long-term effects?"

Shaun had questions, like what was a merc, but Saskia moved from topic to topic so fast it was difficult to keep up.

Shaun smiled affectionately as she took a coffee pod from a basket on the counter and popped it into a single-cup coffee machine. She opened cupboards until she found a mug then hit the green button on the machine.

"No long-term effects," Shaun confirmed. "The poison was ethylene glycol. It's a slow acting poison that I would've ingested around 12 hours before I collapsed since it takes time to metabolize in the system. It's a common poison, easily accessible."

Saskia gaped at Shaun, a forkful of cold cheesy noodles halfway to her mouth. She let the fork drop and straightened on the couch. "But everyone said you were poisoned at the party. If you were poisoned earlier then it couldn't have been a guest, which means..."

Shaun didn't say it out loud. She didn't need to. The perpetrator was either someone in the family or someone close to the family. It could've been one of the servants, but they wouldn't have had a motive unless they were hired to slip Shaun the poison. If the poisoning had happened at the party, it could have been anyone, though the only people in attendance with a reason to want Shaun dead were the Kobas and Giselle, Jozef's ex-girlfriend.

The poison was unsophisticated and easily accessible, though no less deadly for its commonality. It could have killed Shaun if she'd taken more of it or if she'd gone longer without medical care. As a result of the quick actions taken by the Prague General University Hospital staff, Shaun recovered quickly without any lasting effects, which was a miracle considering the poison was meant to specifically target organs such as the kidneys. There hadn't been enough in Shaun's system for the job to get done.

"I vote for mom," Saskia said, shoving a huge bite of food into her mouth. "She can be a ruthless cunt when she wants to be."

Shaun burst into laughter and shook her head as she reached into the fridge for coffee cream. As she was adding it to her delicious smelling brew, she said, "I don't believe your mom would try to kill me, she spent too much time and money on the party."

Saskia laughed, barely covering her mouth in time to stop food from spewing out. "Are you kidding?" she asked incredulously, still choking. "My mother once threw a birthday party for a half-sister she despises. I'm pretty sure she would have murdered Aunt Vasha long ago if she could've managed it."

Shaun took her coffee cup and sat on the opposite end of the couch from Saskia. She took a sip and closed her eyes, inhaling.

Once she'd had her first hit of caffeine, she felt better able to manage a conversation with her guest. She gave Saskia a serious look. "Who do you think tried to kill me?"

Saskia finished her last bite and set the glass dish on the coffee table. Leaning back against the couch cushion, she pulled her feet up in a cross-legged pose and tilted her head to the side, thinking. Her light brown hair was styled in a wild, jagged, edgy cut that suited her pixie-like face and her dark gothic outfit consisted of black leggings, high-top runners, a rocker T-shirt for a band Shaun didn't recognize and a leather jacket.

"I've been trying to work this out for a year and I keep going in circles."

Warmth spread through Shaun. Coming back to Prague felt less lonely, less terrible, when she had Saskia to talk to. It didn't matter that the young woman was a member of an incredibly powerful crime family, she was first and foremost an intelligent, inquisitive and honest young woman. She might be loyal to her family, but she wasn't blind or stupid.

"Give me your best guess," Shaun encouraged.

Shaun hadn't put much thought into who tried to kill her.

She'd been emotionally exhausted by the time she'd gone back to Canada and hadn't been in a good enough place to put her mind to the problem. She assumed the distance she'd put between herself and the Czech Republic was enough to stop a second attempt on her life. Perhaps not smart, but it was where her mind was at a year ago. Now that she was back, close to the scene of the crime, she felt a pressing need to solve the problem.

Saskia shrugged. "I guess my mom or dad are probably the top contenders. When Jozef showed up with you in tow it rocked our tidy little world in a big way. I doubt it's my mom since she was so convinced you would be the perfect bride for Jozef and a possible mother to her future grand-nieces or nephews. She wouldn't have wanted to give that up considering there were no other contenders in sight."

"Giselle?" Shaun asked, somewhat unsuccessfully keeping the snark out of her tone.

Saskia laughed and shook her head. "He might've tapped her before he met you, but he wanted nothing to do with that clingy bitch. Did you know she actually tried to visit him in prison? Oh my god, you should've seen the outfit she wore!"

Both women laughed for several seconds as they pictured the glamorous Giselle showing up at a prison in her heels, slinky dress and fur coat only to be turned away by the very person she was there to see.

"She is persistent," Shaun choked out.

"Also delusional, psychotic, and desperate."

They laughed again and Shaun had to wipe tears from her eyes. It felt good to laugh like that. She hadn't found much to laugh about in the past year.

"Maybe Giselle tried to kill me."

"Too obvious," Saskia said shaking her head. "And too stupid. Whoever did it planned well enough not to get caught."

They sobered and stared at each other.

"They wouldn't let me see you when you were in the hospital." Saskia looked away, her eyes dimming with the memory. "My parents refused to let me visit in case the police tried to pick me up for questioning, but I was able to get away from my security team when I was in the city and I went to check on you. I couldn't even get onto your floor."

Shaun looked at the young woman, her heart cracking over the distress she heard in Saskia's voice. Though they hadn't known each other long, they'd formed a solid bond. Shaun suspected she was one of the few fairly 'normal' influences on Saskia.

"Between Havel and the police, I was locked down so tight I don't think the Queen of England could've gotten into my room," Shaun said apologetically.

Saskia picked at the edge of a hole in her jeans. "Why didn't you contact us after you got out of the hospital?"

Shaun was surprised by the question and didn't immediately know how to answer. She'd thought of Saskia and the rest of the family often over the past year. She would give the best answer she could though, to try to alleviate some of Saskia's sense of abandonment.

"When I went back home, I felt lost and lonely. I was barely able to function. My mom was with me all the time, protecting me but also...." Shaun didn't want to say that her mother had also smothered her with worry. It felt like a disservice to the woman who'd sacrificed so much to be there for Shaun. Shaun looked Saskia in the eye. "I did miss you, very much. Our friendship meant something to me. It helped me get through the ordeal of being kidnapped and forced into an engagement with a stranger."

Saskia looked thoughtful, then brightened. "I thought about you too." She glanced down at her phone and then gasped, hopping up to her feet and rushing to the door. "I have to go, my class started a few minutes ago. If I run, I can make the last half." She grabbed her bag, which she'd dropped by the door, and rushed out while Shaun sat with her mouth open. Saskia stuck her head back in. "I'm taking linguistics at the University and I'm acing it!"

CHAPTER NINE

ood work, Jozef signed to Havel as they toured the new operations center that had been set up on the third floor, above the club. He'd asked Havel from inside the prison to direct the removal of Jozef's belongings and his team from the Koba estate. He'd also asked Havel to create an operations center that would rival what the men were used to when doing jobs for Krystoff.

Havel had exceeded expectations.

The space was designed to look like a high-end office with board rooms, cubicles and desks. The entire floor had been opened up, the removal of walls creating an open concept. One end of the floor was dedicated to their tech equipment and the two men who operated from the office while the teams were in the field.

There, the similarities to an office ended. A locked and coded cage contained their weapons. His men carried personal weapons at all times, but the heavy stuff was kept in the cage. Next to the cage was a sparring area covered with rubber matting. Along the wall was a number of hand-to-hand combat weapons. There was also a fully equipped gym with weight and cardio equipment located on the same floor as Jozef's apartment.

The only room in the office area that was walled in was the main board room. This was where Jozef and Havel would have their private conversations before the team was invited in.

Meetings with clients would occur in the club as they always had.

Jozef called a meeting for 10:00 AM with his entire staff. It was time to meet his new hires and reacquaint himself with the men who'd been acting on his behalf while he was in prison.

He checked his phone, 9:54. Everyone on the premises was expected to attend except for a select few who would keep watch on the club, and Karl, who'd been stationed outside Jozef's apartment to keep an eye on Shaun. Jozef still wasn't sure if he was keeping her in or any potential threats out. He didn't trust her not to run if opportunity presented itself. It was a problem he would have to address in the near future. They couldn't live the way they had a year ago when she'd spent most of her time plotting her escape.

Jozef had been alerted twenty minutes earlier that Saskia had shown up for a visit. He allowed it, wishing he could also see his little cousin. It had been over a year.

Jozef's team filed in first: Havel, Halil, Terek and Nikolay. They'd already had their jubilant reunification on the plane, but the boys made it clear as they shook his hand and talked over each other, that they were happy to have their leader back.

Warmth sparked in his chest releasing some of the tightness that had developed over the past year. He'd missed his men... his friends.

He was tough; tougher than most. He'd had to be to become one of the fiercest enforcers in Czechia. In prison,

Jozef had trusted his men to work for him on the outside while he worked from the inside. He hadn't missed them while he'd been incarcerated but seeing them now made him realize how lonely he'd been. Though his life was one of silence, violence and isolation from society, he'd been surrounded by these four men for the past several years.

His secondary team said their hello's but didn't touch Jozef. They didn't know him as well as the others and respected his reputation too much to pretend they were on familiar terms with the boss. Several new hires shuffled in and sat, eyeing the man they now worked for with curiosity.

The tech team and building security arrived last.

Jozef stood at the head of the room, arms crossed, surveying his men as they talked. There was a serious atmosphere for their first meeting. He didn't blame them. They hadn't seen him in a year, and while they'd been working for him remotely, they were still on shifting ground when it came to leadership. They'd become used to taking their orders from Havel while Jozef was in prison, but that would have to change.

Havel took his place next to Jozef and raised an eyebrow. Jozef nodded and Havel called the meeting to order. The men who were used to working closely with Jozef looked at his hands, the rest looked at his face. Jozef didn't bother attempting to get their attention. They would learn. Havel would have insisted the new hires learn sign language.

Welcome to our new headquarters. If you're in this room, then you have been invited to become part of either my team, our tech crew or club security.

He looked around at the faces, noting the unfamiliar ones. The men who were new were hired by Havel to fill out the B team and building security. Some of Jozef's men had opted to stay with the Kobas, seeing their well-established organization as the more secure option over Jozef's newer organization.

Many of Jozef's team had moved into the newly renovated apartments above the club. He'd also bought a separate building several blocks away, outfitting it with living spaces and armaments, so not everyone was in the same place at the same time if they were attacked.

You are among the best in technology, weaponry, bounty-hunting and mercenary work. If you're in this room then you are elite. You work hard, you follow orders, and you reap the benefits.

The men banged their fists on the table, shouting their enthusiasm. The loudest voices belonged to Jozef's men. It was obvious they were happy to have him back. They knew the score. The machine couldn't work without its main cog, the heart. They needed Jozef, and he needed them.

Havel called the meeting to order. "Let's get started. Jozef doesn't know half of you so we'll start with introductions. I want each man to give his name, position and specialty."

As the men went around the room introducing themselves, it became clear to Jozef that Havel really had hired the best of the best, scouring the world over for his new hires. Jozef was impressed with the caliber of men Havel brought to his table. He'd even heard of a few of them, having worked the same regions while completing contracts for the Koba organization.

Once the introductions were finished, Jozef jumped right into their next job. Havel turned on a wall screen at the head of the room. Both men stepped to the side as all eyes focused on the screen.

Jozef tapped the map displayed, pointing at the capitol of Somalia. Mogadishu. One of the men whistled under his breath. It was one of the more dangerous areas in the world to work in.

This will be ground zero for our next job. He used the

trackpad on the laptop to enhance the map until it was focused on Mogadishu. *A city of 2.5 million people, most living below the poverty line. We have contacts in the area who will shelter us.*

He tapped a section of the city known as the red zone, an area that was so dangerous even the police wouldn't go in. He used the clicker to bring up another image. A large man appeared on the screen. Though his face was neutral, the man had an air of such deadly fierceness that he would rival Jozef's team.

"Sharif Muhammed Radik." The room fell silent as Havel spoke the name of a man everyone had heard of.

Radik was one of the fiercest mercenaries to come out of the Central African Republic, or CAR. He'd retired at an early age, an extremely wealthy man. He'd disappeared from the underworld scene, but rumour had it he resurfaced sporadically to target his enemies before they got to him. While active, he'd been known for his bloody disregard for human life and his ability to move freely through the most dangerous regions on the planet, particularly if those regions were on the continent of Africa.

"What does he want with us?" Halil asked with a frown. "He's more than capable of doing his own jobs, right? Or am I getting the wrong Radik? Didn't this guy level an entire village to get at his target?"

We don't question the jobs, Jozef signed. *Our client has been vetted by our tech team, and they have confirmed the job is legitimate. He's willing to pay a substantial fee for the delivery of a package.*

Halil shook his head. "Hell of a first job to get back in the saddle, boss."

Jozef narrowed his eyes. *You wish to leave the team?*

Halil laughed, the sound boisterous. "Bring it on, Boss. Just wanted to establish that this is the guy who eats babies for breakfast."

Jozef smiled grimly, but it was Havel who spoke.

"We don't question who hires us once the tech team has given the go ahead." Havel focused on a small, energetic man sitting near the back off the room. "Ali, tell them what you know."

Ali stood, pushed his chair back, then immediately tripped over his own feet to get to the front of the room. Used to their technician's clumsiness, the men patiently waited for him to settle in front of the screen. He cleared his throat.

"The job does come from the Radik we've all grown to know and fear." He used the laptop to show the next image. It was Radik's stats. 35-years-old, 6'5", 280 lbs. His mother originated from the Congo, father from the Central African Republic. No other known family. No known home address.

"How the fuck did you decide this job is going to be safe for us?" One of the new men spoke.

Jozef crossed his arms and watched the interaction, curious about his new team members.

Ali addressed the man with a blank stare. "No job is safe. I believe that's the point of mercenary work. We do the jobs legitimate companies won't."

"This looks like suicide," the other man countered.

Jozef raised an eyebrow at Havel who shook his head, turned his back to the room and signed, *his name is C-O-O-P-E-R. American born and raised. Worked as an independent before we picked him up. He has an impressive resume. He can be outspoken but has already proven himself adept. He's particularly good with people. He talked your aunt out of her smartphone password in under ten minutes.*

Jozef nodded and both men continued to observe the conversation.

Ali was speaking. "Radik is dangerous, but not stupid. He knows that there'll be no place on this planet for him to hide if this job goes sideways. He might have an army at his back, but we're better."

"Hell yeah!" Halil shouted with a grin. "Let's get this party started. I've been ready to go on a proper mission for ages."

Jozef snorted and Halil looked guilty. While the men had been working on small jobs over the past year, most of their efforts had been concentrated on a smooth transition away from the Koba organization. This would be their first mercenary-for-hire job in over a year.

Jozef bumped Ali in the arm to get his attention. When Ali was looking, he gave the signal for the other man to continue.

Ali nodded and started speaking again. "Radik isn't a cream puff, but he has a job that he insists only we can do. He sees us as second only to his people. According to Radik's secretary, this job is of a sensitive nature, which means he can't do it."

"What the fuck's the job already," Cooper grumbled.

Ali glared, making his feelings for the American mercenary obvious. "We're to go to a pre-arranged meeting point in South Sudan where we will retrieve the package and deliver it to Nice, France. I believe Radik will be coming in from the CAR while we come in from the west side of the continent. We meet in the middle, do the hand off and head back to Mogadishu."

Cooper started laughing. "Are you serious? We're going from Somalia, one of the most dangerous places on the planet, to South Sudan, a suicidal prospect on a good day, to meet with someone coming in from an even worse place, a certified dead zone. Am I getting this right?"

Nikolay cleared his throat. "You know I love these kinds of jobs, but Sudan? Are you sure? What's the incentive?"

It was Havel who answered. "75 million."

The seriousness of the job settled around the table. It was

an extremely risky mission in one of the deadliest areas in the world with a compensation package higher than any the team had ever collected.

After a moment of silence, Halil asked, "Who's going?"

"Everyone except our home security," Havel answered.

"Even tech?" Ali asked. They rarely took their tech team into the field, especially on dangerous missions.

Havel nodded. "We'll need communications while we're travelling through dead zones. The tech boys will have to be on the ground with us, enabling our equipment via satellite." Havel pointed at Cooper and the men surrounding him. "Our B team will land in Mogadishu ahead of the rest of us to meet with our liaison and secure the safe house."

"Hell yeah," Cooper said excitedly. "Now this is what I signed on for."

Jozef smacked the table and pointed at Cooper, who immediately looked at Jozef's hands. *You will take this seriously.*

The man nodded, his face smoothing into neutral lines.

Jozef looked around the room, satisfied that the others were listening and watching. *In two weeks, I will meet with R-A-D-I-K here on home territory to collect the first payment and work out the details. Any questions?*

"I have one," Nikolay, the quietest member of Jozef's team, asked. "Are we at war with the Kobas?"

Though his question was blunt, there was a wealth of feeling behind it. Nikolay was Krystoff's second cousin, son to one of Krystoff's cousins. He'd grown up on the periphery of the family and experienced the benefits of their loyalty for many years. He'd been uncomfortable with the transition. If any other man had asked the question, Jozef might have taken offence, but he understood Nikolay's concern.

No, we are not at war with my uncle. I made the choice to leave, which was long overdue. We will continue our work undisturbed, maintaining respect with the Koba organization.

"What is our organization called?" The question came from another new member of the team. "On paper I mean, in case someone asks who I'm working for."

Jozef stared at him blankly. He hadn't thought to name his organization. They were the mob, not a daycare.

"We're registered as Guard Dog Securities," Havel supplied.

Jozef nodded and dismissed the room.

Once everyone left, Havel pulled out the files Jozef had been waiting to see. He spread them across the table. Jozef reached for the first one, which was titled, Krystoff Koba. Each of the others had similar titles: Dasha Koba, Leeza Koba-Horáček, Adam Horáček, Saskia Koba, Vasiliy Stanovich, Phantom. Each person who might have had a vested interest in killing Shaun.

Over the next several hours the two men poured over the files, filling in the blanks and going over every possible scenario. Jozef gave Havel instructions on where to look for more information and who to bribe. So far, Jozef hadn't been able to dig up much evidence on Shaun's poisoning, but he refused to give up. He would find the person who harmed her and remove them. He would make Shaun's existence with him as perfect as he could.

CHAPTER TEN

Shaun spent the day alone, growing progressively more frustrated. She paced, she went through the kitchen, helping herself to a lunch of glazed chicken over rice. It was delicious and she wondered again where it had come from. Did Jozef have a cook, or a housekeeper? There had been a ton of staff at the Koba mansion, but here, she hadn't seen anyone in the building except security.

She explored the apartment and came to the conclusion it hadn't been used yet. Except for the bed they slept in, most of the furniture and electronics were pristine. The TV remote control still had plastic over it. She peeled it off and turned the TV on, discovering a variety of streaming services and local channels.

Glancing over the pots and pans, she realized they were brand new as well. So, the food must have been brought in by some kind of catering service. A thorough search told her there was no house phone.

Instead, she found a walk-in closet full of women's clothes, shoes and jackets in her size. A dresser produced underwear, socks and nightwear, including an incredible selection of lingerie. She fingered the delicate fabric and wondered whose job it had been to procure the items. She pictured Havel pawing through the racks at Victoria's Secret and started laughing.

She took a long, hot shower, using the shampoo and conditioner provided. It was the same brand she used at home, which would allow her tight curls to relax into a looser hairstyle. The brand was expensive and had to be ordered from a company in the United States. She tried to decide if Jozef's knowing about the kind of shampoo she used was an invasion of privacy. Yes, it was, she determined, but she was happy to have access to her preferred brands. She wouldn't put too much thought into how Jozef's people found out about her preferences.

When she finished, she changed into a pair of stretchy denim leggings, a loose button-up, collared white shirt and a pair of red ballet flats. She marveled at how well the shoes fit and how comfortable they were when she realized that they were the same brand as a pair of battered shoes she kept in her closet at home.

So, Jozef's men had definitely been in her house at some point in the past year. She supposed she shouldn't be surprised, though it made Jozef's desire to possess her that much more sinister. Was there a line he wasn't willing to cross?

After several hours spent alone, her agitation peaked, and she opened the door to the apartment. Karl was standing in the exact same spot he'd been when Saskia visited earlier. Shaun stepped into the hallway and gave him a wide smile. He gave her a suspicious look in return.

"Let's go for a walk, Karl." She tried to sound decisive so he would be less likely to argue with her. "I feel like reacquainting myself with the river and some of the shops."

He shook his head. "Not today, Dr. Patterson. Jozef has

asked that you stay inside until he's had time to settle you both in the apartment."

Shaun glanced at the apartment with a frown. "There isn't much to settle. There's food and clothing. I figured out the TV, though I would love to get my hands on a phone. Can you help me out with that?"

Karl shook his head.

"Figured. Well, I'm bored. I don't like being idle and I'm not one to watch much TV. I need stimulation, and if I can't go out, then you're it."

Karl looked alarmed and glanced down the hallway as if hoping Jozef would arrive in the next few seconds to save him.

Shaun was amused by his discomfort. The man could probably manage himself in a gun battle, but when a woman asked him for something, he got all hot around the collar.

Shaun didn't want to torture the guy, but she figured he was her only link to answers at the moment and she had a lot of questions.

"I want to talk to you," she said bluntly. "Can you come inside so we can be comfortable?"

"Absolutely not, Dr. Patterson."

"Shaun," she reminded him, "and I didn't think you would. So that leaves me with staying out here with you."

She glanced down the stark hallway for a chair and, finding an empty hallway, shrugged and sank down to sit on the floor opposite Karl. The alarm on his face grew until Shaun was almost ready to take pity on the guy and leave him alone. His face was turning red and the fingers of his right hand, his gun hand she assumed, were twitching.

"Do you eat a lot of red meat, Karl?" she asked him. "When was the last time you got your cholesterol checked?"

He opened his mouth to respond, closed it, then choked a

little. Finally, he said, "My cholesterol is fine. What would you like to discuss... Shaun?"

His accent had thickened.

"Tell me how you came to be here instead of working at the estate. Saskia told me it had something to do with my poisoning. Do you still work for the family, or do you work for Jozef now?"

He thought about her question for a moment, she supposed to determine if there was anything he shouldn't be telling her.

Finally, he said, "Your poisoning was a breach in mansion security, which I was responsible for. After some investigation by Krystoff's security team, it was eventually determined that there was nothing I could've done to stop the outcome. So, I was simply relieved of my position."

Shaun shuddered as she imagined the other possibility. What if the Kobas had decided the poisoning was Karl's responsibility? His death would be on her conscience. She hadn't poisoned herself, but she was the catalyst for a series of bad events: Jozef going to prison, moving out from the family home, Karl losing his job.

"And Jozef hired you?"

He dipped his head in a nod. "Yes, he had Havel pick me up after I left the mansion. I thought Jozef would try to use me for inside information, but he only asked me to take over family security for him. He's a good man."

Shaun nodded thoughtfully. From what she'd seen, Karl was both loyal and good at his job. He took it seriously, but he still connected with his subject. When Shaun had stayed at the mansion, she'd felt most comfortable with Karl as her escort. Perhaps Jozef knew that and it was why he'd hired the bodyguard.

"Tell me about the transition." When Karl glanced at her questioningly, she added, "I mean the transition of Jozef's team, and you, from the Koba estate to here. That would be a huge undertaking. What happened to Jozef over the past year? I know he was in prison, but how did he get out? How did he build all this from inside a jail cell?"

She waved her hand around to indicate the building.

Karl sighed, looked up and down the hall and then sank to the floor to sit opposite her. "I'm not sure I should be telling you this, Shaun."

"What can it hurt?" she urged. "I'm at sea in this situation and more information about the family and your move can only enhance my understanding."

His brow wrinkled. "I'll tell you what I can, but I'm in charge of family security, which is now you. I'm not privy to operational information unless it pertains to my position."

"Whatever you can tell me, I'm sure it'll help."

"Well, after Jozef was taken away, the family scrambled. They were used to him directing everything, including family security, field missions, local enforcers. I think they realized that Havel was in the process of removing the men, along with Jozef's assets. Anything paid for by Koba money remained, but the rest went. It was clear that Jozef had the loyalty of his team, though Krystoff did attempt to bribe them into staying."

Shaun's eyes widened but she didn't say anything. She hadn't expected Karl to be so candid, especially after he'd demurred for some minutes. The faraway look in his eyes told her he was reliving the experience. It must've been very tense, with his own fate likely still undecided at that point. Karl confirmed her belief.

"After the move, I met with Krystoff, who had no choice but to let me go. I think it was a blow considering he'd just lost ten of the best men he had, and his nephew was behind bars. But I'd failed to protect a member of the family and as a result you were injured."

"That's nonsense!" Shaun exclaimed. "You couldn't have done anything. You said Krystoff knew that."

Karl gave her a half smile. "Things don't work that way in the organization. He had to let me go and I deserved the punishment." When it looked like she would argue, he held a hand up. "To be honest, I prefer working for Jozef and Havel. They're both measured and realistic when it comes to security."

Though he didn't say it out loud, Shaun picked up on the subtext. Krystoff was not a measured boss and perhaps had unrealistic expectations of his men. Her experience in the Koba mansion had taught her that Krystoff was a man of changing moods.

"Jozef moved his team away from the mansion taking a large chunk of the Koba security with him," Shaun ventured, while Karl nodded. "What's happening now at the estate? Do they have enough security?"

Karl shrugged. "Mr. Koba hired more people, but good men are hard to come by. Jozef was responsible for filling the security positions. He cast a wide net to find people who were skilled, discreet and loyal. I'm not sure who exactly is working there now, though I'm certain Jozef will have files on everyone by now. He doesn't leave any detail to chance. He still loves his family and if he has any concerns with their personnel, I'm sure he'll approach Krystoff."

Shaun smiled grimly, remembering the ease in which Jozef and his team had kidnapped her. Both from the hospital in Ukraine and the hospital in Montréal. When it came to knowing his job, Shaun had never seen anything less than precision from Jozef.

"I'll tell you one thing, just between you and me," Karl interrupted her thoughts. "It's a damn good thing Jozef and Krystoff don't plan on going to war."

"Why is that?" Shaun asked. Then, thinking of the family, added, "Besides the obvious."

"Because Jozef would bury his uncle under a pile of rubble so deep, Krystoff would never again see the light of day."

Shaun's mouth went dry. "You're that confident he would win?"

Karl didn't hesitate. "There's no doubt, and Krystoff knows this. It's why the family is remaining amicable."

"Amicable," She repeated, her mind on her conversation with Saskia, the speculation over who'd tried to kill Shaun.

"I believe Krystoff intends to hire Jozef's team for jobs, like a broker I suppose."

"And do you think Jozef will go for that?"

Karl shrugged. "Probably. He has no reason not to."

Shaun was deep in thought when a shuddering bang hit the wall, making her jump. She gawked as Karl leapt to his feet so fast, he looked like a blur. She looked down the hall and saw Jozef striding rapidly toward them. He must've banged his fist against the wall to get their attention. Jozef was signing furiously.

What are you doing? His question was directed at Karl.

"My apologies, Mr. Koba, I was answering Dr. Patterson's inquiries."

On the floor? Jozef demanded coming to a stop in front of them.

Shaun rolled her eyes and, standing, wrapped an arm around Jozef's. "I asked him to sit with me. I was bored and wanted to know what's been going on. Or am I supposed to stay inside the apartment and not talk to anyone? If there are rules, I need to know them."

Jozef growled, letting his displeasure be known. He opened the apartment door and pushed her inside, then turned back to Karl, signing, *you don't need to get friendly with my wife to do your job.*

Shaun didn't hear a reply and Jozef slammed the door shut.

She crossed her arms and raised an eyebrow. "Your wife?"

He walked slowly toward her, stalking like a predator eyeing its favourite prey. Though she was no longer afraid of Jozef, he still made heart beat faster. His fierce looks, the tattoos, the sharp cheekbones and hard eyes. When she was with him it was too easy to forget that he was a mobster, born and bred. She craved the life he was offering; she craved his heart. But it was wrong and they both knew it.

You will become my wife. It's as good as done.

"I won't be bullied into marriage, Jozef," she said crisply, backing away from him. "Not this time."

He backed her against the wall of windows and reached for her, but he only caressed her cheek, before letting his hands fall.

There will be a marriage.

"Not without my permission." Her voice was more breathless than she'd intended. His nearness was driving a heated awareness through her. "Not like this."

He nodded. *I can wait.*

"What if you have to wait forever?" she asked. "What if I never settle down?"

His eyes pierced hers and he allowed his guard to drop, for just a moment. She saw the longing there, the pain, the loss. *I live for you. I will wait.*

"If you live for me, then why won't you let me live the life of my choosing?" she whispered. "Why do you keep taking me away from everything that I love?"

She could tell that she'd scored a hint and nearly called her words back.

His eyes became hard once more, and he stepped away from her. *You will grow used to this life and you will learn to love me again.*

He turned and walked away.

She wanted to call out to him. To tell him that loving him was never the problem, but she didn't. There was no point in having the same conversation over and over. Nothing would change until Jozef was ready to make a change.

CHAPTER ELEVEN

When Jozef still hadn't come back by 10:00 PM, Shaun went to bed without him. It felt strange being with him in Prague once more. It was the same as it had been a year before, but also not. Something was different this time; something besides the apartment and their year apart.

As she lay in bed, staring out the floor-to-ceiling window at the sprawling cityscape, it hit her. The balance of power had shifted in their relationship. While she was still Jozef's captive, she wasn't afraid of him. Not like she'd been when he'd kidnapped her from Ukraine and held her at the Koba estate. She'd been terrified of him back then. She's seen him kill two men and she couldn't have said with certainty that Jozef wouldn't kill her.

Now, things were different. He'd gone straight from prison to an airplane, which took him straight to Shaun. He didn't stop to visit his family and he didn't inspect his new apartment. He flew straight to her because he didn't think he could live without her. It was the only explanation.

She was no longer a witness; he'd served time for the crime of kidnapping her and killing two others. Not much time. One day she'd have to ask him how he got out of prison so early. She suspected someone had pulled strings on his behalf; perhaps a state official or someone with equal power.

The shifting balance of power in their relationship meant Shaun would be able to fight back this time. She could let Jozef know how much he was hurting her without fear of retaliation.

She drifted to sleep, her thoughts on the different ways she could leverage her newly discovered power.

Shaun had no idea how long she'd been asleep when something cool slipping across her skin woke her up. She moaned, rolled over and reached for the blanket but it was gone. She decided she'd rather have sleep than the blanket and started to drift again. She vaguely registered something happening around the waistband of her sleep pants but was pretty much asleep by the time they started to slide down her legs.

Again, she wasn't sure how much time passed, but a persistent pressure in her vaginal region started to register. She gasped and woke up, a moan of pleasure on her lips. It took her several more seconds to realize what was happening. She blinked down at the dark head settled between her thighs but was unable to form a coherent thought as a rush of heat scorched a path from her clitoris to her nipples, zapping every brain cell in her head.

"Oh god," she groaned. "Oh fuck, oh fuck!"

She reached down to anchor herself by taking his head in her hands, her fingers sliding through the silky strands of his short hair. She widened her legs, helpless against Jozef's onslaught. His tongue was everywhere, swirling around her clitoris, exploring her labia, thrusting inside her.

She couldn't catch her breath. The world dimmed as her entire focus was on the orgasm building within her. He played her like an expert with his instrument, building the intensity by slipping a finger inside her and pressing it against her g-spot and then pulling back when she was nearly there. By the time she finally exploded, she nearly came off the bed, her body levitating, a scream bursting from her lips.

The heat of Jozef's naked body covered hers as he climbed over top of her. He gripped her head with his fingers, holding her gaze while he shoved her legs apart with his knee. She groaned, her hips surging, her pussy sliding against the rough hair of his leg and sending a new rush of sparks through her.

Jozef held her gaze, his lake-blue eyes speaking of heat, longing and love as he surged into her.

Shaun gasped, her hips arching to accept the slam of his own. The union, after a long separation, felt like coming home when nothing else about their relationship made sense. She clung to him as he pulled back and thrust back into her, a growl of pleasure escaping his lips. She dragged his face down to hers and kissed him, her tongue plowing into his mouth as he took her body to incredible heights.

He picked her up off the bed, dragging her into his lap while still inside her. The change in positions made her feel impossibly full. She arched, pushing her hands against his pectoral muscles. His arms tightened and he pinned her to his chest, his hands sliding down her back to settle on her hips, his fingers digging into the crevice of her ass.

Jozef forced her hips to undulate, pleasuring both of them at the same time. Shaun was mindless, writhing on top of him, digging her nails into his flesh in a bid to both pull him closer and push him away. He took the pain, his own fingers tightening against her hips until she knew she would bruise. She didn't care. In that moment, she wanted his mark, wanted his cum, wanted everything about him.

"Fuck me," she moaned against him, pressing her head against his and thrusting her tongue in his ear.

He groaned and turned his head, slashing his lips over

hers in a passionate kiss. His cock grew inside her until he could barely thrust. He let out a short, sharp bark as he exploded, bathing her with his cum.

Before she could catch her breath, he was shoving her back on the bed, his body pinning hers to the mattress while his hand slid between their bodies.

"No, no, no," she gasped as his fingers found her, sending lightning bolts through her over-sensitized pussy. Pain and pleasure collided as he pinched her clitoris hard enough to draw a shriek from her, before curving his fingers inside her.

Shaun was helpless against the intense sensations, incapable of moderating her responses. She screamed so loud she was sure Jozef's team would bust down the door any second to save their leader. No one came to save her though; she was on her own as Jozef drove her toward the most painfully explosive orgasm of her life.

Finally, she was there.

Her mouth gaped in a scream that grew in crescendo until she was sure even Jozef was surprised, and pleased, if his expression was anything to go by. Her body was so taut she was able to lift him off the mattress as wave after wave crashed over her.

She had no idea how much time passed, but finally the orgasm let go and she collapsed onto the bed, Jozef's body covering hers like a blanket. As she stared at him with wide-eyed blankness, he lifted his fingers and licked them one at a time, his eyes never leaving hers. When he finished, he dropped his hand to her face, caressing her, touching her lips as her breath gradually evened. She caught her own musky scent, along with the scent of his semen. It was a heady smell, one that she had spent a year craving.

After a few minutes of cuddling, Jozef rolled off the side of the mattress and walked naked to the bathroom. Shaun squinted against the light when he turned it on. He left the door open as he walked to the toilet, flipped the lid up and took the age-old male stance. It took a moment, likely still recovering from the sex, before he was able to let out a steady stream.

Shaun sat up in bed, gathering the blanket around herself. Now that she was coming down from the incredible high of being fucked by a master in the art of sex, she was beginning to feel doubts creeping in.

Once again, Jozef hadn't asked her permission. He'd assumed since she was there that her body would be available for his use. Even worse, he hasn't used a condom.

Shaun was done with his high-handed assumptions. If he wouldn't be mature about sex, then she would be. She heard him turn the shower on, then a few seconds later step inside. She climbed off the side of the bed, dragging the sheet with her and tucking it beneath her armpits. She walked toward the bathroom door, purpose in her steps.

She stopped outside the bathroom, some of her conviction draining as she remembered who she was about to confront. The man who held her life in his hands. A man with a lot of personnel and weapons behind him. She wasn't sure exactly where he stood in the Koba organization, but so far, she hadn't seen any evidence that his absence had caused him to lose position or power in Prague. Granted, she had no real way of knowing what was going on, but she was intelligent, and she could guess.

"He's not going to kill you," she reminded herself, stepping into the washroom.

Jozef was scrubbing his face and hair, so he didn't see her stand in front of the shower, her arms crossed over her chest, her eyes narrowed.

"Jozef."

He looked up when she said his name, blinking water droplets from his spiky lashes. Her mouth went dry and her body heated up all over again. If it was possible, Jozef was even harder than he'd been a year ago. Each slab of muscle on his body was clearly defined, the veins popping out like there was so much muscle there was no more room to hold them beneath his skin. His ink was a beautiful and stark contrast against his pale skin.

He was truly a beautiful man.

He was also a kidnapper.

"Don't do that again." She hardened her voice and kept her gaze on his face.

He scowled, his eyes travelling down the sheet swimming around her body. It was huge, large enough for the king-sized bed, so he would barely be able to see the outline of her body. He stared at her, not bothering to communicate. He was going to leave the bulk of this conversation to her.

Very well, Shaun could hold her own.

"You don't get to have sex with me right now. As far as I'm concerned, you don't get my consent until I'm no longer a kidnap victim." She stared at him for a few seconds, giving him the opportunity to join the conversation.

His hands didn't move, but his look became scornful, speaking eloquently for a man who didn't speak for himself.

"No," she repeated. "Orgasms don't make it okay to have sex with me without my permission. You bringing me here against my will is the opposite of consent."

He made an annoyed sound and stepped out of the water, toward the edge of the shower, his body language threatening.

Shaun refused to back down.

"If you want to have any kind of a meaningful relationship with me, then you won't do it again." She paused, waiting for the words to sink in. "If you want nothing more than a mindless sex doll with nothing else to contribute, then you'll have a hell of a fight on your hands." He growled a warning at her that only served to piss her off more. She pointed at him, then dropped her hand to point at his cock. "I know how to surgically remove your body parts, so you better decide if it's worth going to war with me."

Surprisingly, his cock jumped in response to her vicious words as though excited by the prospect of a fight. Jozef looked less agreeable, his thick dark brows drawn low over his eyes. She glared back at him refusing to drop her steady gaze.

When she figured enough time had passed that her point was made, she turned and walked away, saying over her shoulder, "And stop fucking me without protection! We don't need to add a baby to this fucked up whatever it is."

She didn't get to leave the bathroom. In a rush of hard male flesh, Jozef gripped her around the waist, picked her up and swung her around. He dragged her into the shower, uncaring of the now soaked sheet clinging to her body.

"Don't you dare – "

His lips smashed into hers in a kiss that spoke of frustration and anger. He didn't bother to coax a response from her but pushed her lips apart with his. The kiss was both passionate and forceful as he attempted to show her he could use brute force if she resisted.

It went on and on until she couldn't stand it, shoving her fists against his shoulders and whimpering into his mouth. Finally, he lifted his head and looked down at her. She expected to see anger, a point proven; his strength was much greater than hers, he could force her compliance. Instead, his expression reflected the vulnerability she felt. He didn't know what he was doing any more than she did, but he knew she was right. Sex wouldn't solve what was wrong between them.

She slid under his arm and walked dripping from the washroom.

CHAPTER TWELVE

Shaun was nervous.

Jozef had informed her that morning, before leaving to work with his men for the rest of the day, that they would be spending their evening at the Koba estate. Shaun had tried to ask questions, to find out if they would be safe in the mansion, but Jozef had brushed her off, his demeanour distracted, and had left the apartment.

Shaun had spent her day pacing and worrying, wishing she had a phone so she could call Saskia. The younger woman would have no problem giving Shaun the low-down on what to expect. Did the Kobas hate her for ultimately doing what they'd feared she would do; tear their family apart? It didn't matter that it had never been her intention, or that she'd been dragged into the family against her will.

She looked at Jozef out of the corner of her eye. He was driving, his brow wrinkled in concentration. She didn't think he was engrossed in the drive but was thinking of whatever he'd done during the day when they were apart. She'd tried asking him while they were getting changed, but he shook his head and refused to talk.

There was a new distance between them that hadn't been there before their kiss in the shower. She supposed reality had finally sunk in for Jozef. He was holding a woman captive and forcing her into a relationship with him. She wondered if he'd thought their love for each other could overcome any obstacle and was now learning otherwise. Shaun was a realist; at no point did she think their relationship stood a chance. Not when he'd taken her from Ukraine and certainly not now.

She would be lying if she said a part of her wasn't happy to see him when he showed up in the hospital a few days ago. Her body and heart sang when he was near, as if she and Jozef could transcend everything else and be happy. But logical Shaun wouldn't allow it.

Jozef pulled into the long driveway leading to the Koba mansion, ignoring the guard at the gate who waved him in. Their escort of Havel, Karl, Halil and a man named Cooper were in the vehicle behind them. Jozef had chosen to drive his own car, a silver Bugatti sports car.

Shaun knew nothing about cars, but she knew enough to realize that Jozef's car was both very expensive and brand new. It looked as though it had been driven out of a showroom that morning. It made her even more curious about the state of the Koba organization. How did Jozef make his money? Had he saved it while working for his uncle? Or maybe he invested his money smartly.

Jozef brought the car to a smooth halt next the wide stone staircase leading up to the mansion doors, their backup vehicle parking behind them.

Before Shaun could touch her own doorhandle, the door opened, and a hand sprinkled with hair and missing part of the small finger reached for her. Her heart sank as she allowed the owner to pull her from the vehicle. She found herself face-to-face with Krystoff Koba. She shouldn't have been overly surprised considering they'd driven there to have supper with the family, but she felt ill-prepared standing next to the Koba patriarch.

Her heart froze, her stomach clenched and, though she tried to school her features, she must've looked like a scared rabbit who was positive the predator holding her was about to kill her on the spot. He didn't say anything but took her shoulders in a warm grip and kissed both of her cheeks.

"Dr. Patterson, it is our pleasure to have you here in our home once more. We've missed you and worried over your health. It's good to see you again."

She peered at him, glad that her height and heels put her on equal footing with the man. She wondered if he meant what he said. She forced herself to relax and take a deep breath, assembling a weak smile.

His eyes were sharp, watching her every expression, but his face was relaxed into jovial lines. He seemed genuinely happy to greet her and welcome her into his home.

Before Shaun had a chance to completely gather her equilibrium, she found herself being pulled into a perfume-filled hug. She instantly recognized the strong dose of Chanel N5 fragrance and knew she was being held in the awkward embrace of Dasha Koba.

She felt rather than saw Jozef walk up behind her, the warmth of his body reassuring as he took her arm and gently tugged her away from his aunt. The two couples looked at each other warily, neither Jozef nor Krystoff making the first move. It hit Shaun that Jozef hadn't been back to the mansion since the night of their engagement party. He'd been arrested and taken to prison. Unless he'd come back in the past few days, when he'd left her alone in the apartment, but she didn't think so. The stiff reactions told her the family had a lot of healing to do.

Finally, Dasha broke the standoff. "Please, come inside,

the girls are waiting for you in the sitting room. Cook has outdone herself with this meal."

Jozef placed his hand at Shaun's back as they were escorted inside. Shaun wondered if it was weird for Jozef to be in his old home, but this time as a guest instead of as a resident. If it did bother him, he didn't let anything show. His face was settled into unreadable lines, while tension emanated from his muscles. His tension leapt to Shaun, ratcheting up her own worries.

Were they safe? She had to assume they must be or Jozef wouldn't bring her there.

They walked into the sitting room next to the dining room, where Leeza, her husband Adam, and Saskia sat waiting. The three rose when Shaun and Jozef entered the room. There was an awkward moment of silence that was broken when Saskia launched herself at the couple, hugging them at the same time. She stood on her toes and kissed Jozef's cheek.

"I missed you, cousin."

Jozef extracted himself enough to sign, *you should have waited for me yesterday morning when you came to see Shaun.*

She shrugged. "I had class."

He nodded, his gaze softening as he looked down at his much shorter cousin, pride clear in his expression. *Yes, I heard that you're completing a degree in applied linguistics at C-H-A-R-L-E-S University. Are you doing well?*

"Straight A's," she said with a grin, flopping back into her chair.

"Well done," Shaun chimed in with a genuine smile.

A year ago, she'd been stunned to learn that the Koba family wouldn't allow their youngest child to attend secondary education. Shaun had helped Saskia formulate a plan that would convince her parents to let her go. Though

Shaun didn't know the details, she had to assume the plan worked.

"I want to complete my final year in Paris, but mom says I can't." Saskia made a face, while Dasha entered the room, catching what she'd said.

Dasha propped herself primly on the arm of Saskia's chair. "You know that there are far too many security risks for you to study outside of Czechia. Your father has already gone grey worrying about everything that could happen to you on the Charles campus."

"I worry less for her than I do the other students and faculty. Our youngest can cause mayhem by simply breathing." Krystoff stood next to his wife, his hand on her shoulder.

The family looked healthy, happy and peaceful. Dasha looked up at Krystoff, her plum-coloured lips curving into a smile, her eyes soft. Shaun felt a shaft of guilt at her part in breaking up the family. Though she couldn't make Jozef's decisions for him, she was still a major factor in his decision-making process. If Shaun hadn't come into his life, he would never have gone to jail, been torn from his family and forced to make the decision to leave his home.

"It's good to see you again." Shaun accepted a hug from Leeza who smiled pleasantly, though her gaze was guarded.

It was strange, no one seemed to blame her for the strain in the family. Either that, or they were better actors than she'd suspected.

Still, someone had poisoned her the last time she was in this house. She wasn't about to drop her guard again.

As the family chatted, attempting to find some common ground to reestablish the normalcy of their relationship, a servant came to tell them the dining room was ready.

Shaun had a brief moment of hesitation as her plate was placed in front of her and she was faced with having to ingest something in the same place where she'd been poisoned. The memory of her weeks of recovery were sharp in her mind.

Jozef caught her hand and gave it a reassuring squeeze, reaching over with his fork to take a bite off her plate. She watched, fascinated, as he placed a steamed asparagus spear in his mouth, wrapping his lips around the fork, then sliding the food off. He chewed, then nodded. He reached over twice more, trying something from each item on her plate, then taking a large sip of first Shaun's water, then the wine sitting in front of her.

She was so grateful, she could've cried. He didn't care what other people thought. He didn't care that it was ridiculously unlikely someone in the house would attempt to poison her again. He wanted her to feel comfortable and safe while she shared a meal with his family, and he ensured that by taking bites off her plate.

As he set her wine glass back on the table and gave her a significant nod, telling her she could go ahead and eat, Shaun caught his hand and held it against her chest. If he didn't care that others were watching, then neither would she. She kissed his fingertips, showing him her gratitude, before letting his hand go.

Shaun and Jozef may have some major relationship obstacles, but his caring for her was not one of them. Shaun knew without a single doubt that Jozef loved her and would do almost anything for her. His devotion was beautiful, seductive and frightening in its intensity.

"Switch plates with me," Saskia said from across the table, glancing around at her family. "No one would try to poison me."

"Saskia!" Dasha said sharply. "No one here tried to poison Shaun."

Shaun smiled her gratitude at the younger woman. "Thank you, but I'm fine with my plate." She extended her smile to Dasha, though Dasha's own expression was a mixture of annoyance and frustration. "Thank you for this lovely meal, Mrs. Koba, it looks incredible."

It took Dasha a moment, but her expression finally smoothed out and she was able to smile once again. "Of course, dear. We're so grateful to have you back. You weren't here for long, but you certainly made an impact on us."

Though the words were friendly enough, Shaun was left with the distinct impression that Dasha wasn't at all pleased to have Shaun back.

Shaun looked at Krystoff from beneath her lashes, wondering how he felt about her presence. His gaze was on Jozef, a troubled frown wrinkling his brow.

It was becoming clear that despite Jozef's move, intrigue still shrouded the Koba mansion.

CHAPTER THIRTEEN

After they finished eating, Krystoff suggested he and Jozef retire to the study for a drink. Jozef was hesitant. He didn't want to leave Shaun alone. Throughout dinner she'd been tense and jumpy. She was thinking about the poisoning and likely wondering if her would-be murderer was sitting across the table from her.

Perhaps it had been too soon to bring her back to the Koba estate, but Jozef was still family. Though his position had shifted, this had been his home for thirty years. His aunt had acted as mother to him, his uncle a father figure.

Despite their rift, the Kobas were still the most powerful organization in the Czech Republic. Jozef would have to work with them if he wanted his own budding organization to succeed. He'd far rather be on Krystoff's good side than his bad. Though Jozef had been his enforcer for two decades, growing in both intelligence and brutality, he was under no illusion that his uncle didn't still have a few tricks up his sleeve. If Jozef decided to take the old man on, he would have the fight of his life.

Jozef squeezed Shaun's shoulder reassuringly when he

stood to follow his uncle from the salon, where they would leave the women. Adam, Leeza's husband, excused himself to go back to the house and check on his son. It was a bullshit excuse not to linger with the family. Adam didn't care about his son any more than he cared about his wife. The strange pairing was a mystery to Jozef. His uncle had arranged it, but Jozef hadn't paid much attention at the time, having been too young and cocky to want much more than to hang out with his crew.

"Drink?" Krystoff made his way to the bar in his office and picked up a decanter of Scotch, glancing at Jozef with a raised brow.

Jozef nodded and walked to the fireplace, warming himself while Krystoff poured drinks. It was fall, nearly winter. Soon the snow would come, and the mansion would become blanketed. Krystoff would hire local artists to create ice sculptures in his rose garden. Aunt Dasha would throw her annual Christmas bash, inviting half the countryside and beyond. Jozef wondered if he and Shaun would receive an invitation. He hated the idea of taking Shaun anywhere near a crowd after what'd happened at the engagement party.

Krystoff pressed the drink into Jozef's hand and stepped back, his eyes sharp on Jozef's face. He pulled a cigar from his inside suit pocket and lifted it in question. Jozef nodded his permission for Krystoff to light it, appreciating the silent exchange. His uncle knew him well enough that there were few words needed.

Jozef felt a pang in his chest. He'd managed the distance from his family while he was in prison; he'd had no choice. Now that he was out, everything had changed. He no longer lived in the home where he'd grown up. He was dissociating from the organization he'd helped build. His aunt and cousins were wary around him. He had Shaun back, but that victory felt hollow in light of her anger and resistance.

A part of Jozef longed for everything to go back to the way it was, but he knew that was impossible. Change was inevitable and this one had been coming for a while. Even before Shaun, Jozef had been outgrowing his uncle. He'd balked at some of Krystoff's orders as well as some of the missions Krystoff sent Jozef and his men on. A mafia organization was a complex and potentially dangerous undertaking. Having two alpha men, Krystoff and Jozef, at the helm had been ofttimes contentious and stifling.

"Have a seat, son." Krystoff waved Jozef to the armchairs next to the fireplace.

Both men settled into their seats, sipping their drinks and allowing the heat of the fire to wash over them.

"Have you settled into your new home?"

Jozef nodded.

Krystoff took a sip of his drink, a puff of his cigar, then asked, "Would you consider moving back?"

No, Jozef signed.

Krystoff waited, seeming to expect more. Jozef didn't give it to him. His uncle knew the score, knew Jozef's reasons for leaving. Though the older man preferred to have his family close, living in the mansion wasn't necessary to doing business.

"What can I do to convince you? Family should be here, on the estate. You know this." There was an edge of desperation to his voice, making the pang in Jozef's chest flare hotter.

Nothing.

"I don't accept that, Jozef." The strain of the past year showed in the lines around Krystoff's eyes and the new patches of white streaking his hair and beard.

Havel had reported to Jozef on a weekly basis, giving updates on Jozef's people, the move, and their new business connections. He'd also reported on every move the Koba clan made, especially regarding the organization. Krystoff had suffered the loss of Jozef and his team, both financially and in reputation. It was well known the majority of Krystoff's protection came from Jozef and his team. Though Krystoff scrambled to replace them, his new hires didn't have the skill or background with the organization to be nearly as effective.

Though Jozef had no intention of taking over the Koba interests, the past year had shown which way the wind would blow if ever there was a separation. It was Jozef who held the majority of the power.

"I will make you an offer. Please take some time to consider it, rather than outright rejecting it." Krystoff held Jozef's gaze. "Join me as a full partner, we will share our business interests. You will run all operations, as you used to do. I will approve all of our associates, unless you choose otherwise. You can have veto power, and I'll leave the organization to you when I retire. All I ask is that you move back to the estate. I can provide you and your doctor with a separate home if you like. Similar to Leeza's cottage."

They both knew Krystoff would never retire. Regardless, the offer was incredibly generous. The Koba estate and all of its holdings amounted to a vast fortune. Jozef had never thought much about where the organization would go if Krystoff were out of the picture. If he wanted it, he could take it, but he would have to take his Aunt and cousins out of the picture first, not something he'd ever contemplated.

Finally, Jozef signed, *the money means nothing to me*.

"I know, it never has," Krystoff said sadly. "Your motivation was always this family."

Jozef nodded.

"Now you've switched your loyalty to her."

Jozef didn't say anything; he didn't need to. Krystoff was correct. Jozef was now motivated by Shaun. He still loved his family, but he needed to make the move. Before Shaun he'd seen the world from a narrow view. She made everything richer, brighter, clearer.

"She won't appreciate the things you do for her. The security, the jobs, it will all seem dangerous and illegal, which is not something she'll condone. How do you intend to settle this situation in a way that will allow you to keep the woman freely?" When Jozef didn't speak, he added, "We can keep her safe here at the mansion."

For a trump card, it was a weak one.

She was almost killed in this house one year ago, Jozef pointed out, crossing his ankle over his knee. He took a long sip of his scotch, appreciating the burn of fine whiskey as it slid down his throat.

Fury crossed over Krystoff's face, making him look more like the mobster he was renowned for rather than the kindly uncle he wanted to appear.

Jozef watched the older man steadily. He wondered if Krystoff was angry because Shaun had nearly died on his property or if he despised the woman threatening to bring down everything he'd worked for.

"Of course, you're correct," Krystoff said gruffly, ashing his cigar in a crystal tray. "I blame myself. I thought she would be safe in our home, protected by both the family and the security we constantly surround ourselves with. She should not have been reachable. I became complacent and she paid the price."

Jozef believed his uncle was speaking from the heart. From the day Jozef was born, he learned about the importance of family; first from his own father, then from Krystoff when Jozef's father was killed. It was gut-wrenching to now separate himself from the people, who, over the course of his life, talked to him about how family should stick together.

He didn't have a choice. After Shaun's poisoning, he couldn't bring her back to the place that'd nearly killed her.

And Jozef couldn't live without her, which meant he needed to separate himself from the Kobas. Shaun aside, it was time for him to stretch his wings. Like the phoenix tattoo rising up his back, Jozef would rise from the shadows of his family and strike out on his own. His time in prison showed him how quickly and easily he could knock down the competition, replacing the Vory he took out with members of his own organization.

I will not come back, Jozef signed, finality ringing in his silent words.

Krystoff nodded his understanding that the topic would now be closed. Jozef was surprised to see a glint of pride in the older man's eyes.

"I taught you everything I know," Krystoff murmured, settling back into the plush leather of his chair and sipping from his glass. "You have exceeded all expectations. You'll do great things, Jozef. Remember us while you're out there, injecting fresh blood throughout an antiquated underworld."

A smile stretched Jozef's lips at his uncle's praise. It was rare that Krystoff expressed himself in this way and Jozef was cognizant of the generosity his uncle was showing. He'd had to humble himself to admit he wanted Jozef back, and to further humble himself by admitting his pride in his nephew.

Yet, Krystoff was the type of man who could appear both humble and very much in control at the same time. As though his words were a gift given, not dragged through a mire of bitterness.

"I hope that we can continue to work together, building both of our interests," Krystoff continued. "You're still the best in the business, and I have several lucrative opportunities to explore."

Jozef dipped his head in a nod. *We are at your disposal, but our rate has gone up.*

Krystoff chuckled. "Of course it has. I didn't expect otherwise my boy."

The two spoke at length about the jobs Krystoff wanted to commission out to Jozef and his team. Jozef was grateful that his uncle didn't intend to hold a grudge against either himself or Shaun. The older man loved his family, but he was a hard man. If he chose to condemn the couple, they could've faced a difficult road to independence.

CHAPTER FOURTEEN

Leeza's heels tapped against the garden stones in a hushed patter as she made her way back to the cottage, her home on the Koba estates. She wasn't in a hurry to get back; not after the look Adam had given her. He hadn't wanted to come to the mansion for supper, but Krystoff had made the invitation mandatory.

Adam hated the power Krystoff wielded over the family. Adam was often overridden as the head of his and Leeza's house.

Krystoff took a personal hand in the lives of his daughter and grandson. Unfortunately, Krystoff didn't bother to look close enough to see the horrors that went on inside the cottage, which was tucked away on the eastern edge of the estate. After her humiliating marriage to the Koba accountant, Leeza hadn't bothered to educate Krystoff. Not because she didn't think he would care. He would. If he knew what crimes Adam committed against the oldest daughter of the Koba empire, Adam would have become food for the rose garden years ago.

No, the reason Leeza kept the humiliation of her

marriage a secret was to spite the man who'd cold-bloodedly married her off to a man she hated. It wasn't the only reason, but whenever she was forced to kneel at the feet of her husband, her hands stretched across the bedroom floor, his belt raining welts across her skin, she thought of Krystoff. She thought of the way she'd tearfully gone to him begging him to let her marry another, of his refusal and the heat of his fury as he tried to discover who her lover was.

He would be horrified if he saw his daughter at the mercy of the sadistic accountant. It was this twisted thought that'd gotten her through the first gut-wrenching years of her marriage, the rapes and the beatings.

Leeza still didn't know the exact reason behind her marriage. Though Krystoff could be a brutally cold man, when it came to his children, he had the occasional soft spot. She'd been shocked when he'd called her into his office to inform her of her upcoming nuptials to a man who was nearly two decades older than herself. She'd been twenty-one.

Though she'd known of Adam, she hadn't said more than two words to the man. At the time of their marriage, she'd thought perhaps he'd secretly coveted her, but that had proven to be untrue. It hadn't taken him long to show his disdain toward the eldest Koba daughter. Once, she'd asked him why he married her, but his answer had been a sneered, "You wouldn't understand."

As the years passed, she grew stronger in both mind and spirit. While Adam broke her body, thinking she was his cowed wife, she'd been moulding her mind into a machine. A machine that could take the pain, internalize it and twist it to her own purposes. The beatings grew progressively more severe as Leeza became more resilient, until Adam was forced to look elsewhere for his disgusting pleasures. He still occasionally used Leeza, but not often. He couldn't risk marking her in a permanent way that might give their game away.

Perhaps he knew where her mind had gone. He certainly must've wondered why she'd never gone to Krystoff. Maybe he thought she was too cowed. She didn't know because they rarely had a conversation that consisted of more than the weather, what cook was preparing for dinner, and Leeza's shopping schedule.

Adam simply didn't care about Leeza as more than a path for his ambitious and failed climb to power, and an occasional object for his lust. Even that had faded. Her lack of reaction made him feel inadequate so he looked elsewhere to relieve his perverse pleasures.

Once Leeza realized that her husband had no interest in her day-to-day life, the world opened up to her. She was able to go to the gun range and teach herself how to shoot. She hired instructors to teach her krav maga, taekwondo and aikido. She went shopping for weapons as often as she went shopping for clothes. In the privacy of their cottage garage, she'd taught herself how to make pipe bombs and makeshift grenades.

Leeza despised her husband, but he was the reason she was able to attain such a level of freedom. She didn't want to give up the freedom, which meant she had no choice but to stay married to a monster.

She waved at her security man, Igor, who was standing guard at her front door. He acted as her personal bodyguard when she left the estate.

"Nice evening, ma'am?"

"It was lovely, thank you," she said with a smile.

He unlocked and opened the door for Leeza, waving her in. She told him to have a good night and locked the door behind her. There was a note on the dining room table, instructing her to meet Adam in the master bedroom. The room she no longer shared with him. A mutual decision as neither of them enjoyed sharing a bed.

She sighed her annoyance, hand on her hip as she considered ignoring his summons. He would come for her if she didn't show up in his room, but she could easily defend herself. Though she wouldn't, it helped to imagine all the ways she could kill her husband if he wandered into her bedroom.

She closed her eyes and rubbed at the stab of pain between her eyes. She rarely regretted her marriage but spending an evening in the presence of Jozef and Shaun had tried her hard-earned patience. The two were very obviously in love, and though it was clear Shaun still had major reservations over her future husband, her feelings for him wasn't one of them. Shaun was beautiful and gracious, always saying and doing the correct thing. The warmth in her smile and gaze was all for Jozef.

Jozef revolved around Shaun the way the earth revolved around the sun. He checked on her constantly, touched her when she was close and watched her surroundings like a hawk. Where he was vigilant with the care and safety of his entire family, his feelings for Shaun went to a whole other level.

Leeza had never been a jealous person. She didn't care if the people around her were fucking, loving, living. It was none of her business. But when she looked at Shaun and Jozef she felt a tug of longing. She wanted that elusive feeling they had captured. The feeling she had experienced with only one other.

Never with Adam.

Even before she'd found out he was a disgusting pig of a man, she'd hated him. That feeling had grown to a raging inferno until it finally broke her. Now she felt nothing except for her son.

As she climbed the stairs, she considered what she would wear. He preferred her in something rich and sexy but also demure. He liked lace and silk in white or cream colours. He liked innocence. Something she'd had the satisfaction of denying him on their wedding night. She'd been punished terribly, a taste of their future as man and wife, but it had been her secret pleasure to deny him the one thing he wanted most—her virginity.

She closed the door to her bedroom and crossed to the closet, her hands going to the buttons of her shirt. She kicked off her high heels and ran her hand over a row of lingerie, choosing a black teddy that made her feel sexy. It had crisscross ties up both sides, giving peek-a-boos of the flawless skin beneath.

She wore the teddy with long black stockings and black panties with the same crisscross pattern. As a last bit of defiance before sliding into her black heels and pulling on a robe, she sprayed herself with Roja Dove, a heady perfume that was the opposite of everything Adam wanted in a woman.

As she walked down the hall toward his room, she stopped. Gingerly turning the knob on Kristoph's door, she slipped inside. She didn't want to wake her son, nor did she want Adam to know she'd delayed her route to his room. He would beat her extra hard for the way she was dressed, but he would make her bleed if he found out she hadn't scurried to him straight away.

She sat carefully on the edge of her son's bed, a small smile curving her lips. He was such a beautiful child when he slept. When he was awake, he was in constant motion, usually breaking, spilling and causing general mayhem. She loved every moment, but she especially loved these moments.

She brushed the hair from his forehead and bent to kiss him, pulling his blanket higher against his neck. Winter was coming and there was already a chill in the air. Soon she would have to wear stockings with her skirts and place her heeled feet carefully against the cobblestones as she made her way to the mansion.

"I love you so much, *medvídě*."

Kristoph loved the nickname his mother had given him because of his obsession with stuffed bears.

She made the sign for love, lifting her forefinger, thumb and pinkie while folding the other two down. Then she pressed her index finger to her lips, kissed her finger and placed it against his nose. It was a technique that helped calm him when he was having a meltdown. It meant that his mama loved him, and she was fine with him making as much chaos as he needed to let the world know he was alive and healthy.

Kristoph was the only good to come out of her marriage. If it weren't for her son, she might have killed herself years ago, back when she was still fragile, still breakable. Kristoph had saved her, and she would do the same for him by protecting him for the rest of her life. Nothing would touch her son while she was still alive.

She had no idea how Adam felt about Kristoph. He ignored the boy, only showing anger when the child was too loud. Otherwise, Adam rarely focused on the boy in either a negative or a positive way. Something that Leeza was extremely grateful for. If Adam had laid a single hand on her son, Leeza would've had to kill him.

She stood and adjusted her robe tighter around her body. She checked on Kristoph's teddy bear nightlight, dimming it, and then slipping from the room, gently closing the door.

Walking swiftly to Adam's room, she knocked and waited.

He opened the door and waved her inside. He was bare-chested, still wearing his pants from dinner. The belt was missing. From beneath her lashes, she spotted it laid out on his bed.

"What is this?" he demanded, waving his hand down her body.

"I dressed for you, master," she murmured in a low voice.

At one time it had galled her to call him master. Now it felt like she was mocking him when she spoke the word. The man was no master, especially not over her.

"You know how I prefer you to dress," he snapped angrily.

"I forgot."

"That's because you're a stupid cunt, aren't you? Can't remember to wear the white silk." He spoke scornfully, genuinely believing she was stupid enough to forget eight years of the same demand.

He walked swiftly to his dresser and picked up a bottle, shaking a handful of pills into his palm.

She cringed.

He only took Viagra when he was planning on fucking her, and the amount he was taking told her he hadn't had a good fuck in a while. She'd hoped he would just beat her, maybe humiliate her a little and send her back to her room. It looked like he wanted more. Hot bile rose up in her throat as she remembered similar nights. He wouldn't let her sleep. He would tie her up and fuck her for hours, only stopping for the occasional drink, while he deprived her, making her watch as he prepared for another round.

She could handle the beatings. Hell, she could even handle a round or two of his perverted idea of sex, but she despised those tiny blue pills. He used them like a weapon, fucking her until she was nothing but the used-up doll he really wanted.

It was the one thing she'd never been able to think her way through. She knew the trauma of his repeated rapes would be the thing that finally broke her. She supposed she would murder him eventually, then maybe herself, once she ensured Kristoph's future. She wasn't sure exactly how she'd do it, but her vengeful fantasies occasionally horrified even her.

"On your knees, whore."

Leeza sank to her knees on the plush carpet, placing her hands on her thighs and bowing her head demurely, just the way he liked it.

The blow came from behind, sending her sprawling against the side of the bed before she could catch herself. She scrambled back into position knowing she would catch it twice as hard if she wasn't back on her knees within seconds. Her back and shoulder throbbed but she didn't think he'd broken the skin. She glanced at him out of the corner of her eye. He was holding a length of hard rubber pipe, not a weapon he'd used on her before. Smart. It would hurt like a motherfucker, but it wouldn't break the skin unless he really tried.

He was upping his game. As the blows rained down on her back and shoulders, she made a mental note to tell her martial arts instructor that they would also need to train using different types of pipe. She would first learn how to defend herself, then she would learn how to turn the weapon on her opponent.

As the blows increased in intensity, she took a deep breath and settled into the place in her mind that would allow her to accept the pain and use it for her own purposes. A smile curved her lips, hidden by the silken fall of her dark hair.

CHAPTER FIFTEEN

The drive back to the apartment was silent. Out of necessity for Jozef whose hands had to be on the wheel, but Shaun could have spoken. Instead, she gazed out the passenger side window without saying a single word to him.

Jozef was frustrated by the gulf separating them. The feelings were all still there, but the situation had changed. The power dynamic had shifted. Jozef could use physical force to keep her with him, but she didn't have to comply. She could resist his efforts to keep her in line and he wouldn't lift a finger against her.

She was wrong about one thing though. The misery wouldn't last. In time she would settle into the life he wanted for her. She'd started to come around a year ago. The last thing she'd told him before being taken to the hospital was that she loved him. He knew from her counselling sessions that he'd been constantly on her mind during their separation. She wore his mother's ring during their time apart, only taking it off for surgery, and she continued to wear it now.

He wished he could speak to her, which only increased his

frustration. Shaun was the only person he'd ever met who he wished he had a voice for. He wanted to reassure her but couldn't. Not while he was driving and not while she was looking away from him.

So strong was his assumption that she was miserable, that he was surprised when she turned to face him, a grin stretching her lips.

"Your Aunt's face when Saskia told us she was taking sports medicine as an elective. I don't think Saskia was telling the truth, but it was funny."

Jozef barked in laughter, relieved that Shaun wasn't actively angry with him. She had every right, but she could still bend enough to enjoy the small things. This was how he knew for sure that she would eventually settle down. She was too resilient not to.

He reached across the console, picked up her hand and kissed her fingertips. She allowed him to retain her hand, which he placed on his thigh, covering it with his own.

Their peaceful moment lasted less than a minute.

The chirp of Jozef's phone coincided with a message flashing on his dashboard screen. A digital voice said, "Message from Havel: You're being flagged by the authorities. Someone wants to talk to you."

Jozef glanced in his rearview mirror, frowning.

Following his gaze, Shaun twisted around in her seat and stared into the darkness.

At first, the only thing visible was the headlights belonging to the bodyguard vehicle. Then, a set of headlights swung out from behind Havel's vehicle and drove up alongside Jozef's car. He immediately recognized it as a government town car. Someone high up wanted to talk to him.

Jozef growled his annoyance and accelerated the car. If they wanted to talk to him, they could do it at the nightclub. The vehicle accelerated too, shooting past Jozef and cutting in front of him. Another vehicle came up alongside him, blocking him in.

Another text message came through. "What do you want us to do, boss?"

Jozef growled his annoyance and reached out to type the reply.

"Do you want help?" Shaun asked anxiously, her wide eyes on the vehicles surrounding them.

He wanted to reassure her with words, but he couldn't, so he finished his message and then reached for her. He cupped her cheek and gave her a reassuring smile. She didn't smile back, but the frown of terror creasing her beautiful face faded into worry. She could handle worry, but he didn't want her thinking their lives were at risk.

The car in front of them began to decrease in speed. Jozef knew the drill. The two vehicles, with likely a third behind Jozef's bodyguards, would force them off the road so they could conduct a meeting with Jozef on their terms. Of course, he wasn't going to play their game. Not with Shaun in the car; not for any reason.

Driving one-handed he typed out a quick reply to Havel, then sent a message to Karl, who was manning the nightclub.

Jozef gripped Shaun's seatbelt and tightened it until she was gasping. He gave her a significant look, but her wide eyes were blank. She had no idea what he was about to do and he had no way of warning her. He didn't have time, he needed to act quickly.

First, he tapped his breaks twice, telling Havel he was ready. Seconds later Havel slammed on the breaks to his SUV and swerved his car to block their rear tail. Jozef braked so hard, the tires squealed and both the car to the side of them and the one up front shot past. Before the pursuing cars had time to react, Jozef cranked the wheel and hit the gas.

As his car accelerated from 50 km/h to 250 within

seconds, the Bugatti earned every penny of its hefty price tag. Shaun let out a yelp, slapping her hand over her mouth as she was thrown back in her seat. Jozef tried to take the fact that they were being followed seriously, but he couldn't help himself; a grin split his lips. There was nothing quite like watching the world fly past as a piece of beautiful and expensive machinery shot them forward into the night.

"Oh god, we're going to die!" Shaun shrieked, gripping her seat until her knuckles were pale.

Jozef laughed and shook his head, reaching out to take her hand.

"Keep your hands on the wheel!" She slapped his hand away and Jozef laughed harder.

Shaun looked at him like he was crazy then started laughing too. She lifted shaking hands to her face, wiping her fingers beneath her eyes to stop her mascara from running. He didn't think she was crying out of fear, but from the sudden adrenaline rush.

She twisted in her seat to stare out the back window. "I don't see anyone back there; you can slow down now."

Jozef ignored her. Once the pursuit vehicles realized what happened, they would speed up and either try to catch Jozef or beat him to the club. He had to concentrate on driving as fast as he could, as safely as he could.

If Shaun hadn't been in the car it would've been no contest, but Jozef refused to take any risks with her. He was forced to slow down for corners and check traffic, so they didn't slam into anyone. They arrived at the club at the same time as the government vehicles, while Havel pulled up directly behind them.

Jozef flung his door open and strode swiftly to the passenger door, jerking it from Shaun's hands as she was getting out. He took her arm and pulled her to her feet. She stumbled on her high heels as he dragged her back to the curb where Karl, Halil and Cooper were already waiting.

Karl reached for Shaun while Jozef pulled his gun out of the holster beneath his leather jacket.

Shaun gasped as she caught sight of the weapon, but Jozef didn't have time to explain that there would be no danger from government agents while standing on the corner of a busy downtown Prague street. He was merely posturing, showing them his anger at being pursued. He dropped a kiss onto her open lips then nodded at Karl who pulled her swiftly into the building, club security at his back, their sharp eyes scanning for any threats to Shaun.

Havel, Terek and Halil stood at Jozef's back as he stalked toward a man dressed in a black business suit, white shirt and standard issue tie. He had an earpiece, which Jozef would guess linked directly to the Prime Minister's office. From everything he'd learned in prison, the President was incorruptible while the Prime Minister preferred to keep his fingers in all aspects of Czechian society. At the man's back stood two more government henchmen.

What do you want? Jozef signed furiously.

Havel stood at his side, interpreting.

"Why didn't you stop on the highway, as you were asked?" the man in the suit countered.

Jozef sneered his disdain. *You didn't ask me anything. If you wish to play games with me, then you'll end up in the ground. Now, tell me what is so important that you put my fiancé's life at risk?*

The man's eyes dropped to the weapon in Jozef's hand, as though he was only now realizing he needed to tread carefully. He lifted his hands in a peaceful gesture. "My apologies, we didn't know you had a woman in the car. You were never in danger; we just want to talk."

Jozef's fury grew hotter. If there was one thing he

wouldn't tolerate it was someone being careless with Shaun's life. One year ago, he accepted a lifetime of imprisonment to save her life. He would kill anyone who put that life in danger.

You're either a liar or you're stupid, Jozef signed. *If you have men watching me, then you knew my woman was in the car. If you tried to push me off the road without doing your homework on who was in the vehicle then you're a fucking idiot. Either way, your mistake will not be forgotten.*

The man stood frozen for a moment, as though trying to decide what to do. He'd been sent to intimidate Jozef, but it was happening the other way around. He was the one sweating bullets while Jozef was in full control of the situation. Before he could gather himself, Jozef clapped his hands in the other man's face while Havel barked, "Talk!"

He cleared his throat and tried for a conciliatory tone. "It wasn't our intent to frighten your woman. Once more, I apologize. I was sent here by a man who wishes to remain anonymous but would like to speak with you about a job."

Jozef turned on his heel and headed to the club.

"Wait, hear me out." The man hurried after Jozef, attempting to follow him into the club. The bouncers stood ready to block the door once Jozef passed through. "The opportunity will be lucrative. You should listen to what I have to say."

Jozef let out an annoyed growl and turned to look at the man on the sidewalk. His signs were rapid, showing his impatience. *Your patron is Prime Minister N-E-M-E-C. He believes that he can have me and my men at his disposal because he worked to get me out of prison. You are head of his security detail, D-I-E-T-R-I-C-K.*

Havel translated.

Alan Dietrick blanched, taking a moment to recover. It was clear that this conversation had not gone how he'd planned. The Prime Minister hired for brawn rather than brains.

"Is he wrong in thinking that you owe him a favour?" Alan asked, attempting to infuse some strength into his voice while looking nervously at Jozef's men who were surrounding him and his security detail.

I owe him nothing, Jozef signed. Jozef took the few steps separating them and pointed at Alan's chest with his left hand while keeping his gun low at his side on the right. *It was my uncle who convinced your boss to free me. I would have eventually found my way out.*

"You don't want to refuse the Prime Minister's request," Alan insisted, giving up the pretense that his patron was anonymous. "He won't ask as nicely next time."

Jozef grunted and nodded, thinking. Then he said, *if you wish to play games with me, then I will play to win. Take my message to the Prime Minister.*

Alan took a step back, as if sensing Jozef's mood. Before he could get far, Jozef reached for him, gripping the other man by the bicep and digging his fingers into Alan's arm over the artery, cutting off the blood supply and deadening the arm. Alan yelped as Jozef swung him around and slammed him into the brick wall at his back. Jozef brought his gun up and pressed it into the flesh beneath Alan's shoulder blade. It would hurt like a bitch, but it wouldn't take out the entire arm.

Jozef pulled the trigger.

A woman shrieked and rushed past, clutching the arm of a friend. Jozef and his team ignored them. They were noise, as was everything on the street. Jozef was sending a blatant message. He didn't care who came knocking, didn't care where the confrontation took place, he would not tolerate threats.

Jozef let him go, allowing Alan to slide to the ground,

moaning and clutching his shoulder. Jozef crouched in front of him. He looked the man in the eyes and allowed him to see the devil inside, the gangster who thrived off violence and didn't fear death.

Jozef stood, replaced his gun in its holster, brushed the dust from his leather jacket and walked back to the club entrance.

Havel spoke one last time before following Jozef inside, throwing Alan's words back at him. "Next time he won't say no so nice."

CHAPTER SIXTEEN

"Are you sure that was a smart move?" Havel asked, catching up with Jozef. "It was satisfying to see that cockroach bleeding on the ground, but the Prime Minister has powerful allies. We don't want to go to war with him."

We aren't going to war, my friend, we're establishing battle lines. He knows that he can't get away with threats and intimidation. Now he'll try a softer approach. It will mean we can ask for more money.

Havel grinned, flashing his white teeth as they headed onto the club floor. "You know what you're doing."

I know what I'm doing, Jozef agreed. *But if that idiot involves Shaun ever again, his boss will be fishing him out of the river.*

"Agreed," Havel said grimly.

They were headed toward the back of the club when they were waylaid by an agitated waitress. Her name was Yvetta and she'd been working at Zmatek for three years. Though Jozef didn't hire the club staff, except for security, he had complete files on everyone who worked there. He needed to know who the people were that would work physically close to him. If they had unpaid debts, a questionable background or an arrest record.

"There's a woman here to see you," she told Jozef, glancing over her shoulder. "I put her in the VIP booth."

Jozef frowned and signed, *why would you allow anyone to sit at my table? It is to remain vacant except for family.*

"I know," she rushed to say. "But she insists that she's family. She says she knows your girlfriend. If I'm wrong then I'm terribly sorry, but I didn't know what to do. She was insistent and she wouldn't leave. When security confronted her, she kept insisting she wouldn't leave without seeing you and I thought it best to put her in VIP before she could cause a scene. I'm so sorry if I've done something wrong, Mr. Koba."

Before he could question Yvetta further, she rushed away, a stricken look on her face. Impatience rose up in Jozef as he strode across the floor of the club, bypassing the dancing patrons and ignoring the few who called out to him. He wanted to know what woman was so fearsome that his highly trained and armed men couldn't handle her.

He strode up the VIP stairs and flung the velvet curtain open. The sight that greeted him would've been laughable if it didn't strike a note of terror into his heart. The woman on the other side of the curtain was none other than Fatima Patterson. Shaun's mother and his future mother-in-law.

She sat at the table, sipping a glass of wine and looking bored. On the table next to her was a plastic crate with metal bars. Jozef had a suspicion that the crate contained Shaun's cat, Fitzy. On the ground next to Mrs. Patterson was a suitcase, which was bursting at the seams. When she caught sight of Jozef, her bored expression evaporated, fury replacing it.

He watched in shock as she clambered to her feet, the wrinkles in her travelling suit remaining as she stood to her full height, which wasn't much. She was much shorter than Shaun. Her skin was lighter, and her hair was smooth and straight, unlike Shaun's mane of wild curls.

Jozef tried to back up as she catapulted herself toward

him, her finger shaking and her round face creasing with anger. Jozef backed into Havel who, immediately recognizing Shaun's mother, turned tail and ran away, leaving Jozef alone. The big bald bodyguard was having nothing to do with the tiny volatile mother.

Give me back my daughter this instant, she signed, her lips pulling back into a ferocious snarl as she wagged her finger in Jozef's face.

Rather than being insulted or angry, Jozef melted. She hadn't even tried to communicate verbally with him, which meant she knew about him. Shaun had told her mother about him. He didn't know how much, and he didn't really care. In that moment, he loved the mother almost as much as he loved the daughter. They were special. They were fierce and beautiful, and they could communicate with him.

Jozef wanted to hug the woman but thought it might be too soon. The look on her face told him if he tried to touch her, she would tear out his heart with her bare hands.

You may see your daughter, he signed to her.

She stopped short and gaped at him for a few seconds, then she dropped her face into her hands and allowed her shoulders to slump. "Thank god."

He realized that she hadn't really had a plan upon entering the club. Her entire focus had probably been on getting to the Czech Republic as fast as she could and tracking down the man who'd taken her daughter. His heart melted further. She was a fighter.

He risked his life and gingerly took her arm, guiding her back to the table. She jerked it out of his grip and sank back into the booth. Jozef chose a seat across from her. He despised having his back to the curtain, with an entire room filled with people on the other side, but he was willing to make an exception.

When she looked at him, her eyes still glowed with anger, but her face and posture were composed once more.

How did you find me? Jozef signed.

She seemed to mull over whether to answer him or not, then she said, *Shaun told me some things, but most of the information I got on you I got from following your trial.* She picked up her glass of wine, her hand shaking, and took a long sip. She sighed as she replaced it back on the table, appearing steadier. *After I found your name, I did some digging and discovered that you owned a nightclub in the city. I wasn't sure which one, so I tried a few before I was directed here.*

Her ingenuity amazed him, especially since she'd pieced together his whereabouts from across the world. It was her recklessness that surprised and chilled him. If the wrong person had gotten wind of her inquiries, if anyone guessed her connection to Jozef's fiancé, she could've found herself in grave danger.

As if sensing the direction of his thoughts, she defended herself. *I was discreet and careful. I'm not a dummy, Mr. Koba.*

J-O-Z-E-F, he signed the letters of his name.

"Jozef," she repeated his name.

He was transported back in time to the day he met Shaun. She'd asked him for his name, he assumed so she could forge a connection with him and use it to convince him not to kill her. She'd whispered his name to herself, much the same way her mother had just done. Though the two women didn't look a lot alike, except for their radiant beauty, he could easily see the resemblance in personalities.

"You may call me Mrs. Patterson," she said primly, frowning her disapproval at him.

Jozef let out a barking laugh that was loud enough to startle the creature in the crate. It let out a disgruntled growl that vibrated the box and shoved a fuzzy orange paw through the bars. Jozef was fascinated. He'd never had a pet before, never thought much about them, but this one belonged to Shaun and she clearly loved the beast. Which meant he would love it too.

Would you care for another drink? Jozef asked, turning to tell his men to call the waitress. There was no one inside the VIP area. They were too afraid of Shaun's mother to remain at their positions.

Jozef shoved the curtain aside, scowling in annoyance. Halil and Terek stood at the bottom of the stairs looking up at him guiltily. They knew they were supposed to be closer to their principal. Jozef couldn't bring himself to be truly angry with them. A confrontation with his future mother-in-law had not been on his list of things to do for the evening either.

He snapped his fingers and pointed at the bar.

"Yes, boss." Halil took off, not wanting to delay Jozef's drink after screwing up.

Jozef let the curtain fall back into place and turned back to contemplate the problem which had just placed itself in his lap. What to do with a woman who would be determined to take the one thing Jozef was least able to part with. He couldn't bring himself to hurt the mother of the woman he loved, so his usual method of removing the problem wasn't going to work.

He groaned as he realized there would be only one solution to the problem of Mrs. Patterson; she would have to stay, whether she wanted to or not. If Shaun was mad at him before this, she was going to be livid when he explained what he was planning for her mother.

CHAPTER SEVENTEEN

Shaun stared out the window of the apartment, desperately wishing she could see what was happening on the sidewalk. It had been thirty minutes since she was whisked up the back stairs of the club and into Jozef's suite. She'd didn't have a chance to ask what was going on when the door was slammed shut and she was locked inside. That was when Shaun discovered she could be locked in the apartment with some kind of lock that only the person on the other side could access.

Shaun decided she would be angry about it later once she determined that Jozef was safe.

With a sigh she moved away from the window. She couldn't see anything from her vantage point. It drove her crazy that Jozef was doing something potentially dangerous while she was stuck upstairs. What if he was shot? Or what if he shot someone else? She should be down on the ground helping with any injuries.

She walked into the bedroom, reaching back to unzip her dress. She let it fall to the floor and stepped out of it. Changing into a pair of pink sweatpants and an oversized T-shirt from Jozef's drawer, she walked back into the living room and stood looking around helplessly.

"Is this how mob wives feel?" she mumbled, sitting on the couch in a cross-legged position.

She picked up the remote and turned the TV on, switching to streaming service. She used the voice recognition to command the TV to find "Mob Wives." She'd never watched the show, but maybe there would be some tips on how to handle a man determined to imprison her in the name of protection.

She was completely engrossed in the show when she heard the lock on the door click. A rush of apprehension hit her, and she felt dizzy as she pictured Karl or Havel coming in to tell her Jozef had been shot and killed on the street below. Tears sparked in her eyes and her breathing grew shallow. She knew she was overreacting, but she couldn't seem to stop herself.

The door opened and Jozef strode inside. She launched herself off the couch and rushed toward him, throwing her arms around his neck. He seemed startled, but quickly recovered, his strong arms engulfing her in one of the best hugs she'd ever had. Relief flooded through her as she held him.

He was okay. He wasn't dead.

She pulled back to demand he tell her everything, but her gaze strayed past his shoulder.

"Mom!"

She couldn't believe her eyes. Fatima in Prague? It didn't seem possible. Yet, there she was, standing next to a suitcase and a crate with orange fluff sticking out. Fatima's expression looked just as surprised. Shaun thought her mother was shocked more by the hug she'd given Jozef then from actually seeing Shaun.

"How did you get here?" Shaun extricated herself from

Jozef's arms and stepped past him to hug her mother, her expression one of bewilderment.

Fatima hugged her tightly and then held Shaun away from her, her eyes roving over her daughter, looking for any scratches. "I flew over the day after you were taken, and I've been searching since I got here. Are you hurt?"

"I'm okay," Shaun assured her.

"Are you being held against your will?" Fatima demanded. "Did you request this man come pick you up in Montréal and bring you here? Did you ask for any of this? Because if your answer is no, then you are not okay."

Fatima turned the full force of her glare on Jozef, who stood casually aside, his arms crossed over his chest, his gaze neutral.

"You will release my daughter immediately so I can take her home."

Shaun appreciated Fatima's bravado, but she knew her mother. As fierce as she was, Fatima had to be shaking in her shoes. She hated confrontation, and Shaun suspected that would go double for confronting a man like Jozef; someone who made a living off the lives of others.

N-O, he signed. *She stays with me.*

Fatima glared at him. "I will involve the authorities. Give her up now and you won't go back to prison. We'll walk away like we were never here."

Shaun's heart pounded faster as she saw the hard expression on Jozef's face. He was becoming impatient with Fatima, and in Shaun's experience, that meant he was about to get violent.

You will not call the authorities.

"And how do you propose to stop me?" Fatima said furiously, her arm tightening protectively around Shaun's waist.

Jozef's gaze followed the move and his expression softened again.

Shaun answered Fatima's question. "He'll keep you here."

"What?" Fatima said sharply. "He can't do that."

"Of course he can." Shaun let some of her frustration show as she paced away from her mother. "He'll keep you here the same way he's keeping me, the way he kept me a year ago. He has the manpower and brute force to make sure two women stay hidden away. God, mom, why did you come here?"

Fatima looked first shocked and then hurt. "I came for you."

"And you didn't once consider that you were walking into the home of a known gangster?" Shaun argued. "I love you, and I love that you want to protect me, but you had to know this was dangerous. What if he just had you quietly shot, rather than bringing you to me? I wouldn't have known you ever came, and I would never have known what happened to you. Do you understand what you've done?"

Fatima blanched and Shaun could see Jozef's arms jerk out of the corner of her eye. She refused to look at him though. She didn't want to read anything in his gaze. What if he'd thought about killing her mother? It would shatter her, so she refused to contemplate the thought.

"I wasn't thinking about anything but getting to you," Fatima spoke quietly, the weight of her decision settling around her. She looked at Jozef. "Will you really keep me here?"

Jozef stared at her, then answered with his own question, *Will you leave quietly?*

"Not without my daughter," she said swiftly.

Then you both stay.

Shaun saw that he was firm in his decision and wondered if he'd already made it when he realized Fatima had come for her. Which meant he likely never contemplated killing Fatima. The tension inside Shaun eased.

"Please let us go," Fatima begged him.

"Mom, he won't," Shaun said gently, reaching out to take her mother's hand.

Shaun hadn't realized how reconciled she was to staying with Jozef until she saw the devastation on her mother's face. It was how she felt when he'd taken her the first time, the same as a few days ago. Only this time, she knew deep in her heart that she'd made her decision. Seeing her mother standing in the place of her captivity only strengthened her resolve. She wasn't really a captive. The more Fatima begged, the more Shaun realized she wouldn't get on an airplane with her mother, even if she had a choice.

How could a woman of her profession and personality give up everything to be with a man she was morally opposed to? It was a terrible, awesome realization that she would have to unpack later. She didn't need to examine it now, because Jozef was taking her choices away. Almost as if he knew she wouldn't be able to handle the fallout of that kind of decision on her own, so he took it from her hands.

His gaze was on her, hard with determination but also with a flicker of compassion for her internal struggle. Then his gaze strayed back to Shaun's mother and, once she was looking at him, he said his piece.

Your daughter stays with me. There will be no question of her leaving at any time. You will reconcile yourself to this fact.

"And if I can't?" Fatima asked brokenly.

Shaun answered, her words an echo of what Leeza had said to her all those months ago when Shaun had asked a similar question. "You don't want to know."

Jozef didn't answer, instead signing, *I will leave you to speak with your daughter. An apartment on the floor below will be prepared for you.*

Jozef turned to leave, striding quickly toward the door as though he couldn't wait to get out of there. If Shaun had been in a better mood, she might have laughed at his haste to leave the presence of a woman he would consider his mother-in-law. He was a gangster through and through, and though Shaun knew he loved his aunt and cousins, he had no idea how to handle soft emotions.

"Jozef," Shaun called out. "I want to stay with my mother."

He didn't answer, closing and locking the door behind himself as he left. She supposed he didn't need to answer; there was no chance he would let her stay anywhere that wasn't with him.

"I'm exhausted." Fatima's voice was high and thin, as though she was on the verge of tears.

Shaun wrapped an arm around her. "Come on, let's sit down. I'll get you a glass of water?"

"Do you have any tea?" Fatima asked.

"I'll find some."

Shaun pressed a glass of cold water into her mother's hand, insisting she drink it all while Shaun set a kettle to boil and dug through the cupboards until she found a basket filled with different teas. She took a mug out of the cupboard and chose a chamomile honey tea. The calming effects of the chamomile would help with some of the shock her mother was likely experiencing.

She set the cup down on the coffee table and sank onto the cushion next to Fatima.

"I'm so sorry about all this," Shaun said, as Fatima picked up her mug of tea and blew on the steam.

"You have nothing to be sorry for, baby." Fatima shook her head and gingerly took a sip of the brew, closing her eyes for a few seconds as she savoured the hot beverage. "I was the idiot who travelled halfway across the world with a cat and traipsed into mafia headquarters without a plan."

Shaun giggled and then covered her mouth, her eyes

flaring wide. "You brought Fitzy!" She surged to her feet and ran to the crate on the floor, yanking open the metal closure on the door.

A ball of angry orange fluff flew past her and streaked across the floor, headed for the dining table. He huddled underneath a chair, his eyes wide and fearful.

"He hates flying," Fatima said from the couch, taking another sip of her tea. "Peed his crate and meowed the whole way."

"Why didn't you leave him with Monique?" Shaun named her cousin, who reluctantly took the cat when Fatima wasn't available.

Fatima shrugged. "I didn't know how long I'd be gone, and I suspected something like this might happen."

"Mom, you could've gotten yourself killed."

"I know that now," she said defensively. "Thank goodness Jozef loves you too much to kill your poor mom."

Shaun grinned. Fatima was right, Jozef loved her.

She slid across the floor, crawling toward her cat who was still under the table, his fur so fluffed up he looked like an orange poof with eyes. "I don't know if the same can be said of Fitzy. I have no idea where Jozef stands on pet cats."

"He doesn't look like a cat person to me." Fatima shook her head.

Shaun laughed, suddenly feeling better than she had since she found herself kidnapped for a second time. Though the future was still uncertain, it felt a lot less bleak.

CHAPTER EIGHTEEN

After a brief discussion, it was decided that Fitzy would stay with Shaun. Though he tolerated Fatima, he had only ever bonded with Shaun, making his care difficult for anyone else. Jozef didn't seem to mind having the cat in his apartment, though when Fitzy hissed at him, Jozef growled back. After the exchange, the two seemed to settle into keeping a wary and mutual distance.

The next few days passed quickly for Shaun who spent most of her time with her mother. Shaun had been given permission to go between the floors any time she wanted as long as she had Karl with her. He seemed to take his new babysitting duties in stride, diligently passing on all of Shaun's requests.

Unlike their apartment, the one Fatima now inhabited was quite sparse. Shaun suspected it was originally meant to house another of Jozef's men but was currently empty. It was a smaller version of Jozef's suite with an open kitchen, dining room and living room. While Jozef and Shaun's place had two bedrooms, Fatima's only had one.

"It's fine, I don't need any extra rooms." Fatima had

shrugged off the smaller apartment and set about inspecting her new home.

Shaun made a list of things Fatima would need immediately and then the two women started on lists for food and supplies. Fatima loved to cook and would need a kitchen complete with all the accessories and food staples. As they worked, the reality of where they were faded, and they enjoyed the time spent together.

Fatima, on her hands and knees dusting out the bottom cupboards so she could put away the supplies that had started to trickle in, said to Shaun, "You seem more relaxed than I've seen you in a long time."

Shaun, who was preparing two cups of tea, stopped what she was doing. Was she more relaxed? She took stock of herself and realized she was. She felt as though a weight had been lifted off her shoulders. It took another minute of thought before she realized it was because the two worlds she had been attempting to inhabit were finally merging.

The one truth she had carried with her up to this point was that she couldn't have Jozef in her life. No matter what, their separate lives couldn't be reconciled. Yet here was her mother and her cat. Before Fatima left Montréal, she'd talked to Shaun's boss at the hospital and explained that Shaun had to leave suddenly for personal reasons. Her boss had given her the leave but told Fatima he would require a phone call and a letter from Shaun explaining if she didn't want to lose her job.

Shaun would have to talk to Jozef about her next step. She didn't feel like a captive anymore, yet she was acting like one by needing Jozef's permission whenever she wanted something, especially contact with the outside world. She supposed she would have to work with him on creating a more mutually respectful relationship. Perhaps if she told him she would accept his security measures if he allowed her to pursue her career, he might consider it.

Her profession was the one thing she wasn't willing to compromise on. She would relocate to Prague; she would move her mother and her cat. She wouldn't ask questions about his job; not yet anyway. But she refused to give up everything she'd worked so hard to achieve. Being a surgeon defined her and she knew without a doubt that she would never be able to live with the loss if Jozef took that away from her. She just needed to find a way to tell him.

After several hours of working diligently to put Fatima's apartment in order, the two women flopped on the bed together with contented sighs. There was no couch yet, so they would have to relax in the bedroom until one arrived.

"I always wanted to travel," Fatima murmured. "Never really got around to it."

"You went to the Dominican Republic," Shaun pointed out. "And Hawaii. Oh, and you visited Kiev last year."

"Dominican and Hawaii were vacations, and in Kiev, I didn't leave my hotel room. I was too busy waiting for news of you to explore." Fatima rolled onto her side, propping her head up with the palm of her hand, her silver-streaked black hair swirling over her arm. "I never in my life imagined travelling to the Czech Republic. Shaun, we're in Prague."

Shaun was helpless against the look of wonder on her mother's face. Some of Fatima's excitement filtered through to Shaun and she finally thought about the city she would call home as more than the place of her captivity. It was a gorgeous old city with so much history.

"I'll see if Karl will take us out to explore tomorrow," Shaun offered.

Fatima pushed herself up into a sitting position and sat with her back against the headboard. "Do you think Jozef will allow you to go out?"

They looked at each other, some of their pleasure draining away as they contemplated the restrictions involved in Shaun's new life.

"You know you can't live like that," Fatima said quietly. "You'll slowly die inside if you have to ask him for every crumb. You were raised to be a tough independent woman, not the cowed wife of a man who makes all of your decisions for you. When he says jump, you shouldn't be asking how high. What would your father think?"

Shaun blinked back tears at the harsh words. She didn't think her mother meant them to be unkind, but they pierced her heart. Shaun knew her father would never approve of the kind of life being pushed on Shaun. Yet, once again when she thought about leaving, she couldn't imagine a life without Jozef.

She swallowed, trying to dispel the constriction in her throat. "Are you disappointed in me?"

"Oh no, baby," Fatima reached over to cup Shaun's face. Shaun looked into her mother's warm golden eyes, the exact shade as her own, and saw the truth. "You are an incredible woman, and I'm so proud of everything you've accomplished. I'm proud of the way you've handled yourself this past year, your strength and determination to return to work after you were kidnapped and poisoned. I'm proud of the grace you're showing now, in the face of a major upheaval in your life. If I'm disappointed at all, it's for the dreams you'll be losing if you stay here."

Shaun nodded, allowing a few tears to fall.

She was saved from having to delve too deeply into her uncertain future when Karl's voice echoed through the apartment.

"In here," she called, pushing herself off the bed and meeting him at the bedroom door.

"Boss wants you to meet him in the club this evening."

His eyes strayed to Fatima who was standing next to the bed, straightening her clothes. "He wants you to translate for him."

Shaun was instantly transported back to her last experience in the club when she'd translated for Jozef. The drugs, the cavalier attitude toward murder and mayhem, the confrontation with Giselle. She felt the blood draining from her face as she remembered the way Jozef had attacked Giselle in the club washroom.

"No," she whispered.

Though Karl looked concerned, he knew whose orders he had to obey. "I don't think he's asking."

Shaun shook her head, her stomach churning with anxiety.

Fatima caught sight of Shaun's expression and demanded, suspicion in her voice, "What happened in the club? Why don't you want to translate?"

Shaun tried to think of something to say that wouldn't upset her mother, but as always, she came back to the truth. Maybe Fatima should know what kind of a life they were facing if they stayed with Jozef. As much as it would break Shaun's heart if Fatima decided to leave, her mother would be safer in Canada.

"Jozef pulled a gun on a woman who was bothering me. He threatened her life."

Fatima looked alarmed. "Does he do this often?"

Karl smothered an amused look, while Shaun answered, "He seems to do it whenever he thinks someone is threatening me. I've seen it happen twice." She didn't tell her mother that the second time had happened the night before, right outside the club, probably while Fatima was already inside.

"He can't control himself?" Fatima's concern grew.

"No, that's not it." Shaun was quick to correct her. "The

gun is an extension of him. Like a tool that he's so comfortable with he barely notices it's there."

"But do you think he really would shoot someone?"

"Yes." Both Shaun and Karl answered at the same time.

Fatima sat down on the bed, looking shaken. Shaun wished she could ease her mother's fears, but she didn't know what to say. They were living a dangerous new reality where everyone around them was armed and threats were very possible.

She sat next to Fatima and took her hand. "He won't hurt us, Mom. We're safe."

Fatima straightened her spine and pulled her hand from Shaun's, tucking a lock of hair behind her ear. "I know he won't hurt us; at least not you, and probably not me by extension. But I would argue that we are most definitely not safe. He leads a dangerous life and he's dragging you into it with him."

"I know, but there's nothing we can do about it."

It looked like Fatima wanted to argue, but she glanced at Karl and pressed her lips together. Finally, she nodded and said, "Go to the club, but remember who you are. When he says jump, you tell him to fuck off."

CHAPTER NINETEEN

Saskia walked fast with her head down, her books clutched to her chest. Damn, it was getting cold. She was more of a warm weather girl. She preferred sun and beaches, crackling fireplaces and her bed. It was days like this that she regretted her decision to take university courses in the city.

Her parents had tried to convince her to take her courses online at the mansion. She'd insisted that her education would be subpar if she wasn't allowed to take her classes in person. They'd relented and allowed her to go to the Charles University in Prague as long as she kept her guards nearby at all times. Her father had gone to the dean of the university and told him of their unique situation, with a sizable donation to soothe any ruffled feathers.

Saskia hated that her family had gotten involved in the one thing she was attempting to do for herself. She'd bitten her tongue though and accepted her bodyguards. She allowed them to follow her, unwilling to risk her university career on one stupid decision, like running from her guards.

There was only one exception to her no-giving-the-guards-the-slip rule.

She waved at her main bodyguard. She'd tried flirting with the man once and only once. He'd looked at her like she was about as attractive as a rock, then he told her father. She'd gotten a stern tongue lashing and a threat to have her removed from the campus. She hadn't tried engaging the man since.

She pushed open the door to the women's washroom and went inside, locking the door behind herself. She pushed open all the stall doors to make sure she was alone, set her books down and climbed up on the counter. She unlatched the window and stuck her head out.

"Romeo, Romeo," she whispered dramatically, then, catching sight of her prey, said with a grin, "There you are."

Nikolay reached up and pulled himself through the window. He'd made the same move about half a dozen times since Saskia had enrolled at the university and each time made her sigh all over again. The big muscles on his arms bulged as he lifted himself, pulling his body through the window frame and dropping to tiled floor.

He reached for Saskia and their lips met before either said another word. He kissed her hungrily as though he'd been waiting years to do just that. She wrapped her arms around his waist and kissed him back with equal fervour.

He pulled back and growled, "Clothes."

Understanding, Saskia reached for the hem of her shirt, dragging it over her head and tossing it aside. Her hands landed on the button of her jeans, then her eyes caught on him. Or more specifically, the beautifully veined cock he was pulling from the confines of his pants.

It was hard and pulsing, pointing up toward his belly.

Her mouth watered and she reached for him.

"Ah ah." He smacked her hand and, gripping her waist,

whirled her around, forcing her to place her hands on the counter.

She looked at herself in the mirror over the sink, taking in her flushed cheeks and sparkling eyes. She grinned stupidly at herself as she heard the tearing of a wrapper. Seconds later, his hands were groping her waist while he kissed her neck, biting the tender flesh and marking her.

He unbuttoned her jeans and dragged them, along with her panties to her feet. She heard a ripping sound and realized her underwear had torn. A slight pang hit her as she realized he hadn't seen her panties. She'd picked them out specially for him.

As he bent her over and pushed inside her from behind, she reminded herself that it had to be this way. There was no way her father would allow her to be with Nikolay. Not only was he one of Jozef's men, but he was low born. His mother had been a distant cousin of Krystoff's and had married a poor farmer.

Though they were related, it didn't bother Saskia. The connection was distant. She was his third or fourth cousin. Krystoff was considering other matches, some of them with more shared blood than Saskia and Nikolay.

Saskia watched his face in the mirror. The savage lust, the concentration as he pumped, hurtling toward his orgasm. She moaned and was gratified when he looked up and grinned at her. She moaned again, shoving her hands against the counter and pushing herself further onto his cock. He seemed to like it and began slamming into her in powerful thrusts.

She winced, but he didn't notice.

He gripped her chin and forced her head around so he could take her lips in a sloppy kiss.

"Come for me, slut," he growled against her lips.

Saskia rarely orgasmed during their encounters, having discovered in her teens that she was better off fucking herself if she wanted to reach the big O. But when he called her names during sex, every ounce of lust within her dried up.

She hated when he said things like that to her.

Once he'd asked if she was okay with it, and when she realized how much he liked dirty talk she'd agreed. As her heart grew more attached, he became dirtier and dirtier until she felt near revulsion at the thought of sex. She knew she needed to say something, but she didn't want to risk what they had.

She wished she could talk to her mother or her sister, but both women were frustratingly private when it came to sex. Maybe she would try talking to Shaun one day, after they'd spent more time together. Saskia wondered when it was appropriate for girlfriends to start talking about their sex lives.

Nikolay pulled out of her and turned her around. He used his foot to stomp on her jeans, which were bunched around her ankles, and pull her free of them. She winced as she imagined the delicate fabric of her panties being crushed beneath his boots.

He lifted her off the floor and set her ass on the counter, then lined himself back up and pushed inside. She gripped his shoulders as he fought his way past her constricting muscles.

He leaned forward until his face was inches from hers. "I said, come for me, you fucked up little cunt."

Tears filled her eyes, and she flung her head back in imitation of ecstasy so he wouldn't see them. He slammed into her over and over. She closed her eyes and imagined someone else. No one in particular; he was faceless, a tall man, nice cock, big hands that would span her waist as he lifted her.

She grew wetter as she used her imagination to get off. It wasn't working and she could tell Nikolay was close. If she didn't orgasm, he would know and he'd insist on finger fucking her while calling her terrible names, which never worked.

She chewed on her lips, letting out a series of moans and groans. She wiggled her hips as though chasing her orgasm.

"Yeah, you like that, bitch," he growled, falling for her show. "My little whore. Take this big cock like the bitch in heat you are."

She let out a high-pitched yelp, as though she was close and rolled her eyes back.

He grunted, emptying his semen into the condom.

As always, he pulled out of her right away and stepped back. She wished he would hold her, but he turned away to dispose of the condom, using toilet paper from one of the stalls to wrap it.

Saskia slid off the counter, shame burning in her chest, and pulled her jeans back on, while he readjusted his own pants, tucking his cock away and zipping up. She didn't know why she felt shame. She shouldn't. They loved each other; they weren't doing anything wrong.

Saskia wasn't stupid though. She knew there were secrets between them. It was only a matter of time before she discovered his and she was terribly afraid she wouldn't look at him the same when it happened.

Finally, he reached for her, holding her against his chest.

"I've missed you so much, baby," he murmured into her hair.

Saskia sighed, some of her shame receding as he held her and stroked his hand down her back.

They didn't have much time together as Saskia's guards would become suspicious if she spent more than fifteen or twenty minutes in the washroom. It didn't matter though, there wasn't much Saskia and Nikolay could say to each other. They'd agreed early on not to talk about Jozef or the Kobas.

They were on opposite sides of a family feud neither of them wanted.

Nikolay had decided to go with Jozef, which made him loyal to the guard dog.

Saskia's loyalties were split. She'd never known anything other than her family and though she knew they were completely fucked up and amoral, she owed them her loyalty. Didn't she?

They'd let Jozef go without a fight. They'd let him go to prison, then let him split from the organization and she didn't understand why.

But she would find out.

She would find out all of her family's secrets. Then maybe she would finally understand the people who'd made her life a living hell since birth.

"You have to go," she whispered, her heart wrenching at the thought.

Nikolay pulled away, kissing her forehead, and then pulling himself up onto the counter.

He turned to look at her with a grin. "Stay safe, Juliet."

She grinned at him. "Don't fall on your ass on the way out, Romeo."

CHAPTER TWENTY

Shaun stood next to Karl in the elevator, her fingers twining in the skirt of her dress; a slim fitting royal blue sleeveless sheath that covered her from neck to knees and emphasized her height. With her three-inch silver heels she would be as tall as Jozef. She tried to control her breathing as best she could. She was nervous. She couldn't shake the feeling that something terrible was going to happen. The club had featured in her nightmares more than once over the past year. She would dream of men being tortured on the tables and women shot in the head.

She jumped when Karl touched her shoulder.

"You'll be fine. I won't let anything happen."

She looked at him, absorbing the kindness in his eyes. She jerked her head in a nod and tried to smile.

"The boss doesn't want anything to happen to you and he knows you don't like the club. He'll be on his best behaviour." Karl spoke earnestly, turning his big body toward her. "And you have me. I'll be watching you every second."

"Thank you." A real smile touched her lips. "That makes me feel better."

"It should. I won't let anything happen to you, not after...." he trailed off, his body language going rigid again.

Shaun frowned. "After what? The poisoning?"

He nodded. "It shouldn't have happened under my watch."

She touched his arm and waited until he looked at her, his expression one of self-condemnation. "You didn't let anything happen to me. I was surrounded by strangers from catering staff to guests, and if the poison came from inside the mansion, you wouldn't have known. It was a very subtle poison. Easy to access and difficult to detect."

He looked unconvinced. "Krystoff blames me."

She gave him a grim look. "Krystoff doesn't want to accept any responsibility. I think it's probably easier to blame you than it is to look suspiciously at his family and closest allies."

Karl looked marginally better.

"Besides," she continued. "Jozef wouldn't have hired you to act as my personal bodyguard if he didn't trust you completely. Your life is here now, so try to forget about what happened at the mansion."

As the words left her mouth, she realized their significance. *Her* life was there now too, not at the mansion and not in Montréal. Did she need to forget what happened a year ago in order to move forward? Did she need to forget about the kidnapping, forget that Jozef had killed people in front of her, forget everything? And if she did put it behind her, what next?

She was so preoccupied by her revelation that she barely noticed the bump of the elevator stopping on the club floor.

Karl punched in the code to open the elevator and, when the doors opened, they stepped out together. Karl escorted her down the hall to the floor of the club, sticking to her side as she walked into a roomful of glittering strangers.

Shaun quickly scanned the club, taking in the dancers, the drinkers and the general air of merriment.

"This way." Karl took her arm in a light hold and used his body to shield her right side, his other hand hovering over the butt of his gun. "He's in the VIP area."

They wound their way through the throng, making their way up the steps to the VIP section. Karl pushed the velvet curtain aside and waved Shaun inside. She gave him a grateful look and stepped through the curtain.

She smothered a gasp as saw the men assembled.

There were three of them, huge men, dark skin, shaved heads, wearing uniforms. One seemed more important than the others. He sat while the others stood to his side, hands clasped behind their backs, gazes fixed on Shaun. Or perhaps past her, staring at the opening that would lead onto the club floor.

Jozef stood and walked to her, covering her view of the terrifying men. He took her arms in his hands, warming her and leaned in to press a kiss against her lips. It was a light kiss, but it sent arrows of heat straight through her, warming her chest and belly. He led her to the table where one of the biggest men she'd ever seen stood, his eyes sweeping over her in a cold, calculating look. The medals on his uniform rattled as he reached to take her hand.

Shaun usually prided herself on a firm handshake, a necessity for her profession. Her hand felt like a limp noodle engulfed in his much bigger hand. He held her hand for a second too long, squeezing, then let go.

Jozef introduced him. *I would like you to meet my new client, R-A-D-I-K. We'll be doing a job for him in a few weeks. He's taken great pains to come here as it's difficult for him to leave his home country. He doesn't speak sign language so we will need you to interpret.*

Shaun was surprised that Jozef was giving her so much

information. Did she need it in order to properly translate? It made her feel uneasy but elated at the same time. She was pleased that Jozef was willing to share more of his work with her, but it also terrified her. What if she knew too much? She could find herself in the same situation she faced a year ago. Dead witness or live captive.

Radik moved aside so she could sit in between him and Jozef. Before she could slide into the booth though, Jozef took her arm and pulled her to the outside, seating her next to him but closest to the nearest exit. She felt Karl move to stand on her other side. When she glanced up at her body-guard, every trace of the softer emotions he'd shown in the elevator was gone, replaced by a fierce glare.

"You will be able to translate for us?" Radik asked, his voice a deep accented baritone that sent waves of apprehension through Shaun.

She glanced at Jozef who nodded, then looked back at Radik. "Where are you from? I might be able to understand your language too. I've travelled a lot."

"The languages of my birth are French, Sangho and Arabic, but I also speak Amharic, Somalian and English."

"Are you from the Central African Republic then, or Chad?"

Radik stiffened, which caused his men to do the same. His gaze sharpened on her face as if seeing her for the first time. "How would you know this? You are a westerner, no?"

She nodded. "Yes, but I've worked all over the world with Doctors Without Borders."

He seemed to relax slightly. "You worked in one of the refugee camps?"

"Yes, just on the southern border of Chad. I also worked with a team on the detection and rapid treatment of HIV in Mozambique a few years ago."

Shaun glanced sideways at Jozef who was staring at her

with horrified interest. She wondered what was going on in his head. He knew she'd worked all over the world with Doctors Without Borders. She did four-month rotations nearly every year for the past seven years. Yet he looked as though this was the first he was hearing of it.

"I thank you for your service to our country and our neighbors. The regional conflicts have made life difficult, if not impossible, for many of my people. Our citizens would've starved or died in war if it weren't for the refugee camps. Your sacrifice is appreciated."

Shaun refocused on Radik, who appeared to be sincere in his praise. She thanked him and when she looked back at Jozef, his strange expression had passed, replaced by the blank look he wore when he was doing business.

"Should we get started?" Radik leaned back in his chair, his gaze, which was much warmer now, on Shaun's face.

Jozef dipped his head in a nod and began signing while Shaun translated. *You're agreeable to our terms? The first three are non-negotiable; our fee doesn't change, you give us access to regional information we can't access on our own, and my team doesn't do human transport. We can discuss the fourth term if you have a better plan than what we came up with.*

"Your fee is exorbitant," Radik said. "But I'm willing to pay that and more for the safe delivery of my package."

We will see to it, Jozef signed. *You've outlined the importance of this job. We won't fail. I have the best team in the business.*

"You understand what will happen if the package is corrupted either before or after delivery?" Radik's expression grew fierce.

Shaun shivered. She didn't want to know what the consequences of a corrupted package were, but she suspected they were extremely unpleasant.

You have nothing to worry about. We've never failed.

"I don't care about your failure rate," Radik snarled. "I

don't care about assurances. These will mean nothing to me if anything goes wrong."

Radik's gaze strayed to Shaun where it lingered in an assessing way that made her uncomfortable. It wasn't a sexual look, but malignant, as if their pleasant conversation a few minutes ago hadn't happened. She was beginning to wish Jozef hadn't made her part of this conversation.

Then I won't give you my assurances, Jozef signed. *You'll see our effectiveness in action.*

"I like your confidence." Radik switched focus. "Your second demand is also agreeable. I will have the regional maps sent over. You are correct in your belief that what's happening on the ground it largely undocumented. I have access to a satellite that goes over the area every few days. I will have my man send over the images."

Thank you.

"I do have one amendment to our original agreement." Radik looked from Jozef to Shaun, his expression still calculating.

Jozef had been mostly relaxed up to that point, communicating with politeness. When Radik spoke of an amendment, Jozef straightened in his seat, all pretense of relaxation gone. He glared at Radik for a full minute before signing, *N-O.*

Shaun suspected she didn't need to translate based on the uncompromising look on Jozef's face and the belligerent look on Radik's. She didn't understand what was going on. What was the original agreement and how did Radik want to change it? Whatever silent battle was raging between the two, she was starting to suspect she was right in the middle.

"She will remain completely safe while travelling through my territory. In fact, you will likely be safer for having her with you. She is black, she can translate, she has met many people from the region and will understand their culture and traditions. Someone like her can only enhance your objective."

N-O, Jozef repeated, shaking his head and glaring fiercely at Radik.

Again, Shaun didn't bother translating the obvious.

She felt an instant bolt of excitement that took her by surprise. After the trauma she'd experienced a year earlier she hadn't even considered going back to Doctors Without Borders. At least not yet. But now that the men were talking about travel, yes to war torn countries, but also to places she'd worked in and loved, the thought of going back was extremely appealing.

Radik allowed his anger to show by smashing his large fist into the table and making it jump. Shaun felt her chair move back a few inches and glanced up at Karl who gave her a quick wink. He was making sure the table didn't smack into her.

"I am making this term non-negotiable. Either your doctor friend travels with you or we do not move forward with our partnership." Radik was now laser focused on Jozef, speaking directly to the other man. "Which would be a shame. You do not want me for an enemy."

A chill travelled around the table and Havel stepped out of the shadows, startling Shaun who hadn't seen him. Of course, he would be nearby during what sounded to Shaun like a very important meeting. Havel's presence felt reassuring and bolstered Shaun's confidence.

We have many enemies; you won't be any more significant than the rest.

Shaun translated, but Radik didn't look at her.

"You do not have any enemies like me, Koba. Think carefully before you refuse this very lucrative opportunity."

Jozef stubbornly shook his head. *I don't need to think about it. You're proposing I take my woman into one of the most dangerous regions on the planet. The answer is no.*

"She's been there before, which makes her an asset. She will also be helpful in moving my package."

Jozef didn't speak again. Shaun supposed he didn't need to. He'd made his position abundantly clear. She wanted to argue as well but this wasn't the right place to do it. She knew better than to undermine Jozef's position by arguing with him publicly. She would talk to him in the privacy of their home.

Their home. She'd been there less than a week and already she was thinking of the penthouse as their home.

The tension ratcheted up as the two men faced off, neither wanting to back down. Shaun knew Jozef well enough to know that he wouldn't be the one to back down. Not in this instance. He'd made his position on Shaun's safety abundantly clear the day before when he'd pulled his gun on the man who'd been following them.

It was Radik who broke first, his fierce expression melting into a jovial grin.

"We will discuss it no further. I can appreciate a man who will protect his woman, even to the detriment of himself. I feel the same about my women."

The tension around the table evaporated as the men discussed a few more details. Twenty minutes later, Radik stood and shook hands with Jozef and Shaun. He lingered over Shaun, his expression softening.

"If you ever visit my home country, look me up. My protection will keep you safe."

"Thank you," Shaun murmured, pulling her hand from Radik's grip and tucking it against Jozef's arm. She was uncomfortable with the large man. She suspected he was either a military general or a warlord. It didn't matter which. Depending on the region, the two were synonymous.

Once Radik and his men were gone, Havel and Karl stepped outside the curtained VIP room, giving Jozef and Shaun some privacy.

Shaun looked at Jozef, crossing her arms over her chest and narrowing her eyes. "Tell me about the package. What's inside and how dangerous is it?"

CHAPTER TWENTY-ONE

I *don't know*, Jozef signed.

Annoyance crossed Shaun's features. "You'll include me in a conversation like that?" she waved her arm around the table. "But you won't tell me the details."

Jozef reached for her, dragging her onto his lap as he sank back into the booth. He wedged Shaun between him and the table, turning her so she was facing him, but his hands were free.

I don't know the details of the package, Jozef clarified. *According to Radik's original request, the contents of the package are to remain anonymous. If Radik's enemies were to find out what it's worth, they would stop at nothing to get hold of it.*

"Do you think it's dangerous, like a bomb or something?" Concern edged her voice.

Jozef debated with himself. Tell her the truth or leave her in the dark where she was less likely to worry over him. He was elated by her genuine concern for his safety, but she would need to reconcile herself to his job. He didn't walk dogs for a living. Among other things, he was a mercenary for hire.

Yes, the job will be dangerous. Even if the contents of the package aren't dangerous, the danger will lie in moving it through several regions with varying levels of active combat.

Her eyes grew wide. "That's why you don't want me to go."

Among other reasons. You don't need to see what I do for a living. It's not pleasant and I may not be as effective if I'm worrying over you.

"I saw what you did for a living when you took me from the hospital a year ago." There was no accusation in her voice. It was a fact she was pointing out to show him she could handle his world.

Jozef knew otherwise. Though she'd witnessed some terrible acts, most committed by Jozef himself, she was still a baby in his world. She didn't know the worst he could do, and he didn't want her finding out.

That was before I knew you, before I knew I loved you, Jozef signed, trying to tell her of his regret and sorrow over their first meeting. *If I could take it back, I would. I hate that I did that to you and that our relationship will forever be coloured by those first few moments.*

Shaun took his face in her hands and leaned over to press a lingering kiss against his lips. His mouth moved beneath hers, and his arms slid around her back, pressing her tight to his chest. When she lifted her head to look down at him, he allowed her to see the vulnerability inside him. It was all for her. She could bring him to his knees, and she could rebuild him into a better man. She had the hands of a surgeon and he would willingly subject himself to her ministrations.

"I won't pretend that I will ever be able to forget those first few moments when you shot up the hospital, or the way you killed the man in the basement. When you held a gun to my head fully intending to pull the trigger." Her voice was filled with the pain of those moments, every word a strike to

Jozef's heart. "But those memories will dim with time. The fear will be replaced by something else."

Jozef's hands tightened on her to the point where he knew it must be painful. He couldn't help himself, he needed to make sure she wouldn't disappear. She didn't protest.

"I want to be happy." She pressed another kiss to his lips.

He wanted to ask if she wanted that happiness with him, or if she would be happier without him. He didn't know if he could take the answer. He wanted her to be happy; wanted it more than he wanted everything else. But if her happiness was contingent on her leaving him, what would he do? Could he let her go?

No, he couldn't. He couldn't live without her, which meant she couldn't live without him. Selfish, perhaps, but he wasn't raised to be a good, altruistic person like Shaun. He was raised to take what he needed and wanted. To fight for it and to kill for it.

Rather than allow her to continue speaking, he shifted her until she was straddling his lap. He gripped the back of her neck, tangling his fingers in her curls and dragging her face down to his. He kissed her deeply, pushing his tongue into her mouth and forcefully exploring the depths. He didn't release her until she was gasping for breath.

When he finally did let her up for air, she had the most beautifully dazed expression on her face. It made his cock so hard he wanted to tear her dress off and crawl up inside her. He debated with himself for about ten seconds. She'd told him not to fuck her without permission, but he was contemplating doing just that.

Maybe he could get her permission, but he didn't want to take the time to ask.

So he would fuck her without fucking her.

He shifted her on his lap until she was facing away from him. She squeaked and gripped the table when he jerked her dress up her thighs to her waist. Even sitting on his lap, the table covered everything if someone should enter the VIP area. It was unlikely, but Jozef knew Shaun would worry and he wanted her as comfortable as possible while he played with her.

He wrapped one arm around her waist, anchoring her against him. She wiggled her ass, trying to get comfortable while he used his knees to spread her legs as wide as she would let him. She moaned and he paused waiting for her to deny him.

She dropped her head back against his shoulder and turned her face against his, pressing her lips to his ear. She didn't say anything, but he took the softening of her body and her lack of denial as permission.

He slid his hand up her belly to her ribcage, holding her tight against him. He could feel the indent of her ribs. Too thin. Too much weight lost. He would make sure she never worried herself into the ground again. She would prioritize her health if he had to stand over her and make sure she got it done.

He cupped her breast, filling his hand. It wasn't enough. He needed to feel her, the silken skin, the blood flowing through her veins. Everything that belonged to him. No one else. He slid his hand down the front of her dress forgetting his determination that no one entering the VIP area would know what was happening.

It was worth it to touch her gorgeous ebony skin, to feel the warm silk flowing beneath his hand. To watch the barbaric pattern of tattoos across the back of his hand as it contrasted against the beauty of her flesh.

He slid his other hand to her thigh, squeezing before covering her heated core with his palm. He massaged her through her thin lacy panties, driving her wild without giving her what she truly needed, the rough pads of his fingers against her sensitive clit.

"Jozef!" she gasped, squirming on top of him, her ass pressed against his cock, inviting him to ravish her willing body.

He couldn't help himself. He moved his hand up her belly then slid it back down, into the waistband of her panties.

She jerked her legs wider, giving him all the access he could want. She was so wet it made his mouth water. If he could've done it with any amount of ease, he would've sunk to the floor and eaten her out beneath the table. He wanted to hear the moans spill from her throat as he drove her higher and higher with his tongue.

The club was not the place for that kind of play. Not yet, not until she was more comfortable. For now, he would content himself to simply touch. And touch he did, sinking his fingers into the heated wetness soaking her panties and his hand.

He loved that she responded so easily to him, that her responses were unpracticed. Natural. She begged him for more, following words with action as she writhed on his lap and soaked his fingers.

He curled them into the dampness of her heated pussy and played her like a stringed instrument, pinching her engorged clitoris, then sliding through her labia and sinking inside her, thrusting the tips of his fingers against her g-spot.

She bucked so hard, her stomach hit the table, moving it a few inches away. Neither of them paid attention.

Shaun gripped the back of Jozef's head, hanging on with both hands as her body reached for the orgasm he alternately denied her and pushed her towards. He turned his face to hers, thrusting his tongue into her mouth, mimicking the thrust of his fingers in her pussy.

She desperately gasped for breath against his mouth.

He growled and shoved his crotch up against her ass, pressing himself against her. The pleasure zinging through his cock was incredible, relentless and frustrating. He wanted to bury himself balls deep in her hot little pussy, but he had more control than that. He would give her what she needed without demanding anything in return. She made him want to be less selfish.

She keened wildly causing Havel to stick his head through the curtain. Luckily Shaun's head was turned into Jozef's neck. It was obvious exactly what was happening from the way she was undulating on top of Jozef, his hand down the front of her dress while the other one was under the table.

Jozef narrowed his eyes at his second-in-command, but he didn't stop touching Shaun.

Havel's eyes flared with lust, but he disappeared quickly, likely doubling down on his vigilance to let no one else into the VIP area. Jozef ignored the man. He was doing his job, checking on the boss and his woman. The sexual encounter was unplanned and Jozef hadn't warned his people to back off. Havel was a man with a man's responses, but he was also a professional. He would spend a few uncomfortable minutes after what he saw then he would forget.

"I'm coming, I'm coming!" Shaun whimpered, pressing her teeth against Jozef's throat as she opened her mouth wide.

He turned his head and captured her lips, swallowing her screams as she came on top of him, squirming wildly, jerking in his arms, her fluids soaking him.

She collapsed against his chest and tore her lips from his so she could gasp for air.

He lifted her off his lap, smiling at the way she flopped like a limp doll as he laid her down on the booth. He lifted her legs and tucked them against him, then leaned across her to press kisses to her throat and face.

When he touched her cheek, he noticed a tear and frowned, looking down at her. Was she crying?

She touched her face and looked at the wetness on her fingers, then laughed. "It was good, Jozef. Really good. I think I'm crying from relief. I needed that." Then she rolled her head to the side and frowned at the underside of the table. "We could've picked a better spot though. I'm not really into exhibitionism."

Jozef let out a growling laugh and clasped her against his chest, hugging her tightly. She was everything to him. He would do anything to protect her and the feelings she generated inside him. He had learned from his family that loyalty was a strength. Now he was learning from Shaun that love was not a weakness, as he'd thought previously, but just as much a strength as loyalty. Love motivated him like nothing else could.

He reached into his pocket and pulled out the delicate chain with the tiny heart. He draped the heated metal across her cleavage before securing it around her neck.

"Thank you," she whispered. "I didn't know what happened to it."

It's your heart, he signed, his eyes glowing with possession. *I will always keep it safe for you.*

CHAPTER TWENTY-TWO

Word travelled fast between the two Koba households and the next day Shaun and Fatima were invited to lunch with Dasha and Leeza. Jozef reluctantly gave his permission for the women to leave, though he was unhappy that he couldn't accompany them. Shaun wanted to ask what he was doing that he couldn't come, but hesitated. It was that line between his work and her feelings toward what he did for a living. She wasn't ready to cross it yet.

Shaun changed into a cream skirt suit with a rose-coloured blouse underneath a jacket and a matching scarf wrapped around her tightly pinned hair. She added a pair of heels and looked herself over in the mirror. Conservative but stylish. Not her usual, but she didn't want to cause waves. The brief time she'd spent with the Kobas had taught her enough about fashion that she knew how to dress correctly for a luncheon with Dasha.

Fatima was another story.

When Shaun showed up at her mother's apartment with Karl in tow, Fatima took one look at her daughter and said, "Shit, I need to change."

Shaun laughed and followed her mother, who was running through the apartment to her bedroom. Fatima was wearing a pair of jeans and a sweater with a black bear knitted into the grey fabric. It was cute, but definitely not appropriate for the Koba household. The women in that house wouldn't be caught dead leaving their apartments in anything less than formal day dress.

"I never know what to wear to these things," Fatima mumbled digging through her drawers.

"Mom, it's fine. They won't care." They probably would care but Shaun would shut down anyone who dared to comment. "We need to purchase some more clothes for you. You brought enough for a vacation, but not for your day-to-day needs."

"I hadn't planned on staying here long-term." There was an edge of sarcasm to Fatima's voice as she held up a pair of black dress pants, examining them critically. She tossed them on the bed along with a black shell and a formal jacket. "It's dark, but it'll have to do."

"I'll grab a scarf from upstairs and you'll be all set."

Shaun ran back to her suite and rifled through her assortment of scarves, most still with the tags attached, and found a lovely gold and green leaf-patterned scarf that would give Fatima's outfit a splash of colour.

Jozef met Shaun at the door of the club, his eyes sweeping over her, a slight smile curving his lips. She loved that smile. The scar slashing through his lips gave him a sinister edge, but she didn't care. She thought he was beautiful.

Jozef pressed a kiss to her lips and ran his hand over her hair. He touched the necklace at her throat, lingering over the tiny heart. He had eyes for no one but Shaun as he said a private goodbye. It didn't matter that she was only going across the city, or that she would be back in a few hours. He said goodbye like it was the last time. It made her heart soar.

You will listen to Havel. Leave if you're uncomfortable, don't worry about being rude. Text me at least twice.

Shaun laughed and kissed him again before patting his cheek and stepping away. "I'll be back before you can miss me."

I doubt it.

Shaun followed her mother into the back of the waiting car while Jozef spoke with Havel, Karl and Nikolay who would be accompanying the two women. Shaun was used to Jozef giving his men commands, but her mother watched with rapt attention.

"He's quite serious about security, isn't he?" Fatima murmured, a slight frown wrinkling her brow.

"Yes, he is," Shaun agreed. "I've never known him to take any unnecessary risks."

"It seems strange, doesn't it?" Fatima mused. "His career lends itself to dangerous situations, yet he isn't a reckless man."

Shaun gazed at Jozef as she thought about what her mother said. Jozef really did try to mitigate any danger for him, his men, and now for her and her mother. He was an intelligent man, and he used that intelligence to create fool-proof plans that he and his men could execute with precision. Security came as naturally to him as breathing.

The one exception was on the day they met, when he and his men had beaten Gustav until his heart gave out. But a weak heart was not something Jozef could've planned for.

It made her curious about the jobs he took on. How he dealt with all the risk factors of a new region, contacts, etc. She assumed the jobs were dangerous, which made her fear for his safety. Her mother's words made her realize that Jozef was definitely not a reckless person. He planned and he followed through on those plans.

She was snapped out of her thoughts when Havel and

Karl climbed into the front seat of the vehicle. Nikolay followed in a separate vehicle. As they drove, Havel pointed out the various sightseeing spots to Fatima. Shaun was amused by the easy way in which he spoke to her mother. Though she and Havel had found a relative truce, there was still a coolness between them.

Dasha was waiting for them on the steps of the mansion, Leeza a few paces behind her, as they arrived. The two women were perfection. Dasha wore a cherry red skirt suit with rope after rope of gold necklaces of varying lengths decorating her elegant throat. Her hair was twisted on top of her head in a carefully arranged knot. Leeza wore a fitted green patterned dress that stopped at her knees. The high neck and short sleeves made it look severe, but her long wavy dark hair and the string of pearls around her neck softened the look.

"Glad I changed," Fatima remarked drily as they climbed out of the vehicle and approached the two women.

Shaun accepted the double cheek kisses from Dasha and Leeza while Fatima awkwardly accepted the same treatment.

"Welcome to my home, Mrs. Patterson. I've heard so much about you."

Shaun wondered where Dasha had heard about her mother. Shaun hadn't had much opportunity to mention Fatima during her weeks spent in the mansion and they'd only seen each other once since her return. The odd thing was, the words coming from Dasha's lips could have been completely normal, but Shaun heard a hint of threat. As if Dasha had known the moment Fatima stepped foot in Prague and had been tracking her.

Shaun shifted closer to her mother while Havel and Karl protected their backs.

Dasha's eyes travelled to Havel and her smile grew rigid and cold. "Havel, how are you doing?"

"Fine, thank you, ma'am," he answered automatically, keeping his eyes fixed on the space between Leeza and Dasha.

"And how is Jozef?"

It seemed like a strange question considering Dasha had seen her nephew two nights ago.

"He's adjusting well," Havel answered, his eyes finally meeting Dasha's.

Something passed between the two and Dasha's smile became more natural as she said, "Thank you. Of course, you are welcome in our home." She extended her smile to Fatima and Shaun. "Come inside, both of you. Winter is well and truly upon us; there's a chill to the air now."

Shaun squared her shoulders and walked into the mansion. She felt bolstered by the presence of her mother. As though the confidence that naturally came to her, but seemed to disappear around the Koba family, reappeared with an ally in her corner.

"Wow," Fatima whispered as they walked.

Leeza caught the comment and turned with a grin, walking backwards on her four-inch heels, which Shaun thought was an impressive feat. "It's rather gothic, isn't it?"

"Oh stop." Dasha gripped Leeza's arm and forced her to turn back around. "This house was built in 1788 with much of the original structure still in service. Most of the pieces you see, both furniture and art, are from the same time period. I like to keep everything as authentic as possible."

"Like I said, gothic," Leeza piped up, avoiding her mother's light slap. "You can just picture a dastardly villain hiding in the shadows."

They all laughed, but the sound was uneasy. A dastardly villain had escaped the shadows of the mansion to hunt and kidnap a helpless woman whom he dragged back into his shadowy home to force an engagement on her.

"I like authenticity too," Fatima murmured, still looking

around with awe. "My 90's rattan furniture matches my home perfectly. The structure itself was built in the notable, but often tacky era of the 90's."

Shaun burst out laughing. "It's true. She still has some of that awful old furniture. She uses it in her sunroom, where she sits with all her plants and her favourite romance novels. When she has Fitzy, he'll curl up under her feet."

Leeza giggled but Dasha pressed her lips together disapprovingly, as though trying to determine if she was being made fun of.

They entered the dining room where Dasha directed them to take a seat at the massive table. Once again, Fatima's eyes widened as she took in the opulent room, decorated in gold, each place setting immaculate. Dasha directed them to sit at the far end next to the windows. Fatima and Shaun sat on one side of the table while Leeza and her mother sat on the other side.

"Your home sounds lovely," Leeza said, lifting her arms as one of the wait staff smoothed a napkin over her knees.

"Not compared to this." Fatima stared past Dasha at a massive gilt-framed painting that looked like it was an original renaissance something, but Shaun had no idea what.

"I prefer a smaller home. I like to know where my son is." Leeza's voice was flat and her mother gave her a sharp look.

Shaun interrupted before Dasha could say anything to her daughter. She hadn't paid much attention a year earlier because she'd been preoccupied with her own kidnapping, but Shaun suspected that Leeza felt oppressed in the house of her birth. "Thank you so much for inviting us to your home." Shaun smiled warmly at Dasha. "It's so kind of you to extend a welcome to my mother. She's never been to the Czech Republic before."

Dasha turned her megawatt smile on Fatima. "I would love the opportunity to show you around. I was born in Kiev but have lived most of my life in or near Prague. I can show you both many sights only the locals would know about."

"That sounds like fun," Shaun said with as much enthusiasm as she could muster. She wasn't sure her idea of fun was the same as Dasha's. She also couldn't picture the elegant woman, who Shaun had never seen wear anything on her feet other than high heels, escorting them around the city and surrounding countryside.

"Perfect," Dasha purred, dipping her spoon into her bowl of steaming soup.

The serving staff flitted seamlessly through the dining room, setting down dishes and disappearing quickly. Each dish always seemed to land in front of the women just after the last bite was taken from the previous dish.

They finished their lunch a few hours later with promises to see each other again. Though Shaun hadn't looked forward to going to the mansion without Jozef, she had to admit that she'd had a nice time. Strange but nice. Fatima was an easy person to like, alternately jovial and quietly thoughtful depending on the mood of the room. Shaun had never really appreciated that quality in her mother before but seeing her flawlessly navigate the tensions inside the mansion, Shaun realized how adept her mother was at handling new and strange situations.

"Thank you," Shaun said to her as they buckled themselves into the back seat of their car.

"For what?" Fatima asked.

Shaun thought about it for a second, then said, "For being you, for coming here with me today. For flying halfway around the world to find me and then agreeing to live here. I guess, I want you to know how much I appreciate the sacrifices you're making. I'm not sure I could do this without you."

Fatima looked at her seriously. "Yes, you can. You're a survivor, Shaun. You wouldn't be here with me now if you weren't. It's me who can't live without you." She pointed at the mansion and waved her hand around the vehicle. "This is no sacrifice, baby. This is unimaginable wealth being dropped at my feet at the perfect time in my life. No husband, no job and the world at my fingertips. Perhaps you should've gotten yourself kidnapped years ago."

Shaun laughed, though she knew her mother absolutely didn't condone Shaun's kidnapping.

Fatima's gaze focused on something past Shaun's shoulder. "What do you suppose they're talking about? Neither of them looks happy."

Shaun twisted in her seat, catching sight of Havel and Leeza standing on the steps of the mansion. They were arguing about something. Leeza turned on her heel to stalk away but Havel grabbed her arm. From their distance it didn't look like he grabbed her hard, but she jerked away from him, yelping in pain. Her hand went to her arm and she rubbed vigorously.

Instead of letting her go, Havel took hold of her elbow and shoved the sleeve of her dress up. Shaun gasped when she saw Leeza's arm. The bruise on it was so dark and large it was clearly visible from Shaun's vantage point.

Havel's face became flushed until it looked like an angry red beacon. "Who the fuck did this to you?" His bellow was so loud that everyone in the vicinity heard.

The mansion security edged toward the couple on the steps, clearly torn between their loyalty to one of the women of the house and a man who'd once been their boss.

"I don't know," Shaun murmured, answering her mother's question. "But whatever it is, it looks bad."

Leeza snapped something at Havel that they couldn't hear, wrenched her sleeve back down and stormed away.

Havel stalked back to the vehicle, jerking the driver's door open and climbing inside, his body language telling Shaun she probably shouldn't speak to him right now. She ignored his body language.

"Did she say what happened?"

Havel glared at her through the rearview mirror. "Walked into a doorframe."

Shaun bit her lip and glanced back at the mansion where Leeza had disappeared through the door.

"That bruise wasn't an accident," Shaun told him.

"I know," he grunted, starting the vehicle and leaving the Koba mansion behind.

CHAPTER TWENTY-THREE

The days passed quickly and Shaun settled into an uneasy pattern. Even though she spent a good portion of her time alone keeping up to date with professional journals and medical advances, she often found herself restless. It helped to have her mother near-by. She spent a good portion of her days in Fatima's apartment, Fitzy twirling around her feet as she took the stairs to her mother's apartment. The cat seemed to look forward to their daily trips downstairs as much as Shaun did. Fatima always had a snack waiting for both of them.

Fatima had settled into her new life much more easily than her daughter, spending Jozef's money as though she'd been born for online shopping.

"Which one do you think I should buy?" she asked, turning the computer screen toward Shaun. "I rather like the Monet, but the Van Gogh is more expensive."

Shaun choked on her laughter. "Since when do you like classic artwork?"

"Since I visited the Koba mansion and realized my own collection is woefully lacking."

"Maybe you should find out if there's a limit to Jozef's generosity," Shaun pointed out drily.

Fatima shrugged. "I'll let him know when I reach the limit of the credit card he gave me. He told me to buy some things for you too, since you don't seem as interested in spending his money."

"It's not my money to spend!" Shaun protested.

Fatima gave her a stern look. "You were kidnapped and tortured with the knowledge that you were going to die. You were forcibly confined and then poisoned. If that's not enough, you were forced to witness an assault in the Montréal hospital where you should have been safe. Then, you were kidnapped for a second time. I don't care if you love the guy, you deserve to spend his damn money." She paused, then added, "And so do I."

Shaun stared at her mother who was busily trying to choose her new painting.

"I never told you I loved him."

"You love him, not loved. Not past tense," Fatima corrected Shaun, her sharp golden eyes on her daughter. "I suspected when you refused to testify at your own kidnapping hearing. I knew for sure when I saw you two together. I've never seen you look at anyone the way you look at him."

"I'm sorry," Shaun whispered.

"For what?" Fatima said impatiently. "Loving the wrong man? Welcome to the ranks of every woman ever."

Shaun laughed and swiped at a tear threatening to spill. She reached for the laptop. "Buy the Monet; you'll like it better. We'll buy you a Klimpt for the bathroom to offset the lack of expense."

While her days were spent in the company of her mother, her evenings belonged to Jozef. If he was busy with work, he would have Shaun meet him in the club so he could still spend time with her. He didn't ask her to translate again, but he often met with contacts while she was there. At first, she wondered why, since he clearly didn't want her to be part of his job, but she realized he simply wanted her near and this was his compromise.

The men who met with him weren't allowed to so much as glance at Shaun, let alone talk to her. She would have appreciated the gesture if she wasn't becoming so bored. Her only contacts, besides the occasional visits from Saskia when she wasn't busy with school, were Fatima, Karl and Jozef. She occasionally saw Havel, but he didn't have much to do with Shaun.

It was the ever-increasing boredom that finally made Shaun break down and decide to ask Jozef for more freedom. She'd been trying to keep her restlessness to herself. Jozef was a busy man, his workload having increased drastically when he split from the Koba organization. Not only did he have to work with his men to ensure the flawless delivery of all contracts, but he had to handle the logistics of moving his offices into a new building. The security involved in the building and the people housed within was not a small job.

Shaun was also grateful to Jozef for not only allowing her mother to live in the same place as them, but for allowing the two women to freely visit one another without restrictions. She knew that she was fortunate and she didn't want to complain.

Jozef was mafia through and through, yet she'd seen him change so many things in his life simply to ease her mind and make her comfortable. Though she didn't condone kidnapping, or the lives he took, and probably continued to take, she was grateful for the things he was giving her. He could've decided to do things his way. Lock her up and throw away the key. Force her compliance.

All of this was in her mind when she approached Jozef after another evening spent in the club. They'd had a good night, even dancing a little once Jozef had finished with his meeting. She'd gotten the opportunity to see his body move to music. He was graceful and fluid, quite beautiful to watch. He'd tossed aside his leather jacket and rolled up the sleeves of his shirt, showing off the tattoos on his arms and throat.

Shaun had moved with him, brushing against him, allowing the music to flow through her. As much as she despised the noisy atmosphere of nightclubs, she was starting to like Zmatek. It was a class unto itself with its glittering clientele and rich décor.

Jozef's men cleared the floor so there was enough space for Shaun and Jozef to dance. The world disappeared as she whirled in his arms, the skirt of her red silk dress flying to wrap around her legs. He pulled her into his embrace, her back against his chest, his arms wrapped around her middle, trapping her arms against her side. They swayed together, Shaun turning her head so Jozef could kiss her waiting lips.

After a satisfying evening they found themselves curled up on the couch, the lights dimmed, the city spread out below them in blanket of colour. Jozef pressed kisses along her jaw and hairline, sending showers of sparks through her veins. They hadn't had sex again, nor had Jozef given her any more orgasms like he had in the club. He was either respecting her request for no sex until they sorted themselves out, or he was so tired after long days of work that he wasn't interested.

Judging from his near constant erection when he was around her, she suspected it was the former.

"Jozef, can we talk?" she asked huskily.

He moved back so she could see his hands. She felt the loss of his body next to hers like a visceral tearing as his warmth moved away. She almost told him she'd changed her mind and they could talk later.

You're bored, he signed. *Is that what you want to talk about?*

She gaped at him. "Well, yes, but how do you know?" She

thought she'd been doing a pretty good job of hiding her restlessness from him.

I can tell. He frowned, then added, *I can feel it.*

She wanted to know what he meant but she didn't push for answers. She could sense his moods too, even when he wasn't giving any outward signs. They seemed to share some kind of connection that went beyond the obvious.

"I don't mean to complain," she assured him. "I know you're busy and you have a lot on your plate, but I'm used to living a very full life. My work at the hospital consumed me, and when I wasn't working, I was conducting research for my papers. I've been developing new technology to use in surgeries, and I need to publish my findings so other surgeons can begin studying and using the same techniques."

He nodded his understanding and then stood, walking away from her. She knew he wouldn't simply end a conversation with her that way, since it drove him nuts when people did that to him. He couldn't sign at someone's back.

She stood and followed him into the bedroom where he dug a box out of his closet. He'd given her the large walk-in closet and had taken the smaller one for himself. Out of respect for his privacy she hadn't opened it, though she'd been curious.

She and Jozef were in a strange relationship. Even though their hearts recognized each other, had ached from the distance of the past year, they didn't actually know each other well. She didn't know if he would be okay with her rifling through his things and she felt shy asking.

He knelt on the floor next to the box and waved at her to join him.

She sank cross-legged onto the carpet, the skirt of her dress pooling around her, and watched as he pulled books and files from the box. Frowning, she reached for one of the books, staring blankly at the cover. It was a medical textbook.

Then she recognized it, Operating on Inoperable Tumors. She'd written chapter five. Wordlessly she flipped the book open to the correct chapter. A lump formed in her throat as she scanned the pages. Section after section was highlighted and there were remarks written in the margins in what she guessed was Czech.

"Did you read this?" she asked, still gazing down at the book. She pointed at one of the remarks in the margin. "Did you write in here?"

He nodded, taking the book from her and replacing it with a file.

The label on the file read, "The Use of Guided Laser Ablation on Glioblastomas." She'd written the paper three years earlier. It had been published in the American Medical Journal. She opened the file. It was a printout from off the internet. Like the book, there were sections highlighted and remarks written on the top, sides and bottom of the paper. Mouth open, she pulled more files and books out of the box.

"These are all mine." She was stunned.

It looked like everything she'd ever written and published was in the box. Chapters in textbooks, papers, essays. There were even a few that hadn't been published. She didn't want to examine too closely how he'd gotten his hands on them.

"You've read all of these?" she asked incredulously.

He nodded. *In prison. When I wasn't working, or working out, I was reading. I wanted to understand what drives you; why you were so desperate to get back to such a stressful and demanding career.*

Tears filled her eyes. "And do you understand now?"

He tilted her chin until she was forced to look into his eyes, to see the earnestness there. *I do understand.* He tapped her forehead. *Your brilliance should not be kept in the shadows.*

A small sob left her lips and she launched herself at him, sending papers flying in all directions. She hugged him around the neck, burying her face in shoulder. "Thank you."

He ran his hands down her sides and pressed her close against his chest, hugging her in his lap. She wasn't crying, not really. She was overcome with emotion. She'd never imagined finding someone like Jozef. There were so many things between them that could tear them apart, but for the moment, those were not the thoughts crowding her head. She was simply happy.

He set her back on her ass on the carpet. She used the edge of her fingers to wipe the tears from beneath her eyes. When she was able to concentrate once more, he began signing.

I'm asking you for patience. His face creased with apology. *I want to give you more. I want you to be able to pursue this career. It would be a crime to take you away from the medical field.* He paused, a wry expression crossing his face. *More of a crime than any I've committed, I mean.*

Shaun bit her lip so she wouldn't verbally disagree with him. She rather thought murder was more of a crime than forcing her to quit her job.

There are things that must be in place before I can allow you to pursue your career once more, but I want you to know that it's important to me.

"Because it's important to me," she whispered.

He nodded. *You must be allowed to continue your work. It's too important to abandon.*

A flare of hope lit in her chest. "There are so many things I can do, Jozef," she said excitedly. "It doesn't have to be the hospital if you think that's too much of a risk, though I hate the idea of giving up surgery."

I know. He tapped one of the textbooks. *Your theory on improving non-invasive laser techniques is groundbreaking. If I understand correctly, you would throw the laser through the skull, pinpointing the exact location of the tumor and cutting it out without damaging the surrounding brain matter.*

"Yes!" Her heart sped up in anticipation as she realized she could talk shop with Jozef. There were very few people in her life who weren't colleagues who understood the complexity of her work. Her father had been one, which made his death that much more of a blow. "I'm trying to figure out how to remove the harder to reach tumors using this non-invasive technique. It's not possible with the current technology available, but one day it will be."

Someone will weaponize the technology first.

You're not wrong. Shaun switched to sign language. *But if a medical professional is able to build the technology first, then maybe we can keep it out of the hands of the people who would weaponize it.*

Not if I get my hands on it first, Jozef signed with a snicker.

Shaun laughed out loud and smacked his leg.

Together they went through the box, discussing her papers in detail. She discovered that the markings in the margins were questions Jozef had. He asked many of them while they sat on the floor together, clearly enjoying that they could share something of this depth and complexity.

Shaun realized that Jozef was an impossible man not to love. He put so much of himself into loving her that she couldn't resist, even if she wanted to. And it was time to admit that no part of her wanted to resist him anymore.

She stared at him as he continued to flip through the papers and books like an excited schoolboy showing off his homework.

"Jozef." He looked up at her. "I love you."

CHAPTER TWENTY-FOUR

Jozef's revelation was a turning point in Shaun's thinking toward him and the life he led. If he was willing to put so much effort into understanding the things that Shaun loved and had worked so hard to achieve, then she could bend enough to try to understand his world.

It had taken some convincing, but she'd finally talked Karl into spending some time with her in the apartment. He was the only mobster on the premises she saw on a regular basis who was somewhat friendly toward her. Except for Jozef, of course, and he was too busy to help her.

"Would you like coffee or tea?" she asked, glancing over her shoulder at Karl, who stood in her living room looking like he was about to be shot for the infraction of spending time alone with the boss's woman.

Shaun had cleared it with Jozef first. She hadn't told him exactly why she wanted to spend time with Karl, just assured him that her intentions were entirely innocent. She'd been surprised when the usually hyper-possessive Jozef had allowed it without argument. Maybe he thought Karl was too old for

Shaun? Karl couldn't be more than 50, so she didn't think so. She was 35. It wasn't an insurmountable age gap.

She wasn't interested in Karl though, and beyond the job, he didn't seem interested in Shaun either.

"Coffee," he said gruffly. "Black."

Shaun brewed a single cup of coffee with the shiny new Keurig upgrade she'd ordered, taking a page from her mother's book and spending some of Jozef's money. She set the steaming cup on a coaster on the coffee table and curled up on the far end of the couch, holding one of the pillows against her stomach.

Karl continued to stand, his arms hanging at his sides, his expression clearly saying he'd rather be anywhere than in her apartment.

"You can sit down." She tried to keep the humour from her voice.

He looked at the couch where she was pointing and moved to sit on one of the sofa chairs instead.

"What did you want to talk to me about?" he asked warily. "Your mother?"

She frowned. "No... what about my mother?"

"Uh, nothing," he said quickly, clearing his throat and looking away.

"I'm not sure if you know how women work, but you can't say something like that and expect that I'll let it go." She watched shrewdly as his face became flushed. "Do you have a crush on my mom?"

"No," he denied quickly, his flush crawling down his throat. Then he sheepishly admitted, "Okay, yes. She's a beautiful woman, but I don't have any expectations from that quarter."

Shaun couldn't help herself, she grinned. "You like my mom. That's so... so... kind of awesome."

"You can keep it to yourself," he said gruffly, scowling at the floor.

"Of course," Shaun said solemnly, then added, "She likes movies. She's a big-time classic movie buff; her favourite is Breakfast at Tiffany's. She loves gardening too. I'm pretty sure that's what she'll miss most about living in an apartment. You could buy her a plant if you wanted to get your foot in the door."

Though his scowl deepened, he seemed to be absorbing what she was telling him.

Shaun thought it would be best to let the topic go before Karl became too uncomfortable and left before she got what she needed out of him.

"I want you to tell me what Jozef does," she started. At his blank look she added, "I want to get to know him better and his lifestyle is completely foreign to mine. I guess what I'm looking for is some kind of bridge to understanding why Jozef does the things he does."

Karl looked thoughtful and then shook his head. "You won't like it."

"How do you know?" she challenged.

He gave her a skeptical look.

"Okay," she admitted. "I probably won't but I need to start somewhere."

"May I ask why the sudden interest in Jozef's work?"

Shaun nodded but hesitated before speaking.

"I guess there are a few reasons. I want to get to know and understand what Jozef does, especially if this is the life I'll be living with him. I need to know what the risks are." She stopped speaking, trying to find the words to explain what she wanted. "Jozef loves me wholeheartedly and puts in the effort to show me that love. I suppose I want to return the favour."

Her gaze drifted back to Karl and she almost laughed out loud at the look of horror on his face. He was uncomfortable with her use of the word 'love', but she didn't know how else to describe it.

He cleared his throat, then shrugged. "I'll do my best to give you the answers you're looking for, but the medical profession is a far cry from organized crime."

She looked at him curiously. "See, that's the first thing I want to ask. You guys refer to what you do as 'mafia' and 'organized crime'. Doesn't it bother you to know that you're doing something illegal? I would think you guys would try to legitimize it by calling yourselves an organization, or a business."

Again, he shrugged, but he settled back into the chair, his arms draped over the sides. "Some organizations might, but the Koba clan has always been honest about what they do and why. Of course, they legitimize certain aspects of the business, so they and their clients are separated from anything illegal, particularly when there's a politician involved."

"Like the guy who followed us the other day," Shaun murmured. "He works for the Prime Minister's office, doesn't he?"

"How do you know that?" Karl asked sharply.

She smiled. "The guys look at me like I'm some kind of fixture. They're not careful about what they say around me. They were impressed with how Jozef handled the issue and talked to each other about it."

Karl looked alarmed. "Did they discuss the details in front of you?"

She shook her head. "No."

"I'm sorry you had to hear about that. It's not meant for your ears. I'll have Jozef talk to them."

She looked at him curiously. "But Jozef is involved with the Prime Minister?"

Karl looked down at his lap as if debating how much he should tell her, then seemed to come to some kind of conclusion. He leaned forward, his elbows on his knees. "Look, I'll tell you what I think you need to know, but no more than that. It'll help you stay protected if you know who to trust and who to stay away from."

"Thank you," she murmured, not wanting to push her luck by demanding everything and potentially losing her only source of information.

"The Prime Minister pulled some strings to get Jozef out of prison."

Shaun nodded her understanding. She'd figured someone high up must've done something, because Jozef had been looking at life in prison. Getting out in one year would've been impossible without some kind of pardon.

Karl continued. "The PM wants Jozef to do some work for him, but Jozef has refused. As far as Jozef is concerned, the favour was done for Krystoff, who talked to the PM on Jozef's behalf. I think the PM agreed to the pardon because he thought he would have Jozef and his team at his disposal, but Jozef has split from the Koba organization. Krystoff no longer has the resources the PM needs and wants, which leaves both men in a bad position."

"Why doesn't Jozef want to take jobs from the PM?" Shaun asked.

"Two reasons," Karl replied. "First, the money won't be good enough. Though he's a wealthy man, the PM can't offer Jozef the money he receives from his other wealthier clients. The second reason is that Jozef doesn't accept IOU's. He would've rather bided his time in prison than be beholden to anyone for getting him released. Jozef is also very choosy about the jobs he and his team take and IOU's mess with his code. He wants complete control over all jobs."

"So why did Krystoff accept an IOU in order to secure

Jozef's release if he knew Jozef wouldn't accept it?" Shaun asked, a picture of the past year beginning to form. "Why didn't he leave Jozef to figure it out? I assume he would've eventually gotten himself out."

Shaun was getting to know her fiancé well enough that she could say with confidence Jozef wouldn't have spent his life in prison.

Karl's eyes twinkled. "Yes, he was working on a plan. He was systematically taking out the top Vory on the inside, and some on the outside, taking their business and their assets. He would've eventually been able to buy his way out of prison or pull some strings without giving up an IOU."

"Vory?" she asked.

"Head of the crime families," he explained. "They mostly reside in Russia, but there are some scattered across the Baltics. The term has changed over the years. It translates literally to 'thief in law' or a thief who is the law, a legitimized criminal. The thieves in law organized themselves within the Siberian prison system creating a system of underworld laws. They were not allowed to conduct legitimate business, nor could they work inside the prison. If they accepted work, then they would be labelled traitors by their followers. Most Vor didn't have families as they refused to put women and children at risk. Nowadays, the term has loosened to include men who climb the ranks of organized crime outside of prison. The Vor will also raise families now, as there are unspoken rules surrounding non-involvement of families."

She nodded her understanding. Had she not spent the last year in a trauma filled haze, she likely would've been researching all this. It hadn't occurred to her until now. As soon as she was finished with Karl, she would go online and dig up as much as she could to aid in her knowledge. The prospect of a project excited her, even if it was researching the mafia.

"Is Krystoff Koba a Vory?" she asked curiously.

Karl nodded. "As is Jozef. He took the top spot for himself while in prison, using the old methods to achieve his new status. Jozef has always been a bit of a purist."

Shaun swallowed a giggle when she realized Karl was serious. It was difficult to reconcile the term 'purist' with a criminal. Although Jozef certainly seemed to have a code of honour he followed.

"Nowadays, the title of Vor is often passed on through family lines. The son of a Vor will likely become a Vor himself."

"Like royalty."

"Exactly," Karl agreed. "Marriages and alliances are made throughout the families. Dasha is the daughter of a Vor. She was then married to a Vor to strengthen the family connections. Businesses combine and even more wealth is created."

"Can women become Vory?" Shaun asked, suspecting she already knew the answer. "As his eldest daughter, will Leeza one day take over the Koba organization?"

"Though there are exceptions, women are not usually Vory," Karl said. "The system is an old one and they don't accept change easily unless there's a lucrative reason for it."

"Leeza?" Shaun prompted.

"No, she's not in line to take over for her father. Though she is a capable woman, things aren't done that way. Jozef was next in line to take over from Krystoff. Now..." Karl shook his head, "I don't know. Jozef is likely still Krystoff's heir until a better replacement comes along. Perhaps Saskia's husband when she marries. There is now more pressure for her to choose a husband from among the Vory and their sons."

Shaun's heart ached for her young friend that she could be facing such a decision. Saskia was intelligent and energetic. She had so much more to give than an arranged marriage to a mobster so the family wealth could be protected.

"What about Leeza's husband?" Shaun pushed. "Can't he take over the organization?"

Karl's professional mask dropped. Anger flashed in his eyes and he scowled. "That man will never head the organization."

"Why?" Shaun asked, then added, "I don't understand how or why Leeza is married to Adam. They don't seem to like each other, and he doesn't have any interest in the family that I've seen. He's like a ghost; he's there but no one sees him or pays any attention to him."

"I don't wish to engage in idle gossip," Karl said in admonishment. "It's one thing to want to learn about Jozef and his job. We shouldn't be discussing the private lives of the family, other than to draw the connections for you."

Shaun felt chastened, but his answer didn't dim her curiosity. She wanted to know what was going on behind closed doors with Leeza and her husband. The bruise on Leeza's arm told Shaun things were not as innocent as the pair projected to the outside world.

"Sorry," Shaun said. "We'll keep it to business. Can you tell me about the jobs Jozef and his team accept?"

Karl and Shaun continued to talk for most of the afternoon, until Karl was relieved by the evening security guard who would stand outside Shaun and Jozef's door overnight. Karl agreed to continue Shaun's 'mafia' lessons until she was satisfied. He'd told her that after their chat he'd decided the lessons were a good idea. If Shaun knew the ins and outs of the mafia, she would better be able to protect herself and her family. He also told her he thought it was appropriate for a future mafia wife to understand her place within the organization.

Shaun had wanted to correct him and tell him that a woman's place was wherever she placed herself, but she'd kept her mouth shut, thanked him and, after saying hello to her nighttime security guard, closed the door and sat down with her shiny new laptop. She had no idea what Jozef was going to say when he got his next credit card bill, but something inside her thought he would be pleased rather than annoyed.

CHAPTER TWENTY-FIVE

"I don't like this," Shaun repeated, her arms crossed tightly over her chest.

She was watching Jozef fill a hiker's backpack with his necessities: jeans, T-shirts, socks, underwear, toothbrush, toothpaste, soap, razor, Tylenol. It seemed so normal, the things he was putting in the pack. The same sort of things any traveler might pack. She assumed he would pick up his weapons and bulletproof vest from the operations center, two floors beneath theirs.

She didn't know what else to say so she kept saying the same thing. She didn't like it; didn't like that he was leaving her alone in a city that wasn't home to her yet. Leaving her vulnerable. She didn't like that he was placing himself in danger by going to one of the scariest places on the planet. Didn't like that he was doing it for money. Didn't like that he would likely have to use violence to stay safe.

The whole idea of willingly walking into a potentially violent situation seemed absurd. Only adrenaline junkies did stupid things like that. Of course, she knew she was wrong. She'd done the same thing by working with Doctors Without

Borders. She could say she was doing it for far more noble reasons than Jozef, but it boiled down to the same thing; walking into a war zone knowing they would likely experience violence.

Since meeting Jozef, Shaun's perception of violence had shifted. She'd always seen it as black and white. Violence was bad and so were the people who committed violent acts. By working with Doctors Without Borders, she had been actively fighting against that violence. Or so she thought. Being directly faced with Jozef's motivations for working in war zones forced her to look at her own motivations, which wasn't an easy thing to do.

She could say she'd been doing it for altruistic reasons, but what were the motivations behind altruism? She couldn't bring herself to regret working in war zones. She had learned many things about herself and others. She'd discovered different ways of practicing medicine, while teaching others her methods and the methods practiced by her Canadian colleagues.

Shaun wasn't sure if she would ever go back to Doctors Without Borders. She certainly wouldn't be if Jozef had anything to say about it, but it was a question she would need to examine closer if she regained control of her life again.

I'll be fine, you have nothing to worry about, Jozef signed as he finished packing his bag.

Shaun snorted. *Said every dead soldier ever as he left for war.*

She'd gotten so used to switching back and forth between signing and speaking that it seemed natural depending on who she was talking with, the direction of the conversation, which direction she was facing when she was talking. Her transitions were becoming smoother and smoother, her signs less clumsy.

I'm not a soldier, Jozef argued.

You're a soldier of fortune, Shaun countered.

Jozef grinned, picked up his backpack, and slung it over one shoulder before reaching for her. He wrapped an arm around her waist and dragged her in for a lingering kiss.

Shaun melted as heat filled her belly and the ever-present butterflies winged their way through her chest, her pulse quickening. If she and Jozef could bottle their chemistry, they would become billionaires. Maybe Jozef was already a billionaire.

When he broke the kiss, she leaned back in his arms. "Are you a billionaire?"

He looked surprised, then tipped his head back and barked with laughter. She grinned as his Adam's apple bobbed and the tattoos on his neck stood out stark against his pale skin. Despite their harsh origins and the depictions of death, she loved them, particularly the rose peeking from the top of his chest. When he was shirtless, the rose extended down, across his heart, crisscrossing with the Koba family crest. Her name was written in cursive across the top of the rose, which was only partially open, its petals peeking out in delicate supplication.

I'm not a billionaire, Jozef signed. *Are you disappointed?*

Shaun shook her head. "No, I'm relieved."

Why? he asked. *It would be more of my money for you to spend.*

She smacked his arm. "You're the idiot who gave my mother a credit card. How exactly did you think she was going to take her revenge for kidnapping her daughter?"

He grinned at her and kissed the frown between her eyes. *I wish you would spend as much of my money as your mother does.*

"Don't say that around her; she'll take it as a challenge to spend as much as she can."

He stepped back from her, adjusting the strap of the backpack on his shoulder, then signing, *she'll have a difficult time spending it all.*

"You said you're not a billionaire," she said suspiciously.

I'm not, he assured her. *I'm somewhere in the mid multi-millions. Not sure exactly how much. I'd have to ask my accountant.*

"Millions?" she said with a squeak.

Bet you wish you hadn't fought so hard against marriage a year ago. You could own half of my assets if you weren't so stubborn.

She could tell by the barely suppressed grin and the boyish sparkle in his eyes that he was joking. She crossed her arms over her chest. "I don't care about the money. I never have and I never will. I'd rather you stay home and stay safe."

Jozef sobered, his eyes taking on a look she was becoming familiar with. It was stubbornness combined with the need for her to understand his choices. It was getting harder for her to resist that look, to push his reasoning aside and stubbornly stick to her principles. Love was changing her, but would she still like the person she was becoming if she allowed it to change her completely?

I know you don't care about the money, he signed. *But I have to do this, as well as the other jobs. This is the life I was born to. This is what I'm good at.*

"You can find something else, *do* something else. You're talented and highly skilled. There are thousands of things you could be doing that aren't illegal. Why does it have to be this?"

She finally spoke the words she'd been holding in since Jozef took her from Montréal. The words she'd tried to keep inside. Though she was trying her best to understand the mafia, she couldn't bring herself to condone Jozef's business activities. He terrorized, intimidated, killed. He used violence.

Jozef looked annoyed, then disappointed. She hated that look. Hated that he was disappointed in her, that her lack of understanding was causing a rift between them.

I don't want to fight with you, he sighed. *Not before I leave.*

"I don't want to fight either," she admitted.

He lifted her hands and wiggled them, the corner of his lips lifting.

Shaun laughed and pulled her hands away so she could sign, *you'll never change, will you?* She meant both his career and his preference that she speak to him in sign language.

He shook his head and opened his arms. She walked into them, cuddling against his chest and inhaling his scent. He hugged her tight; a warm hug meant to give her some semblance of reassurance, and it worked. She did feel better.

When he untangled himself, he stepped back and stared at her, his expression torn. Finally, he signed, *I'm not ready to leave you. Come downstairs with me?*

Thus far, Shaun had managed to avoid the floor that belonged to Jozef's men and their offices. She didn't want to see anything she would regret, but the way Jozef formed his request as a question instead of a demand made it impossible for her to refuse. She reached out and took his hand.

"I want to be with you too."

Together they left the apartment, Jozef nodding at Karl while Shaun said a cheery hello to her big, gruff protector. He fell in step behind them, following them to the elevator. When he got on with them, Shaun sent him a questioning look.

"I'm paid to protect you, Dr. Patterson. Doesn't matter where you go, what you do or who you're with, I'm your shadow."

Jozef grunted his approval while punching in the code to the third floor of the building. Each floor had a separate code, which Jozef had given her. She'd seen it as a sign of trust that he was giving her the passcode to get to the main floor, the club floor. She could take advantage of the potential escape route, but she wouldn't.

For one, if she ran away, Jozef would find her, bring her back and lock her down tighter than a pearl in a clamshell.

Second, she wanted to be with him, wanted to work on their issues, which seemed less insurmountable than they had a year ago.

They got off the elevator and it was like stepping into another world. Shaun thought her mouth probably fell open, but she didn't care. There were big and muscular men everywhere, packing bags, checking weapons, laughing, talking, joking. It looked like an all-male gym, but with desks.

A hush fell over the men as Jozef led Shaun through the throng.

Havel stepped into their path, his gaze on Shaun, and for once his expression was welcoming. She was almost relieved to see him. A familiar face in a sea of testosterone.

"Welcome to Guard Dog Securities," Havel said jovially, reaching out to take Jozef's bag.

"Guard Dog Securities?" Shaun asked, looking around.

Havel grinned at her. "We do have some legitimate business interests."

She laughed. "Such as?"

"We provide security details to businessmen, politicians, royalty. We provide security for our club as well as others. Bank security. You name it, we're in on it."

Shaun chewed on her lip, but finally said what was on her mind. "You aren't casing the banks are you? For future heists?"

Havel laughed, along with a few others. He shook his big head. "No, Doc, we don't rob our own clients. Sets a bad precedent. We save our robberies for the fuckers who deserve it."

Jozef growled a warning, his arm tightening on Shaun's waist, but Shaun was enjoying herself. The security floor, Jozef's job, everything, it seemed... different from what she'd been expecting. Far less shady.

She supposed she was expecting a torture chamber on the

third floor. Not a classy looking office, with desks, glass partitions and an entire section dedicated to technology. She drifted toward the tech department, Jozef tight against her side.

"Is that laser tech?" she asked excitedly as one of Jozef's men was packing a laptop in a bag.

The guy nodded. "We use it to pinpoint locations, map the terrain and log it into the database. We don't do jobs blind anymore. It's made our lives much easier."

"Hmm, similar to the tech I use to pinpoint a tumour and remove it from the brain."

"Exactly." The guy looked at her closer. "You're the doctor, aren't you?"

"Yes." She held her hand out to him. "Dr. Shaun Patterson. I'm a surgeon."

"My name is Ali." He shook her hand with more enthusiasm than she was expecting. "I read some of your work after..." he glanced guiltily at Jozef, then focused on Shaun again. "Your experimentation with laser technology in the human brain will be revolutionary for both medicine and weapons systems. In fact, I'm attempting to use some of your techniques to better our guidance systems."

"What?" Shaun asked, looking sharply at Jozef who stared steadily back, a shutter falling over his expression, telling her he knew she was going to be angry when she found out. "You guys are already weaponizing my stuff?"

The guy cleared his throat as though just realizing he was about to put his foot in his mouth.

Havel stepped forward to diffuse the situation. "Not sure I'd want someone digging around my brain with a laser."

"You would if there was a tumour sitting on your brainstem and you had a week to live." Shaun turned her focus on Jozef. "Weapons? Were you going to tell me? Is this why you were reading my stuff? To create better weapons? You didn't say anything when we were talking about it."

Jozef shook his head, took her arm and pulled her away from the group of men. Karl trailed behind at a respectful distance. When Jozef and Shaun were once more standing near the elevator, Jozef dropped his hand so he could sign.

I read your papers so I could feel close to you while I was in prison. I didn't lie to you.

She shook her head and glared at him. "But you did use my knowledge and my technology to better your own weapons. You're too smart and resourceful not to." She glanced at the tech corner and added, "Probably your surveillance too."

Jozef sighed and scrubbed a hand down his face. Finally, he looked at her. *Yes, of course I did. Your work with laser technology is brilliant. The only reason no one else has used it is because your work is buried in medical journals that are nearly indecipherable. No one outside of the medical profession would read them.*

She scowled at him, her blood beginning to boil with self-righteous anger. Not only was he stealing her life's work and using it to make weapons, but now he was calling the papers she wrote boring and impenetrable.

She straightened her back and glared at him, signing so she wouldn't be overheard by any of his people. *Did you think about how I would feel when I found out about this?*

You weren't supposed to find out.

I'm not blind or stupid. I would've noticed eventually.

He sighed and reached for her, but she stepped out of his reach and jabbed the elevator button angrily before signing, *every time we establish some semblance of trust between us, you destroy it. How am I supposed to live like this? Every corner I turn there's something new and terrible that I have to learn to live with. Eventually I'm going to find something I can't live with, Jozef.*

Lower your expectations, he signed.

"What?" she said out loud.

The elevator door opened behind her.

Maybe if you stop expecting me to be someone I'm not, you'll learn to live with me.

She stepped into the elevator, her happy mood evaporating. "Maybe if we keep arguing about this, you'll be the one wanting to escape me."

He stepped into the elevator and wrapped an arm around her waist. He dragged her against his chest and kissed her, his lips taking hers with harsh intent. He was imprinting himself on her, his tongue lashing the inside of her mouth in a one-way dance.

As the elevator started to close, he flung an arm out, hitting the metal doors. They opened again. Karl slipped inside the elevator and did his best to look like an uninterested bystander.

Jozef stepped back, his striking deep blue eyes on Shaun's face. *Never. I will never let you go.*

He let the doors go.

Just before they closed, Shaun shouted, "Don't you dare die! We're not done talking about this."

CHAPTER TWENTY-SIX

Mogadishu had never been one of Jozef's favourite places. It was hot and smelled like mildew and dirt. The red zone, where they were currently hiding out, smelled like shit too, from improper sewage disposal in that part of the city. They had to be constantly vigilant so as not to get caught up in the ongoing violence between sectors. The poverty was nearly overwhelming.

Ordinarily poverty in a region he was travelling through wouldn't bother Jozef. He'd travelled the world, seen poverty of every kind.

Now, he was looking at it through Shaun's eyes. Everywhere he looked he saw starving children, women prostituting themselves to feed their families, injustice.

"Ali, go get us something to eat," Cooper said from his cot, where he was laying with his hands twined behind his head, staring at the ceiling. "I'm fucking sick of rations."

"Why me?" Ali demanded.

Cooper pushed himself up to stare down the smaller tech guy. "You're the only one of us who can blend in."

Ali took immediate offence. "Fuck you, Coop. I don't

know if you noticed but I don't look even close to fitting in here. They'll take one look at me and peg me as a foreigner before I even open my mouth."

Ali wasn't far from the truth. Though he was the only person of colour on their team, his skin tone was still several shades lighter than most of the citizens of Mogadishu.

Jozef looked at his team through new eyes. Most were poached from mob families throughout Eastern Europe and Russia. A few were foreign, from the United States, Ireland and Egypt. No women. No one with darker skin than Ali. For the first time he contemplated the advantages of hiring for more diversity. The team could blend in better, depending on the region they worked in. A woman would be able to access places that men couldn't.

Damn. Shaun was getting into his head. Making him think things he'd never thought about before. He wasn't sure if it was a good thing or a bad thing. Of course, he loved having her in his life, but it was an uncomfortable realization. He and the men on his team were far more privileged than most of the people in Mogadishu and surrounding areas.

Ali and Cooper were still arguing when Havel grunted, "No one's leaving. We have enough rations to get us through until we get the green light on our mission. Shut up and relax, boys."

Jozef stood and headed for the door.

"What about him?" Cooper asked. "Why's he allowed to leave?"

"He can do whatever the fuck he wants," Havel growled. "Now shut the fuck up. Some of us are trying to get some rest."

"What happened to lead by example?"

"This isn't a fucking democracy. Now I suggest you do as I say, or you'll be chewing on a bullet next. Don't give a fuck if your team's down a man."

Jozef didn't hear if there was more back and forth. He pulled his ball cap lower on his head, lifted his collar and headed out into the street. His minor efforts at disguise weren't particularly useful. He was pale as fuck with tattoos covering every inch of skin except for his face. He would stand out like a beacon in the night, and if anyone was targeting him, he wouldn't be hard to find. It didn't matter. Jozef hated being cooped up, especially after his stint in prison. In his mind, the freedom to go outside was worth the risk for him. Not for his men though. He needed them to stay inside and stay hidden. He didn't care if the rules weren't fair. As Havel pointed out, he wasn't running a democracy.

Jozef had always been a restless person. He hated sitting for too long. But much of their time in Mogadishu had been spent sitting and waiting. Seven days, so far.

Jozef walked, his feet taking him in the same direction he went every time he stepped foot outdoors in Mogadishu. When he arrived at his destination, he stayed to the shadows, standing just inside an alleyway across the street from the free clinic. As there had been every day prior, there was a long lineup of mostly women and children. Some were obviously sick, while others waited for things like vaccinations and birth control.

Prior to this trip, Jozef hadn't paid any attention to the health care systems in the different parts of the world. But through his observations, it became clear that Somalia had a huge need for medicine and not enough clinics and doctors to fill that need.

The free clinic he was watching was run by Doctors Without Borders. Most of the doctors and nurses going inside were from different parts of the world. He knew Shaun had worked in the refugee camps on the Chad border. He wondered if the conditions were similar but knew in his gut, they were probably worse.

He felt a strange mix of emotions as he imagined her working in this part of the world. Anger and fear that she would put herself in so much danger. He had proved to her how much danger she was in by kidnapping her from a different but no less risky place than this one.

He was also proud of his girl for doing some of the hardest work on the planet. She had brains, guts and beauty. She was truly a rare gift, one he intended to treasure for the rest of his days. A chill ran through him as he thought about how close he'd come to extinguishing all of that greatness.

Shaun had once told him that when he took a life, he wasn't just taking the person, he was taking away their potential. Everything they could've accomplished in their lives. Her words had stuck with him, changed him. Not significantly, he admitted, but enough that he was more careful now when dealing death.

In prison, he'd killed four people. One cellmate and three Vory. The first he'd sacrificed to show the other inmates not to fuck with the mute mobster. The other three were necessary deaths. Steppingstones in his bid to climb to the top. Shaun wouldn't approve those choices, but it didn't matter. Despite her influence over him, he was still the same guy; a born and bred assassin. A killing machine. And now, a mob boss.

Love didn't blind him to who he was, just made him more aware of who he wasn't. A lessor man might leave the woman he saw as greater than himself. Jozef would never let her go. He would keep her and use her as his conscience. She would remind him of the joys in life. Of the value of life.

He turned away from the clinic to make his way to the nearest market to buy some fresh food and sweets for his team. He might not run a democracy, but he still understood the value in team morale. Before he made it halfway down the alley an explosion rocked the ground beneath his feet and threw him off balance. He slammed into the side of a building and landed on his side. He covered his head as debris landed all around him.

He lay on the ground, his ears ringing from the blast and waited for some of the dust to clear. Finally, after several long minutes he unfurled his body and did a quick damage assessment. Scrapes and bruises, nothing more.

He stared up the alley to the spot where he'd been standing moments before. It was obliterated; taken out by a collapsing wall. He'd be dead if he hadn't moved.

A siren rose up, piercing the fog that'd fallen over him. He tried to decipher the noise from the ringing in his ears, but he couldn't place it. He stood, using the wall to drag himself up. He stretched his limbs and then turned away from the explosion, intending to walk back to the safe house.

He stopped.

He knew the target of the explosion was the free clinic. It was the only controversial building on the block. There were foreigners inside. Clinics like this were targeted in this part of the world by different factions intent on using them as an example to both their own governments and foreign governments. As he stood there, breathing in the dust and ash, rage hit him.

Shaun could've been inside that building. If things were different, she would've continued her work with Doctors Without Borders. She could have easily found her way to Mogadishu and gone to work in the clinic, vaccinating patients and providing medical assistance to locals.

The people who worked in that clinic were like her. Innocent victims. He wanted to look down on them as idiot do-gooders who got what they deserved for sticking their noses where they shouldn't go, but he couldn't. Not if they were anything like Shaun. Kind, compassionate, intelligent. In the wrong place at the wrong time, doing a job they knew could get them killed, but doing it anyway because it needed to be done.

He couldn't walk away from them.

Fuck, he thought to himself. *He was as much an idiot as they were.*

He turned back toward the clinic, picking his way through the smoking debris. He had to climb over the pile of rubble, careful not to touch any of the hot stone. Jozef had seen a lot in his time, but he'd never seen anything quite like what was on the other side of the fallen wall.

Where there had once been a lineup of patients waiting to get into the clinic, there was now nothing but smoke and debris. At first his sluggish brain wondered where the people had gone, but then he realized they were most likely dead, killed in the blast. There was blood all over the street and a large hole in the side of the clinic where the doors had been.

People were starting to rush into the streets to help the ones caught up in the blast, but there wasn't much for them to find. He realized what the siren sound was. A child standing in the road, covered in blood, screaming at the top of his lungs. He was so loud Jozef found himself wishing the kid had been caught in the blast, then immediately felt shame for the thought. For all he knew, the kid's entire family had just been wiped off the planet.

Jozef didn't know what he was going to do, didn't know if he could help. Or if he even would. But he felt himself drawn to the clinic. As if he had to see inside, see if the doctors and nurses were safe. Do it for Shaun.

He picked his way down the rubble and was about to walk across the road when the sound of moaning caught his attention. He turned and saw a splash of colour next to one of the stones that had fallen from the building where he'd been standing.

He turned back and knelt down, shifting the rocks and

cursing as they scraped his hands. After a moment he unveiled a woman. Still alive, but badly injured. She was Caucasian, brunette, wearing scrubs. She must've been on her way to the clinic when the bomb went off.

He could tell right away that her shoulder was broken, and she had a bloody head wound, probably from the fallen rock. She was barely conscious and though her eyes were open she wasn't looking at him.

Jozef knew in his gut that she wasn't going to make it. Her breathing was erratic and gurgling as though she was choking on a chest filled with blood. He didn't know what to do. Stay and comfort her? Leave? Get help?

Then she seemed to focus on him. She flailed her arm, and he took hold of her hand before she accidentally hit him.

"Help…" she said faintly, blood trickling from her mouth.

Internal injuries. He'd caused enough to know that there would be no coming back from this. Her insides were probably as much a mess as the streets around them, but he couldn't bring himself to get up and leave. Even though she looked nothing like Shaun, when he looked at the woman on the ground, he saw his love. The possibility that this could've happened to her shook him.

He released her hand and cleared more of the debris, freeing her body. It was worse than he thought. Her pelvis was crushed and there was a gaping wound to her belly. Both of her legs were shattered.

Ambulances began arriving, their sirens drowning out the screaming child.

Jozef looked over his shoulder. He was twenty feet from the nearest ambulance.

He reached an arm beneath the woman's neck and the other beneath her knees. She let out a grunt of pain as he lifted her, then her head lolled back against his arm.

He stumbled with her toward the ambulance.

She took her last breath as he passed her over to a para-medic. Before he could turn away and leave, he took one last look at her face, now slack as death took her. Her eyes stilled. He snatched the name tag hanging from the pocket of her scrubs and backed away from her.

The paramedic turned back to him, his gaze concerned as he took in the blood down Jozef's front, the scrapes and the shell-shocked look that was written all over his face. The man spoke to him in Somalian. Jozef shook his head, turned and walked away.

It took him an hour to make his way back to the safe house. When he arrived, the place was in chaos. His men were on their feet, shoving things into bags and checking weapons. At first, he thought they were preparing to come get him, having somehow found out that he'd been caught up in a bombing, but then he realized no one was paying him any attention.

"Where've you been, man?" Havel demanded. "We just got word. The mission's a go."

Jozef shook his head, trying to shake the ringing and the horror from his brain so he could concentrate on their mission. His men would need a leader whose head was in the game.

"Is that blood on your clothes?" Havel asked, checking his sidearm before shoving it into the holster. "Who did you kill?"

CHAPTER TWENTY-SEVEN

Jozef had been gone for one week, and so far, it was one of the most nerve-wracking weeks of Shaun's life. There was something especially terrifying knowing that the man she loved had walked willingly into a war zone to do something dangerous. The more she thought about it the angrier she felt. He was doing it for money! Was there a worse reason to do something so stupidly reckless?

Shaun knew she was overreacting, but she couldn't seem to stop herself. She was also experiencing a particularly vicious bout of PMS, probably because she wasn't sleeping or eating properly. She was laying on the couch with a hot water bottle pressed against her belly, Fitzy curled against the small of her back, watching the news. An explosion in Mogadishu had taken out one of their free clinics.

The Doctors Without Borders organization had lost three people: two nurses and a doctor. Twelve Somalians had died in the blast and countless others had been injured. The scenes depicted on the television weren't new to Shaun, but they weren't any less horrifying. After the blast, she'd checked obsessively until she was able to come up with a list of the dead. Jozef's name wasn't on it. Not that he would have been anywhere near the free clinic, but she couldn't shake the feeling that her lover was in danger.

They were going to have a talk when he finally got back home. And when she could stand up again without the cramps crippling her attempts.

"Here you are." Fatima set a steaming cup of tea on the coffee table in Shaun's line of sight.

Shaun glared at it. Why did people think tea was soothing when someone was injured or depressed? Tea was tea. It was a weak version of coffee without the amazing coffee taste.

Shaun pushed herself up and reached for the hot beverage. "Thank you, mama," she said politely. She might feel bitchy on the inside, but she would do her best not to take it out on the people she loved.

Saskia snickered and crossed her eyes from the end of the couch where she was curled at Shaun's feet.

Shaun glared at the girl and sipped the surprisingly good tea. Her mother knew just how to make it, with a dash of heavy cream and a liberal tablespoon of honey.

Fatima picked up the remote control from the coffee table, turned off the news, and settled herself in the cozy leather chair next to the fireplace, opposite the couch. She sipped her own tea, a thoughtful expression on her face.

Finally, she turned her gaze toward Saskia and asked, "What happens if Shaun and Jozef have children? Will they automatically become part of the Bratva?"

Shaun wanted to protest that children were not in the picture yet, and wouldn't be for a while, but she was curious too. Saskia had popped by the week before and met Fatima. The two had taken an instant liking to each other. Saskia had called Fatima badass for, "walking into a mobster stronghold with a suitcase and a cat." Fatima saw Saskia as an under-loved urchin who needed a strong dose of mothering when she came around. Shaun had pointed out that the under-loved urchin had access to unlimited funds and resources and frequently used her intelligence for mischief.

When Fatima and Saskia had learned of Shaun's conversation with Karl about the mafia, both had insisted on getting in on the action. Fatima, because she was an intelligent woman who realized that the more she understood how the mafia worked the more power she and her daughter would have. Shaun also suspected her mother might be reciprocating Karl's crush and came around the apartment more often to hang out with Shaun in hopes of seeing him. It was like watching a couple of teenagers circle each other.

Saskia had wanted in on the mafia conversation because she thought she had quite a lot to contribute, and she wasn't wrong. While Karl had been somewhat willing, but mostly nervous, to share information with Shaun, Saskia had been wholeheartedly enthusiastic about the idea. Now, she came over frequently after her classes to spend time with Shaun and Fatima.

Saskia had taught them the word Bratva the day before; it was Russian for mafia.

"Yes," Saskia said around a mouthful of the caramel popcorn Fatima had made for her. When Shaun's mom realized the way to Saskia's soul was through her stomach, the treats had become endless. "A son will learn about the organization from his father in preparation to one day take over, and a daughter will be expected to marry into another powerful family."

"Over my dead body," Shaun had snapped, while Fatima exclaimed, "That's terrible!"

Saskia shrugged. "It is what it is."

"What an antiquated system," Fatima had said with some concern. "Shouldn't the children decide?"

Saskia shook her head at the older woman as if to say,

'what a newb.' "That isn't how it's done here. Even outside the Bratva, children are expected to accept the will of their parents."

Shaun thought about her reaction to Saskia the year before when the girl had told her she was expected to marry, not go to university. Shaun had been horrified at the time, but now realized the Koba family wasn't being deliberately cruel to their daughter, they were following accepted convention.

Saskia had gone as far as to bring a whiteboard with her on one of her visits. It was filled with the names and family connections of everyone involved with the Koba family. She reached over the couch to grab her whiteboard and go through all of the marriages that had been arranged. It was shocking to Fatima and Shaun to see how many mafia families made arranged marriages.

"Arranged marriages make for stronger alliances." The women turned to look at Karl who was standing by the island, his arms crossed over his chest. "Most children are raised to understand their duty."

"Understanding and accepting are two different things," Saskia muttered, then pointed at a name on her whiteboard. "Alexandr Volkov. Head of the Volkov family." She moved her pointer to the name next to his. "Olga Volkov, his second wife. His first disappeared in a tragic yacht accident outside of Moscow."

"There's nowhere to boat outside of Moscow. Unless she died in a paddleboat accident on the canal." Karl frowned.

"Smart man," Saskia said with a quick grin. "He totally killed her, but the official version is that the wife died in a boating accident. The second wife brought a lot more resources and prestige to the family. Volkov was among the lower ranks of the Vory until he married Olga. Now he's sitting among the decision-makers in Moscow."

"And how does this relate to the Kobas?" Fatima asked.

So far everything they'd learned came back to the Koba family who, as it turned out, were intricately connected to most of the other organized crime families.

"Olga is the daughter of Yuri Turgenev, who is the half-brother of Petr Koba."

Shaun figured it out first, the second name ringing a bell. "Your great grandfather."

Saskia nodded. "My father's grandfather. Olga is my third cousin."

Fatima nodded knowingly.

It seemed mind-boggling to Shaun that the families could and did keep track of each other. They were very much like royalty in the way they arranged marriages and stayed connected with each other, many of them wealthy and living among the elite. Some were even married to or descended from genuine royalty.

"Do you think Olga will go the way of the first wife?" Fatima asked, her tone one of curiosity rather than concern, like she was discussing a soap opera.

After only a few of their mafia gossip sessions both Shaun and her mother had reached the point where they were no longer horrified by the things they were learning. Perhaps that should've tipped Shaun off that she was becoming more accepting of the world she refused to integrate into one year ago. She still thought often of the morality involved in giving into the mafia lifestyle, but she reasoned with herself that she couldn't change something if she didn't understand it.

The problem was, once she understood, would she still be standing on the outside looking in with disapproval, or would she be on the inside, her morality as twisted as that of the people surrounding her? It wasn't an easy question to ask herself, and there were no easy answers. For now, everything boiled down to her decision to stay with Jozef and find a way to meet in the middle of what had seemed like an impossible situation a year ago.

Saskia was busy explaining the annual meeting of the Vory when a muffled pop sounded, and the lights went out. Everyone froze as the room was plunged into shadows. It was the middle of the day, but the heavy snowfall outside the windows obscured most of the natural light.

Karl was the first to leap to his feet. "Everyone up, follow me."

Though his words were spoken calmly, he seemed tense. He pulled his gun from the holster that seemed to be a permanent fixture on his belt.

Saskia dragged her purse close and Shaun realized the younger woman probably had a gun tucked inside.

"What's happening?" Fatima asked, alarmed.

"Probably nothing," Karl said reassuringly.

"Maybe something," Saskia piped up. "Where's the panic room?"

"Here," Karl said, ushering the three women into Jozef and Shaun's bedroom. Fatima scooped up Fitzy and carried him.

Shaun clutched her hot water bottle and obediently followed Karl. Her mouth fell open in surprise when he escorted them through her huge closet and opened a panel at the back. She hadn't noticed it before as it blended into the wall. He punched in a code and the back of the closet disappeared as a door swung open.

"You didn't tell me you had one of these," Fatima said accusingly to her daughter.

"I didn't know," Shaun said faintly, following him in.

Karl's phone rang and he answered it quickly. "Alex." He listened intently, then said, "They're in the panic room now. Saskia's here; she can watch over them. I'll cover the door."

Karl hung up and turned to the women. "Weapons," he

pointed at a locker in the back of the small room, then swung his hand to point at Saskia. "You're in charge. There're lights, communications and a door release; code 9037. Food and water in the locker if you're in here for a while." His eyes pierced the three women. "Don't leave this room for any reason."

"Wait," Fatima lurched forward. "Where are you going?"

"To do my job." His gaze softened. "You'll be safe."

"I'm not worried about us," she snapped.

He closed the door, and the room was plunged into darkness. They could hear a lock electronically sliding into place and engaging with a click.

"It would've been handy if he let us turn the lights on before sealing us in," Saskia said, annoyance in her voice.

The women stumbled around the room until they found a light switch, turning it on.

"Must be on a backup electrical system," Shaun murmured.

Fatima set the cat on the ground and he immediately set about licking himself, disgruntlement at his forcible removal from the couch ruffling his composure.

Saskia strode to the locker and started digging through it. She pulled a gun out, checked the chamber then reached for a box of bullets. She loaded the gun with quick precise movements, then tucked it into her waistband. She looked at Shaun with a raised eyebrow holding up another gun. Shaun shook her head. She might be learning about the mafia, but she was nowhere close to wanting to use a weapon.

"Suit yourself," Saskia said tucking it away.

She dug through the bottom of the locker and came up with a handful of snacks. Sinking onto the floor she leaned against the wall and began digging through her stash, opening wrappers and eating as she went.

"You've done this before, haven't you?" Shaun asked, some

awe in her voice at how casual Saskia was about having to hunker down in a panic room.

"Yup," she said around a mouthful of chocolate. "After my aunt and uncle were killed, our parents installed panic rooms in every apartment. Mine looks like a cardboard box compared to this luxury. I used to hide things in there before my mom found out and forbid me from using it as a play-room. Otherwise, I only ever legitimately used it once."

"What happened?" Fatima sat next to Saskia.

Saskia handed her a chocolate bar which Fatima accepted. "It was last year when Shaun was attacked at the party. We didn't know who'd done it or where they'd gone so dad rushed me, Leeza, little Kris and mom into the panic room and shut down the mansion until he could be sure another attack wasn't coming."

Shaun had been so out of it she hadn't considered what was happening to the Koba family in the immediate after-math of the poisoning.

"How long were you in there for?"

Saskia shrugged, but her body language was stiff. "Two days."

"Two days!" Shaun repeated incredulously. "The four of you lived in a tiny room together for two days?"

"It's a miracle we survived," Saskia said with a grim smile. "And I don't mean your attacker. Leeza can be a grade A bitch when she's feeling claustrophobic."

Fatima laughed and shook her head. "How did you go to the bathroom?"

Saskia pushed herself off the floor and hunted around the room until she found a nearly invisible seam in the wall. She pushed hard on the section of wall and it swung out. A basic toilet and sink were in a tiny cubicle that would only fit one person at a time.

"It's not pleasant to do your business on the other side of a very thin wall, but it's functional."

Fatima and Shaun looked at each other. It felt strange to be learning all the ins and outs of the mafia but to still be shocked by something like a panic room with a built-in washroom. Saskia took these things in stride, but she'd grown up surrounded by the accoutrements of the mafia.

Saskia settled on the floor next to Fatima and pulled a dried fruit leather from her pile of goodies.

"Don't you think we should ration the food?" Shaun asked, humour in her voice. "In case we're in here for a while."

Saskia shrugged. "I'll fight you for it."

The three women laughed.

Fatima sobered first. "Saskia, you mentioned your Aunt and Uncle were killed. Was it... was it mafia related?"

"I think so. It happened before I was born so I never knew them. No one knows exactly what happened, or if they do, no one's talking. It was Christmas, thirty years ago. They were preparing to come over to the house for a family meal when they were attacked. Dad thinks it had something to do with a rival."

"Oh, I'm so sorry, how awful," Fatima exclaimed.

"Jozef's parents," Shaun murmured.

Saskia nodded her head while Fatima looked shocked.

"It's how his throat was cut," Saskia supplied. "The attackers went after him too, but they didn't count on a five-year-old boy being just as vicious as the rest of them." The way she spoke indicated Saskia enjoyed this part of the story. Shaun was beginning to suspect Saskia hero-worshipped her older cousin. "He pulled the knife they'd used on him out of his own throat and stabbed one of the guys through the eye."

Fatima gasped, her eyes wide with worry. "Oh, that poor boy. To lose his parents and his voice all on the same night."

Shaun felt the urge to laugh but swallowed it. She didn't think it would be any less traumatic to lose his parents and his voice on different nights.

"Did they ever find out who did it?"

"No," Saskia said around a mouthful of dried fruit. "The body left behind was a low-level street thug. No affiliation to any particular family. I think my dad tried to find out but had to give up and write the incident off as a robbery gone wrong. I think it bothers him to this day that he was never able to avenge his brother."

"What happened to Jozef?" Fatima was Saskia's rapt audience and Saskia was more than pleased to talk someone's ear off.

"He went to live with my mom and dad. They'd only been married a few years, so I think it was rough for them to take in a traumatized child, but I think Jozef turned out just fine."

Shaun did laugh this time and Fatima returned her smile.

Oblivious to the exchange, Saskia continued to eat.

Twenty minutes later someone banged on the door to the safe room, then opened it.

Karl stepped inside, sweeping the room with a serious look. "It's alright. Someone set a firework off in the club which triggered the alarms. Alex shut the lights down in the building to encourage people to leave the club."

Karl frowned as though something was bothering him.

"What is it?" Saskia asked sharply, standing and dusting the crumbs from her jeans.

He shook his head, but finally admitted. "It's a weird coincidence. Someone playing a stupid prank in the club while Jozef is out of town. Almost as if they know he's away and are testing our defenses."

"Do you really think that's what happened?" Fatima asked, fear in her voice.

His eyes softened. "I'm a suspicious man. Have to be for my job. I'm sure it's nothing."

Fatima looked marginally better, but Shaun knew better. And apparently, so did Saskia.

"What aren't you telling us?" Saskia demanded.

He looked at her, his gaze still troubled. "We looked at the footage of people leaving the club. Your sister was here."

CHAPTER TWENTY-EIGHT

Jozef's team ran into very little trouble as they moved through Somalia, travelling down the border between Ethiopia and Kenya, into South Sudan. Ali hacked into and redirected a satellite from a large telecommunications company to survey the region as they moved so they were able to avoid any hotbeds of activity.

Every man on Jozef's team understood the score. They worked hard, paid attention and rolled with the rough living. At the end, the payoff would be worth more than they would have otherwise likely seen in their lifetimes. This was why Jozef took the risks that he took. The payoff.

Yet, something felt different this time. An alarm bell was going off in his brain telling him to step carefully, double check everything, make sure his team was alert. He suspected the alarm was Shaun. She was worried about him, which caused him to worry. He wondered if this new development was a liability or if it might one day save his life.

It was two days into their trek, as they were forced to lay low and allow a paramilitary contingent pass through the valley below them that Jozef realized what the bell with

Shaun's voice was trying to tell him. He had too much to live for to die now.

As they continued to walk over, under and through the rough terrain to the vehicles waiting to take them over the border, Jozef thought about his life. He'd been raised and trained to believe one thing. His existence was for the protection of others at the expense of all else, including his own life. He'd never before valued his life quite the way he did now. His year in prison had been made more bearable by the knowledge that he had little to live for, thus the risks involved in climbing the Bratva ladder didn't faze him.

Now, things were different. Now, when he thought about death, he thought about all the missed days and years that he wouldn't get to spend with Shaun if he died. She was giving him a reason to survive.

"Stop," Havel commanded as they neared the checkpoint.

Jozef's men fell into place, each taking position to watch and attack if they were set upon. Jozef, who had been at the back of the group, made his way to Havel, who was standing next to Halil, their scout for the mission.

Halil didn't hesitate but starting filling Jozef in the moment he was in earshot. "Two transport vehicles up ahead. They look military, but I don't think they are. There appears to be four men with the vehicles, all armed. One is our contact."

Jozef grunted his acknowledgment. Radik had given them a contact for the border crossing. A man named Zeke, no last name. Probably a fake name.

You two come with me, Jozef signed. *We'll take three others. The rest will cover us until we give the go-ahead.*

They'd already gone over the meet, discussing every possible scenario, so every man knew what he was doing. Yet Jozef knew the best laid plans could go to shit in a matter of seconds. He had so many backup plans, his team occasionally referred to him as their mother hen because he worried over them.

Of course, no one said it in his hearing, but Havel was pleased as punch to tell Jozef when his team was making fun of him. Though they would have to respect him to his face, he didn't mind a little ribbing. It strengthened their bonds with each other, which made them more effective.

Jozef, Halil and Havel walked up the overgrown dirt road, their boots kicking up dust. Three of Jozef's men followed several meters behind, covering their backs. It took about ten minutes to reach their destination.

The vehicles and the people around them were as expected. Two military trucks with canvas-covered beds were waiting for them. Their contact, Zeke, separated from the group and strode toward Jozef.

Zeke stretched a hand towards Jozef but spoke to Havel. "Right on time." He glanced around, a frown creasing his thick brows. "Where are the rest? I was told you'd have ten men."

Havel growled his annoyance at Zeke. "You talk to him." Havel pointed at Jozef. "He's in charge."

Zeke's surprised gaze snapped back to Havel. "My apologies, I was told Mr. Koba doesn't speak."

Havel's hand landed on the butt of his gun. "You don't know the difference between speaking and hearing? He's got ears."

Jozef clapped his hands, getting everyone's attention. He'd learned long ago how to hit his palms together just right, so they made a thunderous, ear-splitting clap. It worked well when he needed to communicate and no one was looking at him.

He signed to Havel, his movements rapid, *quit fucking with our contact. We need him and he's not doing anything we haven't seen before. In fact, it's better when they underestimate me. Let's get on with it. I don't want to be late for the next meet.*

Havel dragged his big knife from his belt and tapped it against his fingertips. "Okay boss man, you got it. Gut the fucker if he so much as breathes funny." Havel was messing with their contact on purpose, his protective instincts toward Jozef kicking into gear. Jozef sighed but allowed it. He would talk to Havel later about not misinterpreting Jozef on purpose. They'd had the same conversation multiple times. It never seemed to stick.

"I didn't mean anything by it," Zeke was quick to say. "We should get moving before the next patrol hits this area."

Jozef nodded. *What do you want us to do?*

They talked specifics for a few minutes and once Jozef was satisfied, he gave the signal for the rest of his team to make an appearance. Zeke blanched as he was rapidly overtaken by a dozen mercenaries carrying enough weaponry to wipe a small country off the planet.

They split the teams up, climbing into the backs of the vehicles, seven men per vehicle: two up front and five in the rear. Jozef changed Zeke's original configuration to include one of Zeke's men in the back with Jozef's people and one of Jozef's men up front with the driver. If Zeke's men were split up, they would have a much more difficult time ambushing Jozef's team.

Not that Jozef was particularly worried; his team was too good to be easily taken by ex-bush soldiers turned muscle-for-hire.

Jozef sat in the back of one of the jeeps with Zeke, Ali, Nikolay and Cooper. Halil sat up front with their driver. When Jozef saw Cooper climbing into his jeep, he'd nearly sent the American to the other jeep. The man was fucking chatty and he didn't seem to have an off switch unless he was sleeping. But Jozef figured Havel was far more likely to shoot the man's head off, so Jozef allowed him to stay.

The drive was arduous to the point that Jozef wished Radik had just allowed them to walk the distance. His team was trained for hard hiking and could cover around 60 kilometers in a day with their equipment. Their meeting place was 30 kilometers across the border, but Radik wanted Jozef and his men escorted in and out.

Jozef wasn't sure if the man underestimated them or distrusted them, but he'd been forced to accept the escort if he wanted the job.

The road was bumpy and, in places, so overgrown that there didn't seem to be a road. He knew they were crossing the border at an unpatrolled point, but that didn't mean the military wouldn't have troops checking.

Jozef glanced at Ali who was looking down at his travel laptop, open and balancing on his knees. Ali looked up and caught Jozef's gaze. He already knew what Jozef wanted.

Ali shook his head. "No movement other than us within a ten-kilometer radius of the route. There's a five-minute lag though."

Jozef nodded his understanding. There was, of course, always a lag between the satellite transmission and the ground. Five minutes was a small window for troops to get in and ambush the trucks, but it was possible. Jozef preferred vigilance over faith.

Keep watching, he signed.

Ali refocused on the laptop, occasionally updating Jozef as they drove.

When they arrived at Radik's meeting point, the men climbed out of the trucks and fanned out in a previously discussed configuration. They'd been warned not to engage if they ran into any of Radik's people while in the bushes. Radik had agreed he would be accompanied by only three men, all visible, but Jozef didn't trust the man. Jozef didn't trust any man except Havel, which was why he was still alive.

A slight pang hit him as he thought of his uncle, but he quickly dismissed it. Perhaps he'd trusted Krystoff as a child, but his uncle had used Jozef and his team for years for his own purposes. And while Jozef had been a willing participant in the jobs, he hadn't trusted his uncle to have their health and safety in mind. Jozef had compensated to cover for Krystoff's blind spots. It was better that Jozef had split from the Kobas and took control of his team.

Jozef refocused on the job as they waited for Radik to arrive. Everything went according to plan. Jozef's team arrived exactly fifteen minutes before Radik's. Radik's group arrived in a truck that looked like the ones Jozef's team had taken across the border.

Jozef figured all of the men and trucks belonged to Radik, which put them firmly in Radik's control. Or so the man would think. When Radik had talked about a team coming to pick up Jozef and his men to take them across the border, Jozef had suspected it was Radik's way of putting more of his men in the field than the three Jozef had insisted on.

What Radik didn't know is that Jozef's team had been briefed on every possible scenario including this one. They were expecting an ambush, even though it was unlikely Radik would draw them all the way out there just to kill them. Not when the man had enough resources to blow up Jozef's club and the building it was in, killing most of Jozef's team in one move.

No, Jozef had done some checking on Radik and while the man was one of the deadliest mercenaries in the world with a body count higher than Jozef's, the general word on the dark web was that he didn't double cross his business associates. If he hired Jozef for a job, then he wanted Jozef to do that job. He wouldn't go to the effort and expense of luring Jozef and his team into an ambush.

Havel stood next to Jozef as Radik walked toward them, two of his own men at his back, all three of them carrying rifles.

"Koba." Radik extended his hand and Jozef took it, squeezing.

Radik and Jozef spoke while Havel translated. Jozef respected that Radik spoke directly to him without pausing or stumbling over Jozef's lack of voice. Jozef would bet his cut of the pay for the job that Radik didn't underestimate him either. He knew the silent guard dog could and would strike without warning if provoked.

Finally, they got around to the package.

"You'll have questions, I'm sure," Radik said, his deep baritone voice serious. "Don't ask them. You won't get any answers. Do your job and deliver the package. I'll transfer the pay once I know it's safe."

At first, Jozef was insulted that Radik thought he would ask questions about a job that had already been discussed in detail. Then he felt uneasy. Radik would know that, which meant the package could only be one thing.

Human cargo.

Jozef growled, gaining Radik's attention. He signed swiftly, making sure Havel could see. *I told you, we don't transport human cargo. You better not be fucking with me; I won't take kindly to a change in our agreement.*

Radik had easily agreed to Jozef's strictest term; he didn't transport people. Now Jozef realized Radik had agreed to it too quickly. Most of Jozef's other clients had questions about that term. For most it was curiosity, for some disappointment.

Jozef lived in the underworld of the mafia, which meant he was surrounded by prostitution and human bondage. He'd become somewhat immune to the pathetic men, women and children caught up in the industry, but he refused to participate. His uncle had tried to talk him out of that particular term, arguing that it wasn't Jozef's job to judge their client's activities, that they were leaving money on the table by not accepting human cargo jobs. Jozef had stood firm.

Radik looked angry, but finally nodded. "I know your terms, and you must believe I understand. Even agree, to some extent. But I need you for this job and I'm not willing to compromise."

Jozef let out a vicious growl and lifted his hand to give his men the order to take Radik and his men out.

CHAPTER TWENTY-NINE

"You don't want to do that," Radik said calmly. "I have a missile aimed at this site and, like you, a satellite in orbit. If you make a move, I will have my people fire, and we all die together."

Jozef stared at the man, infuriated, tempted to call his bluff. There would be a five-minute lag between Radik's satellite and his ground communications. Five minutes was plenty of time to clear out if a missile really was pointed at them. Only Jozef didn't think Radik was bluffing. None of his research on the man had indicated he spoke anything but the truth to his clients.

Radik stared Jozef down, finally saying in a low voice. "Is your distaste for human trafficking really stronger than your desire to live? Stronger than the lives of your men?"

Though Havel knew the answer, he didn't speak for Jozef. He didn't need to; Radik could read the truth in Jozef's eyes. He would rather die than transport humans to a life of misery.

Radik straightened, running a hand over his forehead, which was beaded with sweat from the heat of the sun. "You are an interesting man, Jozef Koba. You would judge the business of others, silently condemning, while running around with this ragtag group, setting fire to the world in search of profit."

Jozef raised an eyebrow, not at all bothered by Radik's assessment of his character. He'd seen the pictures of the aftermath of Radik's own operations. He didn't just kill people. He tortured them, psychologically and physically before murdering them and everyone they knew.

Radik laughed, his demeanor growing lighter. "Lucky for us, I do not intend for you to transport flesh intended for the meat market. You will be transporting something far more precious."

Radik let out a whistle. One of his men opened the tailgate of a covered truck and reached inside. Though Jozef didn't move a muscle, his team trained weapons on the back of the truck.

A woman emerged, her head ducked low so she wouldn't hit it as she allowed the man below her to lift her by the waist and set her on the ground. When she looked up, her gaze met Jozef's. Her eyes were a rich dark brown, guileless, yet somehow also world-weary. Her hair was cut short against her scalp with an army green scarf pushed back on her head. She wore a pair of fatigue pants and a militaristic shirt. She was dressed the same as Radik's men, but the outfit did nothing to hide the ripe curves beneath.

Radik reached for her as she approached, taking her hand and drawing her forward. She looked to be in her late teens, perhaps around Saskia's age. She dropped her eyes, staring at the dirt next to her boots. Jozef suspected there was no submission there; that she'd been told not to look at him or his team directly. She hadn't had a problem staring boldly at him when Radik wasn't looking.

Radik continued to hold her hand, but before he could

explain what was going on, she looked up and said something in a language Jozef didn't recognize. It took seconds for Jozef to realize she was angry and not afraid to tell off the giant warlord. She jerked her hand from Radik's and turned to face him, pointing a finger at his chest as she spoke.

Jozef's lips twitched and he had to clear his throat so as not to laugh out loud. Havel was experiencing the same struggle as he ran a hand over his face to wipe his amused expression away. It was fucking hilarious to watch the delicate woman who was at least a foot shorter than Radik tear a strip off him while he looked sheepish and refused to make eye contact, scuffing his shoe in the dirt. Jozef wondered if the woman was Radik's wife and this was why he was sending her away.

After a few minutes of listening to an extremely one-sided tirade, Jozef cleared his throat and stepped forward with a raised brow. Radik reacted swiftly, shoving the still chattering woman behind his back and pulling his weapon, training it on Jozef's face.

Jozef's men reacted, pointing weapons at the pair, ready to fire on Jozef's or Havel's command.

Jozef lifted his hands slowly in a 'peace' motion.

It was abundantly clear that whoever the woman was, she meant a lot to the giant mercenary. He was willing to protect her with his life and the lives of his men. There was no way he'd be selling this woman.

Finally, Radik lowered his weapon, but the scowl remained on his face.

"Ayaan is my sister," Radik explained. "You will ensure her safe passage to her handlers in France."

Jozef stared at Radik and finally nodded. He signed while Havel spoke. *Since you've changed the parameters of our agreement, I will also make my own amendment. I want ten million on top of the*

75 you agreed to, and you will explain why you need me and my team to take the girl to France. I want background before I agree to this.

Though Jozef suspected he could work the reason out for himself he wanted details.

Radik didn't look happy but he didn't have a choice except to answer Jozef's questions if he wanted Jozef's help.

"Ayaan was born out of the union of my mother's second marriage. A surprise to both our mother and myself, but a welcome one. She has been the joy in what could have been a very bleak existence. Both of her parents are now dead and she's my responsibility, which is equal parts a pleasure and a burden."

Radik oomphed and then grinned as his sister punched him in the back and rejoined him at his side.

"I am not a burden," she said in clear English, her accent British.

Radik's gaze softened as he looked at his much younger sister. "Not a burden in the way you mean," he admitted. He lifted a more serious gaze to meet Jozef's. "I have done many terrible things in my life; none of them I regret. But I have made enemies. Though none have managed to turn their threats into fact, they still continue to hound me. It's only a matter of time before one of the attacks is successful, and I will not have my sister around to get caught in the crossfire."

Why don't you take her to F-R-A-N-C-E yourself? Jozef asked.

"I am vulnerable when I travel," Radik admitted. "So, I don't."

"You came to Prague," Havel pointed out, knowing what Jozef would ask next.

"I don't travel from my region of control, except to meet with you." Radik's eyes never left Jozef's. "Protecting my sister is the most important thing I will do with my life. Meeting you in Prague was a small, but dangerous sacrifice to make if it ensures her safe passage. You must understand, you have two younger cousins. Intelligence has it that they are like sisters to you."

Jozef's lips pulled back in a snarl before he could stop himself. He was willing to put up with any kind of shit talk from a client, except when it came to the female members of his family. He didn't care that the Koba family was in upheaval at the moment, that he didn't trust them. His cousins were still his responsibility.

Before Jozef could warn the other man to keep his mouth shut regarding Jozef's cousins, Radik made it worse. "Your woman, Dr. Patterson. Like my sister, she is both beautiful and vulnerable."

Jozef lost his cool, pulling his gun and leveling it on Radik. He would kill this fucker and leave his body behind to bake in the hot sun. His sister could grieve for him.

Radik didn't blink, though he did give his sister a push so she wasn't standing as close to him. "I am not threatening you, Koba. I'm appealing to your softer side, if you have one. You must. I have seen you with your woman. There is love in your eyes for her." Radik gestured at Ayaan. "I want you to protect my sister the way you would protect your lady doctor."

Slowly the red haze faded and Jozef reholstered his weapon. He took several deep breaths to clear his head, catching the concerned look on Havel's face. He shook his head. Jozef was the picture of calm when meeting with clients, no matter what they said to him, yet he couldn't keep his cool when Shaun's name came up. He would have to work on it, or let Havel take lead. He couldn't let Shaun distract him while he was on mission.

Finally, Jozef signed, *I understand. Throw in the extra ten million and we will complete our mission and take your sister to the drop point.*

Radik grinned and wrapped a big arm around Ayaan's shoulders. "You have my gratitude. I will not forget this."

Jozef pointed at Radik. *If you ever lie to me about a job again, I will make sure there's nothing left for your enemies to find.*

Radik laughed out loud. "I think we will become great friends, Koba." Radik sobered as he studied Jozef's face. "You should know, there was some competition for this contract. They bid lower than you but didn't have sufficient manpower to complete the job to my satisfaction."

"Why are you telling me this?"

"They used the Koba name to get a foot in the door."

Jozef frowned and glanced at Havel, who asked, "Krystoff Koba?"

Radik shook his head. "No, someone going by the name Phantom. A woman. I seriously considered her offer as I would have been more comfortable allowing my sister to accompany a woman."

Jozef nodded thoughtfully, then, without another word, turned and stalked toward the trucks, his men falling in with him. While Radik and his sister said their goodbyes, Jozef and Havel came up with a new plan. They now had to figure in an extra body and all the possible variables involved in her existence.

CHAPTER THIRTY

Saskia waited about 30 seconds after she knocked before fitting her key into the cottage door and pushing it open.

"Hello?" she called out.

She waited for an answer, then went inside and closed and locked the door. She hadn't expected Leeza to be home, but she'd wanted to make sure. She'd decided to cut class and come home early.

Leeza had been acting weird lately and Saskia wanted to get to the bottom of the weirdness. Actually, it hadn't been just lately that Leeza had been acting strange, but almost two years now. At first Saskia thought it might have something to do with Shaun's arrival a year ago, but when she'd put her mind to it, she realized it had been going on longer.

Leeza had always been the more serious of the two. As the eldest child of a high-ranking Vory, Leeza had responsibilities.

Saskia wrinkled her nose as she stepped from the entryway into the house. It didn't feel like a house; it never had, which was why Saskia didn't often visit. She and her sister weren't particularly close, which was another reason she didn't visit.

Saskia tried to tell herself that she didn't want a relationship with her sister because Leeza was cold and stuffy, but a guilty voice in her head told her that Leeza would probably be open to a closer relationship if Saskia wanted one. Saskia didn't pursue it though.

There was nine years difference between the two women. Certainly not an impossible number to bridge. Saskia enjoyed her friendship with Shaun, who was fifteen years older than her. But Leeza was different.

Leeza had no interest in furthering any educational or career aspirations. She acted like the perfect wife and mother, but Saskia knew her sister despised her husband. Not from anything Leeza had explicitly said, but from the bruises she took pains to hide, the way she refused to touch, look at or talk to her husband. She didn't even pretend she loved the man. She simply ignored him, like he was invisible.

It was weird. Leeza clearly wore the pants in her little family, called the shots, but then where were the bruises coming from?

Over the past few years, Leeza had grown even more distance, cooler toward the rest of the family. The only joy she showed was when she was with her son.

Saskia had to admit that Leeza was a good mom. She would lay down her life for her son. He was the only person in the world Leeza was willing to stand up to her father for. If Krystoff made any decisions about his grandson, Leeza would not allow them without approval. She'd threatened to move her family away from the estate if Krystoff tried to override her decisions.

It was odd, but Krystoff was willing to back down. Saskia suspected he only gave in to Leeza's motherly protectiveness because Kristoph was autistic. He would never take over the organization and was therefore out of contention for the prized top spot.

Perhaps, Krystoff had once intended for Adam to take the position, but Adam had shown himself to be a weak man. Saskia had always thought Adam's marriage to her sister was strange. Leeza had been prepared to marry into the mafia, to a man of her father's choosing, but why Adam? Why the accountant?

Did he have something on Krystoff? If so, then why hadn't Krystoff gotten rid of him? The Koba patriarch was not one to allow threats to him or his family.

Saskia had decided, in light of her friendship with Shaun, and her desire to find the person who poisoned Shaun, she would investigate her own family, starting with her older sister, who had been acting like a zombified weirdo for the past two years.

Saskia searched the first floor. As usual it was cleaned and shined to perfection and smelled like soap and disinfectant. Leeza had a housecleaner in daily until her house smelled permanently like a cleaner's closet.

Saskia figured anything important wouldn't be hidden on the first floor, so she went over it quickly, not bothering to linger.

She made her way up to the second floor, the family rooms. She wandered into Kristoph's room, knowing there would be nothing in there to interest her. Still, she liked seeing her nephew's things. He was the true innocent in the family and the one thing most of them agreed on. Kristoph must always be protected.

Saskia picked up a teddy bear and pressed it against her nose, enjoying the fluffy sensation against her face. It smelled like little boy, a combination of juice, dirt and baby lotion.

On the rare occasions when Leeza asked Saskia to babysit, Kristoph usually came to her suite. He loved playing with her dolls and stuffed animals. Saskia had passed some truly happy hours sitting on the floor of her suite with her nephew. She wished it could happen more often, but Leeza was protective and didn't often pass her son off to others. Another departure from the mafia world they lived in, and a reason to admire her sister.

When Leeza and Saskia were growing up, they were raised by a team of nannies. Their mother was present, but like Leeza, she wasn't a warm woman. The difference between the two was that Leeza knew how to unbend enough to love her child and be present in his life.

"Then why are you so distant from everyone else?" Saskia murmured out loud, dropping the teddy bear onto the bed.

As children they had been close. They had made it their mission to terrorize as many nannies as they could, tallying who scared which nanny away. The age difference had certainly been one barrier, but Saskia had distinct memories of sitting on her sister's lap, reading books, playing with toys and coming up with nanny plans.

Really, they had stayed close until Leeza married, when Saskia was around twelve. Almost immediately after the wedding, Leeza started pushing her younger sister away. No matter how much Saskia begged, Leeza refused to play with her. She said married women didn't play with children.

At the time, Saskia had been so hurt that she hadn't questioned her sister's about-face. Now, several years later, she wondered if maybe Leeza had been trying to drive her away for a reason.

Saskia had always been curious by nature. She had no problem with snooping through other people's stuff. As the younger daughter, she was rarely included in organizational discussions or decisions. If she didn't snoop, she would never know what her father was up to.

Same with her mother and her sister. Saskia had gone

through all of their private things, rarely coming up with anything interesting. But this time, she was determined to ferret out the reason for her sister's withdrawal. Maybe if Saskia figured it out, she might be able to bridge some of the distance that had grown between them.

Since Saskia started taking classes at the University, she'd been forced to look at the world in a new way. It suddenly became bigger and was filled with things she didn't know but wanted to understand. One of the skills she'd been developing over the past year, was the ability to think critically. She no longer lived in the box her family put her in. She was able to branch out and think about things in a new and different light.

She left Kristoph's room and walked across the hall to Leeza's room. She didn't hesitate but slipped inside, leaving the door open a crack. She was fairly certain she was safe since she knew Leeza's household schedule and it almost never deviated. Leeza left with Kristoph at 9 AM for homeschooling with Kristoph's tutor at the mansion. The cleaning staff came through from 10-12. Leeza took lunch in the mansion then came back at 1 PM to change for her yoga or Pilates class, which she attended daily at a posh studio in the city.

It was now 12:30 pm. Saskia had about twenty minutes to finish up and get out.

She went straight for Leeza's huge walk-in closet. It was filled with women's clothes, even more than Saskia possessed, which was impressive considering Saskia thought of herself as a fashionista. The difference between the two was that Saskia preferred high-end brand name clothes in her particular style, while Leeza preferred to have every type of yoga pants in every colour available.

She also possessed a rack of formal day clothes, mostly

skirt suits and pencil dresses. She had a rack of formal wear including black gowns, dress pants, blouses. Boring clothes.

Saskia closed the closet door behind herself and used her phone for light rather than turn the closet light on. She knew she was being overly cautious but didn't want to take the chance that she would have to have a very awkward conversation with her sister. Of course, she would lie about why she was in the closet, giving some bullshit excuse about having to attend a stuffy luncheon at the university and needing boring formal clothes for the occasion. She preferred not to lie to her sister though. She was good at it and she did it often, but it never quite sat right.

Saskia shoved a rack of jeans that had been colour coordinated to the side and sank to her knees, wiggling further into the closet until she was draped in clothes, sitting next to Leeza's safe.

She hoped Leeza hadn't changed the passcode.

She punched in the four digits she'd memorized the first time she'd broken into the safe; 0115. The years Saskia and Kristoph were born. She'd felt a warm glow the first time she'd punched the numbers in, but that glow had faded over the years as her sister persisted in distancing herself.

She sighed and rolled her eyes when she opened the safe. Leeza was one of those really smart stupid people. She could hit a target better than any man on their staff during range practice. She could work out a solution to almost any puzzle, but she flat out refused to understand technology. She never upgraded her software and she never changed her passwords. She was a hacker's wet dream and Saskia was convinced it was a matter of time before Leeza's security was breached.

That wasn't Saskia's problem though. She was pretty sure if a hacker got in, they wouldn't find anything more interesting than Leeza's yoga schedule and her online mommy chat groups.

Leeza preferred paper trails, which was why Saskia's first target was the safe. She was disappointed though. When she looked inside, it held nothing more than a typical mobster's stash. Piles of cash, a gun, a box of ammunition, a marriage certificate and two birth certificates; one for Leeza and one for Kristoph.

Disappointed, she started shoving the wads of cash back inside.

Something moved on the other side of the closet door. Saskia froze, holding her breath. She leaned back on her heels and peeked through the rack of clothing to the closed door. The knob was turning.

"Shit!" she whispered to herself.

She lunged through the clothes to the back of the closet, dragging the hangers back together so there wouldn't be a gaping hole next to the safe. As the door opened, she tried her best to be soundless as she shoved the rest of the cash, the gun and everything else in the safe.

Leeza's voice startled her and, at first, Saskia thought her sister had busted her.

"I can't leave until Saturday, but I think I can get away overnight. I'll tell them Giana is having a late birthday bash at her weekend cottage."

Saskia reached out to close the safe, using the light filtering through the clothes to see. She'd dropped her phone. Hopefully somewhere not visible to Leeza. The door to the safe was blocked and Saskia had to feel around to figure out why. A stack of bills had wedged itself in the door.

She pulled the stack loose and shoved it down her shirt, then closed and locked the safe as noiselessly as she could. It didn't matter. Leeza was completely engrossed in her conversation.

"I'll try to bring him, but everyone makes such a fuss when I take him off the property. Especially now, with Jozef cutting himself loose." Leeza listened for a moment. "I know, but for now that's how things will have to be. I can't confuse my son; you know I can't."

Saskia peered through the rack of jeans and watched her sister as she jerked a pair of yoga pants off a hanger and strode from the closet, leaving the door open.

Saskia crawled along the back of the closet wrinkling her nose at the smell of carpet cleaner. Seriously, Leeza had the carpets in her closet cleaned too? She was such a weirdo.

A weirdo with a secret.

Saskia grinned and leaned against the wall next to the door, still hidden behind a rack of clothes. She listened intently as Leeza's conversation continued.

"Can you meet me somewhere? I don't think I can find the cottage again in all that wilderness." She paused. "Do you need groceries? Anything you can't get in that tiny village?"

Saskia frowned. Who was she talking to?

"I have to run, Dad," Leeza said, her voice clear as day as she stepped up to the closet, the legs of the yoga pants she'd just changed into visible to Saskia as she started to push the door closed. "I have to get back to Kristoph before he throws a fit. He doesn't like his new tutor."

Dad?

Saskia leaned back against the wall, stunned.

Just before the closet door shut, Saskia heard her sister say, "I love you, too."

Which was how Saskia knew there was no way Leeza was talking to their father. Krystoff Koba did not tell his daughters he loved them.

CHAPTER THIRTY-ONE

"Can I sit here?"

Jozef glanced up and nodded, closing his laptop and setting it in the empty seat on his other side.

They'd made it out of South Sudan as easily as they'd made their way in. Their trip through Somalia back to Mogadishu had been similarly without difficulty. Jozef had worried that Ayaan wouldn't be able to keep up with him and his team during the terrain trek part of their journey, but she'd proved herself as fit and capable as his men.

When a patrol had passed on the road beneath their position, she had been one of the first to take cover, automatically reaching for a weapon. When she remembered she didn't have one, she'd dropped her hand. Jozef had been watching her like a hawk and had noticed her unusual action. She was clearly trained in combat.

Once they'd made their way back into Mogadishu, they'd checked in at their safe house, repacked their equipment and headed to the jet for their flight. They'd been in the air for two hours and had six more to go. Jozef was planning on finishing up his operations report and then sleeping for the remainder of the flight. Apparently, his charge had other ideas.

Ayaan sat next to him, her curious gaze on first his face, then his throat. He wondered if she was looking at the scar that had led to his inability to speak or his plethora of tattoos. She didn't seem to be afraid of him or his men, and they were an intimidating lot. He supposed hanging around her brother would expose the young woman to men who lived dangerously.

"We didn't get a chance to talk when we were travelling," she began. "I want to thank you for bringing me to safety, even though you hadn't originally agreed to it."

Jozef grunted and continued to look at her steadily. He had no quarrel with the young woman; his ire was directed at Radik for deliberately misleading Jozef.

Perhaps Ayaan sensed Jozef's annoyance toward her brother. "You must not blame Muhammed. He knew you wouldn't agree to transport me because you don't deal in the flesh trade. I asked him to explain our situation, but he insisted we had to use deception. He said you wouldn't agree because you don't like to take responsibility for anyone outside of your team and your family. Is that true?"

Jozef nodded his acknowledgment. Radik had been correct in his assessment of the situation. Jozef wouldn't have agreed to the job, even if he'd understood the full story. Quite aside from the potential of aiding in human trafficking, Jozef despised human cargo because they were unpredictable, difficult and often ungrateful.

"I want to tell you my story so you can understand why my brother did what he did." She bit her lip and glanced away.

Jozef wanted to tell her he understood and might have done the same with Shaun or his cousins, had they been in danger. Just because he understood Radik's actions didn't mean he would forgive them. Nor did it mean he wouldn't seek retaliation eventually.

"I know what you're thinking. You are very similar to my brother," she said, looking back at him, her dark eyes meeting his. They were earnest and unafraid. "I've lived with my brother for most of my life, except for a few years of boarding school in England."

Jozef nodded; it was the same with his family. Leeza and Saskia had been raised in the bosom of the Koba family except for a few years each in England. It was considered finishing school for the world's wealthy, where they would go to learn history and politics.

"I understand the dangers of living with a man like Muhammed. He has led armies into battles on both sides of the law. Sometimes he was the revolutionary and sometimes he was the military. Governmental allegiances changed, but he didn't. He has always held the belief that freedom and democracy should take hold and flourish without corruption."

"A dangerous belief, both admirable and naive," Havel piped up from his seat across the aisle. He opened his eyes and pinned Ayaan with his no-nonsense stare.

Havel was in his usual position; several seats to Jozef's left. It was both practical and symbolic. Havel always stood to Jozef's left because Jozef was right-handed and could protect his right-hand side. Havel's position on the airplane also put him closest to the door in case they needed to make an emergency exit.

"My brother is not naive," Ayaan defended sharply. "And neither am I. We know that Muhammed's work is dangerous, but he has also helped many people throughout central Africa. His work is important."

Jozef snorted while Havel laughed out loud.

"We've seen the 'important work' he's done in the villages

he's razed," Havel pointed out. "You won't convince me your brother is anything other than a mercenary."

"Those are lies!" Ayaan said sharply. "Insurrectionists burned those villages and said it was my brother. He was trying to help them, not kill them. What does he want with a burned-out village?"

Havel shrugged, but leaned forward, balancing his elbows on his knees as though interested in the conversation. "To use them as an example to anyone else who refuses to fall in line. Sometimes a few deaths will save many more. Your brother strikes me as a man who would use this type of tactic."

"The villages were no threat to us," she said scornfully. "They were often suspicious and hostile toward the idea of a united democracy, as they had been taught to believe that any form of government was inevitably corrupt and against their chosen way of life. Despite this thinking, many of them welcomed us with open arms. They fed and protected us when we travelled. They did not harm us, and we would not have harmed them."

"We?" Havel asked. "Did you work with Radik?"

Ayaan nodded. "I am... I used to be one of his soldiers."

Havel looked at Jozef in surprise.

It was as Jozef had suspected; the girl had been raised a soldier. She was clearly capable of handling herself, but Radik took some dangerous jobs. Is seemed inconceivable that the sister he'd shown such love for, he'd also put in dangerous situations.

Then, Jozef had been raised with a different way of thinking. Even though his aunt and cousins could handle themselves, it was a family rule that they were to be protected at all times. Cherished. Not directly involved in business.

"I know what you're thinking," Ayaan said, her voice softening as she looked at Jozef.

He raised an eyebrow at her.

"You think my brother could not have loved me as much as he professes if he puts me in danger." He nodded that she had guessed correctly. She settled back in her chair, wiggling to find a comfortable spot. Then she looked back over at Jozef, her eyes sparkling with mischief. "He didn't have much choice. I was a strong-willed child. If he hadn't looked past my gender to the potential within, I would have followed him into battle anyway. I believe he thought training me himself was the lesser of two evils."

Jozef thought she had been indulged as a child and perhaps needed to be strictly curbed. But then, she was right. If a male child within the Koba organization had shown potential, the family would not have hesitated in making them an enforcer and putting them on the streets.

Perhaps the world was changing and women were becoming more accepted into risky careers, such as mercenary work. Still, Jozef couldn't shake his bone-deep desire to protect the women he cared about. He couldn't imagine sending any of them into battle the way he sent Havel, whom he loved as a brother.

"I've given you something to think about, haven't I?" Ayaan said, watching Jozef curiously.

His lip twitched with amusement. If she ever wanted to switch professions from professional soldier to mind-reader, he would give her his endorsement. She was a perceptive girl.

Jozef straightened in his chair and pointed at Havel then at his own mouth. Havel nodded that he understood Jozef wanted him to translate.

If you're as capable as you say, then why are you relocating away from your home? Your brother suggested that you would be in danger if you stayed, yet you're a trained soldier.

She nodded. "Yeah, I thought the same thing when he brought it up. Radik's enemies are always closing in. We've moved with dizzying frequency, tearing down and setting up our lives so often I can be ready to move in a matter of minutes."

Jozef nodded, not surprised. Central Africa could be alarmingly uncivilized. A home could be burnt to the ground and the inhabitants murdered and, depending on the location, it might never be known. The Koba family owned an impenetrable stronghold in the heart of a society too civilized to be a danger to them. They were sharks hiding in plain sight.

Ayaan continued. "The thing is, the threat wasn't coming from my brother's enemies, but another warlord, living nearby our territory. Chinaka."

He threatened you?

"Not at first," she admitted. "Chinaka tried to woo me. He figured if he could convince me to marry him, he could combine his forces with Muhammed's. Only I didn't fall in line with his plans. The man is a real psycho. Those pictures you saw of burned-out villages could have been his handiwork."

"So, we're rescuing you from a would-be suitor?" Havel asked incredulously. "Your brother is willing to pay a hell of a lot to get you away from the guy."

"He was a would-be suitor to begin with," Ayaan corrected. "When I rejected him, he turned from a suitor to a kidnapper."

Jozef frowned sharply. *He kidnapped you?*

"Yes," she admitted. "He took me while I was out on patrol, killing the others in my team." Her eyes dimmed with the memory. "His plan was to force me to live with him until I got pregnant. He figured if he managed to make a baby with me, I'd be more willing to marry him and my brother would fall in line with his plans."

Havel looked uncomfortable and Jozef knew the feeling. This was part of why Jozef hated transporting humans. They were talking, thinking creatures with emotions. There was an emotional aspect to Ayaan's story that Jozef wasn't prepared to deal with. He wished Shaun were there, she had the ability to show compassion to a victim.

Aside from Ayaan's team being killed, she might have been raped, beaten, tortured, any number of things while in custody. Neither man knew how to ask the relevant questions, so finally Havel spoke, finding a way not to ask anything that might be traumatic.

"How long were you in custody?"

"One day," she told them, a smirk curving her lips. "Muhammed showed up on Chinaka's doorstep the next day. Before he could even forward his proposal, my brother took out half of his militia and breached the main house."

Jozef listened intently to Ayaan's story.

"Chinaka tried to use me as a human shield. I stabbed him and ran to my brother." She smiled at the memory, as though stabbing Chinaka had been a true pleasure. Her smile faded as she continued, "Unfortunately, he escaped into the jungle with a handful of his men. Shortly after, he vowed vengeance and has become increasingly more unhinged. He has killed indiscriminately in his attempts to get to me."

Your brother decided it was time for you to relocate somewhere safer, Jozef signed while Havel translated.

"Yes." She nodded her agreement. "I will reside with my caretakers in France until my brother has found and dispatched Chinaka. Once it is safe for me to return, I will rejoin my brother in his fight for fair government for the people of central Africa."

Jozef was impressed by Ayaan. She had far more depth than he'd given her credit for upon first meeting.

Thank you for telling us your story.

"I didn't want you to judge my brother unfairly."

She'd been honest with Jozef, he could do the same for her.

I don't blame your brother for wanting to keep you safe. I am unhappy that he lied to me during negotiations. I work on a strict policy of trust. Any who breach that trust or attempt to double-cross me must pay a price. If they don't then word will get out that I am weak.

She blanched and reached for Jozef's hand, squeezing it between her own hands. "Please don't hurt my brother. He'll do anything to protect me, including misleading the best mercenary in the business to ensure my safety. Isn't there anyone in your life you would do the same for?"

Jozef swallowed a laugh. Manipulative girl, trying to get him to think of her as someone he loved. Of course he would do the same. He had a heart, even if it was black as sin.

I will not kill your brother. Havel raised an eyebrow at Jozef, surprised they wouldn't retaliate for Radik's lies. Jozef signed for Havel alone, *I doubt we could get at him anyway. I have no desire to get into armed conflict with the man while he's buried deep in his own territory. If he comes to ours then we'll cut off his hands and castrate him, thus keeping our promise not to kill him.*

Havel nodded his understanding and didn't translate the last part.

Ayaan looked at them suspiciously. "What did he say?"

"He won't kill your brother," Havel told her.

"Oh thank you!" she threw her arms around Jozef, who froze, leaving his arms loose until she pulled away from him.

"I have something else to ask you...." her voice trailed off and she looked at the floor shyly.

Jozef waited for her to finish. He couldn't ask her verbally to continue and she'd turned her back on Havel, blocking his view of Jozef's hands.

Finally, she looked up at him with a grin plastered across her face. In a rush, she said, "I was wondering if you wanted to have dinner with me? You know, when we land in Nice. You're probably hungry."

Jozef was not hungry. Like everyone else he'd eaten a hearty meal in Mogadishu before they flew out. Perhaps he would be hungry by the time they landed, but he didn't intend to linger in France. He was going to hand Ayaan over to her caretakers and continue on to Prague.

Jozef shook his head, but she persisted, reaching out to take his hand.

"I really think we have a lot in common. You should get to know me better; I think you'll like what you find. I know I like what I've seen so far. I'm really into guys with tattoos."

Jozef's mouth fell open as he realized she was hitting on him and asking him out for a date. He pulled his hand from hers and quickly switched seats, placing his laptop between them. Even if Shaun wasn't in the picture there was no chance in hell that he would've messed around with Radik's younger sister. That would be like signing his own death warrant.

Havel didn't even pretend he wasn't listening. He laughed uproariously until Ayaan stood and stomped past Havel, rejoining the men at the back of the plane.

They handed Ayaan off to her caretakers at the Nice airport, completing their mission. Jozef's men were jovial and asked to spend the night before heading back to eastern Europe.

Jozef refused, eager to get back to Shaun. He signed to Havel, *Get the jet fueled. We're going home.*

CHAPTER THIRTY-TWO

It was 4 AM by the time Jozef arrived back at his apartment. He'd told his men to get some sleep and report back to work at 2 PM for debrief and mission report. They wouldn't have a lot of time to sleep, but in Jozef's experience, debrief needed to happen very shortly after each mission so there were no forgotten details.

The smallest of inconsistencies could lead to a failure in communication, which could lead to a death in the field. Jozef's men were the best for a reason. They were quick, sharp and mission-ready at all times. This included the intelligence that followed each mission.

Along with the rest of his men, Jozef dropped his gear in the storage room of their offices. They checked in all tech and weapons then left to get some rest. Jozef made his way up to his floor on the elevator, saying goodbye to the men who piled out on the fourth floor. His elite team had apartments in the building, on the same floor as Shaun's mother, while the rest resided offsite.

As they walked away from the elevator, Jozef could hear

Havel admonishing Halil and Nikolay. "Mrs. Patterson will be asleep so fucking keep the noise to a minimum."

Jozef nodded at the night security guard on his floor as he let himself into his apartment. He closed the door softly and started to make his way across the floor toward his bedroom.

"Jozef."

His hand automatically went to his gun, even as he recognized Shaun. Instead of pulling the gun, he removed the holster and set it carefully on the counter. He rolled his shoulders back, easing some of the tension that had built up over days of sleeping in a shitty camp bed and on the hard ground.

Shaun was standing by the windows, looking out at the city lights, something she loved to do. It made him happy that he was able to give her this view, sort of an apology for the things he'd done to take the joy from her life.

Why are you still up? he signed when she looked at him. There was enough light filtering in from the streetlamps below that she could see him.

She walked into his chest, burrowing her face against him as his arms closed around her. "I didn't sleep much while you were gone. I was busy worrying about you and thinking about the safe room."

She pushed away from his chest. "Why didn't you tell me about the safe room?"

Jozef knew about the saferoom incident. Karl had sent daily updates on Shaun's activities while Jozef was in the field. He hadn't had time to worry over her reaction though. It was a necessary part of his existence and she would get used to it.

I would have told you eventually, Jozef explained. *Honestly, I forgot. I've had one since I was a child. Are you angry?*

She seemed to think about the question then shook her head. "No, it's fine. I understand why you have one, even though I don't like it. I'm glad you're keeping your safety in mind."

Jozef nearly laughed out loud. She was living in fantasyland if she thought he'd be hiding in a safe room during an attack. It was there for her. He didn't tell her though. He was pleased that she was concerned for him.

"I removed those high sugar, salty snacks and replaced them with dried fruit, fruit cups and some canned vegetables," she informed him. "I also added a can opener, some paper plates, plastic cutlery and some napkins. Saskia made an unholy mess while she was eating in there."

Jozef barked his laughter and Shaun joined in. He loved everything about this woman, even her insistence on healthy eating. He'd fallen in love with her a year ago, but it had taken him more than a year to realize what he loved about her. While in prison, he could see the way her brain worked as he poured over her professional papers. He could see aspects of her personality in his daily reports coming in from the men he had watching her in Montréal. Everything he saw and heard made him love her a little more until he knew he was hopelessly entangled for life.

He couldn't remove her without removing a large piece of himself, and no part of him wanted to do that. She was his muse, his strength, everything he wanted in his life. And if it took the rest of his life to get her to agree to stay, he would spend it showing her how much she meant to him.

He dropped his mouth to hers, tasting her laughter until her amusement turned to lust. He could taste the difference and knew she wanted him as much as he wanted her.

He lifted her against his body as he deepened the kiss, thrusting his tongue into her mouth and sipping at the sweetness within.

She clung to him, kissing him back with equal hunger. She

wrapped her legs around his waist, holding him tight, welcoming him home with her warm embrace.

"I kept dreaming you were dead," she whispered against his lips. "I hated that you were out there, putting your life at risk."

Jozef couldn't respond, couldn't reassure her. His arms were around her, holding her up. He didn't know what he'd say anyway. How could he reassure her without lying? His job was risky and there would always be a certain amount of danger. He loved what he did for a living and he wasn't ready to give it up. If she asked him to, he didn't know what he'd do. He wanted to think that the strength of his love would make the decision easy, but he was learning, from Shaun, that love, no matter how strong, didn't make life easier. Instead, love was messy, complicated and exhilarating.

She broke their kiss. "Please fuck me."

Jozef didn't need to be asked again. He turned to carry her into the bedroom, but she protested.

"No, do it here, out in the open," she said breathlessly. "I want to watch the lights while you fuck me."

If Jozef's dick had been hard before, it was now stone. Her words, her sexual assertiveness, it made him want her with a new kind of desire. He wanted to touch her wildness, wake it up, revel in the barbarism that surged through them when they came together.

He set her on her feet and reached for the hem of his shirt, stripping it from his chest. She did the same, pulling her pajama top over her head and tossing it across the room. He saw her teeth flash in a grin as she hurriedly shoved the waistband of her pants over her hips and down her legs.

Jozef got his belt unbuckled and his jeans unzipped before Shaun launched herself at him. He barked with laughter as she jumped into his arms and nearly knocked him backwards onto the couch. Her impatience infected him, and he realized he wanted inside her as badly as she seemed to want him there.

Shaun rained kisses all over Jozef's neck, face and shoulders as he tilted her back, resting her ass on the top of the couch so he could reach between them and pull his straining dick from his jeans. Her breathing hitched as he spat on his palm and reached down to stroke himself, before lining himself up against her pussy. She was wet and ready for him as he pushed himself through her tight passage.

She moaned, tipping her head back and closing her eyes, enjoying the sensation of him filling her.

He bit her neck, tasting her flesh, licking her sweetness. She tasted like strawberries, warmth and woman. He held himself still inside her, savouring the sensation of her tight squeeze on his cock. She wiggled her hips, trying to get him to move, but he refused. He loved that she was so needy, that she wanted him with such passion.

He'd thought of her often while he travelled, her image lingering no matter where he went or what he did. He thought he was holding Shaun close to his heart but being with her now showed him that the real woman was so much better. She was everything he wanted in life and then some. An unexpected gift he would never stop thanking god for.

"Jozef!" she exclaimed, hitting his chest. "Fuck me now."

He chuckled at her impatience and lifted her in his arms, deliberately bouncing her so she was forced to take all of him. She let out a yelp, then, gripping him tightly, moaned her approval. He moved her to the kitchen table and set her ass on top, tilting her so he was at the best angle to fuck her as deeply as she appeared to want and need.

He began thrusting, slow at first, then building to a furious crescendo. She flung her arms wide across the table, arched her back and took everything he was giving her. The slap of flesh, the grunts and moans, they were a symphony to his ears. He gripped her hips so tight he was sure he would leave bruises. He didn't care. He loved seeing his mark on her, loved knowing that she begged for it.

He pulled out, which made her cry out in protest. He lifted her off the table and pushed her against the window, pressing her hands against the glass. He lined himself up behind her and slammed himself home. His thrusts were shallower, but the tight squeeze of her pussy gripped him so hard it didn't matter.

He wrapped one arm around her waist, holding her tight against him, while he twined the fingers of his other hand with hers. She was trapped between him and the window, but she didn't notice or care. She was so lost in sensation, the moans spilling from her exquisite lips as she begged him to keep going.

He moved his hand from her waist down to her pussy, and strummed her clit, which was slippery and engorged. She keened wildly, throwing her head back into his shoulder.

"I'm coming, Jozef!" she yelled.

He bit her ear, thrusting his tongue into the delicate shell and forcing her over the edge of her orgasm.

She screamed with the force of it, bucking in his arms and smashing their entwined hands into the glass.

He marveled at her strength when she was in the grip of her orgasm. She nearly threw him off, but he was determined to follow her over the edge of bliss. He needed the release, had dreamed of it whenever he fell asleep with her image plastered across his mind.

When they fucked, it was more than fucking. So much more. It was the meeting of their souls. No matter how hot, how dirty, or how frantic, they were in unison during these few moments. They didn't need language because they were so connected that words were unnecessary.

Shaun collapsed, but Jozef held her tight, thrusting,

driving toward his own orgasm. Using her constricting muscles to milk himself inside her.

Pleasure shot down his spine, settling in his tight balls and then releasing. He grunted, filling her with his seed and continuing to pump until he was empty. He pulled out of her and bent to lift her into his arms.

"I can walk," she protested with a laugh, gripping his shoulders so she wouldn't fall.

He strode with her into the bedroom, then into the ensuite. Setting Shaun on the edge of the vanity, he rifled through a basket beside the sink, coming up with a clean facecloth. He wanted nothing more than to lay down in his own bed, resting his head on his own pillow and falling asleep with his woman at his side, but he had to take care of her first. He didn't want her to wake up uncomfortable and sticky.

Jozef ran the sink until the water was warm enough, wet the facecloth and pressed it between Shaun's thighs. She moaned and tilted her hips. Despite his exhaustion, lust shot through him as she involuntarily fucked the facecloth.

He pressed harder, pushing the rough fabric against her sensitive clit.

She gripped the counter tight and tilted back until her torso was resting against the mirror.

Jozef continued to stroke, cleaning her and driving her toward another orgasm. This one hit her within seconds, coming fast and hard. A gush of liquid soaked the already wet facecloth as she came, her face strained, and her mouth opened in an 'O'.

Jozef's cock was ready for another round, but he ignored it. He was pleased to give all the orgasms to Shaun. She deserved them and he loved watching the concentration on her face as she fought her way toward the shining peak.

As she collapsed back against the mirror, Jozef tossed the

washcloth in the sink and picked her up. She didn't complain this time as he carried her to the bed. He set her down and sprawled out next to her. She rolled to face the city lights, her favourite position.

Jozef wrapped an arm around her, their hands twined over her beating heart. They fell asleep together, the city below casting a warm glow over their naked bodies.

CHAPTER THIRTY-THREE

"I've seen that man before..." Shaun trailed off as she stared after the man who'd abruptly turned away and left the bustling Christmas market.

Karl glared after the man. "When?"

Shaun racked her brain until she came up with the answer. "Here, in Prague, a year ago. I saw him watching me when Havel came to my hotel to talk to me, right before I left for Canada. I pegged him for law enforcement."

"Good eye," Karl grunted. "He's Interpol."

Shaun gaped at the place where the man had been standing. "How do you know?"

Karl looked at her. "We have eyes on everyone who thinks they have eyes on our boy."

"Jozef?"

Karl nodded. "Interpol is interested because Jozef often crosses international lines when on the job. While our officials are corrupt as hell and unwilling to pin anything on Jozef, especially after the chaos he caused in prison, Interpol would love to get their hands on him. Charge him for some of the shit he's done while out of country."

"Why don't they, if they know he's committing crimes?" she asked, idly picking up a beautiful tree ornament from one of the craft tables and turning it over in her mittened hands.

Karl grinned at Shaun. "Jozef is too good to pin anything on. He never leaves evidence. Only once, and he paid for it."

"When he kidnapped me."

Karl nodded his agreement but didn't say anything. Suddenly the day, and Shaun's special outing to buy Christmas gifts, seemed less joyful. She was taken back to the tiny basement, where Jozef had demanded she save a man's life, only to turn around and take that life. He'd left fingerprints on a bucket.

And he'd allowed Shaun to live. Perhaps his biggest mistake, although she knew he didn't see it that way.

"You said Jozef caused chaos in the prison." Shaun handed the shopkeeper a handful of Koruna, still unsure of the conversion on the currency. The shopkeeper looked startled and then started making change. While Shaun waited, she asked, "What did he do?"

Karl cleared his throat and shook his head. "You know I don't participate in idle gossip."

Shaun glared at him. "It's not idle curiosity. I think it's important for me to know for my understanding of the mafia."

"I'm not buying it," Karl countered, reaching out to take her change from the shopkeeper who was watching them curiously.

"Okay, if you insist, then it's idle gossip," Shaun admitted. "But as the daughter of the woman you are trying to have familiar relations with, I insist you tell me. What did Jozef do while he was in prison? Did he... did he hurt anyone?"

Karl ignored her question, instead turning an alarming shade of red and sputtering the words, "Familiar relations?"

Shaun was a little worried about Karl's diet if his system

couldn't handle the shock of a fairly innocent question. If he was going to date her mother, Shaun would have to insist on him going to his doctor for a health check. Fatima's heart couldn't handle another man in her life passing too young.

"I have it on good authority...." Her nighttime guard, who wasn't afraid of idle gossip, had told her, "... that you spent four hours in my mother's apartment on Tuesday night after you got off shift. I'm sure she convinced you to watch an Audrey Hepburn movie, but what were you two doing with the rest of the time?"

Karl was staring at her like she was about to whip a chainsaw out of her purse and take him out at the knees. She covered her mouth so he wouldn't see her giggling.

"We were talking." Karl's voice was a mixture of lofty defensiveness and horror. Shaun suspected if he could've run away, he would be streaking through the Christmas market to escape her questions.

As if on cue to save his sensibilities, a voice piped up from behind them. "Shaun, is that you?"

Shaun turned on the spot while Karl went on the defensive, his hand going beneath his jacket, no doubt landing on the butt of his gun.

He relaxed almost immediately as they both recognized Dasha Koba.

Shaun took a speechless moment to remember how perfect the other woman was, no matter where she went. She wore a fur hat perched on top of her long, loose chestnut curls. A grey fur coat was wrapped loosely around her body, while a calf length cherry red pencil skirt peeked from beneath the edge of the coat. She wore soft grey leather gloves and high-heeled leather boots.

Shaun was engulfed by Dasha's perfume as the older woman seized Shaun's arms and pulled her in for a hug, kissing both of her cheeks.

"It's so wonderful to see you," Dasha said brightly. "I've missed you."

"Uh...." Shaun accepted the hug, kissing Dasha on both cheeks, as was expected. "I've missed you too."

It was a lie, and Shaun felt guilty for telling it. She'd actually forgotten about Dasha, Krystoff and Leeza. They had drifted to the periphery as her life was filled with settling herself and her mother into Jozef's apartment building and purchasing necessities. Of course, she knew the Koba family still existed, but aside from Saskia, she didn't see or spend time with them. She suspected Jozef was acting as a buffer.

Despite his insistence that he wasn't at war with his family, there was a gulf between them, one that Jozef didn't bother to try and bridge. He seemed content building a life for himself and his fiancé outside of his family's influence.

"Please, you must have lunch with me," Dasha insisted, pulling her arm through Shaun's and then turning until they faced away from Karl.

"Well...." Shaun hesitated.

She'd come to the Christmas market to spend some time alone outside of the apartment and find some gifts for her loved ones. Now it looked like she was being commandeered.

"Oh please," Dasha begged. "I don't know when I'll see you again. Consider it my Christmas gift to spend a little time with my soon-to-be niece. You can tell me all about your wedding plans."

Shaun wanted to laugh, but held it in. So far, the wedding plans consisted of Jozef insisting they would be married soon while Shaun was insisting she needed more time. Jozef was too busy to set a date and stick to it and Shaun was taking advantage of his distraction by never mentioning her upcoming nuptials.

It wasn't that she didn't want to marry him. She wanted to marry him whole-heartedly and without reservations, which wasn't possible yet. Though he was impatient to make their union official, Jozef cared enough about her wants and needs to give her more time, which was how she'd managed to avoid the alter. She suspected when her time finally ran out, and Jozef was ready to act, she'd find herself in a church and married in short order.

"Alright," Shaun gave in gracefully. "I'll have lunch with you."

Dasha was being kind and it felt churlish to turn her down for a simple lunch.

"Where should we eat?" Shaun tried to peer through the crowd of shoppers, assessing the nearby eateries.

"Let's go to *Kuchařský Stůl*," Dasha said, naming the Koba owned restaurant, which translated to Chef's Table. Jozef had once taken Shaun there on a date. "It's not far; we can walk."

Shaun nodded her agreement but glanced back at Karl.

"I'll have the car brought to the restaurant," he told her, pulling his phone from his pocket and texting their driver.

"You seem to be settling well," Dasha murmured slyly.

Shaun knew what Dasha meant. Shaun was settling well compared to the previous year when she'd fought her role as Jozef's fiancé. Shaun wasn't sure what to say to Dasha so elected to change the subject.

"How is Saskia doing with her classes?"

Dasha's nose wrinkled, but she immediately smoothed her expression. "She's doing well, of course. Saskia was always a good pupil. A little wild, but intelligent."

Dasha's description of Saskia was spot on, but Shaun couldn't detect any note of parental pride in the other woman's tone.

"She has an aptitude for languages," Shaun pointed out, watching Dasha carefully.

Again, Dasha's gaze turned brittle, but she didn't comment, other than to say, "Yes." She led Shaun to the door of the restaurant at the same time as Shaun's vehicle pulled up to the curb. Shaun waved at her driver but followed Dasha inside.

Dasha greeted the concierge coolly and asked for her usual table. A wave of vulnerability washed over Shaun as they were led into the depths of the restaurant. It was starting to feel less and less coincidental that Dasha happened to run into her in the market and decided they should eat lunch at the Koba owned restaurant.

When Shaun caught Karl's eye, she realized he felt the same. His brow was wrinkled in a deep frown and he was on his phone, no doubt texting Jozef. Shaun felt better knowing that Jozef would know where she was.

They were shown to the same table Shaun and Jozef had shared and Shaun felt a pang of longing. She wished she were about to sit down with Jozef, rather than his aunt.

The maître d' took their coats and seated the two women. The server arrived as they were settling in.

"Let's have the most exclusive wine on the menu," Dasha said, smiling at Shaun. "We don't get an opportunity like this often. Let's celebrate."

Shaun wasn't sure what they were celebrating but murmured her agreement. She didn't want to drink wine when it was barely noon, but she couldn't politely decline when Dasha seemed so excited.

"So, tell me...." Dasha placed her elbows on the table and her chin in her hand. It was a smooth move that made her look truly interested in what Shaun was about to say, but Shaun knew the move was an affectation. "Have you set the wedding date yet?"

Shaun should have known that Dasha would want to talk wedding details. The woman was nothing if not single-mindedly focused on her next big party.

Shaun shook her head. "No, we haven't really had time to talk about it."

Dasha frowned. "But my dear, you've been here for almost two months now. Surely you've given it some thought."

Shaun sighed and took a sip of her wine when it was set on the table. She almost instantly regretted it. Not because the wine was bad. In fact, it was incredibly delicious; light and fruity. No, she regretted taking a sip because her mind immediately jumped to a year earlier when she was poisoned. Though she was in a restaurant, surrounded by people, which should be safe, it was Koba owned and controlled.

She discreetly picked up her napkin and used it to spit out the liquid in her mouth, wiping her tongue. She dropped the napkin in her lap and glanced over at Karl who was standing near the table, not bothering to look like anything other than a bodyguard whose entire focus was on his principal.

When Dasha took a sip of her own wine, Karl caught Shaun's eye and tapped his cell phone. Shaun wasn't sure exactly what he was trying to tell her, then her phone rang.

"Excuse me," she murmured, lifting her purse and digging until she found her phone. Jozef's name flashed on her screen.

She frowned. Jozef only ever texted.

"Hello?" she answered.

"It's Havel. I need you to say I'm your mother."

"Hi mom," Shaun said brightly, smiling at Dasha. "I'm out for lunch with Mrs. Koba, can I call you back when I'm finished?"

"Good girl," Havel said approvingly. "We know where you are and we're on our way. We're about fifteen minutes out. Sit tight until we get there."

"Thank you," Shaun murmured. "I'll talk to you later then."

CHAPTER THIRTY-FOUR

Relief rushed through Shaun. It was stupid. She really shouldn't be in any danger sharing a meal with Dasha. Jozef had allowed Shaun to go to the women's luncheon at the mansion several weeks earlier. At the time, Shaun had been surrounded by bodyguards and it was unlikely that the Kobas would attack in their own home, if their intention was to harm Shaun.

She wondered if she was being paranoid, then shrugged the thought away. She was mafia now, or at least mafia affiliated. She had to be paranoid. It was how she was going to survive.

With that in mind, Shaun excused herself and stood to walk to the washroom. She would waste a few minutes in there so she wouldn't have to eat or drink anything before Jozef arrived. Karl moved to follow her, but Shaun shook her head, placing her hand on his arm. "I'll just be a minute. I'll be fine, promise."

He seemed to agree that Shaun couldn't get into much trouble in the washroom by herself. He remained by the table, speaking politely to Dasha as she turned her focus on her former family bodyguard. Shaun wished she could stay and protect him from Dasha's sharp tongue, but she needed a few minutes to herself.

She made her way to the washroom, pushing the door open and going inside. She took several deep breaths, trying to stop her shaking. She felt like she was on the verge of a panic attack, which was ridiculous considering nothing bad had happened.

She felt uneasy though and she couldn't shake the feeling.

Why had Dasha come to the market to find her? It was too much of a coincidence to believe the older woman had run into her without prior knowledge of Shaun's where-abouts. Shaun wasn't sure what the population of Prague was, but she guessed it was high enough that an accidental meeting was unlikely.

"You're okay," she told her reflection, practicing her breathing technique.

When she felt calmer, she turned the tap on cold and leaned over to splash water on her face. She blinked the water droplets away as she straightened and reached for the paper towel in a basket on the counter. As she was wiping the water from her face, she realized someone was standing behind her.

Her brain had just enough time to register Dasha's pres-ence when the older woman whipped her arm around Shaun's neck and swung a blade toward her.

Shaun acted on instinct, hurling herself backward at the same time as bringing her booted foot down on Dasha's.

Dasha yelled and jerked the knife away from Shaun's throat up toward her face.

Shaun twisted in Dasha's hold, swinging her elbow back into Dasha's solar plexus. As she threw herself from Dasha's grip she felt a searing pain down the side of her face.

Dasha gasped as the wind rushed out of her, but she

quickly recovered, jumping to cover the door so Shaun couldn't run past her.

Shaun stared in shock. She'd been told repeatedly by both Jozef and Saskia that it had been one of the Kobas who'd tried to kill her, but she hadn't actually believed the accusation. She couldn't. They'd been good to her, accepted her as a member of the family.

Dasha had always treated her with kindness, even if it had been cold and formal.

"Why?" Shaun demanded as she was backed against the wall by Dasha's advance.

Shaun's cheek was on fire and blood dripped freely down her face, soaking into her sweater.

Dasha didn't answer, but lunged again, completely focused on her task of killing Shaun.

Shaun tried to dive away, but Dasha was faster, managing to sink her blade into Shaun's forearm. Shaun let out a scream of pain as she jerked away from the blade.

Dasha didn't give her time to recover as she took another swing. Shaun threw herself back against the wall and brought her arms up protectively. This time the blade scored her wrist, slicing through the skin until it hit bone.

Dasha yanked it back.

Shaun had to do something, and she had to do it fast or Dasha was going to slice her up until nothing was left.

"Karl!" Shaun screamed at the top of her lungs.

As Dasha swung the blade again, Shaun flung herself to the side, crashing through a stall door and dropping to the floor. She rolled onto her back and kicked the door at Dasha who was running toward her.

The door hit Dasha, throwing her backwards. She stumbled on her heels, hit the counter and fell to the floor, the knife clattering away from her.

Shaun pulled herself to her feet, cradling her bleeding

wrist and ran for the washroom door. She yanked the handle, but the door was locked. As she tried to unlock the latch, Dasha gripped Shaun's ankle and jerked her off her feet. When Shaun hit the floor, Dasha's booted leg crashed down onto her chest.

Pain radiated throughout Shaun's chest and it felt like she was swallowing needles when she tried to take a breath.

Dasha knew exactly what she was doing. The woman had clearly trained in combat.

As Shaun lay on her back trying to catch her breath, Dasha rolled away, reaching for the knife. When Shaun realized what Dasha was after she forced herself off the floor and did the last thing she wanted to do. Every instinct inside her told her to get the door open and run, but she doubted she could open the door before Dasha got her hands on the knife again.

So instead, Shaun threw herself on Dasha's back, slamming her to the floor. Dasha went down with a grunt.

The knife was a few inches from Dasha's fingers.

Shaun leapt for it, grabbing it triumphantly and rolling away from Dasha.

Realizing Shaun had the knife, Dasha rolled in the opposite direction, using a stall door to drag herself to her feet.

"Stay back!" Shaun yelled when it looked like Dasha would lunge for her again.

Dasha remained eerily silent as she watched Shaun, taking in the way Shaun's hands shook and how she was holding the knife. It was clear to both of them that Shaun had no idea how to hold a blade defensively.

Dasha decided to risk it and began stalking Shaun, dancing from side to side, her heels clicking on the floor tiles as Shaun swung the knife. It was a truly amazing and horrifying sight to see the elegant older woman with her hair in complete disarray and Shaun's blood smeared down her white fitted sweater.

When Dasha finally made her move, Shaun was completely unprepared. The other woman swung her leg around in a spinning kick that made her look like a blur. Before Shaun could determine where Dasha was trying to strike, the blow hit Shaun in the side of the head, and she was thrown sideways into the counter. Shaun retained her hold on the knife, but her ears were ringing, and her vision was blurred.

Dasha punched Shaun in the back.

Shaun screamed in agony as her knees buckled. She had no choice but to suck it up before Dasha regained the upper hand. If Dasha got her hands on the knife again, it was game over for Shaun.

Shaun pushed away from the counter, absorbing the next blow and swinging around, bringing the knife up as Dasha lifted her arm to hit Shaun again.

"No!" Shaun yelled as Dasha's arm swung straight down.

Dasha didn't see the knife swinging up and wasn't prepared as it was buried deep in her arm, severing her brachial artery.

CHAPTER THIRTY-FIVE

Dasha fell back, surprise written across her face.

She looked down at her arm, watching as the blood flowed down the limb like a fountain. She dropped to her knees and then fell to her side as shock crippled her.

Shaun dropped the knife and flung herself at Dasha.

"You stupid idiot!" she snapped as she assessed the other woman's injury. She would have seconds to act if she wanted to stop Dasha from bleeding out.

Without hesitation, Shaun gripped the jagged edge of Dasha's sweater where it had been cut. She tore it wide open, drawing a scream from Dasha; the first sound the woman had made since attacking Shaun.

Shaun looked around but there was nothing within immediate reach that would help her. She needed something to tie around Dasha's upper arm to cut off the flow of blood pumping from her heart and out through the wound.

Her belt! She reached down and undid the buckle, dragging the belt through the loops. She swiftly fitted it over Dasha's upper arm, pulled it through the metal loop and yanked as hard as she could.

Dasha screamed again, but she didn't fight Shaun, instead slapping her hand over her own wound to stem the flow of blood. She must've realized Shaun was trying to save her life.

"This is going to hurt like a motherfucker," Shaun warned, sitting back on the floor and placing one booted foot against Dasha's armpit, and the other on her hip.

"Do it," Dasha gritted hoarsely from between her teeth.

Shaun was impressed. Dasha's wound was life-threatening and would be extremely painful, but she was dealing with it better than anyone Shaun had seen with a similar wound.

Shaun wrapped the end of the belt around her uninjured hand, gripped the leather with her bleeding hand, braced herself against Dasha and pulled as hard as she could.

Dasha screamed again then bit down on her lip to stop the cries from spilling out.

Shaun was able to gain another inch of belt. She wrapped the leftover leather around Dasha's arm and secured it. She looked at the wound again and was relieved to see the blood flow had slowed.

It was still bleeding profusely though and Dasha would need immediate emergency medical attention or she could die. Shaun picked up the torn piece of Dasha's sweater and pressed it against the wound, lifting Dasha's hand to cover the makeshift bandage.

"Press as hard as you can until help arrives."

Shaun lurched back and dragged herself to her feet, intending to head for the door. She paused and then turned on her heel and stared down at Dasha.

Dasha lay stoically on the floor, her hand over her wound, her eyes fixed on the ceiling above her.

"Tell me why," Shaun said softly, sinking back to her knees next to Dasha.

Dasha refused to look at her and didn't speak.

Shaun hesitated, not wanting to hurt Dasha again, but she

needed to know why the other woman wanted her dead, and if Dasha died she would never know.

Shaun took hold of the leather binding and shook.

Dasha cried out and rolled her blazing eyes toward Shaun, anger rolling off her in waves.

"Your brachial artery has been severed. This fix is only temporary. Without help, you will die."

Still Dasha said nothing.

"Do you understand, Dasha? You will die and you'll do it without any of us ever knowing why. You raised Jozef as your son. He doesn't deserve this."

Some of the anger drained from Dasha's expression and she licked her lips, wetting them so she could speak.

"Tell Jozef I love him."

It wasn't what Shaun was looking for, but it would have to do. If she left Dasha any longer, the woman would bleed out. She was going to need a transfusion as it was.

Shaun pushed to her feet and ran to the door, but before she could get it unlocked, Dasha spoke again, her harsh voice ringing out. "You'll ruin us all." Shaun looked over her shoulder to see Dasha pull herself up using a stall door. She sat back against the metal. "You already have."

Shaun shook her head. "You've ruined yourself."

Shaun unlocked the door and yanked it open. Karl was standing on the other side, his face reflecting alarm.

"Are you alright?" he demanded. "Dasha got by me and locked the door. I was looking for something to break it down."

Shaun was surprised there weren't a contingent of people on the other side of the door trying to get in. She and Dasha had screamed enough to bring the restaurant down, but apparently the washroom was sound-proofed. Weird, but she didn't have time to dwell on it.

"You're bleeding," Karl said, reaching for Shaun's arm.

She winced as he touched the cut.

She shook her head and pulled from his grip. "We have to go."

Shaun swung around, not waiting for Karl, and hurtled toward the front exit uncaring of the gasps from patrons as a bleeding woman ran past them.

Karl was on her heels and then he was in front of her, pushing people out of the way. Before they left the restaurant, Shaun shouted at the maître d', "Call an ambulance, there's an injured woman in the washroom!"

She didn't bother to wait for his reaction. She had to assume that Dasha had bodyguards inside the restaurant who would manage to organize themselves sooner rather than later. She didn't want to be on the premises when that happened. She had no idea what would come next, if Dasha would try to attack her again.

The driver was waiting outside the car. When he saw Shaun, his face reflected alarm and he reached for the door handle, intending to open the car door for her.

"Never mind," Shaun yelled. "Just get in and drive."

Karl covered her while she jerked the car door open and flung herself inside. She landed on her side and curled her legs in so Karl could slam the door shut. Karl leapt into the front seat and growled at the driver, "Go!"

Shaun felt silly laying down on the seat when there was nothing happening outside the restaurant. She pushed herself up and reached for the seatbelt while the driver accelerated into traffic. He made it into the lane before the rear window shattered.

Shaun screamed as bullets impacted the vehicle. She swung around to look and saw several men running toward the car with their weapons drawn. She hadn't expected Dasha to bring their fight to the street. When the other woman had asked Shaun to tell Jozef she loved him, Shaun thought she'd given up.

Maybe Dasha's men were coming after them for revenge, attempting to take out the person who stabbed their employer. Shaun didn't know and she didn't care.

"Let's go!" she yelled.

Just as the driver tried to accelerate again another spray of bullets came through the back window. Shaun ducked down in time, but the driver didn't. A bullet hit him in the back of the head, and he slumped over the wheel, turning it sharply to the left.

They were flung into oncoming traffic and hit head on almost immediately. Shaun was thrown back, her neck jerking painfully as she impacted the seat behind her.

Her head was ringing, and she had to blink several times to clear her vision. As she was about to lift her head, strong hands gripped her. She looked up and saw Karl who was climbing into the back seat with her, his hands running down her body. He tried to open the door next to Shaun, but it was jammed shut from the impact.

He looked up. "They're coming. Curl up and try to make yourself as small as possible."

Shaun let out a whimper as Karl crawled over top of her, using his body to cover hers and then twisting around to swing his gun toward the shattered window.

As he fired his gun, bullets whizzed inside and around the car. The acrid smell of gunfire burned her nostrils and the pain in Shaun's wrist chose that moment to amplify.

Karl jerked on top of her, his body twisting. He grunted in pain but continued to shoot.

"More bullets on my belt."

His words were laboured but Shaun understood. She did her best to turn over onto her back with Karl's heavy body laying across her. She searched his waist until she found something that felt like a leather holster. She unsnapped it and reached her fingers inside, coming up with a small box of bullets. She maneuvered the box out and opened it, spilling several bullets into her hand.

"I have them," she said.

"Good," he snapped. "I'm out."

With militaristic precision he snapped the gun open and put the bullets in one at a time, taking them from the palm of her hand. It couldn't have taken longer than ten seconds for him to reload his gun, but it was long enough for their attackers to realize they were no longer being shot at.

Shaun saw a head pop up in the window, gun hand extended.

"Karl!" she screamed as bullets filled the inside of the car.

Most of them hit Karl in the chest and stomach. He returned fire, hitting the man in the head. As soon as he dropped, another replaced him. This time, Karl was struck in the head, but not before he was able to shoot the guy, sending him spiraling away from the window.

Karl grunted one last time, then his body went limp on top of Shaun.

"Karl!" she gasped, dragging herself out from underneath him. "Karl."

She pushed him onto his back and let out a moan of despair.

He'd taken a shot to the forehead. His eyes were open, staring, glassy.

Shaun checked for a pulse but knew the truth before she touched him. Karl was dead.

Sobs spilled from her lips as she searched the seat for his gun. She found it still sitting in the palm of his right hand. She pulled it away from him and did her best to crouch down as small as possible, cramming herself between the front and back seats.

Two men converged on the car, guns raised. One was

coming to the side window and one to the back of the car. Shaun couldn't shoot them both. Actually, she probably couldn't even shoot one. She'd never used a gun before.

She lifted it, preparing to shoot.

She hadn't been ready to die a year ago when Jozef had put a gun to her head and she wasn't ready to die now. She would go down fighting if that's what it took.

She held the gun as steady as she could, watching both windows intently and trying not to look down at Karl. His body was pressed against hers, the warmth still radiating from him. She wanted to break down and cry over his loss, but now was not the time.

She could grieve later, if she was still alive.

She used the back of her hand to swipe at the tears blurring her vision.

One of the men lunged toward the window shooting wildly. Shaun squeezed the trigger, and the gun jumped in her hands. She didn't get the guy, but he looked more cautious than he had a moment before. This time he crept up to the window. Before he could try to shoot again, a bullet hit him square in the temple and he crumpled to the street.

Shaun gaped, but swung her gun around to cover the back window where she'd seen the other guy.

Suddenly the car jerked as someone jumped on the hood and then onto the roof. Shaun screamed in reaction and looked up. Bullets thunked into the trunk, then she heard a scream of pain as the guy who'd been attacking her from the rear was shot. A pair of leather booted feet hit the trunk of her car and legs filled her vision.

The man was pointing a gun at the ground. He shot one more time and she realized he was finishing the guy he'd hit when he jumped on the car. Shaun levelled her gun at the guys legs but didn't shoot. She assumed he was on her side, or he wouldn't have shot the men who were attacking her.

He dropped to his knees and looked through the shattered rear window.

"Jozef!" she shouted.

His blue eyes were ice chips when he looked at her, but she could see the relief reflected there.

"Jozef, they killed Karl," she sobbed and reached her good hand out to him, clutching Karl's gun in her other hand.

He took hold of her wrist and pulled, dragging her through the shattered window. He jumped to the ground and picked Shaun up off the car, one arm around her knees and the other supporting her back.

She buried her face against his chest and held onto Karl's gun for dear life as he strode toward his SUV.

Sirens sounded in the distance as they sped away from the scene.

CHAPTER THIRTY-SIX

Nikolay stood in the doorway of his bedroom watching his roommate fuck the woman they'd brought home. He was naked, bathed in the lights of the city coming through the windows. He held a joint in one hand, rolled with a combination of tobacco and *bhang*. While he smoked, he lazily stroked his semi-hard dick.

Sharing women was a common activity they participated in together and they'd banged this particular one a few times. She was a mediocre fuck, but the real treat was in doing fucked up depraved things to such a perfect little princess.

Giselle threw her head back and shouted as Halil took her ass.

Nikolay couldn't tell if she was screaming in pain or ecstasy, but she wasn't begging Halil to stop. She was taking it like the good girl she pretended to be.

Nikolay wondered if he had a thing for messing up pretty little girls who pretended innocence but got on their knees and allowed him to do his worst. Saskia had been a virgin when he got to her. It had been truly satisfying to pop her cherry.

Lately though, their flings had been growing stale. Saskia had been growing more distant, which was a problem considering he had every intention of marrying her and one day taking her father's place at the head of the Koba organization. Maybe it was time to show her some of the other things he enjoyed doing to a woman. He hadn't bothered because he had women like Giselle for the truly fucked up shit.

His semi grew as he imagined Saskia on her knees in front of him, his hand tangled in her hair, his dick deep in her throat as she choked, tears streaking her face. He would take her to the edge then pull back and allow her just enough air to stop her from passing out before he slammed his cock into her mouth again.

He groaned and clenched his teeth around the joint as he squeezed the tip of his dick and then reached under to tug on his balls.

"Oh fuck!" Giselle screamed as Halil lost all respect for her ass and tore into it like a beast.

Halil was usually a gentleman when it came to women, but he was a man of war too. He had the same aggression in him as the other men on their team. They worked hard and played harder.

Nikolay ashed the joint, revelling in the mellow glow filling him. He loved nothing more than these moments when he could truly be himself. He grinned at Halil, slapping him on the back before climbing onto the bed in front of Giselle.

She looked up at him, her face twisted in a mixture of pain and pleasure. They would fuck her hard, multiple times throughout the night. She'd feel it in every joint and muscle by the time they were done with her, but she'd enjoy the experience and likely come crawling back for more.

Nikolay wasn't naive enough to believe she actually cared about either of them. She was using them to get close to Jozef, to weasel her way back into his life, even if it meant giving herself up to the various team members and allowing them to fuck her in ways she probably never imagined. If she had any brains at all she'd let her little obsession go. Jozef wouldn't touch her again. He was too far gone for the doctor.

Nikolay gripped Giselle's head, tipping it up and pressing his thumbs beneath her eyes. He smeared her makeup across her cheeks, giving her a clownish appearance that was at odds with the tears sparking in her eyes and the agonized expression on her face.

"Open," he demanded, pressing his thumb hard against her lips.

She had no choice. It was either open her mouth or allow him to cut her lips against her teeth. He didn't care which she chose. He'd fuck her mouth even if it was filled with blood. More lubrication.

She opened and he pressed both of his thumbs inside, stretching her cheeks and pressing his digits to the back of her throat until she gagged, making a hoarse choking sound.

Nikolay laughed out loud. She looked and sounded ridiculous. A far cry from the sultry woman who was playing 'dirty dancing' on the club floor earlier in the evening. It hadn't been hard to convince her to come upstairs with them. She'd pretended she wasn't sure about being double-teamed, but it had taken only minutes to get her clothes off.

They'd been polite to start, using a vibrator to get her off and get her wet enough for what they had planned. They'd each taken turns after that, taking her vaginally before taking turns at her ass.

Now that she was good and broken in from a few hours of hard fucking, the real play could begin. They'd work their way toward fucking her at the same time, Halil in front and Nikolay in behind. It was their favourite position. The screams of their women, like music, echoing through the bedroom.

She would walk away full of cum, a little pain and utterly satisfied.

But first, Nikolay wanted her mouth, and he wanted it while Halil took her ass. His second favourite threesome position was the spit, where he and Halil each took an end and forced her body to rock and back and forth between them, the momentum carrying them all toward orgasm.

When he'd finished choking her with his thumbs, he replaced them with his now rock-hard cock, slamming himself deep into her mouth before she could take her next breath. She gagged again, her throat closing around his cock in a nice squeeze that made him groan.

She tried to pull back, but he gripped her long blond hair and held her steady, forcing her to gag on him, her throat doing all the work. When her eyes rolled up with desperation, the tears now falling freely, he pulled back, allowing her to breath.

She gulped in a lungful of air as saliva spilled from her mouth. She glared at him and opened her mouth, probably to tell him not to do it again, but he didn't let her get the words out, shoving himself back in and then pounding her mouth, finding a rhythm that worked for both him and Halil.

He hadn't bothered to wash his dick after putting it in her ass. He loved the disgusted look on women's faces when he did that. Maybe they hated him for it, but he didn't care. They would walk away satisfied and most came back for more.

He grunted as his balls tightened.

"I'm close," he told Halil.

Halil nodded. "Me too."

They used Giselle, holding her up between them when she would have collapsed onto the mattress, Halil's arm under her waist as he fucked her ass, while Nikolay continued to hold her head between his hands, forcing her to take every inch of his cock.

The orgasm ripped through him and he pulled out of her mouth, taking his cock in hand and pumping until jets of semen burst from the tip, spraying her across the face. He grinned as she took a load in her eye and hair. She would hate that. Giselle didn't like it when they messed her up.

Halil followed suit, pulling out of her ass and spraying his load across her back. Giselle fell to the bed in an exhausted, but satisfied heap. Halil dropped onto her other side, grinning at the ceiling.

Nikolay lay sprawled on the bed, one arm flung over his head. He wished his joint was closer; he could use another hit.

CHAPTER THIRTY-SEVEN

Krystoff hated hospitals. More than the average gangster hated them. He despised the smell, the arrogant bustling of doctors and nurses, the pathetic patients coughing and sneezing in the waiting room. He avoided them to the point of absurdity, once electing to pay a steep price to have a surgery in the comfort of his own home.

None of these things were in his mind as he rushed through the doors of the Prague General University Hospital. He only had one thought in his head: Dasha. His wife had been transported by ambulance to the hospital, her life hanging in the balance. He still didn't have positive confirmation of her survival.

His understanding from a frantic call made by the maître d' of his restaurant, was that Dasha had been attacked in the washroom and left for dead. He'd confirmed that she was brought to the hospital and immediately rushed out to his car. He drove himself, not wanting to wait on his men to organize themselves.

His heart was in his throat as he approached the hospital receptionist. "I'm here for Dasha Koba."

The nurse's head came up and she stared at him as though he was a ghost and she was struck speechless by his apparition. He was impatient, but not surprised. His family was well known in Prague, as were their shady underworld ties. Most people had heard of him and knew what he looked like from news articles, even if they hadn't met him.

"I'm... I'm... I'll check," the nurse finally choked out, refocusing on the screen in front of her.

"Mr. Koba, sir."

Krystoff turned, his hand going under his jacket until he saw his wife's bodyguard, Rassoul, standing behind him. The man's expression was both bleak and guilty. Rage and fear hit Krystoff with such surprising force he had to grip the counter so his knees wouldn't buckle, sending him to the floor.

He'd spent a lifetime projecting an image of complete calm and control, but when it came to his wife, nothing mattered. He didn't care about his legendary control, couldn't care, until he knew she was safe.

"Where the fuck is she?" Krystoff snarled, carefully taking his hand off the pistol beneath his jacket. He wanted nothing more than to murder the man in front of him, but he wasn't going to do it in public and he wasn't going to do it before he got the information he needed.

"Surgery." Rassoul looked green, as though it was everything he could do to keep his lunch to himself. He knew what kind of trouble was coming his way, but it was a point in his favour that he wasn't on his knees begging for his life.

"Where?" Krystoff demanded.

"I'll take you to her."

No one tried to stop the two men as they moved through the first floor of the hospital toward the operating rooms. Everyone knew who the men were and none were willing to stop them.

Rassoul halted outside of the locked doors of a surgical room.

"She's in there. Has been since she arrived. We... we can't go in though."

Krystoff wanted to tear the man's head off, but the dim place in his brain that still held some semblance of logic knew he couldn't bust down the doors to his wife's surgery. He would contaminate the room with bacteria, or germs, or whatever. He also didn't want the people working to save her life to pause for even a second while they sorted out who he was and why he was there.

"Where do we wait?" he grunted.

Rassoul looked somewhat relieved and pointed down the hall. The two men made their way to a private waiting room. The lack of comfort in the room, the bare walls and metal chairs, were a reminder that Krystoff was standing in a hospital, not something he'd ever intended to do.

He hadn't even visited Leeza after the birth of her first child. He'd fought with her over having the baby at the mansion, but she'd wanted the hospital resources at her disposal. She'd always been an obedient child, but when it came to her son, she could be quite stubborn. Finally, he'd been forced to accede to her wishes. Especially when Dasha had chimed in to tell him to stop stressing out his pregnant daughter.

"Tell me what happened," Krystoff said coldly to Rassoul.

Krystoff inspected one of the chairs, making sure it would hold him, and turned to sit. It creaked beneath his weight but held. He was a big man and he'd taken out a few chairs in his time.

Rassoul paled, but took a chair opposite Krystoff, doing his best to make eye contact as he spoke.

"We went to the Christmas market to find your nephew's

fiancé." He spoke matter-of-factly, but the words seemed to choke him, as though he was pushing them through a throat gone stiff with fear. "Mrs. Koba said she wanted to have lunch with the girl but didn't want to have to go through Jozef."

Krystoff listened in shocked silence. He'd told Dasha to stay the fuck away from Jozef and Shaun while the two men severed business ties. It was a dangerous time. She shouldn't have gone near Shaun without Krystoff and a full team of bodyguards. What the fuck had Dasha been thinking?

"She took me and three others as backup, which was unusual, since, as you know, Mrs. Koba is more than capable of handling herself."

Dasha insisted on taking only one bodyguard when going into the city. She'd always insisted she didn't like the feeling of being followed everywhere she went. Krystoff had balked, but had eventually given in around the time she was able to take his heavy ass down during a sparring match.

"I drove her to the market, she found the girl, then we met them at the restaurant," Rassoul continued. "Mrs. Koba told all of her bodyguards, me included, to remain in the kitchen while she ate lunch. This wasn't an unusual request as she doesn't like us to be seen by the restaurant's guests."

Krystoff shook his head, trying to sort through the information. "Dasha and Shaun went to the restaurant for lunch together?" When Rassoul nodded, Krystoff asked, "Where was Jozef? He doesn't let that girl out of his sight. Why was she at the market by herself?"

"She had her bodyguard, Karl, and a driver with her. I think she was trying to complete some Christmas shopping by herself when Mrs. Koba found her. Jozef didn't come until later."

"Jozef was there?" Krystoff asked sharply.

Rassoul nodded. "I think the bodyguard texted him. He

showed up right after all hell broke loose in the restaurant. He dragged Dr. Patterson away from the scene."

"So, he wasn't in the restaurant." A hint of relief cut through Krystoff's anger. He wouldn't have to go to war with his nephew if he had nothing to do with the attack. "How was the girl?"

Rassoul hesitated, then answered. "She was bleeding but alive."

"She was attacked too?" Krystoff was confused but relieved that it appeared neither Shaun nor Jozef had anything to do with the attack. It must've been one of his enemies, though he wasn't certain who. Krystoff had a strict policy of taking his enemies out before they could get to him. His last one had been Vasiliy, who'd died at Jozef's hand a year earlier.

"Sir..." Again, Rassoul hesitated.

"Spit it out," Krystoff growled in annoyance. There was nothing he hated more than men who chose to cower rather than speak their mind, even if it was unwanted news.

"I was the first to get to Mrs. Koba after she was wounded. The only two people in that washroom were Dasha and Shaun. I think... I think your wife tried to kill the doctor. She ordered us to finish the job before Shaun could leave the premises."

Krystoff gaped at Rassoul in surprise. It was impossible... wasn't it?

Dasha had been the most vocal over the past year about how Shaun had done exactly what they'd predicted, torn the family apart. She'd held onto more anger than any of the rest of them over Jozef's arrest. But lately it seemed as though she got over her anger. When Shaun arrived back in Prague a few months earlier, it had been Dasha who'd suggested inviting Jozef and Shaun over for dinner.

Krystoff cast his mind further back, to the beginning of their relationship. The way she'd dealt with her half-sister's interference had been to poison the girl. Vasha had survived, but her father had cut ties with the Kobas and married his daughter off to another -- Vasiliy.

Dasha had been the one to poison Shaun.

It had to be her.

Krystoff was about to ask Rassoul if he knew anything about the poisoning when the door opened and a doctor ducked inside.

Krystoff lurched to his feet, but he could already tell by the look on the other man's face what the verdict was. His knees buckled and he sat quickly before he fell.

"Mr. Koba?" At Krystoff's nod, the doctor continued. "Your wife has survived the surgery and should make a full recovery. She will need rehabilitation to regain the full use of her arm again."

"Where is she?" Krystoff demanded hoarsely, gripping the arms of the chair until his knuckles cracked to keep himself from launching out the door and tearing down the hospital until he found his wife.

"She's in recovery now. It'll be a few hours until she wakes up. You might want to..."

Krystoff stood and strode to the door. "Show me where she is."

The doctor didn't hesitate, leading Krystoff straight to Dasha's room, Rassoul trailing behind. Krystoff was relieved to find the two men he'd messaged earlier, asking them to get to the hospital to protect Dasha. He nodded at them as he entered the room.

His heart leapt into his throat as he looked at his wife. She looked nothing like the Dasha he'd been married to for over thirty years. She was so pale she looked as though she would fade away if he didn't keep his eyes on her. Dark circles ringed her eyes and her face was slack and haggard. Her hair was pushed back against the pillow, as though someone had pulled the operating cap away from her and left her hair in a bunch.

Krystoff reached out to smooth it against the pillow.

He sat heavily in the chair next to her bed and reached out to touch her arm. He wasn't sure what part of her to touch. She was covered in bandages and the parts that weren't bandaged were severely bruised. She'd clearly fought for her life.

Krystoff didn't understand. Shaun was tall, but she was thin and had no fighting experience as far as he knew. She should have been easy for Dasha to take down. Dasha had been practicing Jujitsu and Krav Maga for two decades. She was skilled in both forms of martial arts and she wasn't afraid to use it if she felt threatened.

Krystoff got his answer almost right away as the doctor slipped into the room and gave Krystoff a rundown of his wife's injuries and what her recovery would entail.

"Her brachial artery?" Krystoff asked, when the doctor described the wound that had nearly killed Dasha.

The doctor pushed the sleeve of Dasha's hospital gown up to her shoulder, showing Krystoff the bulky bandage. "If it weren't for someone's quick thinking she would've bled out within minutes."

A chill ran through Krystoff. "What do you mean?"

"Someone wrapped a belt tightly around her upper arm, cutting off the circulation and slowing the bleeding until your wife was able to be transported to the hospital. The paramedics told us the belt was on when they arrived. If someone hadn't tended to her at the scene, she would likely have died. She has a guardian angel."

"Or a guilty angel," Krystoff murmured.

Though Shaun had spent less than a month with the family at the mansion, Krystoff considered himself a good enough judge of character to understand the woman. She was a simple creature. She held onto her oath to 'do no harm' like it was the only thing worth living for. She would have helped Dasha, even after Dasha attacked her.

A picture of what'd taken place in the washroom began to form in Krystoff's mind. Dasha had lured Shaun to the restaurant under the pretense of wanting to spend time with her. When Shaun went to the washroom, Dasha attacked her.

Only somehow, Shaun had managed to gain the upper hand. Given the imbalance in fighting skill, Krystoff suspected Shaun had accidentally managed to turn the tables and had gotten hold of the knife. She would know exactly what part of the body to cut to stop her opponent. Only once she'd hurt Dasha, she'd probably been horrified, and had done her best to save the other woman.

Krystoff barely registered the doctor leaving quietly, he was sunk deep into his own thoughts. It wouldn't matter that Shaun had tried to save Dasha. The fact was, the girl had tried to kill his wife, making her own life forfeit. Even if he could find it in himself to forgive, he wouldn't be able to spare her.

Jozef would now be preparing to take out the Koba family. Once he knew who'd attacked Shaun, their fates would all be sealed. The family would go to war, and Krystoff wasn't entirely confident he could win. Jozef was the stronger of the two, with better trained men. Jozef wouldn't hesitate to pull the trigger. He'd been taught his entire life to take out the threat, no matter who or what it was.

His only hesitation had been Shaun and twice she had almost died at the hands of the Koba family. Jozef would not forgive them.

Krystoff looked at his wife. Her face almost angelic in

repose, as though she was now above their earthly concerns, despite being the one to cause this mess.

"What have you done?" Krystoff asked quietly, carefully picking her hand up off the mattress and twining his fingers through hers.

CHAPTER THIRTY-EIGHT

Jozef paced back and forth, never stepping further than a few feet away from Shaun. She was laid out on their couch, Jozef's private doctor tending to her wounds. Jozef didn't take his eyes off her as he catalogued every wince, every tear, every sob.

Had he made a mistake in bringing her home? He'd learned from a young age that when he or his men were wounded, they would retreat to home territory where they could get patched up in the safety of their own organization. Jozef had automatically brought Shaun home, where he could defend her if necessary.

Shaun was different though. She should be in a hospital, surrounded by people she trusted to take care of her.

Jozef stopped pacing and stood next to her.

She tilted her chin and looked at him. He felt her hooded golden stare right down to his soul. He reached out and used his knuckles to brush away the tears that spilled freely down her cheeks. She was in pain and shock.

"Jozef..." she whispered and then licked her lips, taking in the salty tears before continuing. "Did I... did I kill her?"

He wanted to scream out that he didn't give a shit if she killed Dasha. That as soon as Shaun was patched up and resting comfortably, he was going to hunt his aunt down, demand some answers, then take her apart piece by piece. But Shaun didn't need to know that. She needed reassurance that she hadn't killed someone.

Jozef shook his head, and signed carefully, slowly, so Shaun could follow, *she's alive and will make a full recovery.*

Instead of happiness, her eyes filled with even more tears and her face crumpled. "I hurt her," she said desperately, the tears spilling over. "I almost killed someone. I... I... oh god."

"Hush, baby," Fatima murmured, picking Shaun's hand up where it was clasped in her own and kissing the back, before smoothing her hand over the delicate skin. "You did nothing wrong."

"I did, I did!" Shaun's voice bordered on hysterical, her breathing laboured. "I broke my oath. I did harm."

Jozef wished more than ever that he could speak, but since he couldn't, he would show Shaun what he was feeling. He dropped to his knees next to the couch and took her face in his hands, forcing her beautiful golden eyes to meet his gaze. He slowly and deliberately shook his head, allowing her to see his thoughts. As he stared at her, he took in a deep breath through his nose and then released it through his mouth. He tapped her lips, instructing her to do the same.

She understood what he was saying, but she tried to shake her head and pull out of his hold. She wasn't ready to forgive herself.

Jozef wouldn't allow her denial. He tightened his grip on her face and dropped his head to hers, making sure she could still see his eyes. He shook his head again, staring into her soul, trying his best to imprint the truth on her. This was not her fault, she did nothing wrong. He was so happy she survived that the knowledge of her survival was the only thing allowing him to hold his shit together.

He tapped her lips again, and this time she breathed with him. Gradually each breath became smoother and smoother, though her tears continued to drip down her face.

"I'm sorry," she whispered. "I've pulled your family apart. I got Karl killed."

Jozef released her head and stood. She refused to understand, to internalize the truth. She'd been attacked, she'd defended herself. She did everything right, even if what was right didn't feel good.

Jozef glanced at Fatima, who'd been quietly crying and trying to comfort her daughter. She seemed to be taking Karl's death particularly badly, inquiring about his family and funeral arrangements.

Fatima looked away from Jozef's stare, focusing her energy on Shaun. She blamed him. How could she not? It was his fault her daughter had been attacked. For the second time. If he hadn't taken Shaun from the hospital in Luhansk none of this would've happened.

They wouldn't have fallen in love and they wouldn't have forged a relationship that destroyed the foundations of his family and set off a chain of events that had shaken up the eastern European underworld.

While he held his aunt almost entirely responsible, he also blamed himself. His existence had caused this. His decisions. His stubborn insistence that he and Shaun could make their relationship work, forcing two separate worlds to collide.

Jozef gripped his head and growled his anger and frustration, his guilt and pain.

He reached for his gun when a hand came down on his shoulder. Then, seeing Havel, he dropped his hand.

"You need to pull yourself together, man." Havel glanced

at Shaun, who was quietly sobbing on the couch, her mother holding her hand. The doctor sat on the coffee table, suturing Shaun's wounds.

She had a deep cut to her forearm, another serious cut on her wrist that the doctor believed had nicked the bone, and a superficial cut to her face. Other than the stab wounds, she had a large bruise on her back. She'd been lucky. Dasha was an accomplished combatant. The attack could have been much worse, much deadlier.

Jozef didn't know how Shaun survived, but he was extremely grateful.

Guilt ate at him as he stared at her. Since coming into her life, he'd caused her a world of pain. And even knowing this, he still wouldn't let her go. What kind of person did that make him?

Havel gripped his shoulder until it hurt and shook him. "Wake the fuck up, man."

Jozef growled and swung an angry glare toward his best friend and second-in-command.

"Good, now I have your attention." Havel's face was set in serious lines, but his voice softened. "You need to put a lid on whatever's going on in there." He tapped Jozef's head. "I get it. Your girl got hurt. You blame yourself. You want better for her, but now is not the time."

Jozef shoved Havel away and signed, *I'm not in the mood for a pep talk. Spit out whatever you're trying to say.*

Havel nodded and got down to business. "Krystoff will know exactly what went down at the restaurant by now. He'll either try to reason with you or take the preemptive strike. You need to be ready for either scenario."

Jozef stared at Havel, his brain sluggish with anger, fear and hate. He shook his head, trying to push away the emotions. Havel was right. He had to wake the fuck up and concentrate. His people would be counting on him as both leader and protector of their organization.

Jozef nodded at Havel and took a mental grip on himself. It was time to start using his head instead of his emotions.

He squared his shoulders and signed, *okay, I'm ready*.

Havel dipped his head in a nod of approval. "We've gotten several reports from the hospital. As you know, your aunt will recover, but she can't be moved. Krystoff is unwilling to leave her side, but I think he'll eventually see the wisdom in mobilizing."

Mobilizing against Jozef and Guard Dog Securities.

Krystoff would know as well as Jozef that if an attack was imminent, his best bet would be a preemptive strike. Hit them while they were vulnerable. Jozef had to think like his uncle in order to neutralize the threat. He had to think big picture.

He signed, his movements fast and precise, *I don't want to hit the mansion. It's too heavily fortified. We'll lose men. When we go to war, we'll take our stand on home territory.*

"Here?" Havel asked.

Yes. We know how to defend our home base, we've done drills. You had the men prepare for this eventuality while I was still in prison.

Havel's phone chirped and he glanced down at it, then looked at Jozef. "He's preparing for war. He's called in every man on his security team to hold the mansion. He's hustling the girls back home. Our guy on the inside doesn't know when the strike will happen though."

Jozef took a breath and glanced at Shaun and Fatima. They weren't paying attention to Jozef and Havel. He nodded at Havel to step outside the apartment door.

Jozef gritted his teeth as the pain of what he was about to say hit him like a punch to the gut. He had to do it. He was the vztekl´y pes, the guard dog. He had to pull the trigger.

As soon as they stepped outside, Jozef made sure Havel was paying attention.

You need to find the location of my cousins and take out Leeza and her husband. Leave the child and Saskia alive and bring them to me. He couldn't bring himself to harm either one. It was gut-wrenching to put Leeza on the kill list, but she was the eldest, could become a problem in the future if he didn't take her out of the equation. *Send a team to the hospital. As soon as my uncle leaves, you will take out Dasha.*

Havel's face hardened and he closed his eyes in a long blink so Jozef wouldn't see the emotion. By the time he opened them, his eyes were glittering with purpose.

"Consider it done, boss." His voice held the same steel that was running the length of his spine. "What about Krystoff? He'll bring reinforcements to the meeting. You won't be able to take him out."

Jozef took a breath as gut-wrenching pain burned through his veins. He took the emotional pain and channeled it into purpose and will, the way his uncle had taught him.

Once he finds out about Leeza and Dasha he'll come to us. He'll be reckless with grief. We'll take him out, right here, on home territory.

Havel looked thoughtful and then nodded toward the apartment. "What about the women?"

As soon as Shaun can be moved, we'll send her and her mother to the safe house.

"She's not going to like it." Havel didn't need to specify which woman he meant. They were both equally stubborn, but Shaun was the one who could argue Jozef out of a perfectly decent plan.

It doesn't matter what she wants, Jozef signed. *She can be angry at me later, once she's healed.*

Havel stared at Jozef for a moment, letting him see his vulnerability. "This is fucked up, man."

Jozef nodded, closing his eyes for a moment and taking a

deep breath, reclaiming his calm. When he opened his eyes, he signed, *I'll send a message to my uncle, asking him to meet. I want you at the hospital. Send the others to take out Leeza. I won't ask you to hunt the woman you love.*

Havel looked shocked. "You know?"

Jozef nodded but didn't respond. He turned away from his second-in-command and reentered his apartment.

CHAPTER THIRTY-NINE

Saskia knew she was in trouble when her guard doubled seconds before her father called. One of the men grabbed her by the arm and hustled her toward a waiting car while she fumbled with the phone.

"Dad?" she asked breathlessly.

"Saskia, are your guards with you?"

"Yes, and a bunch of the estate guards are here too. Since when do I need such a huge escort to get home from the university?" Saskia knew damn well they weren't there just to escort her. Some serious shit was going down.

"You need to listen to every word they say, Saskia. I don't want any of your shenanigans. You listen to your guards and go home to your sister." He paused, then added. "I'm in the hospital with your mother."

Saskia froze, stopping in her tracks. She ignored the frustrated exclamation from her guard.

"What's wrong with mom?" she demanded, yanking her arm and pacing away from the guard. "Is she... is she going to be okay?"

"Yes, she'll be fine," Krystoff snapped. "I don't have time

to talk. You need to go with your guards and join your sister at home. I want you both in the safe room within the hour."

Saskia's brain whirred frantically as she tried to work out what was happening. If Dasha had gotten into some kind of accident, Krystoff wouldn't be trying to rush his daughters to safety. No, there was a very real threat and it had something to do with her mother's injuries. There was only one potential enemy Saskia could think of in the city.

Jozef.

"What did you do?" Saskia demanded.

Krystoff paused, as if he'd been in the process of hanging up when he caught her question. "It doesn't matter. What's done is done. What matters is getting you to safety. Make sure your gun is loaded and ready. Go with your guard. I'll come home once your mother is awake."

Saskia knew she had seconds before her father hung up. She badly wanted to ask after her mother's injuries, but she couldn't. She didn't have time.

"Tell me if it's Jozef."

When her father didn't immediately answer, she raised her voice. "Dad, I need the information. I need to know who you're trying to keep me safe from so I know who to trust and who to shoot."

He grunted his approval and said, "Jozef. Stay the fuck away from Jozef if he shows up. He's separated himself from the family. Gone rogue."

Saskia knew it wasn't as simple as that. If Jozef had gone rogue, then he'd been driven to it. He'd had months since getting out of jail to make a move, but he hadn't. Jozef insisted that he was still part of the family until one of them made a move to show him otherwise. Saskia could only assume one of her parents had finally made that move. Idiots!

"What did you do?" she asked again, ice in her voice.

She glanced around and catching sight of a women's washroom, waved at her guard and pointed. He shook his head and tapped his watch. Saskia rolled her eyes and moved the phone away from her mouth.

"I'm not going to hold it until we get home," she told him. "Either give me two minutes to pee or pick me up and carry me. I'm going."

She didn't wait for an answer but went into the washroom.

She realized her father was still talking. Probably trying to convince her to go home. He wouldn't give her the answers she wanted.

Like most of washrooms at the university, this one had a wide window that could be opened by standing on the counter. She unlatched it and shoved. She stuck her head out and looked down. The drop was bigger than she liked, but she didn't have a choice.

If she went back to the mansion, she would be choosing sides. She'd known this was coming. Could feel the tension in the mansion building since Jozef's release from prison, since he brought Shaun back into the city. Neither of her parents credited her with the intelligence to pay attention. They were wrong. She saw everything.

She'd suspected her mother of poisoning Shaun, had even tried to warn her friend right after she arrived in the city. Shaun was too much of a do-gooder to believe the woman who'd thrown her a fancy party could poison her.

If Saskia had to guess, Dasha had tried to kill Shaun again. Saskia hoped like hell her mother hadn't been successful or they would all burn in the heat of Jozef's rage.

"Dad, I have to go," she said, putting the phone to her ear.

"Jesus, child, I thought something had happened to you!" he exploded.

She winced. He must've realized she hadn't been listening.

"I was... peeing," she told him, swinging a leg out onto the ledge. "Look dad, I need to say something and then I need to hang up."

"Make it quick," he growled. "I need to call your sister."

Saskia wondered why he hadn't called Leeza first, then realized her sister was probably home, safely surrounded by her bodyguards, waiting for Saskia to arrive so they could hole up in the safe room. She would have to disappoint her sister.

"I wanted to say... thank you," she told him.

She shoved the phone into her cleavage, hoping he could still hear as she lowered herself out of the window, walking her sneaker-clad feet down the side of the brick building until they were dangling.

"I'm not thanking you for being a good dad or anything," she said loudly so he could hear. The building was huge, so even if the guards thought to cover the window, it would take them several minutes to get outside and locate the correct window. She would be long gone by then. "Because you aren't a good dad, you never were. You were too consumed by business, power and position to pay attention to your daughters."

She squeezed her eyes shut and let go of the window. When her feet hit the ground, her knees buckled and she fell. She didn't stay on the ground though. She rolled over, leapt to her feet and took off running.

She dug her phone out of her cleavage and put it up to her ear.

"What the fuck are you talking about?" Krystoff roared. "Why is your bodyguard texting that you aren't with him."

"You need to shut up and listen to me for once, because I'm about to ditch my phone and I really don't know if we'll see each other again."

"Saskia, don't you fucking dare," he snarled. "You go back to your guards right fucking now."

The fear in his voice overrode the anger, which slowed

Saskia's steps, but didn't stop her. She'd been preparing for this day from the moment she realized who her family was.

"I won't do that and I need you to stop wasting our time. You know as well as I do that you'll have to get off the phone to coordinate your attack on Jozef. I really, really wish you wouldn't, but I know you too well to think otherwise. You'll hit him before he can organize himself enough to hit back."

There was a pause, then her father said sarcastically, "You think you're smarter than the rest of us, don't you?"

She laughed. "I really am. That's not even a question."

"If you're bound and determined to go your stubborn way then so be it. I wash my hands of you. Just remember, when your cousin is holding a gun to your head, I tried to protect you. You chose the wrong side."

"That's the thing, dad," she said impatiently. "I'm not choosing sides, but if I was, yours would be the wrong one. You know how I know that?"

"How?" he snarled, his rage vibrating down the line.

"Because you want me to choose," she told him. "Jozef cares about me without asking me to choose."

"He will kill you!" Krystoff shouted. "Stupid child."

"Tell mom I love her," Saskia said, slamming the heel of her hand into the gas flap of an older model car. It opened and she fished out the keys. She'd hidden the car and the keys at the beginning of the school year, giving her an out if she needed one while she was at school. "Please try to..."

Saskia choked on the tears rising up and had to stop and breath. She jerked the car door open and slid into the driver's seat. Placing her head on the steering wheel she took several deep breaths until she was able to speak again.

"Please stay safe," she finally said. "I would ask you not to go after Jozef, to remind you that he was a son to you and mom, a brother to me and Leeza, but I know you won't listen."

"Is this why you're leaving?" Krystoff asked. "Don't do this, Saskia. We can figure something out. I need to know you're safe."

She smiled through her tears. "I'm doing this so I will be safe. Tell mom I love her. I love you both."

Saskia hung up and fitted the keys in the engine, relieved when it started. It was an older car and had been sitting for months.

She lifted her phone and hit Nikolay's number. He picked up immediately. "Saskia."

"Niko, are you alone?"

"Uh, wait a minute." She heard rustling, then a door open and close. "Okay, I'm alone."

"You don't have to hide her from me." Saskia rolled her eyes as she put the car in reverse and pulled out of her parking spot. "I've always known you were fucking around. I'm not stupid."

He fell silent and for one tragic moment she thought he'd deny his trysts. Instead, he said, "If you know, then why are you calling? Why didn't you break up with me?"

"It's cute that you ever thought we were going to be a thing." Pain blossomed in her chest as she lied. There had been a time, not long ago, that she'd believed Nikolay would be her one and only. That they might get married and live happily ever after. After he'd given her the burner phone to give to Shaun, she'd been forced to question whether he ever cared about her, or if he'd been using her. "I was using you for sex, Niko, which was pretty bad by the way, and to get info on Jozef and the team, see what you guys were up to."

He snarled something that she didn't catch. She didn't care.

"You can eat your outrage, asshole," she said calmly. "I know you were only using me to get close to my dad and when Jozef split, I stopped being useful. That's around the time the sex started getting really bad."

"Again, why are you calling me?" he snapped.

"I want you to give Jozef a message. Tell him I'm taking off. I won't be a problem and he doesn't need to come after me."

"Why are you telling me this?" he demanded. "Why don't you tell Jozef yourself?"

She laughed bitterly. "Because I wanted one last chance to tell you that you are a below average fuck with a below average dick. Have a nice life, fucker."

She hung up and, without a backward glance, drove away from the university and away from Prague.

CHAPTER FORTY

Leeza checked her gun one more time, glanced in the mirror and then turned away. She stared down at her slumbering son. She'd given him a powerful sedative and it had taken effect. She felt intense guilt for doing such a thing to her child, but the end would justify the means. She needed him to sleep through the events that were about to take place.

She took a deep breath and picked up her bag, slinging it across her shoulders and securing it between her breasts. She picked Kristoph up and held him against her chest, his head on her shoulder.

She took several deep breaths and straightened her spine. She was not a weak person. She would do what she had to do, even if it would haunt her nightmares.

The door opened and her personal guard, Igor, stuck his head in. "Ready to go ma'am? Your sister is on her way to the mansion. She should be joining you shortly."

Leeza was supposed to go to the main house and cower in the safe room with her sister and her son. She had other plans.

She nodded and held tighter to Kristoph, whose dead weight was difficult to manage. Her constant workouts ensured she was both strong and agile though. She knew she could carry him over a great distance if necessary.

"Follow me." Igor turned away from her and headed down the hall to the main floor of the house. "Stay behind me and if we're attacked, run to the house."

"Okay," she whispered.

She reached behind her back and pulled her gun from its holster. As Igor descended the stairs, she shot him, the sound an echoing crack through the house. It was the hardest thing she'd ever done. She hated that she was shooting a man in the back, but she was doing it for her son. She had to get him away from the bosom of the Koba family and she knew her father's men wouldn't allow her to leave.

Though Krystoff would never give control of his organization to Kristoph, due to his autism, Krystoff still considered his grandson his heir. He would override Kristoph's own mother if it meant keeping the child with the family. Now, the family was splintering and so was Leeza's loyalty. She wasn't one of them. She wasn't a Koba.

Jozef thought she was though, which made her a prime target.

Igor lurched forward and fell, sliding to the bottom of the stairs. Leeza hurtled after him. She gave him a worried glance when he didn't move. She'd tried not to hit anything vital, but she wasn't an expert in anatomy.

She leapt over his prone body, Kristoph held tightly in her arms. Before she could leave, Adam shouted from the top of the stairs.

"What the fuck is going on?"

Leeza whirled around and gaped up at him.

"No one told you what was happening?" she asked incredulously and then started laughing. "Oh my god, that's hilarious. No one thought enough about you to tell you we're under attack."

"Who shot Igor?" he demanded, pounding down the stairs to check on the prone man.

Leeza sighed. She'd been so preoccupied with getting Krystoph and herself to safety she hadn't thought of Adam. Fuck. She chewed on her lip. Decisions. Decisions. She could leave him, shoot him or take him with her.

She thought about lifting her gun and putting a bullet through his head. The satisfaction she felt rushing through her was heady, and it was what convinced her not to do it. She'd wielded vengeance once. It had been satisfying, but the consequences were what had led to this moment. To her family splintering and attacking each other.

She wouldn't act on such an impulse again. Not without a great deal of thought.

"Do yourself a favour," she told her husband coldly. "Leave Prague. Go far away and retire somewhere sunny. If you stay loyal to Krystoff Koba, you will die. Probably tonight."

Without waiting for a response, she turned and hurtled toward the front door, jerking it open and running into the night. She could hear Adam calling after her. He wasn't in good enough shape to catch her though. She ran to the family garage, passing by men rushing around the estate with enough weapons to outfit an armory. They really were preparing for war.

Leeza loved her cousin, but she knew she was a target. Her father might underestimate the vicious dog, but Leeza knew better. He was a killer, born and bred. He would take the whole family out for this infraction and he would walk away from the carnage without a backward glance.

Leeza grabbed a set of keys off the wall and opened the back door to her father's Marauder; a rugged truck designed to withstand mine explosions. She sat her son in the child seat. She'd convinced Krystoff to install one in case they ever needed a safe getaway. Krystoff had laughed at Leeza's over-precaution but had allowed the seat to be installed.

She belted Kristoph in, tightening it across his small body and shaking the seat to make sure it was secure. She grabbed the blanket she'd brought along and tucked it around him.

She kissed his cheek and then his closed eyelids. "Stay asleep, baby. You're not going to like this next part."

She slammed his door shut and climbed into the driver's seat. She secured her own seatbelt and then hit the garage door opener. As soon as the door began sliding open, men ran toward it, guns pointing into the garage. The estate was crawling with men. She'd known it wouldn't be easy to get off the grounds.

She hit the accelerator before the doors finished opening and smashed through them.

Bullets thunked into the side of the vehicle and she winced. They clearly hadn't seen her behind the wheel, or they wouldn't be trying to kill her, which made her escape even more dangerous. She'd assumed they would know it was her trying to leave the grounds. That they'd try to stop her but ultimately pull back so as not to hurt her.

She hurtled down the driveway, ignoring the men who were chasing her and accelerated toward the big, reinforced iron gates at the head of the property. There were men waving at her and shouting, but she didn't slow down. They were forced to leap out of her way as she smashed through the gates. The truck jolted and slowed for a second, then picked up speed.

She guided her vehicle onto the highway leading away from Prague. She had another vehicle, one that would blend in better than the Marauder, waiting for her in a nearby car park. She would abandon the truck and take the other vehicle into Poland where she had a hideaway.

She glanced in the rearview mirror to make sure the jolt of hitting the gates hadn't disturbed Kristoph. He remained asleep.

Reaching across to the passenger seat, she opened the zip of her bag and dumped it. She picked up the burner phone she'd activated before leaving the mansion and dialed her father's number.

CHAPTER FORTY-ONE

K rystoff stared at his man.

"Both of my daughters?"

"Yes, they left when we tried to collect them. We don't know where they are. They might've collaborated on this."

Krystoff was stunned. His daughters had betrayed him?

He stared down at his wife and tried to make sense of the situation. His entire family. Gone in a single evening. He hadn't truly known a single one of them.

His wife had tried to kill an innocent woman. His daughters scattered when the family was threatened, and that threat was coming from the one person Krystoff thought would remain loyal until the end.

He wanted to sit down and think, work out what'd happened. Saskia had told him he wasn't a good father, yet he'd provided everything they'd ever needed and then some. Hadn't he?

He didn't have time to think about it. Maybe later he could work out what happened, see if he could repair his relationship with his youngest daughter. He wasn't sure where Leeza had gone but he had a difficult time believing his obedient eldest daughter had betrayed him. Except when it came to her son, she was compliant to a fault.

Wasn't she?

Fuck, he didn't have time to think about it. He had to set his mind to his next move. Jozef wouldn't be taking a time out. He'd be planning his attack. Which meant Krystoff had to beat him to it.

Pain blossomed in Krystoff's chest as he finally allowed himself to accept the inevitable. He would have to kill the man he considered his son. If he didn't, then Jozef would kill everyone Krystoff loved.

A searing anger rushed through Krystoff. He blamed the woman. If she hadn't come into their lives, then none of this would've happened. He should have insisted she be put in the ground the day Jozef dragged her home. If he could, he would take her out himself. Slow and painful.

She might be an innocent in the big picture, but she had destroyed an entire multi-generational crime family. There was no forgiveness in Krystoff's heart for her. Soon she would die, and he could set about putting what was left of his family back together.

Krystoff knelt next to Dasha's bed and gripped her hand, holding it against his lips. "I will finish what you started, my love. I will make this right."

Krystoff stood and stepped away from the bed. He was loath to leave Dasha, but he couldn't stay. He had to lead the men he was sending to take out Jozef at the club. They would need a strong leader if they were to make it out alive. Jozef would not be an easy target.

He stepped out into the hallway to speak with Dasha's bodyguard.

Rassoul turned as Krystoff approached him. "Sir?"

"You stay on her room," Krystoff told the other man. "No matter what you hear reported back from the other teams, you stay on Dasha. Fail to protect my wife again and you can consider your life forfeit."

"Yes, sir," Rassoul said steadily, positioning himself outside the door.

Krystoff arranged for another man to watch the door, then walked away from Dasha. He didn't look back. He couldn't. If he saw his wife, pale and helpless in that bed, he wouldn't leave. He had to join his men a few blocks away from Jozef's apartment complex to organize the strike. To protect his family.

Krystoff had a bad feeling about taking the building. His team of men weren't nearly as prepared as Jozef's would be. Jozef had taken those men from him, the men Krystoff had invested in and trained.

These thoughts helped him build the rage he would need to take out his nephew.

Jozef brought Shaun into the bosom of the family, and like a ticking bomb she was responsible for blowing them to hell. Jozef had insisted on protecting the woman, though his responsibility was with his family.

This was Jozef's war and Krystoff was going to finish it.

He checked his sidearm before climbing into his vehicle and starting the engine. There was a light clicking sound and the engine failed to catch. Krystoff's heart hammered and he carefully took his hand away from the keys and opened the door. He slid out and ran, leaving the door ajar.

Seconds later the car exploded. Heat seared his back, and he was thrown off his feet and into another vehicle. A sickening crunch told him he'd shattered a window with his shoulder.

He pushed himself to his feet and did a quick body check. Nothing broken.

He was impressed. Jozef had never been much of an explosives man. He used them if he had to, but he preferred a more personal kill. Bombs weren't personal. They could be easily misdirected or miscalculated. This one had failed to kill Krystoff, a fact he would take advantage of.

He ran toward the main road, texting his men to send a car.

Then he texted Rassoul and reiterated that the bodyguard was to lock himself in the hospital room with Dasha and call hospital security.

It was the best he could do for his wife. He loved her more than anyone, but he had to focus on the task ahead. Take out the threat to the Koba family.

Leeza peeked her head around the corner and, catching sight of Krystoff, ducked back into the room she was hiding in. The gentle whir of a machine reminded her that she was hiding out in another patient's room. The woman didn't look like she was about to wake up any time soon. The greatest risk was that a family member or nurse could walk in.

It didn't matter though; she'd be out in a minute. Krystoff had no choice but to leave. He had to be part of the strike team preparing to hit Jozef.

Leeza had texted Saskia, telling her to stay away from the mansion if she could manage it. Saskia's response had been, "I've got this. Take care of yourself, sister."

Leeza had blinked away tears as she wondered if she'd ever see her wild little sister again. Saskia was even more secretive than their mother. It was why Leeza didn't really worry about her. The girl had more lives than a cat. Saskia was no longer her concern. Leeza had to protect her child and the woman who had caused this nightmare.

No, Leeza told herself, *you caused this. It starts with you, and now it'll end when you disappear.*

Krystoff thought his daughters would be safe at the mansion. He still believed he was holding onto a strong criminal empire. The rest of them had watched it crumble, one piece at a time, until there was nothing left to hold it together. He believed that as long as he had his family, he had something, but he didn't even have them. His wife had betrayed him and his daughters were scattering to the wind.

Leeza heard quick footsteps coming down the hall toward her. She moved farther back and watched as Krystoff passed by.

She wouldn't have long.

If her distraction killed him then his men would be all over the hospital looking for the bomber. If it didn't kill him, he'd double down on Dasha's security, making it impossible for Leeza to get in the room. She had to move fast.

She placed her hand against the butt of the pistol tucked in the holster at her back, beneath her jacket, and walked toward her mother's room. Her mother's personal bodyguard and another man were standing guard.

"You." She nodded at Rassoul. "Show me to my mother."

His eyes bugged when he saw her. "You're supposed to be at the mansion, Ms. Koba-Horáček."

"Is that so?" she snapped in annoyance. "Well, I'm not. I'm here to see my mom. Now step aside or shoot me."

She walked past him and shoved the door open. Of course, he didn't stop her. If there was one thing hammered into the heads of all staff on the Koba payroll, it was to never touch the women. No matter what was happening, they were not allowed to lay hands on family members. Leeza took advantage of Rassoul's momentary confusion.

He recovered quickly, stepping into the room behind her. It was too late. She pulled the gun and turned, shooting him in the head. The other guard followed quickly behind, but failed to identify Leeza as the attacker, instead waving his gun around the room.

She shot him, too.

Before his body hit the floor, her gun was back in the holster and she was facing her mother.

Her gun had a silencer that muffled the shots, but she could still be discovered by hospital staff if she didn't move quickly. Besides, once the explosion happened, the hospital would go into lockdown within minutes. Leeza couldn't be inside when that happened.

"Wake up," she said sharply, slapping Dasha's cheek.

Her mother's eyelids crinkled, as though she were swimming toward the surface. Leeza slapped her again then took hold of her shoulders and shook her. Dasha cried out in pain as her injury was jarred.

While Dasha was waking up, Leeza rushed to the window, which thankfully had a perfect view of the parking lot. She could see her vehicle, parked illegally against the curb. The windows were tinted so she wasn't worried about anyone seeing Kristoph, but she hated leaving him.

He was still deeply asleep so wouldn't wake up.

"Leeza?" Dasha's thready voice came from the bed.

Leeza rushed back and glanced quickly over her mother. "Get up, we have to move."

"What... what's happening?" Dasha asked, trying to push herself up.

When she put weight on her injured arm it buckled, and she fell back against the pillows. Leeza took hold of Dasha's good arm and jerked her into a sitting position. She looked at the lines that were attached to Dasha, probably giving her lifesaving fluids, painkillers and antibiotics.

Leeza would have to sever the connection, but she had to wait until the explosion distracted the hospital staff.

"You have to be ready to run," Leeza said to Dasha. "We're leaving the second I say."

"Where's your father?" Dasha's voice sounded unusually harsh, like she'd swallowed a handful of nails.

Leeza wanted to shout that Krystoff was not her father, that she knew everything, but now was not the time. That confrontation would come later when they were both safely away from Prague.

"He's going to kill Jozef," Leeza said instead and watched as her mother blanched. "Jozef has a strike team on its way here, which means we need to get out."

She glanced out the window again in time to see a man hurling himself away from a vehicle just before it exploded. Leeza blinked in surprise. She'd built the bomb herself and had been relatively confident that it would work, but she hadn't expected such a large explosion. She was alternately impressed with herself and a little freaked out.

"Time to go," she said urgently, turning back to Dasha.

Dasha nodded, bit her lip and pushed herself up off the bed. She wobbled but she didn't go down. Dasha was a strong woman, so Leeza knew she would do her level best to keep up.

Leeza peeled the tape away from Dasha's arm and jerked the needle out. When she pulled the heart monitor off, the machine started beeping like crazy. Leeza ignored it, pulling her coat off and dragging it over her mother.

"Let's go." She wrapped an arm around her mother and pulled her toward the door.

"Rassoul!" Dasha reached for her bodyguard when she saw him on the floor.

Leeza pulled her upright. She gripped her mother by the shoulders and shoved her into the wall next to the door.

"I'm leaving now, whether you come with me or not. Jozef wants you dead and I want you alive, but I will leave you if you don't do what I say. I have to think about my son."

Dasha stared at Leeza as if she'd never seen her before, then nodded.

"Okay, let's go," she whispered, licking her dry lips.

Leeza opened the door and peeked into the corridor. There was no one at the nurse's desk, which meant they were likely staring out a window, trying to figure out what'd happened in the parking lot.

"Run," Leeza growled, dragging Dasha into the corridor.

Both women ran full tilt down the hallway. Leeza slammed her hand into the stairway door and flung it open, shoving Dasha inside. Dasha reached for the wall to steady herself, but Leeza gripped her around the waist and ran down the stairs, propping her mother up as much as she could.

Leeza flung the door open just as an alarm bell inside the hospital went off, signaling lockdown.

They ran toward Leeza's car, directly through a crowd of bystanders watching the flames of the recent explosion.

"Hey, are you okay?" someone shouted after them.

Leeza ignored the person and used her key fob to unlock the door of her car. She opened the passenger door and stuck her head inside. Kristoph was sound asleep in his child seat, his small chest rising and falling.

She took a deep breath in relief, the tension in her chest easing a little.

She dropped her mother into the passenger seat, lifting Dasha's legs inside before slamming the door shut.

She hurtled around to the driver's side and was about to open the door when a security guard came running toward her. She reached for her gun but froze when he started speaking.

"You'll have to move your vehicle, ma'am," he told her. "The fire department will want to park here."

"I'm so sorry. I didn't realize," she said sweetly. "Of course, I'll move. Is everything okay?"

He shook his head in exasperation. "It looks like some lunatic lit a car on fire. It seems to have exploded in the parking lot."

"Oh, I hope there was no one inside," she said anxiously, looking inside the car out of her periphery.

Dasha wasn't moving.

"We won't know until the fire department puts out the fire."

"Of course," Leeza nodded. "I'll move right away."

"Thanks," he said with a relieved smile. "You have yourself a good night, ma'am."

She slid into the vehicle and slammed the door shut, then she collapsed against the steering wheel sucking in several deep breaths. Everything had gone like clockwork.

She hadn't planned on going back for Dasha, but then she received an anonymous text warning her that there were hits out for her, Adam and Dasha. She'd been hurt but not surprised. She'd gone to the club a few weeks earlier to see Jozef, to pledge her loyalty to him if the family went to war, but he hadn't been there and some idiot had set off a firework on the club floor, driving everyone from the building. Now her loyalty wouldn't matter. Too little, too late. She'd become a target, just as she feared.

Once Leeza realized Krystoff wouldn't be at the hospital to protect Dasha, she'd turned her car around and formulated a quick plan to get her mother out of the hospital. Thank god Leeza had been prepared, with everything in her trunk from a first aid kit to a small bomb. Once she got Dasha away from Prague, they would head for the border. Personally, Leeza intended the move to be permanent. Dasha could do what she wanted when she recovered. If she was smart, she would take the money Leeza planned to give her and retire to St. Barts.

Leeza pulled out of the hospital parking lot in time to see an SUV filled with Jozef's men. She held her breath as they passed. No one looked her way. As she turned onto the freeway, she saw the shadow of a man leap into a vehicle as it pulled over. She couldn't be sure, but she thought it was Krystoff.

So she hadn't killed him with the bomb.

Part of her was relieved. Though he wasn't her father, and he had sold her in marriage to a monster, he had always done what he thought was best for her. For that, she couldn't actively wish him dead.

It didn't matter. Jozef would do the deed for her.

CHAPTER FORTY-TWO

Meet me downstairs.

Nikolay had been expecting the message. He'd been deployed with the rest of the team to secure the building ahead of a possible attack. This was the moment he'd been both anticipating and dreading. The moment when he would choose which Koba faction would be the winning side.

Of course, he'd already thrown his lot in with Krystoff. Had from the moment he agreed to take a burner phone to the daughter, starting the chain of events that would lead him to betray Jozef.

It hadn't been a difficult decision to make. He'd harboured resentment toward Jozef since they were children. They were both related to the Koba clan, though Nikolay was a more distant relation. They were both orphans and they'd both been raised at the Koba estate. The biggest difference was Jozef had been raised in the house, like a favoured son, while Nikolay had grown up in the barracks with the rest of the grunts.

Jozef had chosen Nikolay to be part of his elite hit squad

because Nikolay was unparalleled when it came to target practice. He was good with weapons of all types, but sharp-shooting was his specialty.

He fit in with Jozef's men, never allowing his resentment to show. He laughed with them, worked with them, sweated and bled with them. But he wasn't one of them. He was more important. He was the lost child of the Koba family, and he was about to ensure his future placement with them.

He nodded at the bouncers who had finished clearing the club floor and were going through every nook and cranny to make sure there were no more guests lingering. They were efficient at their jobs which meant Krystoff hadn't been able to get any of his men inside the club before the closure. It didn't matter, he already had a man on the inside.

Nikolay made his way through the kitchen, which was now shut down and abandoned by the cooking staff. They would have been told to leave with the guests so they wouldn't get caught in the crossfire.

As Nikolay passed, he hovered a hand over the grill. Still hot.

He turned and headed down the corridor to the back of the building where the ramp was located for food delivery. He passed Cooper who was walking back to the club, a semi-automatic rifle held to his chest.

"Where're you going?" Cooper turned on his heel to walk backwards as he passed Nikolay. "Already checked the back door. It's locked and rigged to blow if anyone tries to force entry."

Nikolay was glad Cooper had warned him of the explosives, though he would now have to get rid of the American mercenary. The other man would know exactly who'd messed with the back door if it came to light that someone on the inside had let Krystoff and his men inside the building.

"I was ordered to check on the weapons stash in the

ceiling of the supply room. We might need the extra fire power."

Cooper nodded and jogged back toward the club. Nikolay didn't have enough time to take him out before he disappeared around the corner. He'd have to finish the job later, make it look like Cooper was killed by Krystoff's men.

He reached the back door and knelt next to the latch, examining the explosive. There was a C4 pack with a wire extending across the crack of the door. If someone tried to open it, the door would blow, injuring or killing anyone on the other side. It was a basic setup, but effective.

Nikolay took a switchblade from his pocket and carefully slid the sharp knife edge across the wire, severing the connection. He pulled the pack off the door and set it aside.

He unlocked the door and jerked it open. Krystoff stood on the other side, a half dozen men surrounding him.

Nikolay frowned. "Where are the rest? This isn't enough people to take out Jozef. You won't even reach the top floor."

Krystoff gave Nikolay an icy look, telling him what he thought of Nikolay's intelligence, before answering. "We'll meet them at strategic points around the building and let them in."

Nikolay nodded. He recognized the strategy as one Jozef implemented often. Send in a few scouts to secure key areas and let the rest of the team inside.

"Make sure you send men who know how to disarm a C4 pack. All the doors are rigged," Nikolay told him.

Krystoff ignored the comment.

"Is your roommate still upstairs?" Krystoff demanded, entering the building.

Nikolay nodded, his stomach twisting. He knew what was coming next. Had suspected it from the moment Havel called to tell him to be ready for an attack. Krystoff had texted shortly after letting Nikolay know he was on his way.

This was the moment he truly had to pick sides.

"Kill him," Krystoff said coldly. "The fewer of Jozef's men we have to contend with, the better. Don't leave any witnesses."

Nikolay swallowed and forced himself to nod.

Krystoff must've caught onto Nikolay's hesitation. He gripped Nikolay by the back of the neck and pulled him close in a half hug with threatening undertones. "You knew this was coming," Krystoff said in a low voice as the rest of his men passed into the building. "You rightfully chose my side and I promise you will not regret it. In this life, we must make difficult decisions. Jozef betrayed me when he chose his woman over his own family. You will not make this mistake. You will choose loyalty."

Nikolay's gut twisted. If he was choosing loyalty, then why did he feel as though he would regret what was about to come? No, he was choosing money, power and position. He might not be a good man, but the least he could do was be honest with himself.

He pulled away from Krystoff. "It'll get done."

"Good boy," Krystoff told him and then took off with the rest of his men to secure the main floor.

Nikolay ran to the stairs and took the flights two and three steps at a time until he'd reached the third floor. He stopped in front of his apartment door sucking in deep breaths as he prepared himself. The hallway was eerily silent considering what was happening on the lower floors. He wondered if his teammates were dead. Havel, Terek, Halil. It would be better if Halil was downstairs so Nikolay didn't have to do it himself. He knew better though. Halil and Giselle had been asleep when he'd been summoned to let Krystoff in the building.

Once again, the crushing guilt of betraying the team he'd worked so closely with for so long was nearly overwhelming.

He had never in his life felt so conflicted. Now, when he most needed to man up and do what needed doing, he was sinking into a pit of his own feelings.

The irony was, he'd been bottling them up for years. He'd bottled the anger and resentment while working with Jozef. He'd bottled his feelings toward Saskia while coldly wooing her. He'd withheld his glee as Krystoff finally noticed him and made moves toward making a place for Nikolay in the family.

And now those feelings were bubbling up, threatening to strangle him. Threatening to stop him from doing his job.

He ruthlessly set those feelings aside as he let himself into his apartment.

"Thank god," Halil said, relief in his voice. He was strapping weapons to his belt and shoving ammunition into his cargo pockets. "My phone was on vibrate. I didn't see Havel's message until a few minutes ago. He said the building is being evacuated and we're to prepare for an attack."

Halil checked his phone again. "He wants us to secure the weapons locker on the second floor and hold the building until the we can get the women out."

"I want to go now," Giselle said from the bedroom door.

She was fully dressed, her hair a tangled mess and her makeup smeared. She was clutching her purse against her chest as though someone might try to tear it from her arms.

Nikolay took a breath. It was now or never.

"Giselle, you have a weapon?"

She nodded, her hand automatically slipping into her purse as though feeling for it to make sure it was still there. She came from a background of shady politicians and Italian mafia. She likely never left home without a weapon, having been born and raised to expect a threat.

"Give it to me." Nikolay reached a hand out to her. "I want to make sure it's loaded in case we run into trouble getting you out of the building."

"Of course it's loaded." She frowned, but reached into the bag, pulling her pistol out.

It was small, mostly decorative, but it would get the job done.

Nikolay opened the gun and checked. Loaded.

He turned on his heel and pointed it at Halil.

Halil looked up, his eyes widening in surprise before Nikolay put a bullet in his head.

Pain pierced Nikolay as the body of his best friend hit the floor. He barely noticed Giselle's scream of surprise and fear as he was forced to face everything he'd just sacrificed. Halil had been his confidant, listening without judging, his softer personality more compassionate than most of the men on their team. No more boisterous laughter. No more video games and pizza Saturday nights. No more women sharing. Gone in the blink of a bullet. Betrayed by the one man he probably trusted most.

Giselle was still standing next to him, her shrieks bouncing off the walls.

He looked at her. "Run, Giselle."

She didn't need to be told again. She hurtled toward the apartment door and fumbled with the lock Nikolay had engaged.

He strode to Halil's body and picked up the gun he'd watched the other man load seconds before he was killed.

Nikolay straightened and just as Giselle was about to open the door, he shot her in the head. She hit the door face first and slid to the floor, the back of her blonde head a mess of blood, bone and brain. Halil's gun made a much better kill than hers had.

He walked to the door, kicking Giselle's body aside, and jerking it open.

Nikolay took a deep breath and muttered to himself, "You are in control. The rewards will go to the victor."

He ran toward the stairs. He would make his way down a floor and take out anyone else in his way. He would secure the floor for Krystoff's men.

CHAPTER FORTY-THREE

"We have to go," Terek said, pacing the room, his eyes on his phone. "Intel coming in from our guys indicate there was an explosion at the hospital. Must be Krystoff, putting the hospital in lockdown so he can leave and keep Dasha protected."

Jozef nodded at his team member. Terek's orders were to help protect Shaun and Fatima while Havel secured the building with the rest of the men.

Krystoff was thinking on his feet, which meant Jozef needed to be two steps ahead.

He pointed at Fatima and signed, *take her to her apartment and get her packed. You have five minutes. I'll meet you in the lobby.*

Terek jerked his head toward the door. "Time to go, Mrs. Patterson."

She looked up from her position next to Shaun who was sound asleep on the couch. "But..."

"No buts." Terek took her arm and pulled her to her feet, escorting her to the door. Jozef was pleased that Terek was being gentle. The younger man had a mother that he loved and respected; Jozef had no problem trusting him with Shaun's mother.

"Keep my daughter safe," she shouted back at Jozef.

"You'll get to see her in just a few minutes, Mrs. Patterson," Terek assured her, hustling her toward the stairs that would take them down a level to her apartment.

Jozef ran to the bedroom, his eyes grazing Shaun as he passed her. He flung his travel bag on the bed and started packing for her. He wasn't sure how long she would be hiding out at the safe house, but it wasn't well equipped for women. He grabbed a few outfits that looked comfortable, some socks and underwear, her shampoo and conditioner.

Then he looked under the sink and saw her feminine hygiene products. Would she need them? When was the last time she had her period? He couldn't remember. How much would she need? He had no answers to any of these questions and it frustrated him. He should know everything about her if he was to take care of her properly.

He grabbed everything he saw that might be related to her period and shoved them in the bag.

He zipped it and ran back into the living room.

He went down on one knee next to the couch and looked at her face. There was an ugly bandage taped across half her face, beneath her left eye. He touched the warm skin of her other cheek.

Her eyes opened and she looked at him with a surprisingly clear expression. "Jozef," she whispered and tried to smile.

Then, as the pain of her injuries hit, she seemed to remember what had happened. Tears filled her eyes and she stared up at him with a pleading look as if asking him to take it all away. The pain, the anguish, the horror.

Jozef's gut twisted. His fault.

We have to go, he signed.

Her eyes flicked down and he repeated himself until understanding flashed in her eyes.

We have to go quickly. I need my gun hand available so you'll have to walk. Are you able to do that?

She gasped and reached out to grip the back of the couch, pulling herself up. "Why do you need your gun hand?"

He shook his head, not wanting to take the time to explain but knowing she would resist if he didn't.

My uncle will be attacking us very soon. We have to get someplace safe before he does.

"But why?" she cried out, the tears that had brightened her eyes starting to spill over. "Is he angry because I hurt Dasha? Maybe I can talk to him and explain what happened."

Jozef growled his frustration, took her shoulders and shook her. She clamped her mouth shut and stared at him. He didn't want to hurt her, but they had to go. If she couldn't understand how serious the situation was, she might get herself killed.

My uncle is coming here to kill both of us. He has no choice. His wife attacked you, which is an attack on me. He believes I have no choice but to retaliate, so he will strike first in an attempt to take us down while we're unprepared. Jozef didn't tell her that his uncle was right. If Jozef could, he would wipe out the entire organization that night.

Jozef wrapped his arm around her middle and pulled her to her feet. Shaun moaned, then bit her lip, trying to keep the pain inside. She took a few deep breaths, then nodded, holding her bandaged arm against her chest.

"I'm okay," she whispered. "Let's go."

Jozef pulled her tight against his left side and pulled his gun from the holster. He looked into the hallway and nodded at the guard sent to replace Karl. He couldn't sign to the man with his arms full, so he jerked his head down the hall to indicate he should take the lead.

His man understood and they made their way toward the stairwell. Jozef had locked out the elevators, ensuring anyone coming into the building would be bottlenecked. Unfortunately, that also meant Jozef could get caught in the stairwell too.

They made it down to the third floor when the first explosion detonated. He dropped to his knees, forcing Shaun down too and covering her body with his. She cried out and wrapped her arms around her head.

The explosion was small enough that Jozef knew it wasn't a bomb. Probably a smoke grenade or a flashbang. He'd used both in his operations. They were an effective means of confusing the enemy.

The building had been penetrated.

Jozef lurched to his feet, dragging Shaun up too. He pushed her against the wall, covering her with his body. He could hear shouts in the stairwell below them and another detonation.

Smoke billowed up from below. Gunfire sounded in the lower levels of the building. If he hadn't been on the opposite side, he'd be impressed with Krystoff's new team. He hadn't thought his uncle had pulled a team together who had the skills and efficiency to strike this quickly.

Jozef freed his hands, pressing Shaun against the wall so she wouldn't collapse. He turned to his man and signed, *cover us*.

The other man nodded and took position on the landing as Jozef turned to grab Shaun who was coughing from the smoke. He suppressed the urge to cough, needing his ears to hear if the enemy had made it onto their floor.

He took Shaun's good arm and dragged her back to the top floor, swinging her into the hallway. As he walked, he holstered his gun, dragged her into his arms and picked her up. He had to move faster.

He ran down the hall. Once he was back inside the apartment, he set Shaun down and locked the door. He moved swiftly into the bedroom and into Shaun's closet, entering the code to the panic room.

"Jozef..." she said as he turned back to her.

He gripped her face and kissed her hard.

"No, no," she moaned. "You're coming with me."

He couldn't and she knew it. She clung to him, trying to drag him with her as he pushed her into the room.

He shook his head, unhooked her fingers from his shirt and shoved her hard. She stumbled back, a surprised look on her face as she fell. She landed on her butt, flinging her arms out to catch herself and then crying out as she jolted her injured arm.

She quickly turned to stare as Jozef took a last look at her before slamming the door shut and locking her inside. He hoped she was smart enough to stay put.

He made it as far as the kitchen island when an explosion rocked the apartment. The door flew off its hinges, hitting Jozef and sending him crashing into the living room. He leveled the glass coffee table as he fell.

He winced as a piece of glass sliced through his side.

He looked up in time to see Krystoff walk through the smoke, an arsenal of weapons strapped across his chest and waist.

Jozef reached for his gun and realized he'd dropped it in the kitchen when he'd been thrown off his feet. He tried to move, glass crunching underneath him as Krystoff strode toward him.

CHAPTER FORTY-FOUR

As his uncle approached, Jozef had no choice but to lay still, his arms stretched wide, blood seeping from the cuts he'd gotten when he fell through the table.

"I loved you, boy," Krystoff said gruffly, standing over Jozef. Tears dripped down his face, soaking into his beard. He either didn't notice or didn't care because he made no move to swipe them away. "I gave you everything and you chose this over your family."

He waved his arm around the apartment as though to say, he didn't understand the draw.

Jozef remained on his back but lifted his arms to sign. *You would do the same for D-A-S-H-A. In fact, you have. You wouldn't be here if it weren't for her.*

Krystoff nodded, and then did something Jozef wasn't expecting. He sat heavily on the couch, his body collapsing under the weight of his responsibilities. His gun was still in his hand but not pointed at Jozef.

Jozef wondered why his uncle didn't finish him. The more time that passed, the more Krystoff's advantage became Jozef's.

Jozef eased himself up, wincing as glass crunched beneath him. He slowly pulled himself out of the mess of broken coffee table and leaned against the couch on the opposite side of Krystoff.

"I love her," Krystoff said simply. "She has caused both the worst moments and the best moments of my life."

Jozef nodded his understanding. Shaun had done the same for him. The stunned emotion when he took in her beauty of soul and spirit – he couldn't live without her. Yet, she was also the reason his family had splintered. Good or bad, she was reason he now looked at the world a little differently.

"I couldn't allow you to kill her," Krystoff continued, his voice taking on a pleading tone. "She's all I have. Even if she gets me killed, at least I know I died defending her."

Krystoff looked over at Jozef as though silently begging him to understand.

You could have called me, talked to me, negotiated for her life.

Krystoff shook his head. "I've worked with you for a long time, boy. Two decades. You don't leave loose ends. She's a danger to your woman; you won't let her live."

Jozef didn't know how to answer his uncle's charge. Maybe at one time Jozef would have agreed. He wouldn't have left a loose end that could be a danger to himself or those he held dear. But Shaun had changed him, shown him how beautiful and fucked up love could be. He might be more willing to understand, to compromise.

So you decided to take out everything I love, take my life, the life of a man you treated like a son. You don't understand loyalty or love if this is the only way you can resolve your shit.

Krystoff laughed bitterly.

"I'm starting to think you're right," he admitted, his voice betraying his exhaustion. "Both of my daughters would agree with you. Saskia said pretty much the same thing before she slipped her guard and disappeared."

Krystoff looked at Jozef sharply. "Please Jozef, don't go after her. She's just a child. If you can't recall your love for the rest of us, at least remember her."

Jozef was relieved to hear his youngest cousin wouldn't be at the mansion. Though he'd given orders that she wasn't to be harmed, she could still catch a stray bullet. She was a wily and intelligent young woman. She would find a way to keep herself safe until the dust settled.

I have no intention of killing her, he admitted.

"And Leeza?" Krystoff demanded. "You can let her go too. She wants nothing to do with all this bullshit. She just wants to raise her son, be a good mother."

They both knew Jozef wouldn't be able to leave Leeza alive. She and her husband were a direct threat to his takeover. A takeover forced by his uncle. Had his uncle tried to negotiate rather than move against Jozef, he wouldn't have to target Krystoff's eldest child. Now he had no choice. Vory law would insist he take out any potential threats on his bloody path to the throne.

The truth was, Jozef didn't want the Koba seat of power. He never had, and Krystoff knew it.

Fucked up circumstances had forced both of their hands and a part of Jozef wanted to lay down weapons and call a truce. Tell his uncle that no one else had to die.

He knew Krystoff wouldn't go for it. He might be a fair man when it came to most things, but he was still a mafia man through and through. There was no give. He was old-school. He would protect his family no matter the conse-quences; he would protect his wife, even though her machina-tions had brought him to this point.

Instead of answering Krystoff's question, Jozef signed, *what happens now?*

"I have to put you down, boy," Krystoff said heavily, his tears starting once again as he lifted his gun hand. He didn't point it at Jozef but held it loosely between his legs as though trying to find the will to kill his nephew.

Jozef nodded.

Do what you have to do, he looked over at his uncle.

"You're not going to try to stop me?" Krystoff asked, his voice skeptical.

He knew better.

Jozef had never taken the prospect of death laying down. He was ready for every possibility, including being attacked in his own living room. But he needed Krystoff to make the first move so he could act.

Krystoff didn't disappoint. He lifted his gun, saying, "I'm sorry it's come to this."

Me too. Except Jozef thought it instead of signing it, because he was busy grabbing one of the grenades strapped to the underside of the couch.

As Krystoff started to squeeze the trigger, his gun aimed at Jozef's head, Jozef lifted the grenade, yanked the pin and tossed it at his uncle. He dove to the side of the couch, using Krystoff's momentary confusion to drag himself to safety.

Krystoff reacted quickly, diving over the back of the couch as the grenade hit the floor where his feet had been seconds earlier. A second later the grenade exploded, shattering what was left of the coffee table and sending shrapnel into the couch, destroying it.

Jozef hunched his entire body into the couch, which had been reinforced with Kevlar panels. He'd done the same with the bed. Havel had laughed and called him paranoid when he'd ordered the furniture from his prison cell. Jozef wasn't laughing.

He peeked around the side of the couch in time to see Krystoff scramble across the floor, his semi-automatic clutched in his hand. As he swung his gaze back around, he caught sight of Fitzy cowering under the table, his eyes huge and shining with fear. Jozef regretted not moving the cat into the safe room. If it was killed, Shaun would be devastated. He didn't have time to deal with the cat now though.

Jozef reached back under the couch and grabbed his Makarov handgun and yanked it from the straps. He crawled out from behind the couch and took aim at his uncle.

Krystoff must've sensed his imminent death because he rolled onto his back and started spraying the apartment with bullets.

Jozef was forced to duck back behind the couch as he listened to his uncle chew up his apartment. Bullets hit the windows, but they didn't shatter. Bulletproof.

By the time Krystoff stopped shooting, Jozef had pulled an RPG from beneath the destroyed couch and loaded it. Once again he was glad he went with overkill while weaponizing his apartment. There was a panel in the wall behind the TV that held an assortment of weapons, including an Uzi.

Under the stove tray was another cache. Another in Jozef's closet in a hidden panel and more strapped to the underside of his bed.

He'd been preparing for this exact situation, knowing one day that someone would come after him, trying either to keep him from taking his position as a Vory or to take him out and take his place. Revenge was another possible motive for Jozef outfitting himself, but he rarely left people alive who might want revenge.

Family was different though.

He'd been naive to believe he could leave Krystoff's employ, leave his position as enforcer, and not face any consequences.

Now they were in a standoff, and Jozef had the upper hand. He knew where every weapon in the apartment was hidden. He was outfitted to take out an army, instead of a tired old mobster who'd given Jozef the upper hand by not pulling the trigger as soon as he walked into the apartment.

This had been a suicide mission and they both knew it. Krystoff was going to let Jozef kill him. That was why he'd breached the apartment with no backup and why he hadn't put a bullet in Jozef's head when he walked in the door.

Pain gripped Jozef as he realized what his uncle was doing.

It didn't change what Jozef had to do. Krystoff was still dangerous. If Jozef didn't use every skill he had to take his uncle out, then Krystoff would kill him and find a way to kill Shaun. He might be on a suicide mission, but that didn't mean he wouldn't try to take Jozef out if Jozef gave him the chance.

"You still alive, son?" Krystoff asked.

Before Jozef could answer with a grenade, Krystoff sprayed the apartment again, his aim wildly off. As soon as he stopped, Jozef leapt to his feet with the rocket launcher and aimed it at the island.

The grenade hit the marble and exploded. Jozef ducked back down as debris littered the apartment. This explosion was bigger than the one that'd taken out his couch and TV. When he looked around the side of the couch, there was nothing left of the top of the island. There had been no Kevlar to reinforce the structure.

Jozef stood and then had to steady himself as dizziness engulfed his vision. Blood loss was weakening him. He blinked it away quickly, worried Krystoff would take advantage. When his vision cleared and his uncle still hadn't come out from behind the island, Jozef walked slowly toward the kitchen, his gun in one hand and the RPG in the other in case his uncle reached around to shoot him.

No bullets came, and Jozef saw why seconds later as he rounded the island. His uncle was leaning against the cupboards. The island was completely destroyed above

Krystoff's head. Shrapnel had exploded through the kitchen, hitting Krystoff in the face and chest.

He was bleeding profusely from several wounds and a piece of metal was sticking out of his left eye. He was still alive, his chest lifting and falling rapidly as blood poured down his face and chest.

Jozef dropped the RPG and collapsed next to Krystoff, reaching for his chest. He gripped Krystoff's shirt and pulled it away from his body. It came away sticky with blood.

Where is your vest? Jozef demanded. *Where the fuck is your vest? You don't leave for battle without one.*

He shook his uncle as shock pierced him. His uncle knew better. He'd walked into battle without a vest and now he was dying.

"Jozef..." Krystoff groaned. "I need... lay down."

Jozef realized his uncle was trying to push himself away from the cupboard, but his hands were bloody and broken. He'd probably lifted them to protect his face when the explosion had happened, instead getting them torn up by shrapnel.

Jozef set his gun down, knowing his uncle was no longer a threat. Others might come through the door, but Jozef would deal with them if that happened. Easing his uncle's last few seconds of life was more important.

He gripped Krystoff by the shoulders and pulled him down until he was slumped onto his side. Jozef shifted and moved Krystoff until he was lying flat on the floor where his breathing eased.

"Th... thank you."

Krystoff reached out, his bloody hand waving until Jozef took it and held on. He looked down at the stump where Krystoff had lost his finger just over one year earlier. That finger, the kidnapping, had started everything, had led to this moment.

Jozef had been so distracted by his own ambitions while

he was incarcerated that he had stopped looking for the Phantom. Maybe if he'd found her, punished her, given her to Krystoff, he could've stopped all this. It was too late though to give the family a common enemy.

Jozef watched, holding Krystoff's hand, as the life drained from his uncle.

CHAPTER FORTY-FIVE

I t took Shaun a few minutes to find the light switch in the panic room. She was slow and clumsy from the painkillers she'd been given. She realized the dose was far larger than she would have given herself.

Likely Jozef had told the doctor to make sure she wasn't in any pain. And it was working, she hardly felt a thing except for an intense desire to leave the panic room.

Once she found the light switch, she immediately went to the panel, intent on releasing herself. She stopped and stared at it.

Jozef had put her in that room for a reason, so he could do what he had to do without Shaun being in the way. If she went running into the fray without a clue, she could get herself and others killed.

"Oh god," she moaned and gripped her head.

She turned her back to the door and sank to the floor staring sightlessly at the wall opposite.

This was her fault. She hadn't done anything intentional, but she was the cause of the destruction of the Koba family. She'd nearly killed Jozef's aunt, a woman who'd raised him.

Now Jozef was faced with the decision to take out his own family or allow them to kill Shaun. It would have been better for him if he'd put a bullet in her head the day they met.

Then she remembered, the day he took her wasn't the first time he saw her. He admitted that he saw her in the streets of Luhansk with a child. A little boy who'd experienced hearing loss from the percussive force of the bombs dropping on his city.

She'd sat with the boy and taught him several words in sign language.

Jozef had been watching them. Had thought about her and remembered her when he needed a doctor.

A part of him had connected with her before they met.

Maybe this moment was inevitable.

Maybe they were always meant to find a way to each other. God knows, they couldn't seem to stay apart.

Shaun swiped at the tears spilling down her cheeks.

Her emotions and thoughts were all over the place, the drugs making her scatter-brained.

An explosion sounded outside of her little room and Shaun turned over onto her knees, pressing her ear against the door.

It was torture being locked in a room and not knowing what was happening. She hoped her mother was locked away in her own panic room. The two women had explored it once they found out about Shaun's. They were identical.

A minute later another explosion sounded, this one much louder. It rocked the apartment. Shaun felt the vibrations through the floor. She assumed the walls were sound-proofed, or reinforced, or something, since she couldn't hear anything except the explosions.

She was relatively certain they were coming from inside the apartment, which meant Jozef was probably out there.

Was he hurt? Did he need her help?

"Pull your shit together, woman!" she told herself.

She stood on shaking legs and lurched toward the locker that held the snacks and weapons. She pulled a gun out and looked at it. She had no idea of it was loaded and didn't know how to check. Having never shot a gun in her life, she was deeply uncomfortable holding it, but she had to have some protection if she was going to leave the closet.

"Point and shoot," she muttered as she walked back to the panel next to the door.

She entered the digits Karl had shown her when he realized she didn't know about the room. She held her breath, hoping that no one was on the other side. Pointing the gun, she pulled open the door and peeked into the closet.

It was as dark as the panic room had been when Jozef had shoved her inside. She shuffled toward the door, reaching for the knob. Holding the gun up to her chest and pointing it out, she cracked the closet door.

The bedroom was untouched except for what looked like dust in the air. She opened the closet and slid out, her pounding heart making it difficult to hear if anyone was in the apartment.

She desperately wanted to call out to Jozef but swallowed the urge. He couldn't answer her anyway and she might draw unwanted attention. She took a deep breath and glanced around the corner of the bedroom door, sweeping the living area.

What she saw sent adrenaline surging through her. It wasn't the destruction, nor was it Krystoff who was laying on the floor bleeding out, or Jozef sitting next to him, holding his hand. It was the man who stood in the doorway behind Jozef, his gun hand slowly extending.

Without a second thought, Shaun stepped around the

corner, lifted her gun and shot at the man. She didn't hit him, but she startled both him and herself. As the gun recoiled in her hand, she dropped it, leaving herself open as the man swung his gun toward her.

She didn't have time to move, but she didn't have to. Like watching a lightning bolt strike, Jozef scooped up a gun off the floor, rolled to his back and emptied his gun.

The man standing in the doorway was dead before he hit the ground.

"Jozef!" Shaun yelled as her knees buckled and she hit the floor.

She crawled toward him.

He climbed over Krystoff and reached for her, taking hold of her and sweeping her with a look.

"I'm okay. I'm not hurt," she assured him, trying to see around him to his uncle. "I have to get to Krystoff."

Jozef gripped her arm, not allowing her to continue toward his uncle.

He took her face in his hands.

She felt something wet smear across her cheeks and realized his hands were bloody.

He held her and stared at her, his eyes filled with every emotion he tried to hide behind his mafia mask but failed to keep from her.

She always knew how he felt.

Slowly he shook his head and she knew what he was saying. Krystoff was dead.

"I'm so sorry," she whispered brokenly.

He nodded and leaned forward pressing his head against hers. He stared into her eyes allowing her to see the anguish, the pain and the vulnerability. It was killing him that his uncle was dead and it'd happened at his hand.

She wrapped her hands around his shoulders and forced

him against her body. She held him tight and gave him the comfort he needed while he cried. Tears pooled in her eyes and spilled over, mingling with his as they sat clinging to each other, while the world around them imploded.

TO BE CONTINUED...

Thank you so much for reading A Silent Reckoning. I'm working hard on the next book! Grab your preorder for the third and final book in Shaun's and Jozef's story, Goodnight, Sinners (Sinner's Empire Book 3). Available May 18th, 2021.

ALSO BY NIKITA SLATER

If you enjoyed this book, check out some other works by #1 International Bestselling Author, Nikita Slater. More titles are always in progress, so check back often to see what's new!

SINNER'S EMPIRE

Book 1 - Sin of Silence

Book 2 - A Silent Reckoning

Book 3 - Goodnight, Sinners - Coming Soon!

THE QUEENS SERIES

Book One – Scarred Queen

Book Two - Queen's Move

Book Three - Born a Queen

Book Four - The Red Queen (Coming 2021)

Alejandro's Prey (a novella)

The Queens 4 Book Box Set

FIRE & VICE SERIES

Book One – Prisoner of Fortune

Book Two – Fight or Flight

Book Three – King's Command

Book Four – Savage Vendetta

Savage Boss (a novella)

Book Five – Fear in Her Eyes

Book Six – Bound by Blood

Book Seven – In His Sights

Book Eight - Burning Beauty

Book Nine - Chasing Ecstasy (Coming soon!)

Fire & Vice 6 Book Box Set

THE DRIVEN HEARTS SERIES

Book One - Driven by Desire

Book Two - Thieving Hearts

Book Three - Capturing Victory

Novella - The Princess and Her Mercenary

Driven Hearts 4 Book Box Set

THE SANCTUARY SERIES

Book One - Sanctuary's Warlord

Book Two - Sanctuary on Fire

Book Three - The Last Sanctuary

Book Four - The Road to Wolfe

Book Five - Skye's Sanctuary (Coming soon!)

The Sanctuary Series 3 Book Box Set

LOVING THE BAD BOY SERIES

Loving Vincent

Loving Jared

Loving Rico (Coming Soon!)

STANDALONE BOOKS

The Assassin's Wife

Because You're Mine

Mine to Keep (a novella)

Luna & Andres

Kiss of the Cartel

Stalked

AFTER DARK

In collaboration with Jasmin Quinn

Collared: A Dark Captive Romance

Safeword: A Dark Romance

Chained: A Mafia Marriage Romance

Good Girl: A Captive BDSM Romance

Hostile Takeover: An Enemies to Lovers Romance

The After Dark Box Set

Visit ***nikitaslater.com*** for more information
and the latest updates!

Nikita Slater is the International Bestselling dark romance author of the Fire & Vice series, Angels & Assassins series, The Queens series and several standalone novels. Her favourite genre is mafia romance, the bloodier the better, though she loves to write about every subject under the sun. She lives on the beautiful Canadian prairies with her son and crazy awesome dog. She has an unholy affinity for books (especially erotic romance), wine, pets and anything chocolate. Despite some of the darker themes in her books (which are pure fun and fantasy), Nikita is a staunch feminist and advocate of equal rights for all races, genders and non-gender specific persons. When she isn't writing, dreaming about writing or talking about writing, she helps others discover a love of reading and writing through literacy and social work.

www.ingramcontent.com/pod-product-compliance
Lightning Source LLC
Chambersburg PA
CBHW060222100726